BEYOND

THE

FALSE

SUMMIT

BEYOND

THE

FALSE

SUMMIT

Thomas L. Schwenk

Surrogate Press®

Published in the United States by
Surrogate Press®
an imprint of Faceted Press®
Surrogate Press, LLC
Park City, Utah
SurrogatePress.com

ISBN: 978-1-947459-95-3
Library of Congress Control Number: 2024906786

Book Cover design by: Michelle Rayner, Cosmic Design
Interior design by: Katie Mullaly, Surrogate Press®

This book is dedicated to my grandmother, Evelyn Shellenbarger Mumby, now deceased (1908-2001).

Grandma Mumby wanted to be a physician so badly, and she should have been, because she would have been as outstanding as Sarah Fletcher.

She was a constant source of inspiration and support in my early medical career, but more broadly a role model for how to live a principled and purpose-driven life.

I hope she would be proud.

TABLE OF CONTENTS

PREFACE

Park City, Utah, is known to many today as a quaint mountain town with world-class ski resorts, spectacular scenery, mountain bike trails, hot air balloon launches, a resident elk herd, outstanding restaurants, the Sundance Film Festival, and a Main Street that captivates tourists with what they believe to be an accurate preservation of the town's mining history. Accurate, but not of the early days in Park City, the 1880s and 1890s, when Park City was a rough mining town with muddy streets, ravaged by disease and injury, and wracked with business corruption and never-ending mining lawsuits. What the tourists see now is the Park City after the great fire of 1898, a fire that tested whether the town and its residents had the resilience to recover from an event that ended the life of many other mining towns.

Art galleries, bars, and restaurants occupy distressed-brick buildings carrying historic plaques commemorating the rebuilding of the town after the fire that destroyed over two hundred homes and businesses. What little of the town that survived was saved only by blasting a firebreak through the middle of town to stop the fire's spread. Many of the few original wooden homes and stores that survived are protected for historic preservation. They are the only tangible memories of the pre-fire town and its history, particularly the widely-predicted demise of the town that spread like the fire itself before the embers had even cooled.

The town did not die. Its residents were tenacious and resilient, with a commitment to a future that transcended tragedy. This pattern of resilience would repeat itself several times over in the next one-hundred-plus years, carrying Park City through the influenza epidemic, violent conflicts between miners and mine owners, the Great Depression and a few near-great recessions, several crashes in the price of silver, and the final closure of the mines when the pumps keeping the mines dry were turned off. Its most recent incarnation as a luxury mountain town with thriving cultural and recreational amenities is now facing its next crisis of traffic congestion, parking nightmares, and unaffordable housing.

The wave of enthusiasm for the hard rock mining of silver, gold, lead, and other minerals found its way to Utah in the 1860s, first with the discovery of silver ore in Bingham Canyon southwest of Salt Lake City in 1862, just fifteen years after the city's founding by Brigham Young and followers of the Church of Jesus Christ of Latter-Day Saint (LDS). Next came the discovery of silver in Little Cottonwood Canyon, home of the present-day Alta and Snowbird ski resorts, in 1863. The production was low, and the barriers to crushing, smelting, and transporting the ore out of a steep and deep canyon were high. Prospecting continued with little success, until the discovery of silver in December 1868 above Park City in the meadows below Guardsman's Pass, now named Bonanza Flats for the discovery.

The "guardsmen," soldiers from Fort Douglas in Salt Lake City, came over the pass from Big Cottonwood Canyon, now home to the Brighton and Solitude ski resorts, into the meadows above Empire Canyon. Fort Douglas had been established in the northeast corner of the Salt Lake valley, near what is now the University of Utah campus, to oversee the activities of members of the LDS church who had settled Utah and whose religious zeal and beliefs were deemed threatening by the US government. Soldiers were encouraged to explore the mountains surrounding Salt Lake City for precious metals in their off time, in the hopes of encouraging an influx of non-LDS prospectors and miners who would neutralize the dominance of the church.

The discovery of silver led to the filing of dozens of claims throughout the mountains surrounding Park City, facilitated by the previous establishment in the 1850s of a settlement in the meadows north of Park City, now called Snyderville, and extending to present-day Kimball Junction. These settlements, while modest and tenuous, offered the promise of farms and sawmills that could support mining, as well as access to Salt Lake City through Parley's Canyon, named in honor of Parley Pratt, one of the settlers and operators of the Kimball Stage Company and the hotel at Kimball Junction.

The town was also named for Parley Pratt and initially called Parley's Park, which became Parley's Park City, and finally Park City as decreed by another founder, George Snyder, namesake of Snyderville. It was a rough, muddy, violent, and harsh mining camp, with the short summers and long, cold winters characteristic of life at seven thousand feet of elevation and more. The mines attracted workers from across the West, often from other mining camps in Nevada, California, Colorado, Montana, and Arizona that were on the downhill side of the inevitable boom and bust cycle of almost all mining camps. The home country origins of the miners were mostly northern and western Europe, including Ireland, England (particularly Cornwall), Scotland, and Sweden.

Mining successes were infrequent but spectacular when they occurred, leading to fantastical claims of mineral riches, instant fortunes, and the influx of outside investment capital. By the 1880s, Park City was a thriving town with a railroad, a newspaper (the *Park Record*), and a telephone exchange, all of which connected Park City to the outside world and brought it international acclaim. The sinking of hundreds of mine shafts—eventually totaling more than one thousand miles of shafts and tunnels that mostly run underneath the present-day ski resorts—created the piles of crushed rock or tailings scattered throughout the hills above town. The promise of great riches attracted entrepreneurs and developers of every sort.

Most of the prospectors and miners eventually realized they were more likely to be successful developing businesses to support the mines and miners than to strike it big by staking and developing mining claims themselves. Boarding houses were built in town and near the mines to house the hundreds of men attracted to the booming mining economy. Saloons sprung up overnight—over two hundred such public houses over time—usually starting in a tent with a door laid across two barrels as a bar. They each served a specific ethnic group or nationality, sometimes coming and going, and coming again, with every miner of every country origin having at least one bar to call home. The town was proud of its theater, restaurants, banks, blacksmith shops, jewelry stores, meat markets, churches, schools, drug stores and bakeries. Equally prominent, but perhaps less advertised, were twenty "cribs" and larger houses of prostitution that lined what is now the entrance road to the Deer Valley Ski Resort. Three of the original buildings survive, although presumably now serving a different business or residential purpose.

As the population grew, so did the need for medical care to address the devastating illnesses and injuries that characterized life everywhere in the late 1800s. The town's physicians were heroic in their efforts, but their care lacked a scientific basis and was often crude and usually unsuccessful. The city cemetery, located on the hillside along Kearns Boulevard (Highway 248) near a present-day shopping center, and the Glenwood cemetery, established by several fraternal organizations near what is now the base of the Park City Mountain Resort, bear testimony to the ravages of diphtheria, scarlet fever, typhoid fever, influenza, obstetrical and wound infections, mining accidents, avalanches, gunshot wounds, and suicides that characterized life in a mining camp in the late 1800s.

The hard life and hard work discouraged many physicians, but also offered opportunities for those physicians seeking to start a new life and new practice—sometimes because of failures elsewhere, sometimes because of their missionary zeal and sense of adventure. These opportunities attracted mostly men, who constituted almost the entire population of physicians in the United States in the mid-late 1800s, but also caught the attention of some of the first women physicians who trained in and graduated from traditional medical schools in the United States. Despite, or perhaps because of, the groundbreaking entry into the US medical profession of Dr. Elizabeth Blackwell—the first woman physician to graduate from a traditional US medical school in 1849, followed shortly after by her sister, Dr. Emily Blackwell—little improvement was made in the number or quality of woman physicians in subsequent decades. The male medical establishment was hostile to women as physicians, as were many patients, including sometimes women themselves. Medical schools regretted their initial support of accepting women. Some schools that accepted a first woman into medical school did not do so again for several decades. Male medical students were abusive and shaming, often encouraged by their male faculty members. The students' displeasure was particularly personal because the occasional woman in their classes often performed at a superior level. Barriers were many to licensure and membership in state medical societies.

The unregulated, chaotic, underserved, and needy nature of Western mining camps led many to provide more welcoming opportunities to women physicians. The admission of some of the first women physicians to membership in state medical associations occurred in the West, including the states of Utah, Nevada, and Montana, and their medical practices were often based in mining camps. However, the barriers were still considerable, and the disparaging epithet "hen medic" was frequently heard.

The resilience of these women physicians paralleled the resilience of the communities they served, all at a time when the practice of medicine was changing dramatically with the development of infectious disease models of illness, the promotion of antisepsis, the availability of anesthetics, and the teaching of a pathophysiologic approach to diagnosis and treatment. Physicians, both men and women, overcame extraordinary hardship and faced unimaginable challenges to care for their patients in these rough mining towns. Some of these physicians came to Park City well-trained in the curriculum of the day, dedicated, compassionate, and skilled. They brought with them all of their skills, but also the human frailties with which all physicians, like all people, have to cope as they carry out their daily responsibilities. Their care of their patients and commitment to their community contributed to Park City, and similar mining towns, overcoming their own challenges—natural and manmade disasters, political and economic instability—to survive and thrive into the present day.

This is a story of two of those physicians and the town they served.

CHAPTER 1

Park City, September 1897

Patrick Fitzpatrick wondered if he should have paid more attention to the Tommyknockers he had heard in the mine the day before.

He awoke in the dark, four in the morning as always, in one of a hundred rough bunkbeds in the dormitory of his boarding house at the top of Main Street. He could see the faint cloud of frost on his breath and there was wet ice on the rough-hewn walls. It was cold in the dormitory, even in September, with a wisp of crisp, swampy air rising from every sleeping miner. Patrick thought the white puffs would have been charming if he didn't have to smell the air that came from a hundred mouths of unbrushed teeth. Each miner had a distinctive snort or rattle, but every snore came with the same fetid smell. Even then, the rank breath was not as bad as the moldy smells of wet clothes, muddy and manure-splattered boots, and a hundred unwashed bodies. Altogether, it was a truly nauseating way to wake up.

Then he remembered the last thing he thought about before falling asleep the night before—the knocking, creaking, and groaning he had heard in the mine yesterday, the sounds of the living beast that miners believed hard rock mines to be.

Patrick, like most miners, believed that the Tommyknocker sounds were made by small mystical creatures who were trying to warn the miners of one of the many violent events that killed them regularly—falls, collapsed tunnels, explosions.

Each nationality of miner had its own name for these creatures. The Irishman Patrick thought of them as leprechauns. The English called them brownies, the Germans thought of them as mountain ghosts or Berggeisters. The Cornish thought they were the souls of the Jews who crucified Christ and were sent by the Romans to work as slaves in the mines, which is why the Cousin Jacks swore they never heard the sounds on Saturday. Others thought the creatures captured the souls of dead miners and prowled the mines to cause mischief, sometimes stealing lunches and tools, but also sometimes providing warnings of imminent danger. Whatever their name, their origin, or their purpose, they all got lumped together as Tommyknockers.

Nothing had happened the day before, after he had heard the sounds, but the mythic threat still terrified him. He hoped this day would be as safe.

Patrick had come from the Nevada mines in Virginia City a year earlier, following the great migration of miners that traveled the West and moved on to the next boomtown as each mine where they worked failed. He felt fortunate to have secured a bed in the Main Street boardinghouse. Boardinghouses were judged first on their location and proximity to the major mines, to minimize the daily hike a miner would have to take up-canyon to get to work. Some miners were required to live in houses built right next to the mine, so they couldn't get in so much trouble in town. Patrick had been approved to live in this boardinghouse at the top of Main Street, just down the hill a mile, or a bit more, from the Ontario mine where he worked. Close to the mine and close to town, it was the perfect location. After that, it was all about the food, and Gladys was one of the best cooks in town—hearty, simple food, and lots of it.

Patrick had lived rough for the past year after coming to Park City—a heavy canvas-sided tent, open fire for cooking, mud running by and sometimes through the tent flap, snow drifts piling up and collapsing the tent walls, brutal cold, and always the loneliness. He did not have close friends in the boardinghouse, but he enjoyed just having other miners around, however noisy and smelly they were in the dorm. Mining was a lonely job, and mining camps were lonely places.

He worked the mines ten hours a day, six days a week, and drank, ate, and slept the rest of the time, generally in that order. Park City was becoming more of a real town, with a summer baseball league, occasional parades, and one or two public hangings a year. However, Patrick did little but work and drink. Patrick's favorite saloon was the Pat Towey and Co. Livery Stable, mostly because he liked the saloonkeeper and bartender, Barney Riley, who grew up in Cootehill County, Ireland, near Patrick's hometown.

He considered the Livery Stable the best of several saloons serving the Irish. It had started in a tent with a few good bottles and a crude bar, but it had become a high-class taste of his Irish home. He enjoyed the pictures from Ireland, good beer, and better whiskey. It was close, just down Main Street from the boardinghouse, but then almost all the saloons, twenty-seven of them at the moment, were on Main Street. There was a saloon every few doors on both sides of the street, from the bottom of Daly Canyon down to the bottom of Main at the train depot. Of course, any miner would only frequent one or a couple saloons that catered to his countrymen. Saloons were home for many miners, warm in the winter, cool in the summer, and a source of news, gossip, occasional entertainment, and frequent fights.

Patrick splashed near-freezing water from the wash trough on his face, water dripping off his dark, drooping handle-bar mustache. He slicked back his long, stringy, unwashed hair and headed downstairs for breakfast.

"Morning, Gladys," he said.

"And the same to you, son," she said. She liked Patrick because he was a bit chattier than most of the miners.

"What do we have this fine morning?"

"Same as every morning," she said, but with a smile. Gladys put out a hefty breakfast: a bucket of oatmeal, a platter of fried eggs, a pile of fried potatoes, a decent slab of local bacon from one of the ranches in the Snyderville meadows north of town, and fruit preserves to dress up the coarse bread. Patrick was paid three dollars and fifty cents a day as a driller, and the boardinghouse charged him a dollar a day for room and board. It was worth it for a breakfast like this.

The dining hall was filling up, miners bent over their plates, shoveling the food just like they would soon be mucking the pile of rock that was left when they blew the rock face they had worked the day before. Nobody talked at breakfast, or at any meal for that matter. They ate in silence in the warm dining room, heated by the kitchen stove, thinking about the day coming or the day just passed, nothing more past or future. It was still dark out and the lighting was dim in the dining room. Patrick would have rather chatted a bit with someone, just to get the thought of the Tommyknockers out of his mind.

In the absence of any conversation, Patrick shoveled down his hearty breakfast quickly, grabbed his lunch tin, filled the bottom with hot tea from the crockery, and grabbed a meat pasty from the large tray Gladys had put out. He laid the pasty, two pounds of meat, and vegetables packed into a lard crust, on a layer of wax paper on the upper tray of his lunch bucket, where the hot tea below would keep it a bit warm. He stuck the candle cup on top and headed to the front door.

"G'day, Gladys," he said and waved.

"And to you," she said. "See you tonight."

Out the door he turned right and started up the street toward the Ontario mine. The street was ankle-deep in mud, as always, and worse because of a recent cold rain. The weak sun barely penetrated the dank, smoke-polluted air that laid in the valley most every day.

The Ontario mine was the economic and political center of Park City. When Patrick arrived in town, he had heard that the Ontario had already produced more than a hundred million dollars in ore since its claim was filed in 1874. The main shaft had been drilled down more than twelve hundred feet. Drifts branched off along the vertical shaft, each to a stope or working rock face that followed veins of ore as they were discovered. A drain tunnel had been drilled and taken down the hill toward the top of Main Street, dumping its water just above Patrick's boardinghouse. The tunnel drained the ever-present cold water that filled every mine in these mountains, allowing the mine company to sink its shafts even deeper. The tunnel drainage was also the cause of the mud through which Patrick slogged, nearly sucking the boots off his feet. Managing the constant drip, and sometimes a full deluge, of cold water sloshing down the drifts made mining in Park City expensive and frustrating. Draining and diverting water required as much time, energy, and money as the drilling and blasting itself.

Patrick had never quite gotten used to the change in mining from Nevada to Park City. Nevada gold mines were hot and dry while Park City silver mines were wet and cold, a consistent year-round forty-eight degrees. In Nevada he worked in shorts and boots, nothing else, streaked with dusty sweat. He had quickly learned in Park City that he had to get to the mine and changing room early to make sure his work clothes were still there, all of which were essential to maintaining even slight comfort in such a dark, cold, wet, hostile environment.

Patrick reached the top of Main Street and looped over to the entry to the Ontario Canyon road. The sounds of the stamp mill floated up from the bottom of Marsac Avenue to his left, just off Main Street and next to the train depot, pounding away, crushing and separating the rock for transport to a smelter. He had long ago stopped paying attention to the constant pounding of the massive cast-iron stamps. The mill handled the ore from all the mines except the Ontario. The Ontario had its own mill up the canyon closer to the mine, whose pounding would soon replace that of the Marsac mill in his head as he worked his way uphill. The pounding of both mills was just something that was always there, around the clock, forty two-ton cast-iron stamps dropping on a continuous feed of rock every second. Between the two, the pounding could be heard throughout town and up and down the valley. The pounding mills, plus the heavy smoke from coal and wood fires, made daily life in Park City an unpleasant assault on the senses for new arrivals, although most Parkites didn't notice.

The mine was a mile distant and several hundred feet up the hill. He remembered that when he first arrived in Park City, he couldn't get up the hill without breathing hard and fast, his heart racing. The mines in Virginia City, Nevada were at about six thousand feet elevation, but Park City itself was at seven thousand feet and the entrance to many mines a thousand feet higher or more. It had taken him a few weeks to get comfortable.

Patrick arrived at the changing room at the head frame of the mine, along with several other miners he recognized, who nodded to each other silently. He found his work clothes where he had left them the previous night. All the miners waiting to go down in the cage were dressed alike, but no one wanted to wear someone else's stained and sweaty-stiff clothes. He put on a long-legged, but short-sleeved, wool undergarment so he could strip down if he worked up enough of a sweat, unlikely in the cold mine, but possible. Hand drilling was some of the most intense and demanding work he had ever done, but he liked it. He liked working hard, and he wanted to do it well and make something of himself. Over the underwear went canvas pants and a wool sweater, then a waxed canvas slicker. Next came a felt hat that had been boiled hard in resin to make a sort of helmet. Finally, he slipped on high rubber boots that would protect him from the constant stream of cold water that ran down every tunnel.

He grabbed a carbide light, stuck it to his helmet with a wad of mud, and entered the cage that would take him down to work. A bell system connected the cage operator at the top with what was happening at the bottom of the shaft. Two bells sent the cage and twenty miners packed into it to the bottom. In two minutes, the miners dropped more than twelve hundred feet from the bright morning sunshine into the dark, cold, clammy world where they spent sixty hours every week. No one talked on the way down.

At the twelve-hundred-foot level, the cage stopped gently, just short of the hard bottom of the shaft, a measure of the expertise and precision of the lift operator. The men unloaded into the underground station. The station was the center of underground mining life, a large room blasted out of the rock, washed with a dim light from a few small bulbs connected to the mine's electrical system. The station was filled with supplies, tools, spare parts for the cage, back-up drill bits and hammers, and the ore carts that came rolling out of each drift. The rough rock walls and low ceiling created pockets of shadows and soaked up what light the dim bulbs provided. Each miner lit his carbide light and walked away from the cage to their assigned tunnel.

Patrick's light sputtered out its dim glow as he saw his drilling partner, Sam Deanglas, waiting for him.

"Sam," Patrick said with a nod of his head. Sam was a "Cousin Jack" from Cornwall, but not a bad guy. Two-man manual drilling required so much precision that miners tried to find someone they liked, but more importantly someone they trusted. When the team members trusted each other, they stayed together as a team, if at all possible. A miner's life, or at least their hands, depended on trusting the accuracy of the partner's hammer.

The Cornish and Irish had a long and deep history of conflict between their home countries, and now between individual miners even when far from home. The conflict in Park City was mostly manifested in bar brawls. But Patrick liked the Cornish pasties that Gladys made in the boardinghouse, and Sam was a decent guy, paid attention to his work, and showed up every day. He had little ambition beyond that, but Patrick thought that was typical for Cornish miners. An Irish miner was hoping to use mining as a start to something else, to become part of mainstream society, a way to better himself. For the Cornish miner, mining was all there was. Sam and his countrymen saved their wages for the occasional trip home to see their mothers. The Irish miners rarely returned to their home country. There was nothing there for them.

They headed down their drift to the stope they had left yesterday. The dim light of the station was swallowed by the dense black of the drift. On the way down, Patrick looked up along the ceiling so his light would shine on the timbering that shored up the shafts, protecting miners from tunnels collapsing as a thousand feet of rock settled. His light threw shadows across the walls and ceiling, and then just disappeared into the darkness ahead. He could see the eight-inch square cap-and-post timbers. He hoped they were as solid as they looked.

They came to the end of the drift. Patrick pounded a heavy nail into the closest timber near the floor, took his candle off the top of this lunch pail, and put it on the floor. He hung his pail over the candle on the nail. The candle would keep the tea in the bottom of the lunch pail hot and the pasty in the tray above warm.

They found the remnants of yesterday's work as they had left it at the end of the shift, a pile of crumbled rock totaling about six cubic yards and weighing nearly two tons, blown out of the rock face when they lit off their dynamite at the end of their shift. Patrick and Sam looked at each other and silently started to muck the rock pile, by hand, chunk by chunk, into ore cars that they would then haul back on a small track to the underground station. It took them two hours to clean out the rock pile. Patrick had taken off his heavy slicker and still worked up a sweat, even in the cold mine.

They finished mucking the rock and were ready to drill. "I'll check the face," Patrick said, looking for the remnants of drill holes they had drilled yesterday, to make sure there was no unexploded dynamite. 'Drilling into a miss' by putting a drill bit into a hole that still contained a stick of unblown dynamite was not a good way to start the day. An Irish miner that Patrick knew slightly had done that a few weeks before, and the dynamite had exploded, blowing the drill bit straight back out of the hole and through the miner's head. Patrick attended the funeral, as he did for all Irish miners.

Just as they were about to start drilling, Patrick and Sam both heard the Tommyknockers again. First a distant crack, like hard-frozen ice on a lake as it thaws, then grinding, a sort of growl, not like any animal they had ever heard, deep and low-pitched, more felt than heard. Then a pop, just a little pop. And then nothing.

Patrick and Sam looked at each other, eyebrows raised, questioning, worried. Patrick wondered if he should act on the sounds, leave his work, and return to the surface, but he knew his foreman would ridicule him, or worse. He needed this job, but his hands shook as he picked up his eight-pound hammer and Sam picked up his drill.

"Ready?" Patrick asked. He did not want to ask about the Tommyknockers. It might bring more bad luck.

"Ready," Sam nodded.

They settled into their usual routine, fifty strokes with the hammer per minute. Sam turned the drill slightly after each stroke to bring a new edge to bear. Two-person double-jack drilling was as much a dance as it was work, the rhythmic movements repeated precisely and quickly for an hour before the team switched roles. Patrick and Sam were particularly good, one of the best teams in the Ontario mine, partly because they trusted each other so completely. Patrick trusted Sam, even if Sam was Cornish, and Sam felt the same about Patrick, even if he was Irish. The drilling rod was only about an inch in diameter, and the slightest deviation of the bit could cause the miner with the hammer to miss, shattering the partner's hand. Absolute attention to every stroke was critical.

They were starting fresh on the rock face, and they laid out their drilling in the usual pattern. Their goal by the end of their shift was to have a full set of holes, each drilled about eighteen inches deep, room for two sticks of dynamite. They marked the three center holes in a triangle, each angled slightly toward a center convergence so the dynamite would blow out a center chunk of the face. Surrounding this were reliever holes straight into the rock that would collapse the rock face into the cavity left by the center holes. Finally, they marked the edge holes that could clean the face to the edges for a complete blast.

Drilling was exhausting. "Time to switch?" Patrick asked, about an hour later.

"Sure," Sam replied, "but I need to go back to the station and get another bit. This one is getting dull." Sam turned to walk back up the drift.

Patrick backed away from the rock face and slid down the side wall to rest, leaning against the timber. He couldn't get the Tommyknockers out of his mind as he stared at the wall across the drift, barely lit by his lamp. A few minutes passed, and he turned to look back up the drift as Sam returned. Something wasn't right. He couldn't see the rats flitting in and out of the shadows. Their absence always seemed to foretell some sort of disaster. And then the timber directly over Patrick snapped.

He tried to pull his legs back but too late. A chunk of rock the size of a bushel basket, weighing maybe two hundred pounds, dropped directly on his right lower leg, snapping both bones a few inches below the knee. His pants were split by the jagged end of fractured bone ripping through the skin. Patrick screamed and nearly passed out from the blinding pain. Sam screamed as well as he ran up, held Patrick as he leaned back, and laid him down gently to the floor. The rock rolled off Patrick's leg, and he screamed again.

"Help, help!" Sam yelled, but no one came. The station was empty. The tunnels swallowed sound like they swallowed light. He ran back to the station just as two miners came out of another tunnel pushing an ore cart. Sam yelled for them to bring an empty cart and follow him. They pushed it down the narrow track to where Patrick laid. He was moaning and passing in and out of consciousness

"We're here," Sam said. "We need to get you into the cart." The light from their carbide lamps flashed frantically around the walls of the drift. Other miners had heard the commotion, run to the station, and rang for the cage with the emergency code for "miner injured."

"Patrick," Sam said, "we're going to pick you up and get into the ore car."

Patrick just moaned. When they lifted Patrick and laid him into the car, legs dangling over the edge, the moans changed back to screams. One miner tried to hold the broken leg gently, and they all pushed Patrick and the cart along the narrow rails back toward the station. Despite their attempts to hold the fractured leg, it hung over the edge of the car and bounced as they pushed the car. They tried to move quickly, but that just caused Patrick to scream at every bump on the rails.

Between screams, Patrick stared at the jagged spike of bone protruding from his leg and the blood soaking his pants. It didn't seem like it could be his leg. This couldn't be happening to him, he thought. Despite the blinding pain, his mind was working enough for him to realize what this type of injury meant. His leg would be amputated and that would be the end of his life as a miner. He hoped the fracture was far enough below the knee to spare it. He had heard that saving the knee could help him walk better. But he would never swing a hammer again. The cart banged against the wall, and he screamed again.

They pushed the car to the loading area. The cage arrived with more of a jerk than it had just a couple hours earlier as the day started, which seemed so long ago now to Patrick. The cage operator on top knew that something bad had happened, although he could not know what. He just wanted to get the cage down as fast as possible. They loaded Patrick, ore car and all, into the cage. The two minutes to get to the surface seemed so much longer than the same two minutes coming down that morning. Every time the cage bumped the shaft wall, every time the hoist cable jerked, Patrick screamed. He was sweating, as were Sam and the miners with him, but for different reasons. At the surface, they rolled the ore car out to the door of the headframe building into the late morning sunshine and transferred Patrick onto a large flat equipment cart. The three men rolled him down the muddy road toward town. Patrick felt every bump and every rock that the cart hit.

At the top of Main Street, Sam asked, "What doctor do you want to see?"

"Dr. Stout!", Patrick yelled.

"That's all the way to the bottom of Main Street," said Sam. "Not Dr. Wilson? His office is closer, and he is the mine's physician."

"No!" said Patrick. "I heard that the mine manager don't like him. Maybe he's no good. And not that lady doctor, either. Ain't going to be treated by no hen medic!"

Main Street was its usual muddy mess, and even pushing the cart downhill was a struggle. Patrick screamed all the way down Main Street, his stringy hair wet and sweaty even in the cold air. Main Street was busy this time of day, mostly with women shopping. The women stayed on the boardwalk to protect their shoes from the mud, and they stopped to stare. They looked first at Patrick screaming, then at the bloody shard of bone sticking out of his shin, and then away.

One woman, in a fine dress and hat, asked another, "Do you recognize him?"

"No, I surely don't," the other woman replied. "I wonder if he has a wife or family."

"I don't recognize him either," said the first woman. "Probably means he has no family." If he had, they would come together to help. They knew as well as Patrick what it meant for the miner to have a bloody broken bone sticking out of his pants.

They got to the bottom of Main Street, carried Patrick into Dr. Stout's office, and laid him on the table in the front room. Dr. Stout came down from his upstairs living quarters, all three hundred pounds of him, his face covered with a full black beard, shaggy and unkempt hair, a bit greasy. He wore a full wool waistcoat and vest, covered by a once-white, heavy, cotton operating coat, now crusted with the red-brown splatters of old blood from prior beneficiaries in his care. Many doctors were proud of their operating gowns being stiff with blood, as a measure of their successful practice and full operating schedule.

He took a quick look at Patrick's leg and simply said, "Sorry, son, the leg has to come off. No way to put those bones together. They'll just get infected, and the infection would kill you."

Patrick knew this was coming, but it did not help with the shock. "Nothing, doc, no way?" he said, whimpering, desperate. "I can't work without a leg!"

"Sorry, son, just no way to save it."

It was clear to Patrick now that this was really happening, that this was really his leg, and that soon part of that leg would be on the doctor's blood-stained floor. He was scared, not so much about what the doctor was about to do, but about what would happen to his life.

Patrick's despair turned to negotiation. "Where?" he asked.

"I think I can save the knee," Dr. Stout said.

Patrick just nodded, with a little cry, relieved in a perverse sort of way. He would be able to walk, although not enough to go back to mining. He had never thought about doing anything else except mining, although he knew he was smart enough to do other work. Maybe he could operate the lift or work in the machine shop. And then he just sank back on the table, overwhelmed with terror. It was all too much. He had seen what had happened to other miners who had been injured. They drank, wandered around town, did a few odd jobs. Some fell and hit their heads and died. Others just took care of it more directly with a bullet. He vowed he would do better.

Dr. Stout cut off Patrick's pants and prepared his instruments. Surgeons were proud of their speed and skill in performing amputations, mostly because the concept of using anesthetics was new and foreign. Ether was discovered by a chemist in the 1500s who combined alcohol and sulfuric acid to form a clear liquid that put chickens to sleep. Once it wore off, they fully recovered. It was three hundred years before it was used medically in humans. Many surgeons initially opposed its use because they believed the suffering and pain of surgery was healthy for the soul and hastened the healing process. Chloroform was discovered more recently by a chemist working on new pesticides. Before these discoveries, whiskey was the preferred—if wholly inadequate—anesthetic. But chloroform was tricky, with a fine line between loss of consciousness and respiratory paralysis causing death.

Dr. Stout started his career in the Civil War with Grant's Army of the Republic, when ether was more available, although not always. For that reason, Civil War surgeons focused more on speed than precision in amputations, and the end result often reflected those priorities. Forty-five seconds was considered a standard that surgeons should aspire to achieve. It was the longest forty-five seconds in a patient's life. Patrick would not have to suffer like this. Dr. Stout put a stained rag over Patrick's face and started dripping the ether. Patrick was soon unconscious, with deep, slow breathing. The best part of that for everyone else was that he stopped screaming and moaning.

Surgeons in the larger US cities and in Europe were just starting to understand the bacterial causes of infection in surgical patients. The research of Lister, Semmelweis, Pasteur, and Koch led to surgeons adopting the startling practice of washing their hands before surgery. Surgeons started slopping phenol, known as carbolic acid, over the surgical site, and sometimes their hands, to reduce the risk of infection. In the early 1890s, gloves were recommended by some surgeons, including the famous Dr. William Halsted at Johns Hopkins, but more to help protect their hands from the highly corrosive effects of carbolic acid than to protect the patient from infection. To their surprise, the rate of postoperative infections dropped dramatically.

These radical medical advances were adopted, as was often true with any change in scientific paradigm, by younger physicians with more recent and modern medical training. Dr. Stout was not one of those physicians. He was a skeptic who subscribed to the dictum of many older physicians who said that "surgeons are gentlemen and gentlemen do not have dirty hands."

As soon as Patrick was asleep, Dr. Stout tightened a belt around his thigh to reduce bleeding and picked up a scalpel laying in a dish filled with brownish water. He made a continuous cut around the leg below the knee and just above the fracture in a broad, scalloped pattern. It took a good eye and much experience to see how the scalloped skin flaps would come together in a smooth seal over the eventual stump. Blood oozed from the edges of the skin and Dr. Stout soaked it up with some rags, themselves stained with old blood like Dr. Stout's coat. As he cut through the skin, he grabbed the major arteries and veins with forceps and tied them off with suture material called catgut, which was actually made from sheep intestines. He pulled back the skin so he could excise the muscles on the front side of the leg, somewhat above the fracture and above the level at which he had excised the skin, so as to allow room to close the skin over the muscle. He always noticed the similarity between cutting away leg muscles during an amputation and cutting a fine steak at dinner at the American Hotel up the street.

He laid back the cut ends of the front muscles of the leg so as to expose the end of the fractured bone, took his bone saw—not unlike one found on a carpenter's workbench but with finer teeth—and sawed quickly through the tibia and fibula to get a clean and flat end to the two bones. The saw cut was made slightly further up the lower leg than the transected muscles so as to provide room for some cushion by the muscle over the bone ends. With only three hard draws of the saw, he was through the bone, the leg just hanging by the posterior muscles and a few arteries and veins. One of the miners who had brought Patrick down from the mine and had been watching, groaned, slumped to the floor, and passed out. Dr. Stout ignored him.

After he pulled away the sawn bone, he tied off and cut the arteries and veins on the back of the leg. Next, he cut through the now exposed muscles on the back of the leg. The amputated leg fell freely onto the floor with a soggy thump, adding to the long-standing stains in the rough wood. Dr. Stout surveyed the result of his work with pride. He laid the muscle over the bone and sutured the cut ends together. He then drew the skin flaps easily over the stump and sutured the skin in place. Even with anesthesia, Dr. Stout liked to be done within two minutes, a goal he had easily met on this sunny day.

Dr. Stout removed the ether rag, and Patrick started to stir in a few minutes. Dr. Stout let him rest for a bit and then sat him up and moved him to a nearby chair, not yet fully awake.

Patrick looked around the office, confused about where he was and why, and then he felt the fiery pain in his leg, or what was left of it. He saw the bloody bandage on the stump of what used to be his right leg, and it all came back to him. His mind started to race. In his confusion, he wondered if Dr. Stout was going to give him his leg to take home. Where was the leg? Why could he still feel it when he could see it was clearly gone? Why was that miner passed out on the floor? The last thing he remembered was waiting for Sam at their stope, and breakfast before that. Nothing made sense, especially where his leg had gone. He started crying, a soft sob. Dr. Stout looked at him briefly and then went back to cleaning up.

The table and a fair bit of the floor was covered in blood. Dr. Stout's stained operating coat now had a new layer of bloody crusts forming. He opened his medicine cabinet and pulled out a bottle of laudanum to dispense to Patrick for pain. Dr. Stout favored the Sydenham's formula for laudanum that used opium, saffron, cinnamon, cloves, and sherry wine, mixed together and fermented for fifteen days. "Son, use this for the pain when you need it, twenty drops in some water as often as you wish. It'll help you get over the shock. Here, I'll give you some now." He counted twenty drops into a tin cup of water from a basin on the back table.

Patrick downed the liquid, some of it drooling from the corners of his mouth. Dr. Stout handed Patrick crutches and said, "Use both of these for now. You will only need one when you get used to it."

Patrick just nodded, still dopey from the anesthetic, still confused, still not understanding what had just happened and why he needed crutches. As the fog of ether lifted, he cried out again, looked around the room frantically, and saw his bloody leg in the corner of the room where Dr. Stout had swept it. Now he understood what had happened. He started thinking all over again what he was going to do with himself. The miner who had passed out had come to and got up groggily to help Sam and the other miner get Patrick to his feet. He was still wobbly, both in his legs and his head. The three miners helped Patrick toward the door.

"What does he owe you, Doc?" Sam asked.

"I'll send a bill to the mine later," Dr. Stout said. "It won't likely be paid, but I'll settle up with this fellow later. What's his name?"

"Patrick Fitzpatrick," Sam said.

"Very well, get him home now."

As Patrick hopped to the door leaning on Sam, he started to understand what had happened. He knew his mining days were done. Maybe he could fix up a prosthetic leg. Maybe get a job in the Towey Livery Stable and Bar. He vowed he would not let this be the end of his life. There had to be something more for him. He just wasn't sure what.

For the moment, he just wished he had paid more attention to the Tommyknockers.

Chapter 2

Michigan, 1876–78

Thomas Wilson knew suffering and death at an early age, but so did all children. Death was everywhere in the 1800s and touched everyone. Death was an everyday event, explicit, graphic, sudden, and personal. Thomas suffered, perhaps more than most, and the suffering changed his life, in ways he could not know at the time and would not understand until much later.

Thomas grew up in Mendon, Michigan, along the St. Joseph River, a farming settlement on the Michigan frontier that arose in an area first explored by French trappers. The township was officially named in 1831 and the town of Mendon platted in 1845. His parents, Robert and Evelyn, came west shortly after they married in Pennsylvania in 1865. Robert Wilson had mustered out of the 69th Pennsylvania Infantry Regiment, formed from residents of the Eastern Pennsylvania Irish communities and famous for repelling Pickett's charge at Gettysburg. They were also famous for taking some of the most devastating casualties in a war famous for bloody slaughters. By the end of the war, of the one thousand men originally enlisting in the 69th, only fifty-nine remained alive and uninjured, although not necessarily unharmed, to return to their homes.

Robert had seen and heard things he never wanted to see again—piles of amputated limbs gathered behind the surgeon's tent, men screaming for their mothers for hours before they could be removed, men moaning through the night before they went silent—but he was alive. He particularly remembered the smells, bowels ripped open, the coppery metallic smell of blood, corpses rotting because they could not be removed for burial. The haunting images of war returned to him with frightening frequency, mostly at night. He was awakened many times by the screams in his head, heard by no one else. Sometimes, Evelyn found him curled up in the straw in the corner of their barn, whimpering. He could not explain to her why he was there, even if he knew. He had never told her what he saw, but now what he had seen had become his life.

Evelyn tried to understand, but she could not. All she knew was that the war had done something terrible to her husband, and he was broken. He could be kind and generous one minute, and shivering and paralyzed the next. But she also saw a good man who was willing to work hard. He wanted to marry, have children, farm a small plot of land, and not come near death ever again. That was good enough for Evelyn.

They had grown up on adjacent Pennsylvania farms, shyly recognizing each other in the one-room schoolhouse they attended in their small farm community. They knew, or just assumed, that they would marry, even after Robert left for the war. She never imagined he would not come back, but she could not know he would come back like this. When he returned from the war, he was different, moody, dark, but they still married. They tried to start a life in their small Pennsylvania community, but the land was hilly, the ground rocky, poor, and sparse. Robert had no other trade or skills. They had heard of land, abundant and rich in Michigan, with topsoil two feet thick on what was called the prairie.

They loaded their meager possessions in their wagon, hitched the wagon to their horse, and tied the cow behind the wagon. They set off for Michigan, five hundred miles away. It was not a hard trip, on roads and turnpikes cleared across

Pennsylvania and Ohio. They made fifteen or twenty miles a day most days and arrived a month later. Robert staked a claim to a good forty acres, partially cleared with a fast-moving stream. They built a crude dirt-floor cabin and a small barn, started clearing the land and having children, first Thomas, then Steven, and a few years later, Emily.

The nightmares followed Robert from Pennsylvania, as if they had been packed in the trunk loaded in the wagon. Sometimes Robert thought they might have faded away, but then they returned with renewed ferocity, leaping from the corners of his mind and terrorizing his brain. Any death in the community could cause him to remember things he wished he could forget.

Robert's triggers were everywhere in his neighbors and the surrounding communities—a gangrenous leg from an accident with an ax; the profuse watery diarrhea, dehydration, and shock of cholera; the high fevers, kidney failure, and heart damage from scarlet fever; and the internal bleeding and intestinal perforation of typhoid fever. Perhaps most dreaded was the barking cough of diphtheria, with gray pus lining the throat that caused the classic cough and wheezing, and the final strangulation of an obstructed trachea. Robert and Evelyn prayed every day that such tragedies would not befall their precious family.

It was March and the days were warming. The trees were starting to show their green buds and the forest floor thickened with new growth. Thomas's younger brother, Steven, was eight years old when he came to his mother one morning and said in a wheezy, wet voice, "Mommy, my throat hurts."

"Come here, sweet boy, let me take a look," Evelyn said, struggling to stay calm, but shivering with fear that Steven had brought diphtheria home from a recent visit to a neighboring farm family. She mumbled a prayer that her beautiful boy would not, could not, be stricken with this deadly disease. He was so sweet, so perfect, his blond hair always flopping as he ran with a smile on his face. Now there was no running and no smile, just sweaty hair plastered to his head as he came into her arms. Evelyn's fears lurked in the shadows of the candle-light that flickered around the walls of the crude, rough-logged cabin. She had to be strong for Steven, but she was weak and sick inside. She knew the truth. She wiped a tear from her eye when Steven's eyes were closed. She felt helpless, but Steven needed the strength of her soul.

He was flushed, his eyes tired and watery, his skin moist. She gave him a sip of water poured from a pitcher she had drawn from the well behind the back of the cabin. He cried when he swallowed. "Shh, shh," she said. "Take another sip. You'll be fine." If Steven had looked, he would have known his mother did not believe it. Her eyes were red, shoulders slumping. Steven felt her fingers trembling as she touched his hot skin. She wrapped him in a blanket when he started shivering and put him to bed in the overhanging loft where all three children normally slept.

"Thomas, Emily," she said, "You will have to sleep in the corner. Get your blankets and bring them down." Her voice was weak and wavering. Emily did not notice, but Thomas did. He could feel his mother's fear, and it became his fear.

Evelyn went to the cabinet near the large, stone fireplace to find the wooden case containing the home remedies kept by every good mother. She prepared a cathartic with apple juice to which she added powdered sulfur and stirred it into a creamy solution. She had never understood why vomiting should help a child to breathe better, but she did what she had been taught by her mother. She gave Steven a sip in a spoon every few minutes until he gagged and vomited, screaming with pain from his throat. Her skin prickled with his cries.

She wanted to cover her ears to block the sound of his rasping breath. As he laid in a soggy blanket, she had the briefest thought about leaving the cabin, just for a moment, just to be free of the fear that gripped her. But she had to give Steven her strength, and she needed her husband to help.

"Robert," she said, in the calmest voice to him she could manage as he came in from the field, "please put up a fire in the stove and heat some water."

And that's all it took to trigger Robert's visions of death. He heard the same fear in Evelyn's voice that he had heard on the battlefield, the fear that something unspeakable was about to happen, but he could do nothing about it. He froze, paralyzed, unable to even light the kindling laid up in the fireplace. The pail of water sat in the corner untouched.

"Robert," Evelyn said sharply, "Now!" Robert's paralysis gave her focus and pulled her out of her own fears.

"Yes, of course," he mumbled, slowly coming out of his fog. She looked at him, but he could not return her gaze. He busied himself with the fire. He had long stopped crying when he watched so many men die in the war, but his eyes were moist. He made the fire and set the water to heat, but he could not stay in the house any longer, could not stay with the pain. He had to escape. "I have to milk the cow," he said, meekly, knowing he should not leave but could not help himself.

"If you must," Evelyn said sharply, the anger on her face clear. She had seen him do this before, finding a reason to leave when he could not cope with his fear, or her anger, or both. Robert's helplessness triggered her fierce protective instincts. She would take care of her sweet boy, with or without her husband.

Evelyn mixed potash and sulfite of soda, two parts to one, filled the glass with hot water, and gave small sips to Steven to swish around his mouth and spit out. His crying became higher-pitched, harsher, more like a dying rabbit, feral, desperate. Evelyn listened carefully for the dreaded sign of diphtheria, a barking cough that sounded like no other cough, painful to the ear for those who listened, and more so to the one coughing. But it was not there, not yet.

"Mommy," Thomas asked, "what's wrong with Steven?" He stood in the corner of the room, head drooping, eyes red, lips trembling. He had never seen his mother shaking and frightened like this. Thomas was ten years old, old enough to know that something terrible was happening, but young enough to have nothing he could do to help. He felt helpless like his mother but paralyzed, not energized like she was. When Evelyn didn't respond, Thomas asked again, more pleading. "Mommy, what? Tell me."

"Stop!" Evelyn yelled, "I have to take care of Steven, don't bother me! He's very sick. Just stay out of the way! Go outside."

Thomas whimpered with shame and did not understand why his mother was angry at him. *What do I do? How can I help?* His feelings of inadequacy washed over him, his cheeks red with embarrassment. He so wanted to help his mother, and Steven as well, but his mother more. "Why, mommy? Why do I have to go outside?" She did not answer, turning away. *What have I done?*

"Dear Lord, please let my dear boy live," Evelyn prayed, whispering to herself. She tried to convince herself that this was just one more worrisome childhood fever, the kind that passes without harm.

Robert slid hesitantly through the cabin door with a small pail of milk, giving him what he hoped was an adequate excuse for not being inside with Evelyn and his sick son. He knew he should be more helpful to his family, but his memories would not let him. "What do you think?" Robert asked, softly, cautiously.

"Where have you been?" Evelyn asked angrily. "Your son is sick! What can be more important than that?"

"I'm sorry," Robert said, shuffling his feet in shame. "The cow needed milking." He hoped she would need nothing from him because he had nothing to give.

She sobbed, releasing her anger. "He's not worse, but not better. I've tried everything, but nothing helps. Oh, Robert, it can't be diphtheria. We can't lose him," she said, desperate, pleading. Her whole body sagged as she looked at Steven. "You need to fetch the doctor. The trip to town will take at least two hours. I don't know what else to do."

Robert nodded, flooded with relief and guilt at the same time, relief that he had a reason to leave this deathly drama and guilt that he wished for a reason to leave. Ironically, the very thing he hoped would heal him from the nightmares of war—a family and children to care for—were now the source of an even more personal agony than the deaths on the battlefield. He wanted to be far away from the very thing he had hoped would be his salvation.

He saddled the horse and set off in the fading light.

Steven ate a bit, some soft porridge that soothed his throat. As night came, he slept fitfully, crying out from time to time, waking Thomas, but not Emily, his four-year-old sister who innocently slept. Steven's skin was pale, his eyes red and eyelids drooping. Evelyn did everything she knew that might help, using every combination of potions and ingredients she could find in her home remedy book, *The Favorite Medical Receipt Book and Home Doctor.*

And then in the night, Steven finally released the cough that Evelyn had been fearing the most. It was a cough that everyone referred to as barking, but it was really more an explosive, rasping wheeze.

Evelyn broke down, sobbing, "Oh, Steven, no, no," she wept. "Please don't cough like that!" She shook her head back and forth, moaning with fear. She held him tight and rocked, crying out to no one. His hair was wet with sweat, his skin gray, and his eyes closed as he barked and wheezed and fought to breathe. The small cabin seemed to shrink to a gray fog around Evelyn and Steven as the weight of the sickness overtook him.

"Thomas, go down the lane to see if your father is coming with the doctor," Evelyn called out. Thomas heard no more anger in her voice, only fear and exhaustion. Her fear was more painful to him than her anger. His mother seemed small, resigned, grasping at the hope that the doctor would fix everything.

Evelyn held a candle up to Steven's face so she could see down the back of his throat. "Oh, no, no, not that!" she whispered with hushed panic. What she saw was a gray, leathery membrane of pus layered across the back of his throat, covering his tonsils and extending up the back of his throat. As she looked, Steven coughed, gagged, and spit a thumb-sized chunk of the membranous pus into Evelyn's face. His breath was fetid, and Evelyn gagged with the humid stink, like stirring up rotting vegetation at the bottom of a swamp pond. Steven gagged again, along with Evelyn, and choked, his face turning blue. He stopped breathing. Evelyn screamed and shook him, and he started breathing again, barely, in raspy bursts.

Robert and Thomas both heard Evelyn's scream as they walked up the lane. Breaking into a run, they entered the cabin just as Steven started breathing again. Robert looked at his son's pale face. He had failed, failed in comforting his wife, failed at caring for Steven, failed in finding the doctor. "I'm sorry, dear, the doctor was not at home. His wife said he was out with another sick child."

And just at that moment, as Robert awkwardly tried to comfort his wife, Steven died. He took one short rattling breath and stopped breathing. Evelyn shook him again, but no new breath came.

"Noooo, please no!" Evelyn shrieked, rocking Steven gently and sobbing. He turned cold quickly in the cool cabin air, his face graying as the blood ebbed away. Evelyn's face was the same gray and nearly as cold. She stared unseeing at Steven, then at Robert, pleading with her eyes for him to help. But there was nothing he could do, or anyone could do.

Thomas slid away to the dark corner of the room, terrified by his mother's scream. *Why couldn't his father make things right? Why did Steven die? Why does anyone die?* His father had always been so strong. He had always known what to do. But not now.

Evelyn held Robert's shoulders and sobbed, unable to believe that her son was gone. Then she shook Robert off and pulled herself away. She was beyond angry at Robert, or anyone. She was angry at life, at how unfair it was, unfair for Steven, unfair for her. She had failed at a mother's most important task, protecting her child.

Robert collapsed in dry heaving sobs, as he had done on the battlefield, overwhelmed and frightened. Death had followed him into his own home. It could not be escaped.

All Robert could think to do was feed Thomas and Emily, something simple, something basic, something where he did not have to think. He boiled potatoes, and they ate in silence while Evelyn sat in the corner rocking and sobbing with Steven. Robert told Evelyn he was going out to dig a grave, just like he had left before to milk the cow, anything to get away, any way to distract him from the pain he could not bear. She barely looked up, nodding slightly. He left the children sitting at the table and went outside. It only took a few minutes to dig such a small grave in the ground thawed by the spring winds. Then he came in to get Steven. Evelyn still clung to her son and would not let him go.

"It's time," Robert said gently. Evelyn looked at him with empty eyes and finally nodded, nearly imperceptibly. Robert took Steven's limp body and kept it wrapped in the sweaty blanket. He led the family out the door. They walked through dwindling patches of snow and came to the place where a small, shallow grave waited to receive Steven's body. Robert gently lowered the body into the ground.

"Dear Lord," Robert said, awkward, numb, not knowing what to say. "We give this small boy to your care and hope he will awaken from this terrible sleep in Heaven." Robert then read a short scripture from the Book of Matthew, something he had heard read at funerals of other children. He never imagined he would have to do so for his own child.

"At that time the disciples came to Jesus, saying, 'Who is the greatest in the kingdom of heaven?' And calling to him a child, he put him in the midst of them, and said, 'Truly, I say to you, unless you turn and become like children, you will never enter the kingdom of heaven. Whoever humbles himself like this child, he is the greatest in the kingdom of heaven. Whoever receives one such child in my name receives me.'"

Robert and Evelyn looked at each other silently. There was nothing more to say. They stood side by side, not touching, facing the grave. The cool morning wind rustled the dead leaves left on the trees. The words from the Bible seemed small, but it was all they had. Robert shoveled dirt over the blanket-wrapped body. Only a few shovels full were needed. Evelyn turned to Thomas and Emily with dry, red eyes. "We love you," she said flatly.

Robert could only nod.

"Please remember your brother in your prayers," she pleaded.

Robert nodded again.

They turned and walked back toward the cabin. Thomas reached out to hold Emily's hand. He had to touch someone. His little sister looked at him with trusting eyes.

Robert and Evelyn grieved Steven's death, but in very different ways. Robert buried his grief in working the farm as summer came, breaking up the rich soil and planting, and he always had the cow to milk twice a day. He just worked harder and longer, cleared more land, found chores even when there were none, and pushed the memories of Steven to the corners of his thoughts. However, he could not escape the night, Steven's suffocating breaths roaring in his head as he laid awake staring at the dark ceiling, night after night.

Evelyn went the opposite direction, to a different place, slower, sluggish, like wading through a swamp. Her eyes were empty and their blackness absorbed the light that came near. Any task, no matter how small, was more than she could manage. Just thinking about her daily chores, like making supper, overwhelmed her. Each day, she tried to keep up with her duties, failed, and sunk into a deeper melancholia from her inadequacy. The children would often pick up on her unattended tasks while she spent the entire day sitting in a chair, staring at nothing. Evelyn sucked the energy out of Robert and the children. It disappeared into her soul, lost to all of them.

Then a new exhaustion settled on Evelyn, and her stomach was unsettled. She vomited one morning and knew she was pregnant. She felt no joy. "Robert," she said a few days later, pale, with a flaccid face and voice, "I think I am expecting a baby."

Robert hoped this might bring cheer to Evelyn. "Perhaps this will give us a fresh start," Robert said, unsure how Evelyn would greet this news. "Our family must continue to grow and thrive." And he immediately knew he had said the wrong thing as he saw her face.

"I don't know how you can say that!" she snapped at him. "We have already failed once as parents. How can we do better this time? I have failed as a mother," she said, and paused before adding the final cruelty, "and you as a father!"

Robert shrank in the face of her anger, but more than anger, her hopelessness and her helplessness. He was watching his beloved wife's soul turn to dust before his eyes, blown away by the winds of her desperation.

Evelyn watched Robert with horror at what she had said, watched him absorb her cruel anger as his love for her faded. *What have I done? I failed Steven. I am failing Thomas and Emily. And now I have failed as a wife. I cannot be the mother I am going to be again.*

Robert turned and shuffled out the door to the barn to milk their cow. Evelyn watched him go with the deepest sadness but did not call him back. "Children," Evelyn said as they stood frozen, watching, confused, scared. "I am going to be a mother again. You are going to have a new brother or sister." Her despondency was obvious to even Thomas and Emily. The household turned cold and life became meager, dwindling on aimlessly. Thomas and Emily were left alone for most of each day. They did not understand why Evelyn had stopped being their mother.

One day, seven months after Steven died, Evelyn sat in the chair, her pregnancy growing and uncomfortable. She stared at the rough log walls and lost track of Emily as she played outside. Robert was running the family's horse to the small barn where it was kept. Emily was playing in the straw on the packed dirt barn floor. Robert could not see her from behind the horse. Emily screamed as the horse thundered into the barn. The horse startled, reared high, and its heavy hooves came down hard on Emily. She died instantly from a crushed skull.

Robert screamed, like he screamed silently in his nightmares but now a loud wail. He collapsed in a heap on the barn floor. The metallic smell of hot blood flashed red in his brain. He was lying on the battlefield, shells bursting all around, the sound of musket balls hitting skulls like thumping on a hollow drum. He started shaking, a near seizure, uncontrollable, and grabbed his head trying to make the screams stop.

Evelyn came running when she heard the screams and saw Emily lying crumpled on the barn floor. She collapsed on the floor next to Robert but did not touch him, her screams even louder than his. Thomas followed behind and saw his parents weeping and clawing at the straw on the floor. Thomas did not understand what was happening until he came closer and could see Emily lying in an expanding pool of blood.

He saw the horseshoe print clearly visible on Emily's crushed left cheek. A new feeling, strange and embarrassing, welled up to fill the void. He was curious, curious about Emily's injuries, about what happened inside her crushed and lumpy head. He saw bits of pale wormy tissue seeping out of the torn scalp. He had never seen a brain before, and it fascinated him. Her blond curly hair was matted with clots of dark blood. He knelt by Emily's head and reached down to touch the blood dripping down her neck and face as it soaked the straw on the barn floor.

His father slapped his hand, and screamed at him, "Don't touch her, it's disgusting!"

Thomas knew it was strange to want to touch her blood and bits of brain, but he didn't think it was disgusting. He didn't know if it was right or wrong, but it just was. It's not that he wasn't shocked by Emily's death, and he started crying as well, his lips trembling and his stomach churning. But lurking in the corner of his sadness was this curiosity. *Why does blood smell like that? What does brain feel like? What happens to a heart when it stops? Why do these things happen? Why did they happen to his family? Why did Steven stop breathing? What did Emily feel as the horse's hoof came down on her?*

Evelyn lashed out at Robert. "How could you let this happen?" she hissed, hateful and vicious.

"I, I don't know," Robert replied. "I didn't expect her to be in the barn. I thought you were watching her." Anger and accusation of each other flashed in their eyes, and then their eyes went cold. They were both exhausted, and neither had the energy to hang onto their anger. Evelyn thought there was fault, and it was Robert's. Robert thought she was responsible, but not at fault. But neither cared much anymore, about blame, about fault, about each other. The tragedies of life and death had triumphed over love and dreams.

❈·❈·❈·❈·❈

Thomas remembered little of the next four months. He took care of himself, helped his father where he could, tried to cheer his mother without success, and finally just suffered through the fall into the late winter. Attending school was his only solace. He did whatever chores his father had for him, carried in wood and kindling for the dinner fire, brought in water when his mother asked. His father asked little of him as he bustled about his never-ending chores. His mother asked little of him because she asked nothing of anyone, including herself. The three of them could go days with only a few words. Thomas often sat in the corner with a book.

Evelyn went into labor on Thomas's eleventh birthday in February. Labor should have gone quickly and smoothly, but it did not. The baby wouldn't come. Robert went to fetch the midwife, but she was attending a delivery elsewhere and unavailable. Robert continued on into town to find the doctor. Evelyn suffered through hours of contractions without progress before the doctor arrived.

"Evelyn, I'm sorry," the doctor said. She just looked and barely nodded, consumed by pain. "The baby is looking up, not down, sunny side up like we say." he said with an awkward chuckle. "The baby won't come down in that position, even with your other deliveries going well. It's stuck. I need to turn it before it can deliver. If I don't do anything you will eventually get infected, or your womb will rupture. Both you and the baby will die."

"Do whatever needs to be done," Evelyn whispered, barely able to be heard by the doctor. She was resigned, numb all over. The doctor pulled back the blanket and reached into her vagina, without a thought of washing his hands.

Evelyn's doctor found the baby looking up and slightly to Evelyn's right side. He laid his right palm and fingers along the right side of the baby's head, over its right ear, with his fingers along the baby's neck. He gently rotated the baby's head counter-clockwise as Evelyn pushed. The baby's head rotated easily, and the body followed. Now looking down, with the top of its head starting to appear in the vaginal opening, the baby was easily delivered. The doctor guided a healthy, screaming baby boy into a silent home. Evelyn managed a wan smile. Robert was grateful the demons stayed away for now, and he managed a loving look at the baby. He and Evelyn did not look at each other.

Thomas had been told to go outside while the doctor worked. He crept back in through the door, knelt quietly and watched. He was in awe of the physician, who looked so powerful, so commanding. The doctor knew things that saved his mother's life and brought his new baby brother into the world as if by magic. Thomas wished he had that magic.

Three days after delivering the baby, just as Evelyn's milk came in and the baby started nursing, she felt hot and feverish. Perhaps it was just from nursing, perhaps from breast engorgement as sometimes happened. Later that day, she felt an intense wrenching pressure in her lower abdomen, and a rush of foul greenish fluid expelled from her vagina, thick with blood clots. Evelyn screamed, "Thomas, get your father!" He ran out the door to the field where his father was clearing brush.

"Father, something terrible has happened. Please come!" His father ran in and found Evelyn writhing in pain. Robert pulled back the covers and saw the sheet fouled with blood and pus. He pulled the sheet off the bed and handed it to Thomas.

"Take this down to the stream and rinse it out," his father said. Thomas gagged as he took the putrid blanket. He tried to wash it out as best he could. He brought the wet blanket back into the house but could not look at his mother moaning and writhing on the bed.

Robert touched her lower abdomen lightly and Evelyn screamed with pain. "Don't, please don't," she cried. Her skin was hot and the slightest touch of even her clothing was painful. "I am so tired," she said. "Please help me."

"I don't know what to do," he said, the same helpless feelings welling up again. Their life had been cold for the past year, and now he was failing her again. She was pale, and her heart was pounding in her chest, fast and fluttery. As the sun waned and set into evening, her skin became even hotter, almost burning to Robert's touch. She stopped responding to his questions. He tried to sit her up, but she passed out. He laid her back down gently and her eyelids fluttered.

Her consciousness faded as twilight was lost to the darkest night. "Dear, please try to take some water." It dribbled down her cheek. She looked at him as if he were a stranger, eyes wide and wild but unseeing. He put the baby to her breast, but the baby cried because Evelyn's skin was so hot.

"Thomas, you will have to watch her closely while I go to find the doctor."

"Yes, father, but what do I do?"

"Just be with her, hold her hand, give her some water if she will take it. I don't know, just do the best you can."

Robert made the trip once again to fetch the doctor. The doctor was in his office but would not come. "There is nothing I can do," he said. "I am sorry. Puerperal fever, infection after a baby is born, has no treatment. It just happens and we do not know the cause or the treatment."

Robert cried and pleaded, "Please doctor, please do whatever you can to save my wife!"

"I'm sorry," he said. "I have no treatment to offer. It just happens," he repeated. "She is now in God's hands." *God's hands,* Robert thought. *Whatever happened always seemed to be in God's hands.* Neither the doctor nor Robert could know that whatever happened came from the doctor's dirty hands.

Robert returned, out of his mind with fear, whipping his horse along the trail from town, ducking the low branches along the trail, desperate and frantic, making the trip in less than the usual two hours. He ran into the house breathless, saw Evelyn gray and silent. He thought she was dead, but she stirred slightly. "Thomas, fetch some warm water from the fire."

"Where is the doctor?" Thomas asked, looking hopefully behind his father as he had come into the cabin. He expected the doctor to arrive and save his mother's life as it seemed he had done before at the delivery.

"He said there is nothing he can do for this type of infection. Whatever happens now is God's will." He paused, and a bitter scowl came across his face. "I am sick of hearing about God's will. When it is up to God, someone always dies. Just get the water." He tried to do what he knew from caring for their cow, rinsing the vagina and uterus, running a tube with warm water containing a few drops of carbolic acid from a bucket. The discharge became less foul, but Evelyn did not awaken. He felt her pulse. It was thin and slow, a dying pulse. Her skin turned cool.

Robert fell back in the chair next to the bed, wrenching his head from side to side. The demons had returned, and their screaming intensified as Evelyn's pulse slowed, beat by beat, until it stopped. By then, the screaming in Robert's head was so loud he could not think or talk. He looked at Thomas, eyes wide, mouth open, and just shook.

"Father, what is happening?" But Thomas knew, and he ran from the cabin, ran as hard as he could into the woods, collapsed on a pile of loose snow and cried into the icy pellets. Everything good about his life had ended. The deaths of Steven and Emily seemed at the time to be the worst things he could imagine, but only because he could not imagine his mother dying. And now she was gone, the one light in his life, even in her deepest melancholy, extinguished. He started shivering, from the cold and from the bleak life that gripped him. He got up slowly and walked back into the cabin to see his father staring blankly at the fire.

Thomas tried to hug his father. His father sat in a sodden heap and did not respond. He sat staring at the fire into the night. Robert held the baby but had nothing to offer, no warmth, no milk. The baby cried, hungry, and they tried to drip milk from the cow into the baby's mouth. He took enough to stop crying. They dripped more milk and then all three of them fell asleep.

Robert woke Thomas as the faintest dawn light came through the dirty window. "We have work to do, Thomas. Fetch the shovel and axe from the barn."

But the ground was frozen. They tried unsuccessfully to dig a grave deep enough to bury Evelyn. So they chopped ice from the pond and packed it around her body in the barn, surrounded by straw for insulation. They worked without talking, each lost in his own misery and loss. Thomas stared at his mother's cold face. It did not look so different from the face he had seen for the past year, and he ached for her love. He wondered what happened at that moment when someone was alive and then not alive.

The baby needed to be fed. He was pale and listless, weakly sucking Thomas's little finger. Neighbors were few and distant, and Robert knew of no woman who could serve as a wet nurse. Thomas and his father tried to drip milk as they had done the night before, but it was not enough. They fashioned a leather pouch with a spout and tried to drip milk into the sucking infant. The pouch worked well enough but became infected and the milk contaminated, with severe diarrhea the inevitable consequence. They knew of many remedies for diarrhea in older children and adults—castor oil, white oak tea, or subnitrate of bismuth. Laudanum was often used. But none seemed right for a newborn.

"Thomas, keep trying to help the baby suck," Robert said. They looked silently at each other, terrified, unable to believe how much tragedy swirled around them. The baby sucked weakly on the dripping milk, but it was not enough to keep up with the diarrhea. His skin dried and became scaly. Thomas and Robert slept little, milked the cow and ate together silently as they watched the baby slowly fade away. He stopped urinating, his eyes were dark and shrunken, and he died ten days after he was born.

Robert and Thomas wrapped the baby in a clean blanket and carried him out to the barn, now two bodies to pack in ice and insulate with straw. "Thomas, your job now is to keep the ice fresh until we can do a proper burial," Robert said. Thomas took his responsibility seriously, mopping up the water from the melted ice, chopping new ice out of the pond. The weather warmed, the ice melting faster but the ground also thawing. "Why did mother die?" Thomas asked his father several times.

"It seems that God wished for it to be so," his father replied. "If our lives are in his hands, and those lives seem to end so tragically so often, then it must be his desire. Why I do not know. I used to put my faith in God. No more."

They dug graves near Steven and Emily, the baby's grave so sadly small compared to Evelyn's. Robert had never given the baby a name, so he was buried with a rough wooden marker. Thomas used black paint to write "Baby Boy Wilson" on the cross piece. Robert said nothing as they threw dirt over the blanket-wrapped bodies. Thomas carved the sweet face of a lamb in the wooden grave marker.

Chapter 3

Michigan, 1876–78

However deep Robert's depression was before Evelyn and the baby died, it found a way to sink even lower, a bottomless pit of melancholic despair. He ate little, lost weight, slept fitfully, stumbled through the farm work and chores, sometimes not saying a word through the entire day. He avoided town and sent Thomas to the store. Thomas heard him moaning almost every night, rustling and rolling in the bed.

Thomas tried to bring his father out of his misery, just as he had tried with his mother, and, as he soon learned, just as unsuccessfully. Robert's black hole was unreachable and untouchable. Thomas's attempts to find the bottom were exhausting.

"Father, please come to the store with me. It would be good for you to see other people."

"No, you go," he said, flat and slow as always. "I need to stay here and take care of the farm." Each word seemed to be a struggle for Robert. Thomas's loss of his mother was magnified now by the loss of his father, who might as well have died for all that he was available to Thomas.

Underneath Thomas's grief was another layer of sadness, a different grief from Robert's. Robert blamed God, or a vengeful God, or the lack of a God for their family's tragedies. Thomas blamed himself, not in so many words, but he felt inadequate in some vague way. As a now nearly twelve-year-old boy, he was unable to say in words what he was feeling, but then he had no one with whom he could talk anyway. The feelings of failure bored into him and found root in his deepest parts, embedded for the rest of his life. He had tried to be helpful but believed he had failed. He could not say exactly what he should have been able to do, but he hated feeling inadequate and helpless. The feelings flashed in his mind at strange and unpredictable times as he went through the day, waves of putrid smells from the blanket his father asked him to wash, the feel of the splintered wood as he carved the face of a lamb on his brother's cross, and always the sticky sweet smell of Emily's blood.

Thomas and his father were both miserable, but there was a difference that would change Thomas's life. He knew he needed something, or someone, to help him find his way back to a new life. That someone turned out to be Clara Easton.

While Robert staggered through the day, he let Thomas attend school, at least most of the time. The town of Mendon had a one-room school for children of all ages. Attendance varied with the ebb and flow of farm and home responsibilities. The teacher, Clara Easton, was young, energetic, and passionate about her students, of whatever age. She was paid by donations from the local families and might see ten or twelve children in her class at the most, fewer in the summer at the height of the farming season. Rarely did a child attend school past the age of twelve. But she was entirely devoted to them, for whenever and however long they were present.

Clara could see that Thomas was troubled, for what seemed to be obvious reasons. But she felt like there was something more, and she was determined to find out what it was. Clara knew of other children at school who had seen death and had lost family members. They did not seem to suffer like Thomas was suffering. Death was a fact of life, and Clara saw most people grieving, in many personal ways, but eventually moving on. Disease and injury were everywhere, and the explanations meager or nonexistent. People were not in denial, just realistic about life and the mysteries of the death that often followed, early and tragically.

Thomas was not moving on, perhaps because he had nowhere to go. He had become, in many ways, an orphan. Clara saw Thomas's father rarely, but she saw him enough to know that Thomas had been left with a father who barely spoke, was present only physically (and barely that), and was incapable of either expressing or understanding his own grief, let alone being able to help Thomas with his. She vowed to see if or how she could help.

"Thomas," Clara said one day in class, "could you stay after school for a few minutes, please?"

"Yes," Thomas replied, immediately nervous. *What have I done? Why did the teacher want me to stay after school?* Students kept after school had usually misbehaved. He never misbehaved.

"Thomas," Clara said, after the other students had left, "You are doing very well in school. I will tell you that you are the best student I have ever had, although admittedly my teaching career is somewhat short," she said and smiled awkwardly.

"Thank you," Thomas said, embarrassed but relieved that he did not seem to be in trouble.

"I am so sorry about your family's terrible losses. How are you and your father doing?"

"I guess we are getting along," he said, reluctantly, starting to wish he had been in trouble instead.

"Tell me more about how the two of you get along. Have you talked about the terrible tragedies in your family?"

"No, I don't think he wants to talk about what happened."

"Why do you think that is?" she asked.

"I don't know, just is." Thomas was much happier talking about school. He had read every book in the classroom, sometimes more than once. *Tom Brown at Oxford* was his most treasured. Life at an English university seemed so exciting and so magical. He dreamed of attending a university, although he really had no idea what that meant. Perhaps learning and education could offer some answers to his vague discomforts. *I have so many questions,* Thomas thought frequently. *Why have I seen so much death? Why my family? Why couldn't the doctor help? Why didn't God care? Why couldn't my father help? Why couldn't I help!?* Thomas was starting to understand that he wanted to find a different world from the one he lived in now, a world without so much sadness and loss, a world with purpose and the ability to do good. Maybe that different world was college.

"Have you thought about attending college?" Clara asked, as if she could read Thomas's mind. "You are certainly smart enough to do so. There are many exciting possibilities with a college education, including being a teacher yourself, like me! Would your father at least let you stay in school for another year or two?"

"I so wish I could," he said, "but I think my father needs me on the farm." He made it sound like it really wasn't his decision, but then he had no idea what his father thought, since they never talked.

"Your father has seemed supportive of you staying this long, longer than most children. Maybe you could discuss this with him." She was being very careful. She did not want to be the source of more conflict between Thomas and Robert, but she knew that the longer he continued to come to school, the more opportunities she would have to plant the idea of college. She didn't know why Robert had allowed Thomas to stay in school this long. Maybe he just didn't care. He barely talked to her, and what he said was vague and mumbled. "Perhaps I should be the one to discuss this with him sometime," she said gently. "I could also raise the possibility of future college attendance, perhaps at the University of Michigan in Ann Arbor. I was one of the first women admitted there to study to become a teacher," she said proudly.

"I would like that very much," Thomas said, "but my father needs me." Thomas could not let himself think that college was even possible. It was easier to just blame his father.

Clara could not tell if this was Thomas or his father talking.

Thomas was resigned to his fate. His brief spark of excitement about a future in school, and away from the farm, died quickly as he thought about his father struggling on the farm alone. However much he wanted to be somewhere else, anywhere else, other than the farm, it seemed to be his responsibility for now to keep the farm functioning as best he could. *He may think he can take care of the farm, but he just can't. Maybe the farm can't survive anyway, even if I stay home. I just want a new life, any life, a life away from so much misery.* Thomas sighed to himself and left the thought of college to wither in a distant corner.

The next February came, nearly a year after Thomas's mother and baby brother died, the days short, the nights dark and cold. Robert did not seem to remember that it was Thomas's twelfth birthday, but then the day was no different than any other day anyway. Each day started in the dark, milking the cow, followed by the anticipation and excitement of heading off for school for a few hours, even trudging through sleet and snow, sometimes fighting a biting wind. After school, he plodded back home for chores in the barn, his step slower and dragging. The day ended in the dark at supper. They ate together in silence. School was the only place where he felt right.

But then after dinner, on his birthday night, his father spoke. Thomas had heard his father's voice so infrequently that it startled him.

"Your teacher came to see me today, while you were out in the field working. She has an idea you should think about college."

Thomas could barely think, his mind spinning, happy and frightening thoughts racing around. His father had never talked about school, let alone college. Thomas could barely control his excitement. The flat and lifeless tone of his father's voice might indicate what he thought of the college idea, but then he always sounded like that. Thomas replied cautiously, "But I would have to go to school regularly. I can't leave the farm. I shouldn't leave the farm. You told me you needed me here to work." He so wished that his father would say he was not needed, that it was more important for Thomas to seek a new life elsewhere.

"I do need you, I guess," Robert said.

Thomas's shoulders slumped.

"But I don't really know anymore what I need, or what the farm needs. Not sure I care either. The teacher—what's her name, Miss Easton?—suggested the possibility of having her tutor you, separate from school, just for you."

The idea of tutoring seemed so special to Thomas, a fantasy almost beyond his imagination. He wished Miss Easton was there so he could give her a hug. He was overcome with excitement and just blurted out, "I would so much like to do that, but how?"

"She proposes to come here three days a week, after school is out. There would be an extra fee. You would have to earn some of it."

Thomas's excitement could not be contained, and it flooded over the supper table. "Yes, yes, yes!" he said.

Just this much conversation, more words than his father had said in total in the last few months, seemed to exhaust Robert. But he had more to say. "Miss Easton thinks you could attend a university, and tutoring would help get you there. I don't really know what that means, what happens at university, really even what a university is. But she is very persuasive. She says you are bright, and you could have many opportunities." He paused, looking away, searching for his next words. "Your mother would be very proud." He used every bit of his remaining emotional energy on those last words. It was the longest speech Thomas had ever heard his father make.

Thomas said, "But that means I would be leaving the farm permanently. Don't you need me?"

"Yes, but it's not up to me. You are twelve now and have to start deciding these things for yourself. I won't encourage you, but I won't stop you either. If you think it's the right thing to do and you can make something of it, go ahead. You are the only one left in our family. If the family has any future at all, anything like what your mother and I dreamed about so long ago, I guess it's in your hands now." He paused, forming the words for one more thought. "Perhaps you will come back to town after college, some new job, a job that amounts to something."

Robert seemed to have used all the words he knew or for which he had the energy to speak. Thomas felt the enormous burden that suddenly came with this extraordinary opportunity. His father was sacrificing everything for Thomas's future. Thomas would have to sacrifice everything to make sure he was worthy of his father's support.

Tutoring started the next week.

CHAPTER 4

Michigan, 1884–1897

Thomas lived in two worlds with two lives after his father allowed Clara to tutor him. He struggled to keep them separate. The tutoring was somewhat sporadic, dependent on the needs of the farm and the season of the year, more in the winter, less in the summer. But every moment he was with Clara, at home or at school, was precious and bright. His father kept his promise, and Thomas kept his by earning part of the fee by delivering groceries from the store in town on weekends. Clara was demanding because she cared, cared about Thomas's education, cared about him as a young man growing into adulthood. Her demands were matched with love. She became the mother Thomas had lost.

"Thomas, you know why I am demanding so much of you, don't you?" she would say from time to time.

"Yes, Miss Easton, I guess." He knew she wanted him to do well, to be fully prepared if or when he applied to the University of Michigan. *Is this what my mother would have been like if she had not died? Is this what a mother does?* He would never know, nor would Miss Easton, but she acted how both of them thought a mother would. She was strict about his studying, congratulated him when he performed well, and then made the next test even harder. She expected so much of him.

Thomas grew and thrived under her watchful, motherly eye. He responded in kind, feeling her support but also her expectations. The school's resources were modest, but Clara made the best with what she had. He read every book, more than once, and could recite some of them from end to end. She sometimes bought an extra book for him with her own money. His father bought a book as well when he was feeling better, a precious event that became increasingly rare over time. Each day at school glittered with excitement, and then he had to go home. He would set off for the walk home with a brisk step, the same step that brought him to school in the morning, but he was trudging and kicking at the dirt by the time he got to the cabin.

Clara opened his world to new possibilities, which made the torn and tattered daily drudgery with his father even more miserable. His expanding world at school contrasted sharply with the increasingly closed and dark sadness he continued to feel at home, especially for some reason at the death of Baby Boy Wilson, the baby brother without a name.

His life at home was unpleasant, but his father was not mean. Thomas sometimes wished he was. It would be better than just not being there at all. His father mumbled about chores that Thomas needed to do and then said nothing more when Thomas completed them. His father never looked at him when he spoke. Thomas started to realize that he was doing the same thing. Their brief and infrequent conversations mostly occurred with their backs turned to each other. He sometimes told his father about something special that happened at school that day, a test or new book. His father acted like he had not heard Thomas. He could not wait to leave for school each morning.

They suffered alone, together. His father's mental exhaustion allowed, or perhaps encouraged, only a mindless focus on work. He was constantly in motion but accomplished little. His energy declined, along with his health. He complained of chest pains from time to time but would not see the doctor.

He said it was nothing, even as he pressed his fists hard against his chest. They spent long periods together at dinner and in the evening without speaking, just sitting in front of the fire as the light of the flames danced around the shadows of their dark faces. His father sat in his rocking chair and stared into the fire, somewhere else, or maybe nowhere at all. His life force just seeped away before Thomas's eyes.

By the time Thomas left for college, his father was barely keeping the farm working. Getting up in the early morning to milk the cow was more than he could manage some days. The cow's milk eventually dried up, and she was sold to be butchered. He worked vigorously but unproductively to keep the land plowed and tilled, but somehow he could never quite finish all of the planting. The cold fall wind blew across the barren fields where weeds were the only crop. The floor of the house was dusty and littered, and the trash piled up in the woods just a few feet from the cabin door. Leaving for college was a relief in certain ways, a way to escape the black hole into which his father and everything around him had fallen.

On the day Thomas left for town to board the stagecoach for the ride to Kalamazoo where he would catch the train, he assumed, or at least hoped, that his father would come to see him off. He did not. He watched Thomas pack a small, cloth bag with his few clothes.

"Well," Robert said, "I guess this is it."

"I guess so," Thomas said. "I am very worried about you, father. The farm is more than you can manage. I wonder if it wouldn't be better if you sold the farm and moved to town where life would be easier."

"No, no! How can you say that?" his father exploded. "Our whole family is buried in this ground! Our blood is in this ground! I can't believe you could even say such a thing."

"I'm sorry," Thomas mumbled. But he was not sorry. He was angry. *Is this the best he can do?* Thomas thought. *He barely talks and now he uses his precious words to shame and criticize me?* Whatever worry he had about leaving his father blew away like the brown fall leaves.

"As you wish," he said. He turned and walked through the door without a goodbye.

The painful departure from the cabin in Mendon faded in the face of the excitement of his trip to Ann Arbor. He had never ridden a train before and it was so exciting, especially knowing where he was going. He arrived in Ann Arbor, settled into a boarding house, and began his studies. Ann Arbor was a huge town compared to Mendon, people bustling around, elegant carriages, shops with fancy clothes, even restaurants. Thomas was overwhelmed.

He felt the greatest awe and excitement at his new world of learning and was proud of how well he was doing, but it was all tempered by guilt about his father. Clara had prepared him well for his studies, but she had not, and could not, prepare him for handling his feelings that he had failed his father by leaving. He had no good idea how he could have helped if he had stayed, and his father's hurtful words when he left made it easier. But the more he enjoyed and succeeded in college, the more guilt he felt. At some level he believed he was actually killing his father by leaving home and exploring new directions in his life. He could not really blame his father as the source of his guilt. It was all his.

On top of the guilt, the reality of college life, the foreignness of it all for a farm boy from Mendon, took its toll. At home, Thomas had lived his dual lives in school and on the farm. Now, he lived dual lives in the classroom, where he excelled, and the rest of the day, where he was increasingly isolated, constantly confused by the ebb and flow of college traditions. He was surrounded by hundreds of students, all of whom seemed to know exactly how to behave, how to dress, how to enjoy the freedom of college life. He knew none of those things and was alone and lonely.

Thomas's only source of support was his professors. They recognized his superior academic performance, and at least one recognized that something else lay beneath that performance. Clara's guidance and support were replaced by the mentorship of Professor Silas Douglas, Professor of Chemistry at the University of Michigan. Professor Douglas was trained as a physician but had not practiced, preferring instead to develop his research as a chemist. His mind was dazzling and his interests wide-ranging, from the chemical properties of acids to how to keep plants from freezing. Thomas sought his advice with increasing frequency over time, especially about the strange ways of academic life and the behaviors of his fellow students. Professor Douglas consented to meet with Thomas weekly as his studies progressed, and Thomas took full advantage of this special time.

"Thomas, tell me how you are adjusting to university life," Professor Douglas requested at one of their meetings early in Thomas's second year. "You are doing very well in your studies, but I sense you are not entirely comfortable here."

"Uh, yes, you are correct, professor. I am embarrassed that you noticed. Life here is exciting, sometimes almost too much so, at least academically. Sometimes it is a bit overwhelming, all the new ideas, the stimulating discussions in class, your lectures," he said with a slight smile. "It is all quite a shock compared to my former school, if you can call it that. It was very small and very poor. But my teacher, Clara Easton, took an interest in me, and her tutoring and support prepared me well for my studies here." He paused, and the professor could tell there was something more. "But the rest of it, I am not so sure."

"The rest of what?" Professor Douglas asked.

"Oh, you know, the other students, the parties, the drinking. It's not the way I grew up. I am just not sure I really fit in here or belong."

"Well," the professor said, "most college students do have a certain style. You seem more serious than most of them. I am guessing you think they are somewhat immature, always carrying on with silly pranks. Do you find them annoying?"

"Yes, I do," Thomas said. "Or perhaps the opposite. Maybe I just wish I could be more like them."

"Hmm, tell me more about your life growing up."

"It was fine." Thomas suddenly looked away, his chattiness lost as he went to a different place. He looked back into the professor's steady gaze.

"I sense maybe there is more, something that was not fine?" the professor asked.

"I worry about my father. Sometimes I think I should leave here and go back to help him."

"Oh, I hope that does not happen. You have tremendous potential with your studies here."

"It's the past that's the problem," he said softly. "I wish I could just forget the past."

"Why would you want it to go away? The past is what it is. What matters is what you learn from it, what you make of it. What have you learned from your past?"

"Guilt, shame. My brothers and sisters will never have what I have." He did not say more.

The professor looked at him quizzically. He was certain there was more but did not probe further. "The great sadness of your life, whatever it may be, has had the fortuitous and perhaps paradoxical outcome of forcing you to focus on your studies, making you a particularly exceptional student, able to take advantage of the many opportunities here."

"But what does that mean for the future? Where do I go from here? I think often about those questions but have found no answers."

"I think we need to lay out a new academic plan for you so you can see the possibilities of where you could go from here. We should organize new experiences in my laboratory, like opportunities to teach lower-level students, extra tutoring in the chemical and biological sciences, perhaps even some surreptitious exposure to the dissection laboratory in the new medical building. All of this would be done to prepare you for medical school."

"Medical school?!" Thomas was stunned. He had no idea now where this conversation was headed, but he was sure he disliked the direction. The uncaring physicians, God's will, his father's anger, his mother's gray and cold face. They all competed for his anguished attention. "I have never considered such a thing, nor would I," he replied, with an irritated look on his face. "Doctors are the source of all my family's misery!" He almost yelled.

"But I sense you have a desire to care for people, to apply your scientific mind to the benefit of people around you." The professor was shocked by Thomas's vehement response.

"I think you have misinterpreted my passion for learning," Thomas scoffed. "I have seen the medical care provided by physicians. It was crude and disgusting, and nothing helped. People died."

The professor sat up, even more shocked by Thomas's simple bluntness. "Died? Who died?" He could see he had stirred up an unexpected sadness and anger and was shocked by Thomas's opinions about the medical profession.

"Everyone. My brothers, sister...my mother," Thomas said softly, the anger draining from his voice. "Not my father. He is still alive, sort of." Thomas started crying.

Professor Douglas gasped, unable to help himself. The magnitude of Thomas's loss was incomprehensible to him. The professor could not remember a student ever crying in his office, and he did not know how to respond. He reached out and touched Thomas's shoulder, but Thomas did not seem to feel it. He sat and stared out the office window, tears running down his cheeks. He was somewhere else. Professor Douglas withdrew his hand and sat quietly until Thomas returned.

"I am so sorry, Thomas," Professor Douglas said softly.

"The doctor and my father always said it was in God's hands. Every time they said that, someone I loved died. Why would I want to become a physician and be equally useless?"

"Perhaps not every situation is so futile. The field of medicine is changing rapidly, new discoveries, a more scientific approach, not the strange theories followed by doctors in the past. You might find new opportunities to improve the lives of your patients."

Thomas was skeptical, but the professor's sincerity and clear concern for him was disarming. "I appreciate very much your kindness in discussing this, and your guidance."

"I am not being kind," Professor Douglas said sternly. "It is my responsibility as a professor to bring out the best in my students, to help them reach their fullest potential. You have that potential. To not make the most of it would be a failure on my part. Let us begin to plan together to reach that potential."

"Please give me some time to ponder what you have proposed. I cannot promise anything, but I will give it serious thought." Thomas walked out of the professor's office, the conversation having stirred up the dark images of the past: Steven gasping for breath, Emily's beautiful face lying in a pool of blood on the barn's dirt floor, and his mother, gray and unresponsive to his pleas. But the flashes of the past now came with something new, a fuzzy image of himself, wearing a white coat, looking solemn and wise, standing near a patient lying in bed. The patient in his dreams appeared to have recovered from some unnamed illness because of what Thomas had done. Thomas could start to see the new life he had craved, a new direction, a new purpose. He was still not sure Professor Douglas's assessment was correct, but he was willing to see where it took him.

The University of Michigan Medical School was widely admired for the rigor of its new curriculum and the fame of its professors. It had announced a new, three-year curriculum that placed it in the forefront of the most rigorous and demanding medical schools. Most medical schools offered only a one-year curriculum of lectures, without laboratory or cadaver dissection experience. Sometimes they offered and charged tuition for a second year that was simply a repeat of the first. Thomas was impressed with the progressive nature of the medical curriculum at the University of Michigan and submitted his application.

He wrote to his father to tell him of his plans. His father did not respond.

He had worked throughout college in a local grocery store, sweeping floors, delivering groceries to customers, taking out the trash. It was just one more reason he felt different from other students who seemed to have no need to work to support their lavish lifestyle. He could do the same to pay for medical school. He was easily accepted, older than most applicants, more mature, and better prepared. All of these differences manifested themselves on the first day of medical school in 1887.

Thomas was intrigued by the presence of the woman student as she entered the lecture room. His fellow students had a different reaction. The students had heard rumors that a woman had been admitted, but they could not believe such an elite medical school would do something so outrageous. Their skepticism turned to disgust when the rumor was proven true that first day. Thomas himself was neither disbelieving nor disgusted. Rather he was saddened, then angered, by the same childish behaviors he had seen in his undergraduate classes now being demonstrated in the reaction of his fellow medical students to her presence as she walked in. Their loud, babbling behavior was embarrassing. The embarrassment was compounded by the stern lecture their behavior had drawn from their professor. Thomas had not joined in on the juvenile behavior, but he also had done nothing to stop it. He was equally embarrassed about that.

As the students worked through their first year of classes, it became clear that the woman, Sarah Fletcher, was brilliant, a star student, organized, smart, always prepared, always ready to do more. She was serious, if not sometimes severe. She had her hand up first when a professor asked for answers, but also first up when he asked for questions. She worked in the lab of Professor Sewall and was widely, albeit secretively and sometimes begrudgingly, admired for her scientific curiosity, creativity, and hard work.

He had never known a woman like her. He idolized his mother, but she was gone before he could understand her love and integrity as an adult. Clara Easton was an accomplished and serious woman, and a wonderful teacher and tutor, but Sarah Fletcher was another matter altogether with her level of accomplishment and sophistication, a level to which he aspired but was uncertain of his ability to achieve. She was stunning in appearance, tall, a dramatic angular face, shining black hair. She always wore intense black dresses with lace collars and cloaks, which combined to make her even more mysterious and intimidating on top of her extraordinary academic achievements. He was quite certain he was as smart as she was. He performed equally well in his studies, scored at nearly the same level on exams, and was quite brilliant in his medical and surgical skills. But he was not the person she was. He lacked her depth and gravitas. He didn't know why.

She was fierce in her commitment to becoming a physician, confident in her abilities, clear in her ambitions. He was none of those. He had not yet found himself, not yet come to understand who he was as a person, and therefore as a physician. His memories of his helplessness in the face of his family's deaths continued to drag on him.

Thomas graduated near the top of his class, just behind Sarah. They went their separate ways, seemingly to never see each other again: her to the New York Infirmary for Women and Children, him back to his hometown. Thomas had no good idea for where he should go to practice. In the absence of any plan, the default was to return home. His father had asked him to return as soon he finished his studies, and for that reason alone, he tried to avoid it. But he had no other plan, good or otherwise.

Thomas walked down the stairs from his shabby living quarters on the second floor of his office building to his equally dreary consultation room on the ground floor. The furnishings of both were rustic, to be generous: worn upholstery, a chipped enamel wash basin, and dirty globes on his kerosene lamps. He wondered, as he did every morning, how he was going to get through the day and what he could do this day to build up his meager medical practice.

The town of Mendon was small and poor, lacking both patients and economic vigor to support two physicians. He arrived in town, not happy with the plan of returning home, but trying to conjure an image of himself as a respected physician in his hometown. He had tried hard to be available, to be compassionate, and to be a new resource for the community. But he saw only a couple patients each day and was often paid in vegetables or chickens or not at all. He was frequently called out at night for sick children, infected teeth, bar brawlers who needed stitches, sometimes even a sick cow or horse, but he rarely saw the patients again, or received any payment on their bill. They returned to the other physician in town whom they had not wanted to bother with their emergencies.

The other physician, Dr. Ernie Clark, was, in fact, often drunk and not in a condition to be bothered in the first place, but his patients overlooked that fact in favor of his commanding and authoritative presence when he was sober. He had graduated from the Michigan School of Homeopathy and Surgery, a short-lived proprietary medical school in Detroit that opened in 1863 and closed only a few years later due to its poor quality. The school was a victim of more prestigious universities expanding their modern scientific curriculum, the curriculum completed by Thomas at the University of Michigan.

More importantly to Thomas, he was the physician who had attended to his mother when she delivered his baby brother. Thomas now knew, from his studies, that Dr. Clark's dirty, unwashed hands, had killed his mother as surely as if he had shot her. Now, when flashes of his dying mother intruded on his thoughts, Dr. Clark was often there as well. He had hoped that returning to Mendon, close to his family's graves, would cause the images to fade over time. They hadn't. Now, every time he saw his mother's face, he also saw Dr. Clark's dirty hands.

He confronted Dr. Clark about this on more than one occasion, but Thomas doubted that Dr. Clark even remembered because of his daylong alcohol consumption. The townspeople of Mendon, who continued to die at Dr. Clark's hands, did not seem to appreciate Thomas's more modern approach to medical practice. Dr. Clark was frequently wrong in his diagnosis and treatment, but never in doubt, a certainty that inspired misplaced confidence in the minds of many townspeople.

Thomas had seen just such a patient last month. "Fred, your leg doesn't look good. Tell me what happened."

"Getting to be a clumsy old man," Fred had said. "Stumbled and fell against a piece of rusty metal. Usually see Dr. Clark, so I went to him. He sewed me up, but it doesn't look good now."

"Well, I should say. You have a raging infection and it's moving up your leg. Why didn't you go back to Dr. Clark."

"Sorry, doc, had no choice. His wife said he was out of town for a few days and told me to see you. I wouldn't have bothered you, but the leg looks pretty bad."

"It's worse than that. You could lose the leg, if it doesn't kill you first," Thomas had said. "Happy to help. I am going to have to cut into this pretty deep to clean out the infection."

"Do what you have to do," Fred had said.

Thomas had washed his hands thoroughly, washed Fred's leg and was about to put him under with ether.

"Never saw Doc Clark wash his hands like that," Fred had said.

"I'm sure you haven't," Thomas had said. "That's why you're infected."

Thomas had excised a large portion of the farmer's thigh, removing all of the infected tissue, packed the wound, and left it open to heal without more infection. Fred had been scheduled to return to the office the next week but had not appeared. Thomas saw him on the street the next day. The farmer purposely crossed the street to the other side, awkwardly shambling along on his weakened, but still attached, leg. His cap was pulled low across his face, clearly trying to not see or be seen.

Thomas had the fantasy of leaving Mendon as a bright young local boy and returning as the bright new physician in town. The scene with the farmer, repeated many times over the past seven years, had extinguished every dying ember of that fantasy. He was failing, and he did not know why. And worse than that, he thought that coming back to his hometown would help establish a new relationship with his father. Just one more disappointment.

"Thomas, I just don't see how you think you can compete with Dr. Clark's experience and seasoning," his father had said just last week. "You're so young and inexperienced." His voice had strengthened over the years since Thomas had left, but he still spoke as if every word might be his last.

"Father, you do know, don't you, that I have studied medicine and graduated near the top of my class at a very prestigious medical school. Dr. Clark is a horrible physician who is actually killing patients with his antiquated practices."

"I understand you did well at school, but you are still competing with a long-established and highly-experienced physician."

"Who is usually drunk!" Thomas almost yelled. "He graduated from a third-class medical school that doesn't even exist now, and my guess is he graduated at the bottom of the class at that! You do know that he killed my mother, don't you?" Thomas had purposely never brought this up with his father, but he couldn't stand it any longer.

"What? How do you mean? That's not true. He came to take care of her when she couldn't deliver the baby."

"You remember when he examined her and turned the baby? His hands were dirty, and he didn't wash. That's how she got the infection that killed her! It's what I learned in medical school!"

Ignaz Semmelweis, a Hungarian physician, had vigorously promoted his theories of antisepsis in the 1840s and 1850s, including hand washing when delivering babies and cleaning wounds. His ideas were rejected by the medical establishment as radical and heretical. He was widely criticized and sanctioned until he suffered a nervous breakdown and was committed to a mental asylum. He was beaten by guards, suffered wounds that became infected, and died of overwhelming sepsis in 1865, a death that might have been prevented if his wounds had been treated the way he himself recommended. Midwives adopted his theories more readily than physicians, and their patients fared better than those of physicians as a result.

"I don't believe it. You are just blaming him because you can't compete with him." Robert had run out of words and energy, and he slumped back into his chair. "Have you been to your mother's grave lately? I never see you there," he said, doing what he always did, bringing up the sadness and memories of the past.

"Yes, of course, every week like always," Thomas replied sharply. "You don't see me because you are usually sitting inside." His father could not move past his memories. He still thought of Thomas as a scared eleven-year-old cowering in the corner. Apparently, so did many of the townspeople who avoided his care. He could not escape his past, but it was more than just his past. He was damaged in some way. Something important about him was missing. He did not know what it was or how to find it, but he was determined to do so.

In whatever way that discovery was going to be made, Thomas found out the next morning that he was going to have to make it without his father.

A neighbor of his father's ran breathlessly into his office, "Doc, doc, come quick, something has happened to your father. I found him collapsed outside the front door of his cabin. I brought him in the wagon."

Thomas ran outside to find his father lying on a blanket in the back of the neighbor's wagon. "Father, father!" Thomas touched his cheek and saw the faintest flutter of his father's eyelids. He heard a whisper and leaned down to put his ear near Robert's mouth.

"I llllov…," and the fluttering stopped. Thomas could find no pulse. His first thought was medical, that his father had suffered a massive heart attack. His second thought was personal, that his father's heart had killed him, but in a different way. He knew what he hoped his father was trying to say, but he also knew he would never be certain. A swirl of contradictory emotions flew around him: sadness, anger, relief, guilt, all mixed up in a soup of loneliness. He was now the sole survivor of what had once been a family full of hope and promise. Now he had no reason to stay in this miserable town any longer.

Thomas dug a grave next to the others, behind the cabin, his movements leaden and his heart empty. "Dear Lord, whoever you are. I give you my father, a good man, or at least he tried to be. He tried to do the right things, to take care of his family, to be a good husband and father. I hope you agree. I'm not sure I do. Anyway, please receive him into the Kingdom of Heaven." He thought back to when his father buried Steven. Just like his father then, Thomas did not cry. He felt empty, not angry, not sad, just resigned to the reality of how his family had been destroyed by cruel fate.

Thomas's exhaustion was why he noticed an article in the Mendon newspaper a week after his father died, an article that he would have otherwise ignored. The newspaper reported on the boom in silver mining in several towns in the West, following the well-known boom and bust of the gold mines in California and Nevada of the 1850s and 60s. Several mines in Park City, Utah, in particular, were producing at record levels. Dividends were generous, millionaires were being made, and the opportunities were endless. The newspaper painted a glowing picture of a town that was prospering and growing, with opportunities for teachers, doctors, engineers, and entrepreneurs, anyone who had skills and was looking for a fresh and adventurous start. The mountain climate was invigorating, the town and its people welcoming, and the opportunities endless.

CHAPTER 5

Michigan, 1885–1887

Sarah Fletcher wanted more than anything to become a physician. That dream was about to be realized. The mix of excitement, gratitude, and anxiety nearly overwhelmed her as she walked into class on her first day at the University of Michigan Medical School. She had worked long and hard for this day. The barriers to a career as a physician were many and high for a woman, but she had overcome them. Or so she thought.

She approached the red brick medical school building on the Michigan campus in a light drippy rain and walked through the door, then up the creaking stairs to the lecture hall. The building was a bit of a disappointment, not quite as grand and inspiring as she had imagined, but maybe she expected too much in her awe of physicians and medicine. The paint was peeling a bit, the floors worn, the dark, aged wood on the paneled walls fading. Despite all that, it had a sort of moldy gravitas and gave off an aura of learning, of secrets to be uncovered, of scientific problems to be solved. The high windows let in shafts of a wan light that could be seen in the dusty air, giving the building the feel of a dream, gauzy and serious. The quiet air gave proof of the solemnity of the moment, until she got to the top of the stairs where she could hear a rumbling roar coming from the lecture hall.

She opened the door in the back of the hall and was greeted with a chaotic mob of students standing in the aisles, shouting across the room, shoving each other, punching arms as boys do when they are full of energy that has nowhere to go. She was the only woman in the room, just her and one hundred forty-nine male classmates, all of whom were behaving like bumptious and raucous adolescents, their nervousness on this first day of medical school spiraling into a frenzied rabble. The somber academic weight of the physical surroundings was contaminated by their childish behavior and crude language.

Then they all saw Sarah as she settled into one of the few empty seats in the top row. The room fell awkwardly quiet as every student turned to stare at her. Some students were grabbed and turned by their friends to witness this odd apparition. The male students were confused, first startled into silence and then intrigued. She was tall with shining black hair, sharp cheekbones, and an angular face that some might call classically beautiful but most would say was at least handsome and memorable. Her dark eyes were alert but calm. Several of the male students were confused by her presence, but all were pleased that, whoever she was, she was stunningly attractive.

Sarah could feel the admiration in their stares and despised it. It did not interest her, at that moment or really ever. She had frequently resented how she had been seen by men in her undergraduate classes: for her appearance but not for her intelligence or her professional commitment. Based on the intrigued, but perplexed, looks on one hundred forty-nine faces staring at her, she realized the same resentment was about to play out all over again in medical school, at an even higher level of intensity.

"My name is Sarah Fletcher," she said as she nodded slightly to a student sitting next to her. The room was so quiet that her resonant voice could be heard across the room.

"Edgar Miles," the student next to her replied, with the same slight nod. "And who might you be?" He did not speak in an accusatory way, but he was truly confused as to what this woman was doing in the medical school on this first day of class. Perhaps she was the Professor's assistant, or maybe part of the housekeeping staff.

"A fellow medical student," Sarah said, with a cold smile, "assuming you are one as well."

Then the room erupted again. The students were stunned by the sheer impossibility that this woman could be a member of their class. How could a woman become a physician? Why would she want to do so? How could a woman master the extraordinarily grisly and brutal nature of medical practice?

Edgar turned away from Sarah to talk to his friend, acting like she was not sitting next to him. "Do you think she's the one?" he asked his friend. "I heard that the school admitted a woman this year, but I assumed it was just a rumor. If she's it, they at least picked a real looker!" His friend just nodded, mesmerized by looking over Edgar's shoulder at the side of Sarah's handsome face.

"You do know I am still sitting here, right?" Sarah glared at Edgar. The friend could not bear her gaze and turned away in embarrassment. "I also assume you know that the University admits women to medical school. The first one was in 1871, I believe."

"Yes, yes, of course," Edgar stammered. "We just thought it wouldn't happen to us," he said, the last words mumbled and faint.

Edgar turned away from Sarah to talk to his friend again. Sarah ignored them. "I heard that the faculty tried to block this," Edgar said, "when the Board of Regents voted to admit women to medical school. The faculty said that women couldn't function as physicians when they were semi-invalids for much of each month. But the Regents approved it and here we are. I guess she's it."

"I heard they changed the entry requirements because of women, as well," the friend said with some bitterness. "She's why we all have to now have a full four-year degree to get into medical school. And just to be a physician at that. It doesn't take that much education!"

Had Sarah even tried to overhear their conversation, it would have been impossible as the adolescent cacophony in the lecture hall rose to a deafening level, with hoots and jeers and arms waving in disgust. A few students threw wads of paper at her. Their faces were flushed, contorted, full of their privilege and arrogance.

But it was not every student. Sarah calmly surveyed the chaos below her as she sat at the back of the sloped lecture hall, her maturity flowing down the rows of seats. She noticed one student who was silent, not objecting to the behavior of students near him or trying to subdue them, but not contributing to the riot either. He looked older than most of the students, a round shy face, perhaps kind, she could not be sure. His hair was shorter than that of most students, clean shaven, his clothes a bit dowdy, a baggy coat and pants, not the high, starched collar and puffed ascot of most students. He looked like he had just arrived from the farm and was a bit lost, but he also showed a certain simple calmness, like he found the behavior of his fellow students perplexing, maybe even embarrassing. He looked at her with an open, curious face.

Sarah's gaze lingered on the student briefly and then surveyed the rest of the room calmly and confidently, not frightened, a bit curious, a bit annoyed, somewhat amused. Her excitement at finally realizing her dream of becoming a dedicated physician and scientist could not be even slightly dampened by the students' rude behavior. She was confused about why her fellow students should expend so much energy on her presence, instead of focusing on the excitement of this first day of their new lives as physicians. She was already thinking of the possibilities of where this life would take her. The rowdy students did nothing to weaken her ambition. The students sensed her resolve and were subdued by it. The strength in her face and her commanding presence were like oil on water, quieting the swells and froth of her classmates' exuberance. The shouting settled into murmurs as her dark eyes swept the room, and the humbled students settled into their seats.

Professor Henry Sewall had witnessed the entire unruly incident from a back corner of the lecture hall. He strode down the center aisle of the lecture hall to the front. He wore the traditional outfit of an accomplished and distinguished faculty member: long-waisted, heavy wool coat, equally heavy wool vest with a gold watch chain visible between the folds of his coat, a narrow tie on a spread false collar on his white shirt. His droopy salt-and-pepper mustache matched what little unruly hair he had. He commanded immediate respect, tall and somewhat imperious with a military bearing, a sort of Colossus of Rhodes as he might in fact describe himself based on his liberal education in the humanities. Because of his height, he peered down at nearly everyone over his reading spectacles.

He had been recruited to the University of Michigan in 1880 and was the first person in the United States to earn a doctoral degree in physiology, studying under three prominent physiologists in Germany and England. As part of his recruitment, he received support to develop an active physiology research laboratory, albeit in a cramped, low-ceilinged, and damp room under the lecture hall where he now stood. He worked on a technique to make pigeons resistant to the bite of venomous snakes and demonstrated the principle of antitoxins, mysterious compounds that could be used to combat the adverse and often fatal effects of a snake bite. He theorized that these mysterious chemicals could also neutralize the toxins in serious infectious diseases that plagued humans. A German physiologist, Dr. Emil von Behring, performed similar studies a year or two later in which he infected horses with the diphtheria germ and then injected the horse serum into sick children, reversing their disease. Von Behring received the Nobel Prize for his work, and Professor Sewall was bitter for the rest of his life.

Professor Sewall looked askance at this new class of noisy and ill-behaved medical students. His withering stare could bring students to tears without him saying a word. A deep and immediate silence swept away the last murmurs, partly because of the students' fear of Professor Sewall and partly from the piercing stare of the woman student sitting in the back row. This first day of medical school was one they would remember.

Professor Sewall's voice was soft, menacingly so. The students in the back of the hall, including Sarah, strained to hear. "Gentlemen—and the lady—welcome to the opening day of the curriculum in medicine at the University of Michigan Medical School. You are here to become excellent physicians.

You will be judged by your commitment to, and success in, meeting that objective, nothing more but also nothing less. Any behavior detracting from that commitment will be judged harshly. Part of the professionalism the faculty expects from you as physicians of maturity and education is to show respect to your colleagues, and to model a decorum in behavior consistent with your status in society. Both of these qualities, respect and decorum, were sorely lacking as I entered the class this morning. I trust I will not be embarrassed by your behavior again."

As Professor Sewall spoke, Sarah felt the briefest moment of regret, then a bit of relief, and finally anger—regret that she had chosen to commit herself to what was clearly going to be an arduous journey to overcome the resistance to women becoming physicians, relief that Professor Sewall acknowledged her presence and indirectly her commitment to becoming the excellent physician that he expected every student to become, and anger that he needed to say anything at all. Her height and appearance had always drawn stares. Now she felt even more conspicuous.

But then she remembered again, as she had several times in her journey to this point, her meeting with Dr. Elizabeth Blackwell, the first woman to receive a Medical Doctor degree from a traditional US medical school. She especially recalled the promise she had made to herself after meeting with Dr. Blackwell. She would do whatever needed to keep that promise.

Sarah had been raised in a liberal, free-thinking family whose parents not only tolerated but also encouraged the exploration of independence by their children. She lived with and through books, *Five Weeks in a Balloon* by Jules Verne and *Little*

Women by Louisa May Alcott being two of her favorites. She was inspired by the bold adventure of flying a balloon across Africa, but she was even more entranced by and identified strongly with Louisa May Alcott who was, like Sarah, raised in a free-thinking abolitionist family. She read and re-read the book, focusing in particular on the character Jo, who seemed almost certainly to be based on the author herself. Her independent mind and self-awareness were breathtaking.

On top of her sense of adventure and independence, she was fascinated with science, with biology, with anatomy, with how human bodies worked and didn't work, and with their excreta and fluids. Although, her interest was not just theoretical, not just a curiosity about the rapidly developing knowledge base of human physiology. She wanted to put that information to use for the benefit of patients, to relieve suffering, perhaps even to cure disease and save lives, however primitive and often unsuccessful the methods to do so were in the late 1800s.

Sarah and her family lived in Albion, Michigan, an agricultural community founded in 1835. The progressive enthusiasm for a liberal education that was sweeping the country before the Civil War led to the Wesleyan Seminary being founded in Albion in 1843 by the Methodist Church. The Seminary launched the Albion Female Collegiate Institute in 1850. The merger of the Institute and Seminary in 1861 led to the birth of Albion College as a full, four-year degree, granting institution for both men and women. Albion College promoted itself as a bastion of liberal, forward-thinking higher education, which fit perfectly with Sarah and her family's values.

The combination of economic opportunity and the presence of Albion College attracted abolitionist and free-thinking families, including Sarah's. Her father had a prosperous leather goods business that supplied the Union Army soldiers in the Civil War with their leather cartridge cases. He had decided he could best support his abolitionist fervor with his business expertise. His business also afforded him the privilege of buying himself out of military service and not having to go off to war himself. He regularly attended presentations by traveling speakers and experts on a wide range of topics, often sponsored by the college. His lack of service in the army also led to Sarah's birth in 1865, just as the Civil War ended.

As Sarah grew up, she was captivated by the ferment of ideas about health and medical care, the origins of disease, and competing theories about the most effective approaches to medical and surgical treatment, all of which had been heightened by the care of hundreds of thousands of injured and ill soldiers during the war. The Civil War was the first conflict in which the armies and their governments developed a sense of responsibility for the care of their injured soldiers, leading to dramatic changes in the care of gunshot wounds, amputations, and the use of new anesthetic compounds.

Sarah was fortunate to live in a vibrant and thriving community where learning about these developments was so available. At the same time, she was exposed regularly to the destruction of lives young and old and to the devastation and misery that ripped through families wracked by disease, poverty, alcoholism, illiteracy, and madness. Sarah found solace in coping with their misery by helping to reduce it. Volunteering to help families with sick members, even at an early age, taught her that the tragedies of life and frequent deaths in the 1800s could be buffered by her sense of accomplishment as a caregiver.

She became comfortable draining wounds, soothing coughs that expelled bloody gobs of pus from tuberculosis, and easing the discomfort of the massive swelling of the legs and abdomen caused by a heart failing with dropsy. She learned to cope with the ravages of epidemics of diphtheria, scarlet fever, cholera, and typhus. She watched an eight-year-old girl die of diphtheria when Sarah herself was only ten. She would never forget the shocking trauma of watching the child strangulate in her own pus. She vowed that if she ever had the opportunity, she would develop new ways to treat these often-fatal infectious diseases.

Her compassion was matched by her fascination with science, with how bodies worked or, more often, didn't work. She dissected every dead animal she could find, sometimes boiling away the carcass to study the skeleton. The smell of a boiled opossum lingered long in the family kitchen. The lingering smell tested even the tolerant and liberal approach to child-raising espoused by her parents.

"Sarah, what is that disgusting smell?" her mother asked more than once.

"I found a dead raccoon this time," Sarah had replied, cheerily oblivious to the rank odor wafting through their home. "I wanted to see how its organs compared to an opossum's," she said. "So far they are very similar, although the liver seems a bit larger."

"Well," her mother said, "I hope there is some value to this, because the raccoon seems to stink even more than the opossum!"

Sarah's compassion, humanism, and love of science led her to attend Albion College, with the hope and intent of proceeding on to medical school. And that is how she had the opportunity and good fortune to both hear Dr. Blackwell speak at an invited lecture and meet with her afterward, due in part to her father's influence as a generous donor.

The President of Albion College opened the evening with a generous introduction of Dr. Blackwell. "It is with the greatest pleasure that I introduce to you this evening, Dr. Elizabeth Blackwell. As I am sure many of you know, Dr. Blackwell is the first woman to graduate from a traditional allopathic US medical school. She is a pioneer, forging a new path for women to seek a career in medicine. She graduated from the Geneva Medical College in 1849, and I am sure she will tell you more about that experience. She went on to a distinguished career in Europe, and she now travels the United States encouraging the next generation of women physicians. Please welcome Dr. Elizabeth Blackwell!"

After the applause subsided, Dr. Blackwell began, "My path to a medical career was not quite as smooth as was described in that generous introduction," she said. "I sought admission to every traditional medical school in the US in the 1840s, without success. I had done everything I could to break through the onerous barriers faced by women seeking a professional career. I studied privately with prominent physicians in Philadelphia, but even their recommendations had not helped. I could have attended any of several homeopathic, eclectic, or other alternative schools that promoted all manner of spurious theories about disease—botanical, water, and hot-cold cures—but I had no interest in what I saw as second-class training that lacked scientific rigor. I was particularly appalled by schools promoting a curriculum devoted to mesmerism, the theory that disease was caused by disturbances in a person's magnetism. I applied to the Geneva Medical College in Albany, New York in 1847, a somewhat obscure but traditional medical school, mostly because there were few other places to explore at that time. Not, as I should note, because of any particular enthusiasm for rural upstate New York.

The audience laughed.

She continued, "The dean of the Geneva Medical College was so amused by my application that he thought it might be entertaining to present it to the entire student body for their consideration. He hoped to enhance his reputation with students as being an open and receptive dean interested in student input, a trait for which he was not otherwise known."

More laughter.

"The idea of admitting a woman to the medical school was so outrageous and outside his boundaries of comprehension that he thought it safe to give the students the power to decide my fate."

A man in the audience raised his hand. "Did you know about this at the time?"

"No, not until much later when the Dean shared the story with me, with some embarrassment, I might note!"

"Apparently, the students took the dean at his word," she continued, "and, despite their own feelings of dismay at the notion of admitting a woman, proceeded to consider my application with their own perverse twist. As I learned later, most medical students, meaning men, are not the most sophisticated or serious people."

She heard a few nervous chuckles from the audience and continued. Her stern face did not soften.

"They apparently thought this entire process to be quite amusing and treated it as such, culminating in an evening meeting of all students in which the attendees competed amongst themselves to deliver the most outrageous and insincere endorsements of my application. The vote was called, and the students, believing the dean would not actually act on their recommendation, gave my application unanimous support, short one dissenter who was immediately pummeled into submission. The students reported to the dean their full endorsement. The dean, now feeling obliged to honor his request for their support, reluctantly notified me of my admission."

The room erupted in applause, some women cautiously standing and cheering. Dr. Blackwell looked out over the room with pride, although one would not necessarily be able to tell with the same fierce look on her face.

Another question from the audience: "Did you ever discuss this story with the students once you were admitted?"

"No, I just got the top grades on all the exams," Dr. Blackwell said, still with that hard look. That got even a bigger laugh, but the audience could see this was not a joke to her. "In 1849, I became Dr. Blackwell, graduating at the top of my class. I was somewhat disappointed by the ease of the coursework. I will also say that some of my classmates were not the most impressive in their commitment to excellence, with, of course, occasional exceptions."

An audience member stood with another question, "I assume that by breaking down this barrier, you have made the way easier for women coming after you?"

"I wish that were the case, but sadly, it is not. Following my graduation, nearly every traditional medical school in the country felt compelled to repeat the experiment, but with little commitment as it turned out. Most schools accepted what often turned out to be a token woman whose admission was then not repeated in subsequent years. The outcry by the faculty, all men of course, caused deans to conclude that this liberal inclusivity was an experiment they did not wish to repeat. The number of women in medical schools has since languished."

Dr. Blackwell continued on to describe her career in Europe, the battles she fought, and mostly lost, in the United States for hospital privileges, and her new focus on teaching women how to care for their families, with a focus on cleanliness, nutrition, clean air, and exercise. She had concluded that she could have the most influence by teaching about health, rather than actually caring for patients.

Sarah watched Dr. Blackwell with equal parts awe and discouragement. In awe of her strength, commitment, and leadership as a role model for aspiring women like her, and discouraged both by the continued barriers to being accepted to medical school and by her apparent lack of interest in taking care of sick patients, which is what Sarah most wanted to do. She would have to ask Dr. Blackwell about that in the private meeting her father had arranged for her after the lecture.

Sarah and Dr. Blackwell settled into their chairs in a small room off the auditorium after Dr. Blackwell had finished her talk and taken a few questions. Sarah was encouraged by her parents to be direct in her conversation, not a common characteristic among women but one that Dr. Blackwell prized, and she spoke before they had barely sat. "What caused you to want to become a physician?"

Dr. Blackwell answer shocked her. "I thought little about being a physician, let alone being the first woman physician. It simply never occurred to me that a woman could not be a physician, or anything else she wished to be. My interest in becoming a physician was just to show that it could be done."

Sarah was disappointed. "I am so inspired by the role of the physician, by the good they can do, by the respect they command. Are you not similarly inspired?"

"Not really," Dr. Blackwell replied casually. "I find most physicians, meaning men, to be mediocre in their intellect and their commitment. They are unserious and often frivolous in their approach to their responsibilities, sometimes cruel to their patients, especially women, arrogant without having the credentials to justify such behavior, lacking in curiosity, occasionally boorish, and showing little dedication. Sadly, the same is sometimes true, more often than I would like, for the women who have followed me."

"How do you mean?" Sarah asked, not entirely sure she wanted to hear the answer. "I would have expected you to be more supportive of women who wanted to follow your inspiring vision."

"That's the problem, they don't," said Dr. Blackwell. "They are equally uncurious, lacking in rigor, lacking in character, and frequently leaving the profession after only a few years so as to marry."

Sarah had heard that Dr. Blackwell was blunt, even belligerent, about her commitment to maintaining her unmarried status. "But you have not married, so how can you judge their motivations and commitment?" Sarah asked. She feared she had overstepped as a mere college student challenging someone so widely admired and famous.

The doctor was kind in her reply. "I am aware of that, and I try to be more forgiving. But it is difficult when they choose the easiest paths to becoming a physician, then confine their practice to women and children, rarely develop their surgical skills, and work only with poor patients because they do not work to build a proper practice."

"How do they choose easy paths? Nothing seems easy about becoming or being a physician," Sarah said.

Sarah could see in Dr. Blackwell's face, especially the hard, black eyes, that she had hit a topic of some emotion. The doctor was famous for her piercing stare. Sarah was now its target. "Yet another problem! Easy paths to becoming a physician have unfortunately developed for women, in particular the appearance of women-only medical schools. Some enthusiasts seem to think this will enhance the opportunities and standing of women. Quite the opposite. The education is inferior, the professors are mostly women who themselves are poorly trained, the demands of the students are low and the standards even lower. We are creating a second-class category of physician, and they are all women!"

Sarah felt obliged to defend the honor of women physicians. "But the reason there are medical schools only for women is that traditional schools are not willing to accept women. Where else can they go?"

Dr. Blackwell was unmoved and casually dismissed Sarah's defense with a wave of her hand. "The fact that those schools are indeed unwilling to accept women means we have to be just that much better, just that much smarter, just that much more dedicated. We have to study harder, work harder, take on the hardest cases, and push our way into the traditional schools, resistance or not. We just have to be better."

Sarah's liberal education caused her to be even more provocative than usual, confrontational to the point of rudeness. "I have read about your opinions of medical practice, that you sometimes find medical practice to be abhorrent, that you are uncomfortable with sick patients. I have heard it said of you that patients who have a myriad of symptoms for which there is no explanation are annoying to you. You said yourself tonight that you now rarely attend to an actual patient."

Dr. Blackwell's face flashed for just the briefest moment with annoyance, perhaps even anger, but softened, "I do not consider the direct care of patients to be the highest calling, or the way that physicians, particularly women physicians, can best serve society. I have devoted my life to teaching patients, especially women and mothers, how to manage their households, how to care for their families, about diet, and about hygiene. I want women physicians to rise above the menial, mercenary, arrogant conduct of most physicians, meaning men!"

Sarah sensed that she had pushed the conversation about as far as she should, perhaps farther than was appropriate. She was confused by the doctor's attitudes about caring for patients, which is what she most wanted to do. Dr. Blackwell had said women should develop their surgical skills and care for the most complex patients, yet she herself was promoting patient education as the proper role for women. She was saddened to hear Dr. Blackwell's criticism of most women physicians, but she knew there was a message in those criticisms she should heed, however painful.

She had to work harder, be smarter, do whatever needed to gain admittance to a traditional medical school. She also knew she wanted a different career path than what the doctor had described. Teaching hygiene and lecturing about women's health were fine, but she wanted to care for actual sick patients, the sicker the better, to become an expert in the bloody, grisly reality of medical practice of the day. She wanted to be as good as the best male physicians and to go places and care for patients where other physicians would not. She thought little, if at all, about what this meant for her personal life, if indeed one was even possible according to Dr. Blackwell's strong opinion on the topic.

As her attention snapped back to Dr. Sewall's lecture and her first day of medical school, her recollection of the meeting with Dr. Blackwell fortified her. Her acceptance to the University of Michigan Medical School, what many considered to be one of the best schools in the country, was a good start and consistent with the doctor's pointed advice about how women should fight for the best education. Professor Sewall's support on this first day of school was fine, but her objective was to excel to the point that she needed no such support or defense. She now had to prove her worth and abilities to her professors, to her male student colleagues, and, perhaps most importantly, to herself. She would be the best—not the best she could be, just simply the best.

CHAPTER 6

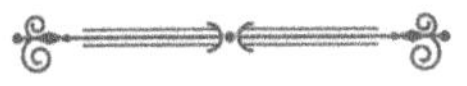

New York City and Park City, 1897

"Emily, could I have a word?" Sarah Fletcher, now Dr. Fletcher, asked. She had just finished seeing her last patient for the day at the New York Infirmary for Women and Children, one more mother living in the depths of poverty, no education, no money, a worthless husband who was usually drunk, and a dirty home with five unwashed children who were poorly fed. The New York Infirmary was a dark and brooding building, rusty stains dripping down the walls from the metal roof, windows so dirty they admitted nearly no light, but it was all her patients had, and more than most poor New York women had.

Dr. Emily Blackwell, Elizabeth's sister, had founded the Infirmary after receiving her training in Europe, exactly the opposite approach of that pursued by Elizabeth. While Elizabeth left for Europe because she could not gain hospital staff membership in New York, Emily trained in Europe and returned to the United States so she could establish the New York Infirmary and have control of a hospital facility where women physicians could practice. Also, unlike her sister Elizabeth, Emily cared for patients with passion and enthusiasm. She successfully assembled a board of well-intended, community-minded philanthropists whose desire to do good took the form of substantial financial support. Donors, unlike local hospitals and medical practices, were impressed with the name and fame of Emily's sister upon which Emily drew heavily. The donors' enthusiastic support also grew out of their sense of guilt about the miserable living conditions of so many poor women and children. The New York Infirmary was one vehicle to address that misery and assuage the donors' guilt at the same time.

"You know how proud I am to work here," Sarah said. "You have done a great service for so many poor women by founding this clinic. I wonder sometimes if I am really doing any good, whether anything changes permanently for these women, but at least we are trying."

"I hear a 'but' coming," Emily said. She was as blunt and severe as her sister, perhaps more so, and conversations with her were usually short.

"You are correct," Sarah replied, smiling at how transparent she had been in her approach to Emily. "I just feel like something is missing. I have this lingering regret that I am not the complete physician I so badly want to be. That regret lurks just beneath the satisfaction I also feel after a day in clinic. But I wanted you to know that I do truly appreciate working here."

"What about the private practice you have developed? You seem very successful there, building a strong practice on the side. You know that this helps us financially by supporting a portion of your work with the Infirmary patients."

"Yes, I am aware of the financial benefits, but sometimes I feel like I am doing even less for those patients. They mostly are worried about minor symptoms for which I can find no cause, or they are simply boring with their confined lives. Those with more serious conditions will not agree to receive care or undergo surgery at the Infirmary, and they often seek care from a physician with a more elegant practice. I have so many medical and surgical interests that just find no outlet here. I want to take care of seriously sick and injured patients, to be immersed in the most complicated medical cases."

"Hmm," Emily mused. "I am not sure what we can do about that. We can do only so much at the Infirmary."

"There are some good aspects. I have, in fact, performed occasional surgeries here, as you know, a couple appendectomies and hysterectomies, but I know that is stretching the boundaries a bit. I just want to do more. The other issue is that I have made little progress in the research I started in medical school. I want to explore new approaches to treating diphtheria, for example. The children from poor families we care for are terribly susceptible to that dreaded disease due to their poor nutrition and crowded living conditions. I want to continue the work I did in medical school with Professor Sewall on antitoxins, but that requires a laboratory and access to horses to develop the antitoxin. All of that would be quite expensive. The patients themselves are also a barrier. When I share a bit of this experimental approach with some of my parents, they look horrified, as if I was mad!"

"Well, you must admit it does sound quite farfetched! But you are correct, we really have no way to support that type of research."

"Even worse," Sarah said, "my private patients often want nothing to do with more modern treatments for their ailments. They are obsessed with strange fads and what I consider to be completely unfounded theories of illness. The practice of medicine is changing so rapidly, and is so exciting, and they still want to be treated with truly barbaric agents. Crystals, magnets, it is all just so uncomfortable for me. A patient recently asked if drinking radium water would help her arthritis. Another asked for a small electric contraption to put in her bathtub to cause a mild electric current to pass through her. She had heard it would help with her headaches. She was the same patient who wanted some sort of vibrating machine to help with her fainting and anxiety. I didn't even ask where she proposed to place it. One mother was just exhausted taking care of her four children and asked for heroin to subdue them, as well as herself. I was so shocked I could barely speak. And some still want to be bled!"

"I understand," Emily said. "It can be quite frustrating. Somehow, I have a feeling you have considered some solutions to address your frustrations?"

"Oh, I don't know. I just wanted to share with you what I was thinking. I have no obvious plan, and I do indeed appreciate the opportunity you have provided. This is a remarkable institution that is doing so much good. I will let you know if I see any way to address this issue."

Sarah really did have no plan. She was just so frustrated with her practice. Her energy had no productive outlet. It was a measure of the depths of those frustrations that she picked up a copy of the bulletin from the local medical society, an organization to which she had only recently and begrudgingly been admitted. She knew the bulletin carried announcements of new postings, and she read one she would have otherwise ignored:

PHYSICIAN WANTED
ONTARIO MINE
PARK CITY, UTAH

The Ontario Mine in Park City, Utah, one of the most productive and successful silver mines on the Western frontier, seeks to hire a physician to care for its miners. Applicants must have a full medical degree from a recognized US medical school, an excellent academic record, and at least two years of experience in a full medical practice. Applicants should reply with their credentials and recommendations from the candidate's medical school and a professional colleague.

Signed
J. S Gibson
Manager
Ontario Mine

Sarah barely knew where Utah was, and Park City not at all. She knew nothing about silver mining, what miners did, their medical care needs or the job of a mine physician. There was a complete lack of connection between the advertised position and her training, background, and life experience. But it all sounded so exciting! She was mesmerized by the adventure of it all. Her confidence was unbounded, and she had a sense that this was the type of practice where she could use her full range of skills. Surely, a Western mining town would be full of violence, injury, and severe illness for which her services would be appreciated. She could be the complete physician she always wanted to be, caring for patients with complicated problems for which she could actually do something! She imagined Park City itself must be a quaint mountain town, fresh air, a healthy environment and beautiful scenery.

Reality kept poking itself into her fantasies. How could she possibly imagine applying for the job as a physician caring for hundreds of men doing something she knew nothing about, in a mountain town more than two thousand miles away in a place she knew nothing about? What was she thinking?

She never really answered that question. She asked again to meet with Emily to let her know of her intent to apply and ask for her help.

"I am disappointed, of course," Emily said, "but I understand what you are seeking. I am so appreciative of what you have done here, and I wish you the best. How can I help?"

"I need to compose a letter of interest," Sarah said, "and also secure two letters of recommendation. I had hoped one letter might come from you."

"Of course," Emily said, "but I have a suggestion. Your letter should come from 'S. Fletcher, MD', and my letter should be written with the same reference. I will sign my letter as 'E. Blackwell, M.D., Director and Founder, New York Infirmary for Women and Children.'"

"Ah, of course," Sarah said. "I understand. Very clever." She sat down that evening and carefully composed a letter summarizing her education, her class standing, and her experience. The scratch of her precious, self-filling fountain pen, a gift from Emily, and the flow of ink on the blank note paper, were entrancing, as if her new life was scrolling out before her very eyes. She tried to write in the hand of a man, although she could really see no difference between her bold and forthright penmanship and that of any man she could recall. She signed the letter, "S. Fletcher, M.D."

Sarah wrote to Professor Sewall and asked him to also provide a recommendation, which he was happy to do. He did not really understand why Sarah asked him to refer to her as "S. Fletcher, M.D.," but he happily complied with a glowing letter on his official University of Michigan stationery, signed with his full name and prestigious title.

A month later, after receiving the letters of recommendations, she sent them off with her letter of inquiry. She was so excited, but she was also acutely aware, in her occasional moments of realistic thinking, that she was unlikely to be selected, or perhaps to even receive a reply. She would likely have to be satisfied with enjoying the moments of imagination of what the life of a mining physician must be like. It was an enjoyable distraction.

She was also amused by the sly way she had structured the entire process. She had little expectation of any good coming from her deception, but two months later, she was thrilled, scared, and amazed all at the same time to receive a letter from Mr. Gibson himself, addressed to "S. Fletcher, M.D." Mr.

Gibson enthusiastically acknowledged her query and offered her the job. She responded immediately with her acceptance, her hand trembling slightly as she signed her reply "S. Fletcher, MD." She began to make plans for a move.

As her stagecoach pulled up in front of the Park Hotel, a grand, brick structure, Sarah looked out the open side window to a sea of mud covering Main Street, piled up on the edges of the wooden boardwalk like waves on a beach, with small mud ripples running downhill. She looked from the mud up to the barren hills above town, scarred with hundreds of rotting stumps where tall pine trees had once stood. Above the low hills, a lid of wood and coal smoke settled over the town. Large wagons filled with chunks of rock clanked and rattled down the street. It was all so frightening and disgusting. She thought she had made a terrible mistake.

Growing up in Michigan and then living in New York City had not prepared her for the drama of the western mountains. She had seen stunning country coming across the plains and into the Rocky Mountains, reinforcing her image of Park City as a picturesque and pleasant town nestled in dramatic mountain scenery, surrounded by green hills cut by cheerful cold streams. The only stream she saw now was running down the middle of Main Street, and it was filled with debris and smelled like manure. She wondered how soon her stagecoach would leave to return to Salt Lake City and whether she should be on it.

When she left Salt Lake City that morning, the skies over the mountains were blue and clear. As the coach rolled past the farming community of Snyderville outside Park City, she looked ahead and got a first look at the smoke filling the canyon in which the town sat. A prosperous looking businessman riding across from her in the coach could see her concern.

They had nodded politely to one another when they boarded the coach. Now he spoke. "It's from all the coal and wood burned in town," he said. He wore the standard dress of a successful businessman, heavy wool coat, vest, and watch chain, and sported a thick mustache and beard cluttered with a few crumbs from lunch.

"I guess you could see my concern," Sarah said.

"Indeed," he said. "Martin's the name. John Martin. Coal and wood are burned for everything—cooking, fireplaces, boardinghouse kitchens. Even the steam dynamo that produces the town's electricity is itself powered by coal. My sister lives in town, and she says that the smoke is so acidic it burned holes in the clothes she hung outside to dry. She sends her clothes to a Chinese laundry now."

"Hmm, thank you for the explanation," Sarah said. "It was not quite what I was expecting." As the coach got closer to the canyon in which the town sat, she could hear a pounding, but really more a continuous crashing that was quite frightful. "What is that terrible pounding?" she asked.

"It's the Marsac Mill where they crush the ore before it is sorted and sent for smelting. One of the best in the West, forty one-ton cast iron stamps, raised and lowered a hundred times a minute. It can handle everything coming out of all the mines except the Ontario. They have their own," he said with great pride. "We are proud to have two mills in town! The pounding is the measure of the town's success, the sign of silver being produced, the mines making money, the miners getting paid, and dividends making investors rich. I happen to be one of those investors." His considerable girth expanded a bit more with pride.

"Oh, the Ontario," she said. "That mine is the reason I am on this coach. I am coming to assume my new position as the Ontario Mine physician."

"Really?" John said, not so much curious as stunned. His boastful chatter suddenly ran out of words.

"Yes, I have an offer from a Mr. Gibson."

"Oh, yes, of course. Everyone knows Mr. Gibson. So you are," he paused, "a doctor?" The idea seemed to baffle him.

The coach arrived at the hotel just in time. "Pleasure to meet you," she said, ignoring his question.

She couldn't tell how deep the mud was that covered Main Street as she grabbed her bag from the rack and stepped down from the coach. It was only three steps from the coach to the wooden boardwalk in front of the hotel, but three steps was all it took for the mud to cover her ankle-laced shoes and overflow the top, dripping down inside. The mud was an ironic contrast to the thick layer of dust that covered her clothes and luggage from the stagecoach ride.

Her dusty and muddy arrival in Park City was the culmination of a three-week trip, most of it by train, which fascinated, energized, exhausted, and disgusted her. She saw spectacular country unlike anything she had ever seen in Michigan or New York, the train running through the Platte River valley of Nebraska, climbing into the high plains of Wyoming and crossing over the Continental Divide at Evans Pass, 8,200 feet high. She was lightheaded in the thin air.

The route skirted the Utah border through Evanston, Wyoming, close enough to just barely see the peaks of the Uinta Mountains to the south as the train dropped into Utah. Herds of bison pounded beside the train, not entirely eliminated by the hunters feeding the train crews that had built the railroad. Clusters of pronghorn antelope grazed more gently and seemed unperturbed by the train belching smoke as it rumbled by. The train stopped at each little town, where she saw every imaginable Western character, all new and exotic—ranchers, cowboys, roughneck workers, Indians, businessmen, ladies with parasols, and ladies of a different sort soliciting customers. Some of the men looked at her, traveling alone, as if she might be a practitioner of that same profession.

She slept on trains filthy with coal soot that sucked in through the open windows from the train's smokestack. She eventually gave up trying to stay clean and wore the smears of black soot across her face as a sign of her excitement about her new life. The puffed sleeves of her day dress were equally stained, and she had long-ago given up on a proper hat, having traded it for a flat straw model at one of the train stops.

Her train adventure ended in Salt Lake City and her stagecoach adventure began. She saw little of the trip into the mountains because the coach was swallowed by a dense cloud of fine, powdery dust from the rough road up Parley's Canyon, an eight-hour ride from Salt Lake City. The washboard road was rutted, and the stage lurched from side to side, moving not much faster than a brisk walk. But the mud, the smoke, the pounding stamp mill, the annoying businessman in the coach, none of it could detract from her excitement and inspiration. This was her new home, her new community, and, most importantly, the home of her new medical practice. She was full of knowledge and skill, bursting with a commitment to help those in need. She felt ready for any challenge the town could throw at her.

She tried to scrape the mud off her shoes as she walked through the hotel door, but with no luck. The slab of mud weighed heavily on her feet as she half-slid to the front desk.

"I would like to arrange for a room, probably for the next several nights until I can secure more permanent housing," she said to the hotel clerk, a bright-looking young man with tousled blond hair.

"Certainly, ma'am. Your name?"

"Dr. Sarah Fletcher. I have just arrived in town and intend to establish my medical practice here," she said. She was not sure why she felt the need to tell the clerk of her plans. She was just so proud to be here.

"Of course, ma'am, er, doctor," the clerk said. "Is Mr. Fletcher coming along behind?" he asked, as he looked toward the front door expectantly.

"I am traveling alone," Sarah said, with a sharp glance.

"Oh, yes, well, of course," he said. "Please excuse me. We are not used to women traveling alone. Although I don't know why it should matter. I was just taught to ask. So you say you are a doctor?"

"Thank you," Sarah said. "I do not know why it should matter either. Yes, I am a physician coming to set up practice here."

"Well, then, welcome," he said. "Park City can always use another physician. The mountains and mines are dangerous places. You are the second physician to have arrived in the last couple weeks. Please just give me your name on this card."

Sarah paid no attention to the comment about another doctor. She was just so excited to get settled and visit Mr. Gibson. But first things first. Excitement and inspiration were fine, but she needed a bath.

Fresh from her bath, kindly drawn by the hotel manager with water heated on the wood-burning stove in the kitchen, she put on a clean dress and scraped the mud off her shoes as best she could. She started up Main Street to the south, on the few blocks of wooden boardwalk that ran along the main business center of the street. The wood smelled and looked freshly-cut, as if the boardwalk had just been built. She walked past shops of every kind, a butcher shop, jewelry store, dry goods shop, what looked like a fine clothing store, and saloons that were dark and quiet inside waiting for the work shifts to end. She reached the top, where the boardwalk ended, and was dumped back into the Main Street mud. In three steps she could not tell that she had cleaned her shoes or bathed her legs for that matter. The mud splattered along the bottom of her long dress. She quickly saw that the dress requirements for a professional woman, at least what was expected in New York City, were entirely inappropriate in a western mining town. Her first stop after meeting the Ontario Mine manager would be the clothing store she had just seen to buy pants and boots.

She turned left toward Marsac Avenue, named, as the hotel manager helpfully explained when he had given her directions, for Sophie de Marsac, a friend of a group of Michigan entrepreneurs who had developed the original Flagstaff mine in the 1870s. As she crossed over to Marsac Avenue, she passed the hollow that lay next to Main Street. The stamping mill filled the hollow at its bottom, just up from the train station where the train tracks ended. Its explosive roar flowed up the hollow like a dark wave. Sarah looked down the hollow toward the mill and saw a single dirt road lined with brightly-colored cottages. She wondered who lived down there. The houses were tidy and the neighborhood clean and prosperous looking.

As she passed the top of the hollow, the pounding slowly faded to just a background thumping that followed her up Marsac Avenue into Ontario Canyon. Then she started to hear the Ontario stamp mill, increasing in intensity as the Marsac mill faded. It was just a mile to go to the mine, but it seemed so much farther. The hill became increasingly steep, and her brisk step slowed. She now understood, at a more physiologic level, what it meant to live in a town at seven thousand feet of elevation, plus she was walking up another thousand feet above that. She thought of herself as quite fit and active, but she could see she would need to acclimate to the rarefied air of the mountains.

She moved to the side of the rough road up Ontario Canyon several times as wagons overflowing with crushed rock came down the hill, on the way to the train depot. The wagons were barely in control, lurching from side to side, the six-horse teams jerking forward and back. The wooden slats on the wagons' sides bowed out from the weight of the rock and seemed about to rupture at any moment. Sarah could see that she had a lot to learn about mining, about the jobs miners were required to do, about the risks of those jobs, and the role of the mine physician. She also wondered why she was getting such strange looks from the wagon drivers as they went by.

The buildings for the Ontario mine were long and low, built with unpainted and weathered wooden siding and steep metal roofs. She peered into each dimly lit building looking for someone to ask for directions. There was a warehouse full of supplies, equipment, and unworked iron sheets and rods, but no one to ask. Poking her head into a metal shop revealed a worker welding a bar to what looked like a large cage, but the sparks were too intimidating for her to interrupt him. She saw what she thought she had read was the mine's headframe, rising up forty feet above a large square hole in the ground. She saw cables running from a large winch powered by an engine belching black smoke, up through pulleys and down into the hole. A lift operator was working the controls of an engine that strained to bring up a cage. As it cleared the floor of the headframe and popped into full view at the top of the shaft, she could see it was full of large metal carts filled with big chunks of rock. She waited until the cage had stopped and the rocks were dumped into the same type of wagon that she had seen coming down Main Street. She got the attention of the lift operator. He was startled when she waved at him, and then by her voice.

"Sir, where might I find Mr. Gibson and the mine office?" Sarah asked.

He looked genuinely frightened by her presence, and confused by what she was asking, as if she was speaking some alien language. Several seconds passed as he struggled to regain his composure. "Ma'am," he said as he tipped his hat. "Uh, uh, Mr. Gibson should be in his office, just that way." She couldn't tell if he was waving her away or waving her toward the office building, but she could see he clearly hoped she would go somewhere.

"Thank you, sir," Sarah said. She didn't know what to make of the strange contortions on his face, but then everything she had experienced in her short time in Park City seemed so strange, exotic even, a completely different world. She had been looking for adventure and she had certainly found it.

She followed the wave of the lift operator's arm to the building with a sign marking it as the Administration Office. She gathered herself and her dress, excited at the opportunities that lay before her, and walked confidently through the door where she was hit with a blast of cigar smoke. As she peered through the thick smoke, she was confronted by the raw and swollen face of John S. Gibson. His face also had a tortured look, but not like the lift operator's. Not fear, just annoyance.

Gibson was imposing in all ways, a large man with a large head, hair sparse and slicked back, a full reddish beard, scraggly and unkempt. He was at one and the same time enigmatic and explosive. Energy poured out of him but without revealing its source or purpose. He was attired almost identically to John Martin, her stagecoach companion, apparently the standard uniform of successful businessmen. She couldn't imagine how he could stand the heavy, double-breasted, wool coat, wool vest, and high starched collar in the hot, smoky room. Despite his heavy beard, his annoyance was visible and obvious to Sarah, making this now two faces in ten minutes with strange looks. It was all quite puzzling.

Sarah announced herself, "Sir, I am Dr. Sarah Fletcher, and I am here to accept your kind offer to serve as your new mine physician."

Like the lift operator, Gibson reacted as though she were speaking in tongues. "I'm sorry, ma'am, I have no idea what you mean. Who are you?" He seemed quite perplexed, struggling to catch up to what she was saying, and then struggling, unsuccessfully, to be civil.

Sarah produced the letter she had received offering her the job. "As instructed in your offer letter, I am reporting to you for instructions on my role."

He looked at the letter and said, "But this is addressed to Dr. S. Fletcher, I assumed Steven or Samuel, or some such."

"No sir," Sarah said, "I am Dr. Fletcher, indeed, but Sarah is my name."

"Then you, Sarah, er, ma'am, have deceived me," Gibson said. "I would never offer such a job to a woman. In fact, I never considered that a woman would apply for such a job. For that matter, it's astonishing to me that a woman can even legitimately call herself a physician. It would never occur to me to even ask if 'S' stood for something other than a proper man's name."

"Nonetheless," Sarah said, "you did indeed make such an offer, and I am indeed a physician. I am also a woman." She worked hard to quell the rising anger at his attitude. Her first day excitement was fading quickly.

Gibson replied, making a half-hearted attempt to explain himself, "Your references said nothing about you being a woman."

Sarah said, "If I am correct, they made no comment either way. They simply, and I might add, strongly endorsed my training. I believe they were particularly positive about my academic standing at graduation and my clinical experience."

"Yes, of course, of course, dear, I meant no disrespect," he said. Sarah's brow furrowed as she tried to ignore the blatant lie, and a condescending one at that. "I was quite impressed with your credentials, having no idea, of course, that your background was entirely irrelevant to the far more important fact that you are a woman. But, no matter," he said, dismissing the entire conversation as a mere courtesy. "It is simply impossible for you to be the Ontario's mine physician. The men will not have it. I will not have it."

"Why does it matter?" she asked. "I do not understand the problem." She started to fear where this was heading.

"I'm sorry, ma'am, it matters a great deal. Mining is a rough business, a man's business. You do not have the constitution or stamina to deal with what goes on here. Besides that, you will never be allowed in the mine. Women are considered bad luck in mines. Bad things happen when women are around, explosions, cave-ins, floods, and more. It's bad enough you are even here in this office."

She had first winced at being called "dear," and the reference to her as "ma'am" just made it worse. She also noticed the comment about women being bad luck in mines, presumably explaining the look on the mine operator's face as well. "Well," she said, as calmly as she could, "be that as it may, I am here and ready to work."

"And I am telling you that will not happen," his voice rising in indignation. "You have come a long way for no purpose, and, I might add, under a cloud of false representation." With that, he walked out from behind his desk to the door and waved for her to leave. There was clearly nowhere for her to go with this argument, at least for the moment, so she walked through the door, grabbed it from him and slammed it hard, stomping away through the dusty ground.

Sarah had long suppressed the reaction to cry at the many insults she had experienced in her short career as a woman physician. She came close as Gibson's disrespect flowed through her, but she was much more focused on the rising heat of her anger.

The trip back down the hill to the hotel was a fog. She was hurt, confused, and angry, all roiled together. She did not notice the mud or the pounding of the stamp mill. She did not notice her rapid and raspy breathing. She was just mad. By the time she had come down Main Street to her hotel, the confusion had resolved itself into clarity about who she was and the strength of her credentials. The anger had turned into a deep commitment to prove Gibson wrong about his beliefs. She understood whose problem this really was, and it was not hers. She was, above all, a physician, and she would find a way to serve the community and its patients. All she needed was an office.

She took dinner in the hotel dining room by herself, causing a stir among the guests as she walked in. The host asked when her husband would be joining her. When she said she was dining alone, he barely suppressed a scowl of disapproval and seated her in a far dark corner of the restaurant, presumably to minimize the exposure to what he clearly thought was a scandalous situation. She was well-dressed and quite attractive, further confusing the dining guests. Sarah took no notice of their murmuring because she was making plans for the next day.

CHAPTER 7

Park City, 1897

The next morning, Sarah went straight to the offices of the *Park Record* to get a copy of the paper and its rental space advertisements; her disgusting meeting with Gibson almost forgotten after a good night's sleep. If anything, his reaction just added to the adventure she felt in starting a new life in a mountain town so far from her former one. All she needed was a home and an office, and she knew exactly what she wanted. The idea that she could create her own office and build her own practice was so energizing she couldn't stop smiling. She wanted a two-story building, living space above, modest but comfortable, with a consultation room on the first floor. She expected to be performing surgery, so the space needed to be sufficiently large for a proper surgical table, with good light. She needed cabinets for her instruments and equipment, and a stove to boil water for sterilizing her instruments and washing her hands before surgery.

She learned quickly from the newspaper and the ads that Chinatown was what she saw when she was looking down the hollow toward the stamp mill, immediately to the east of Main Street and bordering Rossie Hill. Having worked with the poorest women in New York City, she knew Chinese patients well and assumed she would be caring for the residents of Chinatown. But there was no office space in Chinatown. Rossie Hill was really Millionaire's Row, lined with the mansions of the wealthier business owners, including the home of

J. S. Gibson, as she had learned from Mr. Martin on the coach ride. Nothing in that direction would work.

She found five possibilities, all up and down Main Street or on Park Avenue, one street to the west.

She set off to visit each property and talk with the landlords. Her energized smile would last about as long as her conversation with the first landlord.

She knocked on the door and it opened barely a crack.

"Sir," she said, "I am interested in discussing the property you have for rent. I am looking to establish an office. Might I have a word?"

"An office? Why? For what?" a man shouted through the crack. "Who are you?"

"I am Dr. Sarah Fletcher, sir. I am a new physician in town and would like to establish my practice."

"A practice? What kind of practice?"

"A medical practice, sir. As I said, I am a new physician in town."

"Well, I just don't know what is happening in our town. In our society for that matter! Women are not physicians. How could that possibly be? Brazen women think they can do anything these days. Go away!" He slammed the door. She ignored him. She had heard it all before.

The second landlord was kind enough to let her into the house. He introduced himself as Mr. Edward McLeod. "I am the proud owner of the finest jewelry store in town," he said with a wide, self-satisfying grin. "Perhaps you might stop by someday. I would be honored to show you a few pieces."

"Perhaps," Sarah said.

"You have a fine neck for a particular necklace I have in mind. Now, ma'am, please tell me again. Why are you looking at office space."

"I am a new physician in town," Sarah said coldly, "and wish to establish my medical practice." She could barely contain her disgust with his condescension.

"I see, I see," Edward said, "most impressive. But you understand I couldn't possibly rent the house to you. I can see you are a serious professional woman, but my neighbors would almost certainly assume you were setting up, shall we say, a different sort of business, being such an attractive woman and all."

"I assure you that this will be a most reputable medical practice," Sarah said. Her self-control was fading quickly.

"If I may, you should consider Heber Avenue, a road that branches off the bottom of Main Street and runs up toward Frog Valley, as a place to establish your practice. There is, um, considerable traffic, shall we say, through that area because of the nature of the businesses along the road. I am certain you would be busy quite quickly."

"Thank you, no," Sarah said as she turned away. It was her turn to slam the door.

The third landlord thought she was a midwife and was confused about why she needed an office at all. Midwives practiced their profession in the home of the laboring patient, as he explained, as if she was a child.

The fourth welcomed her graciously to Park City and seemed immediately quite solicitous of her business. "Fred, Fred Nelson's the name, finest butcher in Park City. So pleased to meet you, ma'am, er, doctor." He offered his hand which Sarah shook briefly. "So pleased to see a new doctor in town, especially a woman," he continued. "What a modern world it is that a woman can become a physician, and such an attractive woman at that! And right here in Park City. My, my. Tell me about your education and training."

Sarah did, a very short version. She already found Fred annoying.

"And a family, are you married? If you are, I am sorely disappointed, but congratulations to your lucky husband. If not, it would be quite scandalous for you to be out and about as a single woman without an escort. I would be honored to serve in that role."

"Thank you, no," Sarah said. It was becoming a common response. She excused herself quickly before she hit him.

She introduced herself to the fifth landlord, a Mr. Miller, who said he was ill and could not see her. "I'm sorry, ma'am, I am indisposed and cannot discuss this matter, whatever your intentions are for renting my property."

"I am so sorry, sir," she said. "I am in fact a physician intending to establish my medical practice. Would I be able to help?"

"Thank you, but I will just watch it a bit. I am having pain in my tummy here," waving at his considerable girth. "The pain came on earlier today, but I trust it will pass. Perhaps we can talk tomorrow."

"As you wish," she said. "I am happy to attend to you if you change your mind."

"That is very kind of you. I will keep it in mind. But I must defer our discussion for now."

She returned to her hotel room, discouraged but unbowed. She would persist until she found the right house. She had heard various versions of what the first four landlords had said many times before. Their reactions meant nothing to her. She had long ago recognized that the world contained a lot of small-minded men, not to mention a few such women. She had learned to rise above their pettiness, and certainly so now as she launched herself into this new adventure.

As she settled into another steamy bath, an experience she was learning to appreciate in the cool mountain evenings, her dreamy thoughts floated with the steam. *Today was annoying and exhausting, but still so exciting. This is my town. This is where I am going to become the physician I so much want to be. I am actually out on my own, working on my own, creating my own future. It is all going to happen! I am so happy I left New York!*

Relaxed from her bath, she settled into a dreamy sleep. It lasted only a few hours.

There was a soft knock on her door. "Ma'am, uh, doctor, uh, hello?" came the low voice at the door.

"Yes," she replied, raising up groggily from the envelope of her feather-filled mattress, "this is Dr. Fletcher."

"Doctor, there is someone downstairs who has asked for you, and needs your assistance."

She knew she was just waking up, but this was very confusing. "Someone asking for me? Are you sure?"

"Yes, ma'am, er, doctor."

"Very well, I will be right down," she replied. She had visited the clothing store the afternoon before, the one productive thing she had accomplished after so many annoying conversations, and she was pleased with her new look of dark twill pants, practical leather boots with a touch of style and fashion, a colored blouse with some embroidered decoration and a light wool jacket. She already felt more like a Western woman.

In the hotel lobby, the clerk waved her to a young man sitting in the lobby. The young man stumbled around a bit about why he had asked for her. "Ma'am, are you the lady who called on my father yesterday afternoon?"

"Well," she said, "that depends. I called on several people yesterday. Who is your father?"

"Mr. Miller. He said you asked about renting a house he owns, to set up a medical practice." He paused and could not contain his incredulity. "Are you really a doctor?" he finally blurted out.

"Yes," she said. She was really getting tired of the question. "I am indeed a physician. And your name?"

"Samuel," the boy said. "Samuel Miller. They call me Sammy."

"And what is the problem with your father, Sammy?"

"My father's abdominal pain has continued to progress since yesterday. He said you offered to be of service. He is sorry he declined your generous offer and wonders if you might attend to him now."

"I recall your father now. I am happy to help but is there no other physician in town?" she asked. "I have no office, or equipment, or assistant, or anything?"

"Dr. Stout is our long-standing local doctor, but he is away in Salt Lake City visiting family," the young man said. "Another doctor arrived recently, but we don't know anything about him. My father was impressed with meeting you and would be most appreciative if you could come with me."

"Very well," she said. "I have a small medical bag. Let me get that and I will be right back."

She went up to her room and came back down quickly with her bag. She followed Sammy up Main Street, dark with a cold wind blowing down-canyon. She remembered the house to which the man guided her. As she entered, she saw Mr. Miller lying still and quiet on the couch.

"Thank you for coming," Mr. Miller said, slowly, carefully. Just the act of speaking seemed to be more movement than he could tolerate. "Miller, Peter Miller," he said as he offered a weak, sweaty hand. "Doctor, I was wrong to decline your services yesterday. The night has gone badly, and I am having terrible pain."

Finally, Sarah thought, *I can just be a doctor for a change.* "I am happy to help. Tell me what you are feeling, Mr. Miller," Sarah said.

"I lost my appetite yesterday morning," he said, "and that is something for me," waving again to his considerable girth with a weak smile. "I had a little discomfort up here," pointing to his upper abdomen. "Then the pain moved down here," now pointing down to his right lower abdomen.

"Are you vomiting?" she asked.

"Yes, once, and the pain was so severe when I did that I almost passed out."

"May I exam you?" she asked.

"Of course," he said, but his behavior suggested otherwise. He sank back a bit into the couch and carefully crossed his arms over this abdomen. He was desperate for her help, but maybe not *that* desperate.

She approached the couch and gently but firmly removed his hands to his side, unbuttoned his shirt, and laid her soft but strong hands on his abdomen, toward the upper-left side away from the pain. Even that touch caused some discomfort. As she moved down toward the right, he grabbed her hand to stop.

"Please don't touch, it is so painful," he said through gritted teeth.

"I will be gentle," she said. And she was. Just the lightest touch and she could see how much pain he was having. Just the lightest flutter of her hands as she released the pressure on his abdomen caused him even more pain. She grabbed his hips and gently rocked him from side to side. He screamed again in pain.

"Mr. Miller, I am afraid you have an inflammation of the appendix, in your digestive system, what we call appendicitis. Based on your pain, it is possible the appendix is about to rupture, which could kill you. Your appendix must come out."

He looked at her for a moment, not as a patient but as the businessman he was. His eyes slightly narrowed as he weighed the positives and negatives of the decision he was about to make, as if it was a contract to sign. *She is really quite impressive,* he thought. *A very direct manner, confident, easy to talk to. But what do I really know about her? She just arrived in town. Maybe she isn't even a doctor.* He stared for what seemed like minutes but was really just seconds as he came to his decision. "Alright, let's go ahead."

"Oh," she said with a startled gasp. "I did not mean I could do that. I have no office, no equipment, no assistant."

"But you're a doctor, so you do know how to perform the operation, correct?" he asked. He was long past assessing her diagnostic abilities. He wanted the appendix removed, now, by her.

"Of course," she said, with just the slightest arrogance that she hoped simply portrayed her confidence, as she regained her professional demeanor. "I have substantial surgical experience, and this is a relatively easy operation." She had perhaps overstated her experience just a bit, but she was not about to reveal any insecurities, and she had, in fact, performed this operation a few times.

What she did not tell Mr. Miller was that, while the operation was first performed in the early 1700s, it gained little traction until ether and chloroform became available in the 1840s. The operation became more common in just the last several years, and she was fortunate to have seen several such operations and performed a few. The diagnosis was clear. What was also clear is that Mr. Miller would die of overwhelming infection if she did not remove the appendix.

"Good, then please proceed," he replied.

"But how? Where?" she asked.

"I have some influence in town. We will ask Marshal Bennett to open up Dr. Stout's office."

Mr. Miller sent Sammy to the home of the marshal, toward the top of Park Avenue just over from Main Street, not too far up from the office that Mr. Miller had advertised in the *Park Record*. Sammy explained the situation, and the marshal came down the street to open Dr. Stout's office at the bottom of Main Street. Sammy then went next door and woke the neighbor, asking for some assistance in carrying his father in a cart down to Dr. Stout's office.

Sarah was appalled by what she saw as she walked into Dr. Stout's office. His blood-stained operating coat hung on a worn wooden rack. The creaking, heavy-planked floor was red-brown with blood stains, as was the wooden surgical table. She found some instruments in a tray filled with cloudy and scummy alcohol. There were no clean rags. The dim electric light bulbs washed the room with a faint glow.

"Mr. Miller, please get onto the table if you can," she said. "Sammy, can you find some clean rags?"

"Certainly," he said. "I can just run up to the Park Hotel."

"Oh, that is where I am staying," Sarah said. "Why there?"

"My father owns it," Sammy replied.

She rummaged around and found the glass-doored medicine cabinet with a bottle of ether and an array of pain concoctions in small brown bottles, several with droppers.

"Mr. Miller, are you still certain you are comfortable with me doing this operation?" she asked.

"Absolutely," he said with a forced smile, more of a grimace, "even more than before, the sooner the better. Just crawling onto the table has caused me tremendous pain." He had settled carefully on the table with a small thump and a groan.

Sammy returned with several clean white linen napkins from the Park Hotel restaurant. Sarah placed a cloth over Mr. Miller's face and began to drip the ether drop by drop. His face relaxed and the tension eased away. When he was asleep, she left the ether rag on his face and searched for the instruments she needed.

"Sammy, are you able to watch this, perhaps even help? I will need some assistance so I can perform the procedure."

"I, uh, guess," Sammy said. "I have never done anything like this."

She assembled the instruments she needed and opened up Mr. Miller's shirt and pants. She washed her hands, told Sammy to wash his, washed his father's abdomen, and laid out some clean rags around the site where she would be operating. She imagined a line from Mr. Miller's belly button to the bony protuberance from the pelvis on the lower right side of his abdomen. She poised over his abdomen briefly with the scalpel, composing herself and running through the steps of the procedure one more time.

She made an incision perpendicular to and across the line she just envisioned, about two-thirds of the way along the line from the belly button to the pelvic bone. The incision was about four inches long. She grabbed a rag to mop up the blood, and carried the incision down to the thin, glistening membrane lining the abdomen, through a thick layer of yellow fat. Mr. Miller did indeed have a generous diet.

As she entered the abdomen, she was met with more globs of fat, but she pushed it aside with a flat metal retractor blade and gave it to Sammy to hold, keeping the wound open. The inflamed appendix cooperated by popping into the wound.

It was grossly distended, red, and angry, and it looked like it was about to rupture. It remined her of the fat tomato worms that she used to see in her garden, but red instead of green. She showed Sammy where to hold the retractor. He was barely holding on, both to the retractor and to last night's dinner.

She threaded a catgut suture on a needle, grabbed the thumb-sized swollen worm gently with forceps, passed the needle through the tissue at the base of the appendix where it attached to the intestine, circled the appendix and tied it tightly around the base. Her supple fingers moved quickly and precisely. She did the same with another suture next to the first, maybe a quarter inch away toward the tip of the appendix. She was afraid the appendix would rupture with the pressure, but it held.

She picked up the scalpel and cut between the two sutures, pulling the appendix out of the wound as carefully as she could, with only a drop of pus from the cut base falling back into the abdomen. She dropped the inflamed appendix into a clean dish she had placed with the instruments. She took the retractor from Sammy and cleaned up the wound and abdomen. The bleeding from the wound had slowed, and she applied more pressure on the bleeding vessels until they stopped. She placed a few sutures in the membrane lining the abdomen, then a few more in the fibrous tissue underlying the skin, and finally closed the skin itself. She covered the wound with a clean rag and removed the ether cloth from Mr. Miller's face.

As she cleaned up the room, she made a mental note to remind herself to meet Dr. Stout soon and thank him for the use of his office. She somehow had the sense he would not be happy about it. She wondered if he would notice that the room was cleaner than when he left it. Probably not.

Mr. Miller started to stir, took a deep breath, and opened his eyes. He immediately grabbed for his abdomen, but she stopped him.

"We're all done, Mr. Miller," Sarah said. "Please don't touch your abdomen."

"Yes, ma'am, uh, Doctor," he mumbled, still a bit foggy.

"That was so impressive." Sammy said, "Thank you." He was looking much better now, the light reflecting off a faint sheen of sweat highlighting his pale pink skin.

"My pleasure," she replied.

"What do we do now?" Sammy asked.

"Let's get him home to bed. No food for two days, but he can have sips of water. It won't hurt him to be hungry for a bit. He can be up and about in a couple days as well, but I will come by tomorrow, well, actually, later today, to check on him."

She was exhilarated by what she had done. *Think of it, not even two days in town and I have already performed my first surgery. Here, in this frontier town, no hospital, no assistant, and in someone else's office! I am so glad I came to Park City.*

As he was helped away, Mr. Miller said, "Thank you, Doctor. When you return, we will discuss that office you wanted to rent."

She thought he was still a bit giddy from the ether.

Sarah walked up the wide stone steps of Mr. Miller's house later that afternoon. The light was fading in the canyon, but Sarah was still savoring the excitement and satisfaction of the surgery she had performed in the early morning. She had taken a long nap in what was turning out to be much more comfortable accommodations than she had reason to expect for a frontier mining town. To find out that Mr. Miller owned the hotel seemed so fitting, a good omen. She would have to tell him how much she was enjoying his hotel. It was proper that she should have a restful sleep in a hotel owned by a man whose life she had just saved!

She was excited to see how her first Park City patient was doing, but she knew better than to make assumptions. There were many ways the surgery could have gone wrong. She was not certain what she would find as she walked up the steps, and that made her anxious despite her excitement. She hoped she would find him recovering and as rested as she herself felt, and that he was pleased with her care, but she knew she had taken a chance doing the appendectomy. She could have easily declined, given the circumstances. Mr. Miller would have had to be transported down the canyon to Salt Lake, a gruesome trip over the rough washboard roads with an inflamed appendix about to rupture, but it might have been the proper thing to do. Maybe the suture had come off the appendix, and it was leaking pus and fecal matter into his abdomen. Maybe the wound was getting infected. Maybe he regretted that he had pushed her to operate now that he was feeling better.

As she entered his bedroom and walked to Mr. Miller's bedside, she saw that none of those disasters had come to pass. She found him resting comfortably in bed, a glass of water on the bedside table. His color was good, he was smiling, and he greeted her in his usual booming voice.

"Good afternoon!" he said.

"And to you," she said. "Is it good?"

"Indeed, it is!"

"And the pain?" she asked.

"Some. After all, you did cut a hole in my belly. But far better than yesterday!"

His loud energy overwhelmed Sarah, and she had an urge to lean over and hug him, but she recovered her professional dignity.

"You know you are supposed to be resting," she reminded him, having a hard time being as austere and professional as she thought she should be. His mischievous smile was just so cute.

"Yes, Doctor," he said, a bit sheepishly. He seemed to enjoy emphasizing her title. "I have and I will, but I feel so much better, thanks to you!"

"May I exam you?"

"Certainly," he said, and he whipped up his shirt and pulled down his pants. He was getting more comfortable with being cared for by a doctor who happened to be a woman.

The wound was clean, slightly red on the edges, with no evidence of infection. His abdomen was soft, a bit of discomfort around the wound but none elsewhere. It was a far different picture than just a few hours earlier.

"Have you passed any gas?" she asked.

"You mean did I fart?" he asked, knowing full well what she meant but enjoying pretending that he didn't.

She nodded, equally amused.

"I did indeed, just before you arrived!"

"Good, that means your intestinal system is starting to function. But you should wait another day with just sips of water, then you can have a bit of light food, perhaps some oatmeal. After I see you again, you should be able to start a more regular diet. Just keep drinking water. Everything looks quite good and just as I expected," although, if she was being honest with herself, she was not entirely sure what she expected. "I'll stop by again tomorrow."

"Do you still want to talk about that office?" he asked. He moved quickly and smoothly from patient to businessman looking to make a deal.

"Of course. I thought perhaps your offer was just the effect of the ether wearing off," she said with a little laugh.

"Not at all," he said, "I am deeply in your debt and would like to see your practice get established and become successful. I'll tell anyone who will listen how pleased I am with your care."

She really had no idea how to negotiate a lease and what would be proper for a contract and its cost, but Mr. Miller was encouraging and persuasive. He seemed to be acting with good will in helping her get established. She asked him about the property that had been advertised in *The Record*, a cute house in a good location, 401 Park Avenue, just over and down a bit from his house. He told her that Fourth Street was a busy intersection, and she would be easily available to her patients. It was a fine house, clean and tidy, painted a very attractive light blue. He thought the first floor would work well for her practice, and the upstairs had a comfortable bedroom and kitchen. She was so excited and just trusted him to offer a fair agreement.

She marveled at how extraordinarily fortuitous the events of the last day had come together to her benefit, that Mr. Miller happened to develop appendicitis just as she was looking for office space, that Dr. Stout was unavailable, that the operation had gone smoothly, and that her patient had done well. So many links in that remarkable chain of events could have broken, the most important of which was that she might not have had the confidence to perform what was, in fact, a risky operation under highly adverse circumstances. But she had performed it well. Her confidence was justified. It was a calculated risk, but then wasn't medical judgment always like that?

Physicians were always forced to weigh complex risks and benefits with information that was never certain and never complete. She had made that assessment, acted on her decision, and taken full advantage of the opportunities that resulted. She thought this was a good omen overall for the decision she had made to come to Park City, irrespective of the way she had been treated by Gibson. She was beginning to think that Gibson's horrid behavior was the best thing that could have happened to her.

"Thank you, Mr. Miller, I will take my leave now and stop back again tomorrow."

"Park City is really growing up," he said, somewhat offhandedly as she was on her way to the door. "It is wonderful to see two new doctors coming to town at the same time."

She remembered now that the hotel clerk had mentioned a new physician in town, as had Sammy, but she had not paid attention to either of them. Now she did, and she was surprised at her response to Mr. Miller's casual comment. *I know he intended the comment as casual and friendly chit-chat. Somehow it feels more threatening than that. But why? I arrived two days ago, and now I feel threatened because another physician just came into town as well?! Why? I should just be happy the operation went well, and Mr. Miller is recovering.*

There was a quickening of her pulse, a flush in her face. "Oh, how do you mean?" she asked, trying to sound equally casual and offhanded in her response. She hoped she did not betray any particular concern.

"I heard that a Dr. Thomas Wilson came into town and just rented an office up toward the top of Main Street, just up from us a block or two. Came from Michigan as I understand it. I hear he is just getting settled. We might have called on him last night, but I was impressed with your offer of help.

And my judgment was correct. I am glad I took advantage of your availability."

"I am pleased that you did so as well," she said, her previous excitement and warmth turning flat. She hoped he did not feel that his praise was being ignored. She was not reacting to his thanks but to the name she had just heard. "I shall have to meet Dr. Wilson."

However, she did not have to meet him, because she was certain she already knew him. *How many Dr. Thomas Wilsons are there from Michigan? I recall him very clearly. He ended up graduating just behind me in class rankings. He seemed bright, brilliant even, expert clinical skills, well-trained in medical diagnosis and therapeutics. I saw him in surgery, outstanding surgical skills. But somehow we just never seemed to connect. There was something about him, something missing, something lacking as a physician. He was just not that confident or comfortable with himself, maybe damaged in some way. And now, of all people, he was here, showing up just when I did! How could that happen? And why do I care? Because I like it here. Because I want it to be my town, my fresh start!*

"I shall have to meet Dr. Wilson," seemingly unaware that she had already said that.

Mr. Miller wondered why she looked so annoyed.

CHAPTER 8

Park City, 1897

Thomas had felt an enormous weight lift from him as he departed Michigan, the weight of his medical practice, his father's death, his memories, and his former life. He was stunned by the tremendous boost of energy that propelled him into his new life. He had followed the same train and stage-coach route as Sarah would two weeks later, and found the same muddy, dusty, smoky town. He explored the *Park Record* ads for possible locations for his office and talked to some of the same landlords that Sarah would meet. They treated him far differently. The landlords could not have been more supportive and generous. They were, to a person, excited to welcome a new physician to town, and they were honored that he might rent office space from them. He had to show little in the way of his credentials or reveal much about his plans in order to engage in serious discussions with several landlords.

He picked a building at 221 Main Street, toward the top of the street, with easy access to the Ontario Mine, the Judge Daly mine up Daly Canyon, and others up the hillsides to the west above Empire Avenue. It was a perfect location to build a practice. Several boarding houses were nearby, as were other businesses that appeared prosperous. Their proximity to the mines and the boardinghouses gave the entire neighborhood the look of success. Thomas hoped that would contribute to his success as well.

He found a carpenter to make a sign for his new office, a nice piece of finished pine with *"Dr. Thomas Wilson, Physician and Surgeon,"* painted in bright yellow. He placed a small notice of his arrival in town in four weekly issues of the *Park Record*.

> *Dr. Thomas Wilson is pleased to announce that he has recently established a medical practice at 221 Main Street and is accepting new patients. He trained at the University of Michigan in the full spectrum of medical care for patients of all ages and has several years of subsequent experience in a medical practice in Michigan.*

Sarah missed that notice in her perusal of the paper two weeks later. Thomas sent a letter to the Utah State Medical Association to learn about membership, and he let the city marshal know of his availability for emergencies if he was needed.

Thomas had amazed himself by his uncharacteristically impetuous decision to up and leave Michigan. He had left it all, his hometown, his practice, four graves overgrown with brush and one new and fresh. It was all such a whirlwind, but it felt like a good whirlwind, a fresh start, a new home, new possibilities, new opportunities. He had taken this leap into so many unknowns. It was not like him. Launching himself cross-country on such a grand adventure made him realize how discouraged he had felt in his Michigan practice, how he had failed to become the complete physician he knew that he could be. It had seemed easier to start a new life in an entirely new place, without the burdens of so much history and so many memories.

He had felt no emotion when he left Mendon. He packed up a small bag of clothes and a larger one of medical equipment, climbed on the stagecoach headed south toward the

Michigan border where the train would take him to Chicago and on west from there. He sold the farm to his father's neighbor, said goodbye to all five family members buried in the ground near the family cabin, and rode off having no idea what adventures awaited him in Park City. But he didn't really care. He was free of his old life. He hoped it did not return.

The burst of energy propelled him to think seriously about why he had failed in Michigan. He thought about his classmates, especially that woman, Sarah Fletcher. *Why do I not feel her confidence? Why did my father think so little of my skills? That's it! My father. His melancholy life, and then his miserable death. What words were on his lips when he died. Was it "I love you?" Maybe. Did he? Why did he not show it? Why did he not say it before he took his last breath?*

He was starting to understand that his childhood had scarred him. He had hoped that the scar tissue would have become less inflamed, less raw. It would always be there, as was true for all scars, but most scars also faded over time. This one had not, at least not yet, because his father had kept picking at it. But his father was gone, and he was in a rough town full of wild dreams, glittering opportunities, and spectacular successes. His scars would not matter here.

His mind wandered back to Sarah Fletcher. *I want to be more like her. I graduated near the top of my class, right behind her. She was so impressive, from the very first day she walked in class. Commanding, intimidating, so comfortable with herself. She had looked upon the class, especially their initially rude behavior, with a powerful mix of disdain and amusement. Her comfort with herself and her responsibilities as a physician had just grown even stronger from that point on.*

It was all quite a mystery, a mystery he was committed to solve.

Despite his feelings of insecurity, he had learned to portray an outward sense of confidence and competence to those he met. He enjoyed a positive reception by business owners as he introduced himself around town. There was an excitement about the town that caught him up. The Sherman Silver Purchase Act of 1890 had stabilized the price of silver and stimulated new exploration. The old mines were continuing to produce at high levels with new drainage tunnels that allowed deeper exploration. Silver veins often came with a high lead content, and lead was becoming nearly as important a source of revenue for the mines as silver. New businesses were popping up in town on a regular basis. A new school was built last year, and more teachers were being hired as families moved in. The rough mining camp still existed in many places, but there was a new air of respect and influence about town.

Transportation to Salt Lake City and railroad links to the transcontinental railroad north of Ogden connected Park City to the wider world. Extravagant claims of silver lying on the ground and millionaires being made every day brought speculators, sometimes with money, sometimes with bluff and bluster, to Park City. New people, new ideas, new money and new energy were arriving every day. He felt the excitement and felt like he was part of it. He was determined to take advantage of the sense of opportunity and possibility that pervaded the town. Here is where he would become the physician he wanted to be.

He had been in town just two weeks and a day when those opportunities and possibilities became more explicit, walking through his new office door in the form of J. S. Gibson, an exuberant man who blew in with a burst of energy. The wooden slats on the boardwalk groaned from his considerable heft. The dusty air and the glare of the sun through the dusty windows made it hard for Gibson to see much as he scanned around the modest office, fitted out with only the barest of office furniture and equipment. It looked a bit shabby to him.

"Dr. Wilson?" Mr. Gibson asked.

"Yes, sir, how may I help you?"

"I have a very specific need, although probably not of the sort you may expect," Gibson said in his most persuasive and gracious voice. He stood just inside the door, seemingly fearful to step farther into the meager surroundings.

Thomas motioned to a chair. "Please, sir, have a seat."

Gibson swiped a finger across the dusty seat. "Thank you for your hospitality, but I will only take a moment. I am the manager and superintendent of the Ontario mine, as you may know, and I am in need of a physician to provide medical care to our miners. I understand you are new in town, and I wonder if I might prevail upon you to consider that opportunity." He paused slightly and then said, as much to himself as to Thomas, "I thought I had a physician lined up, but it didn't work out."

"I know little about mining and even less about what you might require of me," Thomas replied, "but, as you said, I am new in town, and am interested in exploring all possible opportunities." *Amazing,* he thought. *I have barely arrived and good things are already happening!* "But I understand Dr. Stout is long-established here. He would seem to be a more suitable candidate."

"Dr. Stout is indeed established and doing well. That is exactly the problem. He has no need or interest in being connected to a single mine. I thought perhaps this would be a way for you to get yourself established in your new practice." The insincerity in his voice would have been plain to anyone, but it was not to Thomas in his reverie. Gibson cared little about helping Thomas's practice, but he was trying hard to be as charming and welcoming as he could. *If Stout hadn't been so arrogant and unpleasant,* he thought, *I wouldn't have this problem in the first place.*

"Tell me what would be required," Thomas said. "I know little about mining, as I said, but enough to know that such a position could be very difficult and demanding. I understand mines are very dangerous places, wet, dark, and dirty. I have heard, even in my short time in town, grumbling by miners about how mines are run, with little regard for their welfare. I am sure, of course, that such accusations would not apply to you or the Ontario mine!" But in fact he had heard that particular accusation directed specifically at Gibson and the Ontario. Gibson himself had been heard to say, when a miner died from a tunnel cave-in due to inadequate timbering, that *"miners are cheaper than lumber."*

On the other hand, he thought, *this offer from Gibson could be a tremendous boon to my practice, and a steady source of patients and income. But something doesn't feel right here. Gibson's cheery demeanor seems so false, like it actually pains him to be so welcoming. Look at him right now, awkward and uncomfortable, rocking back and forth, like he can't get out of here fast enough.*

"Perhaps it would be best if I gave you a tour of the Ontario and showed you some of the risks the miners face and how you could help," Gibson said. "My owners have expressed a desire to have dedicated medical care to serve the miners and care for their medical needs." Thomas had to suppress a smile at how uncomfortable Gibson was speaking the last sentence.

They agreed to meet at the mine headquarters the next morning.

The morning was bright and warming nicely despite the ever-present blanket of smoke over the town. Thomas walked up Main Street, turned left past the hollow running down the hill parallel to Main Street where the Chinese lived, and continued up the hill into lower Ontario Canyon. The stamping mill was pounding away, as always. Thomas was getting used to it. As he walked up Ontario canyon, he gradually rose above the smoke. Even with the hills barren of trees, the mountains were stunning, rising steeply above the town and covered with the aprons of crushed rock tailings that had been pushed out of the dozens of shallow and now unworked shafts covering the hillsides.

The tailings spilled down the hill everywhere, evidence of the early frantic digging of every outcropping of rock containing even a little quartz. Prospectors believed that where there was quartz, silver would follow. They were usually disappointed, but even a small amount of silver found in the samples by the assayer could lead to a bountiful sale to an unsuspecting buyer. Salting the diggings a bit with silver found elsewhere didn't hurt to generate enthusiasm, but that chaotic and unregulated era of development was over. Most of the energy went into a relatively small number of mines that could track silver veins deep into the mountain. It was all backed by investors who could support the extraordinarily expensive business of sinking shafts, pumping water, tunneling new drainage, and transporting crushed and sorted rock to a smelter. Park City was starting to look like a settled and thriving small town, set in a stunning canyon. Main Street was busy and bustling, the shops full of customers, the rumble of ore-filled wagons coming down and empty wagons going up a measure of Park City's wealth and economic vitality.

One of those ore wagons came by just at that moment, and Thomas stepped aside. He was looking forward with anticipation to touring the Ontario mine, but the nagging worry about Gibson kept intruding. There was just something wrong with Gibson and his offer. He hoped he could figure out what it was as he reached the Ontario Mine and called upon Mr. Gibson in the Administrative Office.

Mr. Gibson seemed to have forgotten about the meeting with Thomas. He looked confused about why he was there and was about to send him away when he caught himself. He lifted his ponderous body from his heavy desk chair. "Welcome, welcome!" he said in his usual booming voice. "Let's go across to the changing room and take you down." They walked across to the headframe where several miners mumbled their greetings. Gibson tried to smile in return, but Thomas could tell it was an unaccustomed response. His smile looked more like a pained and sinister grimace. Gibson pointed to a clean and folded set of work clothes for Thomas to wear.

"Cleaned just for you, Doctor," Gibson said.

Thomas slid carefully into the heavy canvas pants and wool shirt, followed by a waxed yellow rubber slicker, high rubber boots, and hard felt hat. Thomas noticed how clean his clothes were compared to those of the miners around him in the changing room.

They walked to the shaft and climbed into a metal cage, maybe eight or nine feet square. The metal mesh and struts were gleaming in the morning sun, almost unnaturally clean, Thomas thought. Gibson slid the gate shut and motioned the lift operator to let them down. The bright sunny day quickly disappeared in the absorbing blackness of the shaft. The grinding noise of the winch engine faded as they dropped away. All they could hear was the rasping squeak of the cable as the cage swung from one wall to the other. Twelve hundred feet down and two minutes later they arrived at the station. Thomas looked up to see the tiny dot of light at the top of the shaft from which they had descended, like the only bright star in a dark sky. He was impressed with how tidy everything seemed,

"I am impressed with how clean the mine is, Mr. Gibson," Thomas said. "Equipment stacked carefully along the edges, the floor recently swept. I had been led to believe that mines were cold, dark, and dirty places."

"We try to run a clean and tidy mine," Gibson replied. He had finally found his charming demeanor and had settled into it. "It is safer and leads to happier miners."

He gave Thomas a carbide lamp to carry, indicated a tunnel to the left, and off they went, a slight downhill incline to the drift, water dripping off the ceiling and down the walls, running into a small trench in the middle of the tunnel. Thomas could see in whatever direction he pointed his helmet and the attached carbide lamp, but not to the sides. The blackness of the tunnel soaked up any extraneous light. The darkness was oppressive, close, and threatening. The silence of the tunnel was broken only by the constant drip of water and, increasingly, a loud pounding as they walked along. Thomas was sweating in the cold and clammy air. He heard the scurry of small animals that he could not see.

Thomas had no basis to judge the construction of the tunnel, its timbering or its safety, but it looked substantial; heavy eight-by-eight inch posts topped by a cap of the same size. He felt the weight of twelve hundred feet of solid rock above him and was disoriented by the shadows that jumped in and out as he turned his head. As they approached the end of the drift, the pounding of a mechanical drill became explosive. Thomas could barely think it was so loud. Gibson motioned for the team of two miners working at the rock face to stop.

The hammering drill slowed its pace and finally quit, and Gibson explained about the wonders of the mechanical drill. "This drill has transformed mining," he said proudly. "We are installing them as fast as we can in the Ontario. They are three or four times faster than a double-jack hand drilling team, even the best team, which basically translates to three or four times more ore and the same increase in revenue. Hand drilling is still necessary in some stopes because of limited space and awkward angles."

One of the miners spoke up: "We still miss the old days. Nothing like a good day of double-jacking to pass the time." Thomas saw Gibson shoot the man a sharp look.

The two miners had set up their drill bolted to a heavy steel beam anchored in the floor and ceiling with screw jacks. The drill was attached at about waist-level and pointed to the rock face. An air hose that ran down the tunnel from a compressor in the underground station was attached to the drill. Rapid opening and closing of a valve released high-pressure air into a chamber behind a piston attached to a steel bit, slamming it forward into the rock. A trip lever diverted the air to a chamber in front of the piston and slammed it back, then rotating the bit an eighth of a turn to bring a fresh edge to the rock. The miner operating the drill slowly advanced a large screw feed to keep the drill bit at the most advantageous depth in the hole, so as to get the most out of each strike. At two hundred strikes per minute, the noise was deafening—painful even. The stamping mill was nothing compared to the drill in the close confines of the tunnel.

It was the huge cloud of hard rock dust that got Thomas's attention the most. He made a mental note to ask Gibson about the dust and the health dangers it might pose. He himself started coughing as soon as the drill started up. He couldn't imagine how the miners could do this several hours a day, day after day. He was also interested in the black streaks of rock that seemed to run with the glittery crystals of quartz in the vein the miners were working. The streaks looked greasy, and Thomas assumed it was lead.

"Sir," one of the miners said, "we are just finishing the last hole and about to place the dynamite and blow the face. We will be headed back to the station very soon." They carefully slid two sticks of dynamite into each hole and attached rat-tail fuses to the second stick. The fuses were of different lengths so the dynamite would explode in a sequence that would best bring the entire face of rock crashing to the ground. The shortest one would give them about ten minutes to get to the surface. One miner went back to the station to send a signal, five bells, to the lift operator to indicate they were about to blow a face. He came back and announced that the lift operator had signaled he was ready.

The miners lit all the fuses and made sure they all stayed lit. All four men made their way to the station at a careful but rapid pace. Tripping and falling could be fatal if they could not get to the cage in time. They loaded the cage, signaled the operator, and up they went, exiting the cage at the top just as they heard, then felt, the concussive wave of the explosion. The timing was close, maybe a bit too close, Thomas thought. The miners went back down in the cage to muck the rock, haul the full ore carts out to the cage, and start drilling a new face.

Gibson and Thomas returned to Gibson's office.

"Mr. Gibson, I am intrigued by your offer, but I have some questions," Thomas said. "I noticed the clouds of dust produced by the mechanical drill. I wonder what your thoughts are about that and whether the dust might be harmful to the miners' health. I, myself, started to cough as soon as the miners restarted the drill."

Mr. Gibson waved his hand dismissively. "There is no evidence to my knowledge that the dust is of any concern. There has always been dust produced by drilling, whether manual or mechanical, and we have no knowledge that drilling causes any known health problems. Most miners live a personal life that is far more dangerous than mining—drinking, whores, bar brawls, sometimes knife fights. There are a lot of reasons for them to be sick or injured that have nothing to do with the mines." His self-satisfied smiled tried to make him look sincerely concerned but failed spectacularly. "There is no doubt mining is a dangerous occupation, but we know of no specific harms."

Gibson knew very well there was a problem. He and other mine managers suspected that something in the rock dust was the cause. "The miners are demanding that we bring a water line in to wash down the dust and keep it from forming. That would be prohibitively expensive, and we see no need." The insincere smile became more pronounced. He appeared almost giddy as he tried so hard to seem unconcerned.

"What was the black rock that seemed to be mixed with the quartz vein?" Thomas asked.

"Lead," Mr. Gibson replied. "Lead ore is often found in the same formations as silver-bearing rock. It is becoming almost as important as silver as its demand increases, and therefore its price."

Thomas tried to feel reassured by Gibson's smooth talk, but he knew at some subconscious level that something was wrong. That suspicion was balanced by the heady opportunity to potentially benefit the miners in their desire for better medical care. Perhaps this was the time he could step forward and do something important. He was enthused, perhaps more than he should have been, about the way this position could help establish his practice and provide a guaranteed source of income. He told himself that the remarkably convenient timing of this opportunity was confirmation that leaving Michigan was the right thing to do, that this proved he was turning his life in a new and positive direction. However, he couldn't shake the fear that he was responding to the wrong job for the wrong reasons. He still pushed ahead.

"I would be interested in the details of your offer, Mr. Gibson."

"Very well, I will put together a formal offer and we can discuss the details tomorrow. Thank you for coming." With that, Thomas could tell that the meeting was over, and he was dismissed.

He walked back down the hill to Main Street, debating with himself whether this was a fortuitous way to advance his practice or a bargain with the devil. He answered the question in entirely contradictory ways with each step. The morning was jumbled with thoughts about his family, about Michigan, about Sarah Fletcher, and now about a job offer that could be seriously flawed. He was so lost in his troubled reverie that he nearly walked headlong into Dr. Sarah Fletcher, the last person he could imagine seeing on the Park City boardwalk.

CHAPTER 9

Park City, 1897

As the doctors walked toward each other on the Main Street boardwalk, Thomas was as surprised to see Sarah as she was annoyed to see Thomas.

"Doctor Fletcher," Thomas said, offering his hand.

"Doctor Wilson," Sarah said, barely touching it.

"What a surprise as well as a pleasure to see you. You are one of the last people I could imagine seeing here. If truth be told, I am somewhat amazed to find myself here, but seeing you is another level of astonishment!"

"Well, no less a surprise for me," Sarah said, with as little warmth as possible, barely polite. "I learned of your presence in town from Mr. Miller just a short time ago. I think you may know him and may have discussed renting office space from him."

"Yes, I did look at that house and office but ended up elsewhere, in fact just there," he said, proudly pointing north a few houses down the street. His newly-painted sign was swinging gently in the morning breeze. He looked at it as often as possible. She had missed it as she came up the street.

Sarah looked at the building and the sign and could not control her resentment. She was barely processing the news from Mr. Miller about Dr. Wilson and trying to understand why it was so upsetting. Now he suddenly appears in front of her, all cheery and friendly. She was not ready for that. The whole scene just put a damper on the pride and exhilaration she had felt in her care of Mr. Miller. Thomas's office location on a prime part of upper Main Street plus the quality of the polished wood and hand-painted sign just added to her misery. *Why do I care about this so much,* she wondered. *I have no basis for this resentment, and no claim to this territoriality. I'm annoyed to see him here, and annoyed that I am annoyed!* The flat look on her face darkened further.

"Yes, I looked at that house as well. The landlord was more interested in serving as my escort. He said it was unseemly for a woman to be out and about, alone as I was. He gallantly offered to keep me respectable. His was one of the more annoying responses I received as I tried to establish an office for my practice. But then you wouldn't know anything about that, nor I suppose would you likely care." She felt immediately shamed by the cruelty of her response and wasn't even sure why she had said it. She just couldn't help herself when she saw how easy it was for him to get established. She hoped he might care a bit about her struggles, based on her positive memories of him from medical school, but she didn't really expect he would.

Thomas was taken aback by her anger and the harsh comment. *I would certainly admit I don't understand her experience as a woman physician. All I know is how in awe I was of her performance in medical school. How could anyone treat her with so little respect when she was so brilliant? In any case, it's certainly not my fault!* "And did you find a suitable location?" It was all he could think of to ask.

"Yes, just this morning, down the street a bit to Fourth Street and left up the hill to Park Avenue. Mr. Miller was very gracious to lease the space to me after I operated on him last night, well actually early this morning, although not in that office." Sarah said this as if she was describing a trip to the store for groceries. Her cruelty had transformed into arrogance, somewhat purposely just to calm her rising aggravation. She wanted Thomas to believe that the surgery was just another part of her normal day, however much of an exaggeration that was. She was just tired of even the possibility of more disrespect.

"What? What did you do?" Thomas was stunned by the casual way Sarah referred to caring for Mr. Miller, but he was even more interested, out of sheer medical curiosity, in what she said.

"Took out his appendix, went quite well," she said, as off-handedly and casually as she could, now with only the barest hint of arrogance. "I, of course, had no office at that point because of the way I had been treated by several landlords. The town marshal had to break into Dr. Stout's office who was away. Mr. Miller was aware of your arrival in town but seemed taken by me and the immediate availability of my services. Dr. Stout's office, by the way, is disgusting, blood stains everywhere, dirty instruments, and an operating coat that looks like he works in a butcher's shop."

And with just that brief reporting of Sarah's adventures over the last several hours, Thomas felt the welling of inferiority and inadequacy that characterized his time with her in medical school. Her confidence flowed from her words and her face, a certainty about her skill and a command of her profession that seemed so comfortable to her and so foreign to him. An appendectomy was not necessarily something he couldn't do, and in fact he had done so quite skillfully a few times, but to do so in an office, not even her office or with her own equipment, alone, without assistance, was remarkable. The nonchalant report of her success mixed with the accusatory hurt of her comments about how unfairly she had been treated by landlords threw him straight back into the state of anxiety that he thought he had left behind in Michigan.

However, his anxiety could not match his sheer medical curiosity about how she performed an appendectomy under such adverse circumstances. "How did you manage the need for retraction and keeping the field exposed?"

"I enlisted the help of Mr. Miller's son, Sammy, although not entirely voluntarily. Nice kid. He looked like he was about to pass out, but we made it to the end."

"That must have been quite an experience for Sammy. I wish the marshal had notified me. I would have been pleased to serve as your assistant." His admiration was sincerely felt, however disingenuous he sounded. He hoped his offer of help would be received in the way he intended.

It was, barely. Sarah cocked her head slightly and stared at him for several uncomfortable seconds. Thomas was just so nice. It was hard to hold her resentment for long. As her resentment cooled, she understood that none of this was really his fault.

His curiosity took the discussion in a different direction. "How is it that you found your way to this remote place? The last I heard you were caring for poor women in New York." He didn't mean it to sound like he was discounting what she was doing, but it seemed to come out that way.

Sarah had calmed down enough that she chose to not react to what she first thought was a criticism of her indigent infirmary practice. She realized it was not intended that way. There was also something lurking in the back of her mind about Thomas, something more positive that buffered her resentment. *Why do I remember him so positively, she wondered. Ah, I remember. The first day of school, when nearly everyone was heckling me. But not everyone, not Thomas. He seemed shy and looked as out-of-place as I felt, but in a different way. Most importantly, he was the only medical student who had not behaved in the immature and boorish way I had been treated by the rest of the class.*

A small smile slowly crossed her face. "Yes, I had a very busy practice in New York, both in an indigent infirmary for women and children, as well as a private practice on the side. But it was just not as comprehensive and fulfilling as I wanted. I surprised my colleagues and partners, and perhaps more so myself, by responding to the posting of a job as mine physician at the Ontario mine. The advertisement just seemed to pop up when I was in a particularly adventuresome mood. I wanted to get a fresh start, in a new place, and this seemed like an especially dramatic way to make all that happen. I just felt like I wasn't the physician and surgeon I wanted to be, and my skills were not being fully utilized in New York. I thought there would be many new opportunities in a town like Park City, especially as a mine physician. It hasn't turned out quite like that, but I am still happy with my decision."

This was way more sharing than she had intended, but somehow it felt right. She was surprised to find herself enjoying the opportunity to share so much about herself and talk with a fellow physician about her motivations. Her friends and family had not understood her decision, and Thomas somehow seemed more sympathetic and interested. Her colleagues in New York could not imagine why she was doing something so unthinkable, perhaps even a bit scandalous, when she boarded the train for St. Louis.

"So I applied, sent my references and credentials, and the Ontario manager, a Mr. Gibson, sent an offer. When I presented myself at his office two days ago, he was, shall we say, not pleased. He was just horrid, rude, dismissive, and finally angry. He basically threw me out of his office. He clearly did not have someone like me in mind when he made the offer, and he refused to hire me, so I started looking for an office." She could not conceal her bitterness, although she hoped Thomas was now not taking it personally.

Thomas's face and shoulders sagged, he hoped not visibly to Sarah. *How can I possibly now tell her about the visit from Gibson? She will not be pleased. Or maybe she won't care. Why do I care?* "Well, um, I share your excitement about a fresh start in this adventurous place. But I should tell you that Mr. Gibson offered that position to me this morning. And I, um, well, I have tentatively accepted."

"Well, good for you," she said sarcastically. Her previous comfort with the conversation was gone in a flash. "After the way I was treated, I wouldn't work for him anyway. Even in my short time here I have heard a lot about how little he cares about his miners' welfare, particularly about the dangerous conditions in the mine. I have already heard all manner of stories about deaths, explosions, cave-ins, drownings, all because of Gibson's policies. I think you are going to have a lot of business, although not necessarily for good reasons."

"I actually thought the mine seemed quite safe." Thomas knew he sounded a bit defensive. He couldn't help it. "He took me on a tour just now and the miners seemed satisfied with their work. The mine itself was clean and tidy and looked well-maintained. I did ask Mr. Gibson about one issue, the clouds of dust created by the mechanical drilling, but he was quite reassuring. He professed no knowledge of any problems with the dust, and he said he simply wanted to hire a mine physician to improve the health and welfare of the miners."

"Well, now I feel really fortunate I did not get the job," Sarah said. "Especially after the way he treated me. I am strongly doubtful of his sincerity, and you should be as well. There is no evidence that mine owners and managers care a thing about the welfare of their miners. The state law is clear that mine owners have no responsibility for the welfare of miners except to pay them, and the mine takes full advantage of that lack of regulation."

"I understand, but I found Gibson to be quite proud of how safe his mine is. The tour was fascinating in a scary sort of way, clean and tidy as I said, but also wet, dark, and cold! I think the job could be quite interesting." For some reason, it mattered to Thomas to show Sarah that he was taking his job seriously. He felt he had to defend his decision, despite his concerns, but he certainly did not want to defend Gibson himself. He could already see how difficult that was becoming. It was not entirely comfortable even now, just a day after accepting the offer.

"I will certainly be looking closely at any health risks," he continued, "but I have no evidence at the moment to be concerned about the mine operations overall." He knew how weak, even deceptive, that all sounded. "Besides, I don't know why it would make much sense to expose miners to any danger. Without miners there would be no mines, no ore, no profits, and no dividends. Gibson seemed to want me to improve the quality of medical care and the miners' overall health. I am hopeful I can do that." Now he was trying to convince himself more than Sarah.

"Well, you clearly have talked yourself into believing that Gibson is sincere in his concern about the miners," Sarah said. "I think you are a fool to believe it." She felt no need to be discrete. "Miners are indeed essential to the mine's success, but not necessarily the same miners. I understand there is a steady stream of miners seeking work, especially as the Nevada and California mines play out. One dies and another takes his place. The more we talk, the more I feel fortunate that Gibson couldn't cope with a woman serving as the mine's physician. Bad things happen down in those mines, and you are going to be responsible for it. You seem to think you can make a difference, but I highly doubt you can. You should think hard about whether it is truly possible."

She was not sure why she even cared what he did, or why she was getting into such a heated conversation in the middle of the boardwalk with someone she barely knew. The conversation was entertaining in a perverse sort of way, but she was done with Thomas and had things to do. She abruptly brushed past him. "It was a pleasure. Best of luck in your new job."

She headed on up Main Street. He was left standing alone and confused on the boardwalk as shoppers walked past. He knew at some level that she was accurate in her assessment of Gibson, and she was probably right about the job as well. But the position, the new equipment, the fancy office, the ready-made and busy practice, and a steady income were so seductive. He wondered now whether it was all too seductive.

The most upsetting aspect of this whole encounter, he thought, *was that it involved Sarah. Why does she have to be here? The one student in my class who was particularly intimidating. I was almost afraid of her in medical school. She was so brilliant, so serious, so talented. Just as I try to restart my life, why does she have to appear in Park City? And look at what she has done already, in all of two days, an appendectomy, alone, in a strange office with a kid for an assistant. She was just too dazzling!*

Sarah spent the next few weeks getting her office established, ordering equipment from medical supply stores in Salt Lake City and creating an atmosphere in her office that was comfortable, welcoming, and professional. She hung her diploma on the wall, as well as a framed letter from the mayor of New York City that commended her for caring for the poor women of the city. She tried to be as visible as possible in town. She attended events and public meetings to make her availability known. The reaction was the same everywhere, men looking askance at her or worse, questioning her morals, her education, her experience, her skills, her mental stability, anything and everything. On the other hand, women flocked to her with relief and appreciation that there might now be a physician in town who would pay attention to their needs. They felt ignored and dismissed by Dr. Stout and his predecessors, and they had no confidence that the other new physician in town, a Dr. Wilson, would be any better. They had a long history of being treated rudely and roughly by men, with poor outcomes and poor health. They hoped for something different from Sarah.

One day, a woman walked into Sarah's office to ask for a consultation. "Are you the lady doctor I heard about?" the woman asked. Even though she knew she had come to the office of the new woman physician in town, the sheer amazement of seeing a woman dressed as a physician, in a medical office, surrounded by medical equipment, was difficult to fully digest. Perhaps she had heard wrong, perhaps this woman was a midwife, or maybe the wife of the real physician, but she was desperate, tired, and sick. She needed help. She seemed about to slump to the floor just from the effort of walking up the steps and through the door into the office.

"I believe I am indeed that doctor. Dr. Sarah Fletcher is my name. And yours?"

"Flora," she said. "Flora Richmond."

"You look like you are about to faint, Flora," Sarah said. "Please have a seat here. Now how can I help you?

Flora wore a simple dress and hat, a lady of modest means, but she had a determined look on her face. She gave off a quiet moan as she settled into the chair. The heavy rouge make-up on her cheeks could not hide the pallor of her forehead and neck, making it even more obvious to Sarah.

"I, I guess I don't know," Flora said. "I saw Dr. Stout, and he sent me to a doctor in Salt Lake City. They both said there was really nothing wrong that they could help with. Maybe they are right."

"Just tell me a bit about what is troubling you," Sarah said. "Let's start there.

"My husband, James is his name, says it is nothing and I should just get on with what I am supposed to be doing. I think something more is wrong. I feel weak, sometimes like I can barely get out of bed. Sometimes I think I am just going to fall down and never get up."

"What did the doctor in Salt Lake suggest?"

"He gave me a machine that I am supposed to use to massage, uh, I'm sorry, down in my private area. Dr. Stout suggested a bath with some sort of electric current running through it, but I didn't know how to do that. James doesn't know I saw a doctor, so I can't ask him for help." She paused, partly from the exertion of telling her story and partly because she wasn't sure her story would make any more sense to Sarah than it had to the previous doctors. "I'm sorry, maybe I shouldn't have bothered you."

"Not at all, I would like very much to help," Sarah said. "Tell me a bit about yourself. What does James do?"

"He works at the Ontario mine. He's a driller, started on one of those new fancy mechanical drills a few months ago."

"And a family?"

"Oh, yes, five children, now. Was six but we lost a girl two years back. Scarlet fever. I still miss her." Her eyes reddened. "I'm sorry." She paused. "The children are ten, eight, six, three, and almost a year old."

"I am so sorry to hear about your daughter. Scarlet fever is a terrible disease. That's quite a family, enough to make you tired just taking care of them. But I think something else might be going on. You look like you are low on blood. Have you lost blood anywhere?"

"Oh, yes, I am bleeding all the time, sometimes heavy, from, um, my private area. It never really stopped after my last baby. My husband doesn't know, and the doctors didn't seem much interested to hear about it."

"It would help if I could conduct a medical exam. May I do so?"

"Yes, please, anything that would help you find out what is wrong. I am tired of feeling so poorly."

It was immediately apparent to Sarah that Flora was markedly anemic. Her pulse was weak and fast, her skin pale, and the loose conjunctival tissue around her eyes even more so. Sarah had equipped her office as she was trained, including a syringe and needle with which to draw blood. She also had a hemocytometer, a device invented and enhanced by several European physicians over the prior several decades. She had been taught in its use by her medical school professors.

The technique was tedious, but she followed the proper procedure. She washed the skin of Flora's arm at the elbow, drew a syringe of blood and placed a drop onto a glass slide divided into finely-etched grids. It would take some time to do a full and accurate count of red blood cells, but she could tell just by looking through her new microscope that Flora's red blood cell count was shockingly low. She estimated that the concentration of red blood cells had been reduced by half or more from normal. Flora was severely anemic. Sarah was amazed that she was functioning at all.

When she examined Flora internally, she discovered a uterus that was four times the normal size, similar to a three-month pregnant uterus. She feared cancer, but perhaps the enlargement was simply from benign uterine muscle tumors.

"Ma'am, you are severely low on blood because you are losing so much from your uterus, your womb. It is remarkable that you are functioning at all with such a low amount of blood. Your uterus is very large, the reason for which I cannot tell. But what I do know is that it must come out. I am afraid your time for having children is at an end. Without an operation, you could become even more severely ill, and I could not be certain of the outcome."

"Well, I will have to ask James," Flora said.

"Why?" Sarah blurted out, and then regretted her abrupt response. She knew it was not appropriate. But she persisted. "There is no question about the diagnosis or the treatment, whatever his opinion. You are an adult woman and have the right to make this decision." Sarah could see that her response was upsetting.

"I understand," Flora said, staring at her feet, feeling shamed, "But, still, I must discuss it with him."

"Yes, I'm sorry, I understand. I apologize for what must have sounded like criticism. It is perfectly appropriate for you to discuss this with your husband. Please do so and let me know."

Flora nodded her acceptance of the apology, still feeling the sting of Sarah's criticism. "Thank you. I would feel more comfortable if I talked with him. Not having more children will not be an issue for either of us. We can barely take care of the five we have now. And lately, he has had little interest in intimate relations anyway." She would never have said such a thing to a male physician. She was starting to feel more comfortable.

"If I may, can I ask about his health as well? I am worried about him," Flora continued, "since he started drilling with this new machine. He seems forgetful and he is sometimes a little unsteady. Also, he is difficult to understand when he talks. He sort of rambles and slurs his words. I assumed it was just because of the drinking that he does with friends, but it seems to be getting worse. Could he have low blood like I do, for a different reason of course?"

Sarah was both concerned and curious. "I doubt it. Your description might fit other troubles. Would he be willing to consult me?"

"I will ask. Thank you, Doctor, for your help." She took Sarah's offered hand with both of hers and just held it for several seconds, warmth in her eyes. She walked out of the office straight onto the mud of the street. Park Avenue was not yet of sufficient prominence to deserve a boardwalk.

Sarah was pleased with her assessment of Flora. Cancer of the uterus would certainly be possible, but Flora's overall health and young age argued against it. If Flora, and apparently James, agreed, a hysterectomy could mean a complete cure, a restoration of her blood count, and a return of her energy. However, that all depended on her talking with her husband and returning to the office. Sarah was concerned that the conversation would not go well, especially because James was experiencing what sounded like substantial disorientation and a decline in his mental functioning. She had an idea that he might be suffering from lead poisoning, and she was pleased that he might consult her. She supposed that James probably should be consulting Thomas if he had become the mine physician, but that was not her problem. She was prepared to help any patient who consulted her.

The thoughts about James's possible poisoning caused Sarah to wonder how Thomas was doing in his mine job. She had not seen him since their meeting on the boardwalk, and she had not heard a lot about what was happening with medical care at the mine, nor about whether his medical practice was becoming established. Her resentment at his arrival in town had faded, especially as she was becoming more established herself. She felt less threatened and defensive. She was also enjoying the tremendous energy in the town, its sense of optimism and possibilities, and what those possibilities meant for her. Despite her initial discouragement and disappointment, she thought this was turning out to be a very interesting place to practice medicine.

She thought more about their conversation on the boardwalk. She felt that he had been overwhelmed by her report of the appendectomy. He seemed to actually shrink in front of her as her euphoric success flooded over him. *Maybe I was a bit excessive in how I portrayed the operation. But not really. The procedure was difficult under the circumstances, and I performed it well. I didn't really talk about it any differently than I would in any discussion with another physician. But his reaction was so perplexing. I know he is smart, brilliant even, and certainly as skilled surgically. He just seemed overwhelmed by what I said, like he couldn't imagine having performed the surgery himself. I wonder why. And now it matters because I am going to need an assistant for Flora's operation.*

A hysterectomy is a large and complicated operation, and she would need particularly expert help, which reminded her that she needed to introduce herself to Dr. Stout and thank him for the use of his office. She was certainly not going to ask Dr. Stout to assist. She had seen enough of his disgusting office to know that she wanted him nowhere near her patient. She did need to thank him, though, and have at least a passing relationship with him, given there were only three physicians in town. In any case, Dr. Stout aside, Thomas's surgical skill would be perfect. It pleased her for reasons she could not bring to consciousness that they now had a reason to work together as fellow physicians, and not in just a small way. She was hoping he would agree.

The next day, Sarah walked down toward the bottom of Main Street to Dr. Stout's office. She knocked on the office door and walked in to be met with a wave of memories from operating on Mr. Miller. The recall of the operation was exhilarating, the memories of the office disgusting. She saw the same stained floors and table, the same crusty white coat on the rack. She heard heavy steps coming down the stairs from the living quarters above, and Dr. Stout's bulk filled the stairway.

"Dr. Stout, I am Dr. Sarah Fletcher. I have been severely neglectful in introducing myself as well as thanking you for the use of your office a couple weeks ago."

"Welcome to town," Dr. Stout said, as he offered his hand. "Horace Stout, please call me Horace. It's a pleasure to meet. I was, of course, aware of your arrival, but I knew you had much to get settled before we might meet. I understand you have come from New York after medical school in Michigan."

"That is correct. I was at the New York Infirmary for Women and Children for some years. I left and came here based on an offer from Mr. Gibson to serve as the mine physician. As you no doubt know, that did not work out as planned, but my practice is thriving."

"Yes," Stout said, "I had heard from Mr. Gibson about your interaction. He and I have conversed regularly over the years. He has asked more than once if I could serve as his mine physician, but I declined. He seemed somewhat shocked by your arrival in his office, not quite what he was expecting. I, of course, have no concerns at all about a woman pursuing a career in medicine, as long as she is competent."

Well, Sarah though, *I am at least as competent as he is, based on the disgusting state of his office.* "I believe my patients to this point have been quite satisfied," she said, barely able to conceal her resentment of his condescension. "Mr. Miller has been quite laudatory about my skills with his appendix. He requested that I operate on him that night I arrived in town, but I had no office or facility. He prevailed on the town marshal to open your office for my use. The operation went very smoothly. I trust I cleaned and left your office in a satisfactory condition."

"Yes, indeed, quite satisfactory. I was impressed with your confidence in taking on this operation without assistance when I heard the story from the marshal."

"Well, Mr. Miller's son, Sammy, helped a bit, close to fainting but not quite!" Sarah said with a smile.

"Well, congratulations. Mr. Miller was fortunate that you were willing and able to attend to him. I look forward to working together. As you know, I have a somewhat different background, starting as an army surgeon in the war. This is a fine town and I have enjoyed practicing here. I hope the same for you and wish you the best."

"Thank you so much, sir. I look forward to a collegial relationship."

As Sarah left the office, she thought Dr. Stout was about as pompous as he was obese, and his name was perfect. He was collegial enough, but not more. A polite working relationship would be more than enough.

Chapter 10

Park City, 1897

"Doctor," Gibson nodded nearly imperceptibly, barely looking up from his heavy desk at Thomas as he entered Gibson's office. They met from time to time, more often than either of them wished.

"Mr. Gibson," Thomas replied, with only a slightly more cordial acknowledgement.

"Any problems in my mine?" Gibson asked.

"Nothing new, but I have the same concerns about the lung disease as I have previously described."

"And I have the same reassurance that I provided previously," Gibson said. "We will continue to replace manual drilling with the new mechanical drills as quickly as we can. Am I clear about that?" He didn't wait for an answer. "Now tell me about other troubles."

"I have cared for several miners with minor injuries from falls, and two with more serious injuries from small cave-ins. The most serious injury occurred in a miner who fell several feet in an open side shaft. Fortunately, it was not one of the main shafts, or he most certainly would be dead. There were no barriers to prevent his fall. You really need to restrict access to those shafts with appropriate fences."

"Yes, yes, of course. Feel free to speak to the foreman about that. I am very sorry to hear about the falls and other injuries. Please pass my condolences on to the injured men, but mining is a dangerous business as you know. Excellent report. You are doing fine work," Gibson said with hearty and entirely insincere goodwill.

"I am pleased you find the work adequate, but I am going to pursue further my concern about the lung disease."

Gibson had already stopped listening and waved Thomas toward the office door.

Thomas's practice was booming, and every time he saw a new patient, he felt guilty. He felt particularly guilty when he saw a patient from the Ontario mine, as he replayed in his mind the boardwalk conversation with Sarah. He knew she was right. Gibson was not at all interested in the miners' health and welfare. He just wanted to look like he was.

Gibson tried to say all the right things, however painful it was for him to say, and for Thomas to hear, such egregious insincerity. Thomas could tell Gibson didn't mean a single word of it. He had hired Thomas for show, to demonstrate to the miners that the Ontario and its owners really cared about their welfare. Thomas was tired of being used in this way. He was tired of being a fraud, yet he also thought he was doing some good in his own small way. Perhaps he could do more, but how to keep doing good while not being used? He didn't know.

Sometimes miners died just because—bad luck, wrong place, wrong time—but sometimes they died because of Gibson's policies. Gibson was confident there was a supply of replacements, but it would not always be so. He made clear to Thomas that his job was to make the miners happy. Thomas and Gibson actually agreed, in a strange sort of way, about the goal of keeping miners happy, but their definitions of "happy" were radically different. Gibson just wanted it to seem like the mine physician was doing something. Thomas wanted to *actually* do something.

Later that day, the shift foreman sent a messenger to Thomas's office to come for an emergency.

"Doc, the foreman asks that you come to the mine as quickly as you can," the messenger said. "A miner smashed his hand."

"I'll be right along with you," Thomas said. "Just need my bag." He had a very impressive set of instruments bought by Gibson, in an equally impressive black leather bag. It stood tall with several compartments that folded out holding medications, a bottle of ether, suture materials, bandages, and a small bone saw if needed for emergency amputations.

Thomas and the messenger walked into the outer room of the Administration Building, just outside the door to Gibson's office, where the injured miner had been brought by the foreman. The miner lay quietly on a bench, his right hand wrapped in a greasy rag, blood soaking through.

"What's your name, son?" Thomas asked.

"Charlie," he said.

"Tell me what happened, Charlie."

"My partner was thinking more about drilling the prostitute he saw last night than about drilling the rock face. Stupid Cousin Jack anyway. Not my usual partner. My hand is smashed, don't know how I will ever work again."

"Let me take a look," Thomas said. He unwrapped the bloody bandage. The initial look was not encouraging, fingers mangled and the entire hand covered in blood. "Let me clean this up and see what we have," Thomas said. He saw two crooked fingers broken in two places, a nail ripped off, a partial thickness of skin on the back of the hand peeled off, and two large and deep lacerations over the tendons. "I think we can fix this up right here," Thomas said, "Save you a trip down the hill." He got a bowl of warm water to wash up from the basin Gibson used, and he cleaned the hand vigorously with soap, with attention to the tissue around the tendons where infection would be particularly dangerous.

"Well, that looks a lot better," Charlie said.

"I think we might be able to put this back together in pretty good shape," Thomas said. He washed his own hands in the bowl and laid out his suture material and equipment on a clean cloth. "Bite down on this," Thomas told Charlie as he gave him a clean rag. "This is going to sting a bit."

Charlie declined the rag. He said he didn't need it. Thomas placed several sutures in the big lacerations and pulled the skin together. Charlie barely grimaced and didn't flinch. His hands were so scarred he didn't feel the needle. "Bite down again," Thomas said. "You will definitely need it this time." He grabbed the ends of the two fingers with the fractures, pulled hard and quick, and the bones fell into alignment. Charlie yelped. Scarred hands or not, broken bones hurt. Thomas taped the fingers together and then to their neighbors to provide support, and applied splints and a bulky dressing over the entire hand.

As he finished up, Gibson opened his office door and came storming out. "Sorry, didn't know you were all out here." He nodded to Thomas, barely looking at Charlie, and didn't offer even the slightest word of condolence as he left the building.

Charlie watched him go with disgust. "That's about what I would expect," Charlie said. "He doesn't care a thing about us." The foreman nodded in agreement.

"I think this will heal up just fine," Thomas said. "Come and see me in a week. We'll take the stitches out and see when you can start work."

"Thanks, Doc," Charlie said. "Never thought I would be able to work again. But I'm getting a new partner now."

"Thanks from me too, Doc," the foreman said. "We appreciate the good things you are doing."

The good news of Thomas's care travelled fast, and the flow of patients increased.

One day, a miner showed up in his office, sent by the same shift foreman. The miner was gaunt and sweaty. His clothes hung on his malnourished frame. His sodden shirt had a smear of blood on the front.

"What happened this morning? Why did the foreman send you over?" Thomas asked.

"Been coughing at work, harder and harder and then couldn't stop. I got all sweaty and couldn't breathe. Then I spit up a huge clot of blood. Wiped my mouth with my shirt, and that's what the foreman saw. Told me to come and see you."

"Tell me how you are feeling overall," Thomas said.

"Just miserable, Doc, so tired I can barely stand. Fever, can't sleep. Just a mess."

"Have you lost weight?" Thomas asked.

"Yep, a lot, maybe twenty pounds. Can't seem to eat enough to keep it up. It's like something is just chewing me up inside."

"Do you have the sweats at night as well?" Thomas asked.

"Yes, sir, bad sweats, wakes me out of a sleep. Just tired, tired all over. Can't think."

The man looked pale. He was wasted, his ribs showing through his shirt, sunken cavities above his collarbones. "How can you work a double-jack team? You look exhausted!" Thomas asked.

"Don't know, doc, just try to do the best I can. Have to feed my family."

"Are they ill as well?"

"No, sir, they're fine. Why do you ask?"

Thomas replied, "I am worried you have tuberculosis. We believe that the disease comes from transmission of a germ in the air or by touching some of the pus. It would be possible for your family to become ill as well."

The miner's face startled at the word "tuberculosis," and he heard nothing after that. He knew it was a death sentence. He had seen several friends die of tuberculosis, years of misery before an agonizing death, wasting away to nothing, often drowning in their own pus and blood. Thomas knew what the miner was thinking. He couldn't help the truth.

"Let me have a listen to your lungs," Thomas said. He brought his stethoscope to the miner's chest, a new model with rubber tubing that split into two earpieces. Thomas heard what he feared. The normal breathing sounds were absent, only the faintest sounds of air passing in and out. Louder than those breath sounds were wet crackles on both sides of the chest, especially toward the top of the lungs, like waxed butcher paper being crumpled.

As he listened to the wet lungs, he suddenly saw the face of his brother, Steven, and heard his deathly breathing, different from this miner's lungs, both fatal. The flashes of his family's faces had continued to plague him. He had hoped they would recede when he left Michigan. If anything, they were worse. But he had to focus on the bad news he was about to deliver.

Thomas palpated up and down the patient's spine and found one spot in the middle of the patient's back that caused him to wince from pain. It took a lot of pain to make a miner wince.

"I'm sorry, I know this is bad news, but I am afraid I am right about the diagnosis. You almost certainly have tuberculosis. It has infected your lungs, but it has also spread to your spine. It is not good news, as you know. Because it can be passed from one person to another, you should isolate yourself from your family, preferably in another building. You would be best off going down to Salt Lake City to the tuberculosis hospital there, where you can rest and hopefully recover."

"Is there any cure?" the miner asked. He already knew the answer.

"No, I am afraid not, but with rest, good food, and sunshine, the disease sometimes burns out and stabilizes, and you can live with it. But if you continue to work in the mine, in those wet, cold, clammy conditions, it will kill you. I am so sorry. I wish I could do more."

"Isn't there anything you can do, Doc?" the miner asked. "If I can't work, what happens to my wife and small boy? What can I do?"

"I'm sorry," Thomas sighed. "I really don't know." He felt helpless because he was.

The miner barely mumbled a thanks and dragged himself slowly out of the office.

The following week, the *Park Record* reported that a miner, his wife and their young boy were discovered shot to death in their meager one-room shack up the canyon above the Ontario. The city marshal reported on his investigation. He concluded that the miner was known to have sent a letter back to his family in Ireland telling them he loved them, then shot his wife and young boy before shooting himself.

Thomas recognized the name immediately and just stared in shock at the story in the *Park Float,* the newspaper's weekly column of gossip and news. He was devastated, and he felt responsible. It was his sharing of the tuberculosis diagnosis that had killed the family. Maybe he should not have told the miner. But then what would have happened? The miner would have wasted away, eventually quitting the mine and dying in his bed, leaving his wife to fend for herself and their child.

I wish there had been another way to deliver the bad news or help the miner, he thought. *The physicians caring for my family wouldn't even come to the house, wouldn't explain what was happening, just said it was in God's hands. I suppose everything is in God's hands in some way, but that doesn't mean I shouldn't be able to be more consoling even if there is no treatment. I vow I am going to learn to be better than the physicians who cared for my family!*

His practice ranged from the trivial to the catastrophic—a stream of patients with back pain, skin rashes, and headaches, interspersed with shocking tragedies. One day, a drilling team blasted through a rock face to be met by a flood of cold water blowing through the hole in an icy rush. The two miners were swept back up the drift, got caught in the rising water, were trapped under the tunnel ceiling, got their last breath as their faces hit the roof of the tunnel, and drowned. After the water found its way to a drain tunnel and the miners' bodies were recovered, Thomas's only job was to pronounce them dead.

On another day, he was called to the mine to attend to a miner who had fallen to his death. The miner had finished his shift, looking forward to a hearty dinner in his boarding-house and then a night at the saloon catering to his Swedish brethren. Maybe a trip to the row of red-light houses on Heber Avenue. His mind wandered as the cage ascended from the underground station. As it neared the top, the miner leaned out over the waist-high fence that surrounded the cage platform to look up at the shaft opening, anxious to get to the top and be first out of the cage. His rubber slicker got caught on a spike that was protruding from a shaft timber, and the miner was pulled out of the cage as it continued up. He fell nearly the full twelve hundred feet and splattered on the floor of the station, although not all in one piece. In the nine seconds it took to fall to the bottom, his body bounced from wall to wall, first ripping off one leg and then his head. His body parts all hit bottom at about the same time, blood dripping after in a small shower. The miner's leg had nearly hit a man who was standing near the cage platform. The parts were scattered across the floor of the underground station when Thomas arrived, coming down on the same cage that the miner had been taking up. The miners gathered around and helped Thomas collect the parts in a box so they could be taken up for a proper burial.

Then he was called to the mine to attend to miners who died in an explosion.

Shortly after the day's shift started and the miners arrived at the cage to descend to the underground station, Jack Edwards, young and newly hired, started loading sticks of dynamite to take down to his rock face.

"Don't bother with that," the foreman said. "Dynamite's already down there."

"Isn't it supposed to be kept up top?" Jack said. "Dynamite's supposed to be kept in a special steel locker, safer that way. That's the way we used to do it in Virginia City."

"Takes too much time to come and get it," the foreman said. "Better to just keep it close to the drilling."

Jack shrugged and headed down. He wasn't sure he liked the policies in this new mine.

An hour later, the workers heard a distant rumble, then felt the concussion of an explosion deep in the mountain as the blast wave travelled through the tunnel system. There had been no warning as there would be if miners were blowing a rock face. Several miners in the underground station were hit with a blast of smoke, dust, and toxic gases. When the smoke and gas had cleared, they found only shreds of Jack and his partner, bits of muscle and tissue stuck on the walls and hanging from the timbers, and part of someone's head on the floor.

They couldn't say whose it was. Thomas was called, but there was nothing for him to do.

"What happened?" Thomas asked the foreman.

"Don't know," the foreman said. "The miners went to their drilling face and a little later we heard the explosion. Maybe they dropped a candle in their dynamite."

"What was the dynamite doing there in the first place?" Thomas asked. "It's supposed to be kept in a secure locker on the surface until it is brought down and placed in the drilling holes."

"Not my call," the foreman said. "Take it up with Mr. Gibson. He makes the decisions."

"Maybe I will," Thomas said.

Several miners overheard the conversation and started whispering among themselves. The explosion was one more example of how there was danger at every turn in a mine, but the Ontario was worse than most. It was common knowledge among the miners that Mr. Gibson was only interested in the monthly productivity reports that he delivered to the mine owners. The miners had nowhere else to turn if they wanted a job, but this new mine physician was someone who might listen, someone who was asking questions about their safety. Maybe they should tell him about the really big issue, the strange lung disease that was killing miners. No one knew why it happened, but they all knew it was real and dangerous. The manager and owners wouldn't talk about it. Maybe this new doctor would.

Miners started coming to his office to ask about their lungs. First one or two, then several showed up at his office, all with the same pattern of symptoms: a hacking cough and shortness of breath. One miner reported that he was fine until the mine brought in the new mechanical drills. The dust that the drill threw up was choking, and he went home every night coughing. Now he was short of breath all the time.

"What did the shift foreman say?" Thomas asked one miner.

"He said maybe I had tuberculosis," the miner replied. "I hope he's wrong."

"Do you have fevers or sweats at night?" Thomas asked.

"No, just coughing, but a lot of coughing, real dry and scratchy. Wakes up everyone in the boarding house. They may kick me out."

"Have you lost weight?"

"Not really, maybe a little," the miner replied.

"I think the foreman is wrong. Doesn't sound like tuberculosis to me. May I examine you?"

Thomas heard little in the miner's chest, not only no wet, crackling lungs like the patient with tuberculosis, but not much air moving at all. What he did notice was that the man's lips were blue. He had read about this finding in medical school, it was reported to be a sign of not enough oxygen in the blood. The patient was a bit underweight, but not like the malnourishment of the miner with tuberculosis, not the same look of wasting and cachexia. The picture was entirely different.

"Do you know other miners with this condition?" Thomas asked.

"Oh, yes, a lot of my mates," the miner said. He was from Australia. "It seemed to start in all of us at the same time, when the new drills were brought in. The only ones I know are miners who work at the rock face. Don't know any lift operators or foremen who have it."

Thomas said, "I don't know what is causing this, but it is different from tuberculosis. I don't think it is contagious, but you have to take good care of yourself, as best you can. Can you tell your friends who are having trouble to come see me?"

"I can do that," the miner said. "But what can you do to help me? The cough is terrible, I can't sleep, and I am so tired I can barely work."

"I will prepare a potion for you. It might help. It contains ipecac root, spirits of nitre, and paregoric. Takes some time to brew up. I will give you a small dose of laudanum as well. It will suppress the cough at night and help with sleep," Thomas said. "In the meantime, I am going to dig deeper into this and try to find out what the disease is all about."

As the lingering sunny fall gave way to winter and heavy snow started to fall almost daily, Thomas began a detailed and methodical investigation of the miner's lung disease, identifying more than a dozen miners with what appeared to be the same problem. He described the symptoms reported by the miner in detailed notes, listed what were essentially the same physical findings for every member of the group, and prepared a detailed assessment. The disease appeared to occur only in miners who worked mechanical drills. He could identify no patients with the same disease who worked the many jobs on the surface—the lift operators, the foremen, the stamp mill workmen, or those who worked in the machine shop.

He asked all of his miner patients who came in for other problems about their breathing.

"I used to be a driller," one lift operator told Thomas, "But I started to see that my friends working at the rock face were beginning to get sick. Then a couple of those friends died. I asked to be removed from drilling and took a job on the surface running the lift. It pays fifty cents less a day, but it was better than getting sick. Rather be old and poor than young and dead."

Thomas noticed that he wasn't coughing. "I think you were smart," he said. "I am concerned that there is something about the mechanical drills causing the breathing troubles you have seen."

The investigation captured Thomas's curiosity as a scientist, and he felt a passion to pursue an investigation that he had not felt before. He was feeling the fire that he had seen in Sarah's eyes in medical school. Her dedication to her laboratory work with Professor Sewall had always intimidated him but now served as a role model. The feeling was new and exciting. The scientist in him started to suggest several hypotheses about the nature of the lung disease and its cause. The excitement of the scientific chase led to confidence in his work and the rightness of pursuing it, and the confidence led to more energy, a self-generating cycle of passion and purpose that he had not felt before. It was intoxicating. It was also dangerous.

He was ready to address the issue with Mr. Gibson and approached Gibson's office on a dark day of blowing snow, hoping that he could frame this conversation according to what Gibson had told him he was hired to do, helping to make the mine and miners safer. His surge of confidence waned as he approached the door to Gibson's office.

"Mr. Gibson, may I have a word with you?" Thomas asked.

"If you must," Gibson grumbled.

"I would like to bring to your attention some work I have been doing on the lung disease that seems to plague several of your miners."

"I already told you. I think there is no such disease related to the mine or to mining. They either have tuberculosis or pneumonia. Most of them are just stirring up trouble and trying to get the miners to strike or bring in a worker's union."

"I think there is more to it than that," Thomas replied. "I have conducted a detailed study of more than a dozen of your miners." He kept emphasizing that these were "Gibson's miners," as if that would somehow make him feel more responsible. Gibson was only half-listening, looking down at the heavy, bound ledger on his desk. Thomas pushed ahead. "They all seem to have the same disease. It is not tuberculosis or pneumonia. They are severely short of breath, and most or all will eventually have trouble continuing their work. They show signs of having too little oxygen in their blood. Perhaps most significantly, all of them are drillers using your new mechanical drill."

"I care little about whether they can continue to work. That is their choice. There are many men who would be happy to replace them. As I told you before, I have no concerns about this problem. I think it has nothing to do with the work and nothing to do with the mine. Therefore, as the mine's physician, it has nothing to do with you."

"It has everything to do with me," Thomas said, his tone rising. "This is what I was trained to do as a physician, and especially now as your mine physician. These men are severely ill, they are quitting because they can't work, they can't care for themselves, and they can't care for their families. They are dying!"

"Not my concern, nor yours," Gibson said casually with a dismissive wave of his hand.

"Are you telling me to not pursue this matter further?" Thomas asked, knowing that was exactly what Gibson was saying. He just wanted Gibson to say it, which he did.

"That is exactly what I am telling you. The mine owners, town leaders, and, most of all, I do not want to hear more about this. That will be all."

Thomas was sweaty, his heart was racing. He was breathing quickly and deeply as he left the office, a mixture of shame and anger. Gibson's denials had frustrated him, but he also felt encouraged. He replayed the conversation with Gibson in his head, and he knew now even more strongly that he was right, right about his investigation, right about conducting it and right about its likely conclusion. He had never before felt inspired by his work or passionate about medicine like this. He liked the feeling.

He thought back to how tedious and uninspiring his work had been in Michigan when he returned to his hometown to practice medicine. The only reason he had returned to Mendon was so he could visit his family's graves and comfort his father. He had felt guilty leaving his father to go to college, and hoped his return would absolve that guilt. He knew at the time it was probably foolish to expect all this, and it was not long in practice before his foolishness was clear. He took good care of his patients but had never really felt committed to the town. The town reminded him every day of the tragedies of growing up there, sapping whatever drips of confidence he could muster. He had seen his father every week, watching him shrink and fade with the passing of every season. Robert's life had become so small that his death was almost invisible. And nothing Thomas did could ever change after that.

He marveled that his confidence in himself had found new roots fifteen hundred miles away from his hometown, alone, knowing no one. He was pleased to find that he had knowledge and skills that were previously unknown to him, that he could bring his passion and dedication to bear on something serious, something important. He understood now, more clearly and strongly than ever before, what Sarah felt about fulfilling her mission to serve her patients, first at the New York infirmary, and now with her Park City practice. He knew investigating this lung disease was important, important to the miners, important to the mine, and, perhaps most particularly, important to his sense of himself as a dedicated physician. If only the nightmares would stop.

William Bennett was feared by everyone in Park City, feared often by his children, sometimes by his wife, and always by the drunken and rowdy miners he threw in jail, which was exactly what the townspeople had hired him to do as the town marshal. He was a miner before he took the job of town marshal, big, rough and strong, with an unruly black beard to match. He had been famous for fishing the local streams with an unusual technique, throwing a lit stick of dynamite into the stream and collecting the fish that floated to the surface after the explosion. One day, the stick of dynamite he used was old and the nitroglycerin unstable. It exploded prematurely as it left his right hand, and the explosion took his hand and part of his arm with it, just below the elbow. The townspeople felt sorry, not so much for him but for his wife. She was widely liked by the other wives in town, as well as pitied for her burden of being married to Bennett. He was installed as the town marshal so his poor wife and four children could survive.

There was always a fight to break up, a drunk to put to bed, a prostitute to arrest and fine. Much of his work revolved around the prostitution business in the row of brothels lining the road to Frog Valley. The town felt it prudent to not shut them down entirely. Town leaders viewed the brothels as a harmless diversion for the miners, as a way to blow off the agitation of a day in the mines, an outlet for the pent-up tensions that might otherwise lead to bar fights and violence. The town leaders shared a mutual delusion that it was only the lower classes of Parkites who frequented the brothels, that the town leaders were not themselves part of the steady clientele. The truth was far different, and the town leaders secretly knew it. It was in everyone's best interest that the prostitution business be kept clean and scandal-free.

The miners were too poor to afford the services of the prostitutes, especially the attractive ones. The regular clients of the brothels, especially clients of the higher-class establishment run by Rachel Beulah Urban, known to all as Mother Urban, were the town leaders themselves. That was why the brothels thrived and were not shut down. Park City was, after all, becoming a fine family town, at least for some, and that fine family town required a source of revenue for all of the new cultural and recreational amenities that had sprung up. The brothels provided the second largest source of income to the town in the form of taxes and fines. The smooth continuation of both of those benefits needed a town marshal to police the prostitutes and miners while ignoring the prostitutes' wealthier clientele. For the price of a fake arm, the town got one.

Thomas was replaying in his mind his meeting with Gibson and pondering how to proceed when he became aware of a light tapping on the frame of his office door, a strange tapping, not like someone knocking, more of a wood-on-wood sound. He looked up to see Marshal Bennett standing in the doorway, his fake arm thumping in a hollow rhythm.

"Dr. Wilson, might I have a word?" the marshal asked.

"Of course, marshal. What can I do for you?"

"I understand you had a chat with Mr. Gibson at the Ontario today," he said.

"Indeed, I did. News travels fast. What matter is it of yours?" Thomas asked in a mildly accusatory tone. He had a sense that his newfound passion and dedication were about to be tested.

"Everything in this town is my matter, doctor," said the marshal in his most shallowly polite way. "Mr. Gibson is concerned that you may be stirring up the miners unnecessarily, about things that can't help them, but might hurt the mine. Anything that hurts the mine hurts the town."

"I would think you would be interested in helping to solve a problem that could be causing great trouble for many miners, some of whom are likely your former workmates. These are the men who make this town run, who make the mine owners and Gibson wealthy, and who give you a good job. And you used to be one!"

"All of that may be true, but Mr. Gibson tells me you are wrong, and that you are causing trouble. That's all I need to know. It would be in your best interest to not pursue this matter further. And besides, the miners here are simply a necessary evil. They come and go and contribute little to the town. There is a steady supply of bodies to replace them when they leave. I assure you that the good people of this town, the real Parkites, very much want you to drop this issue."

He moved a step closer to Thomas. He could feel the threat radiating from the marshal's body, like heat from a roaring wood stove. The grimace on his face was not a smile.

"Thank you for your advice, Marshal." Thomas said. "I will take it under consideration."

"Do more than that, if you know what's good for you." He turned abruptly and walked out, his wooden arm banging on the door frame on the way out.

Thomas was shaken, but the marshal's visit made it even more clear that he had uncovered something important. He was now certain about his commitment to do the right thing for the miners. He needed an ally. But who?

CHAPTER 11

Park City, 1897

John McFarlane ran one of the two livery stables in town, but he was also the unofficial town veterinarian. He had no formal training, but he just understood animals, especially horses. He liked horses, more than he liked people. He thought horses were smarter and more trustworthy than most people he knew. He also knew that the townspeople of Park City made fun of him as a "horse doctor," but he didn't care. Apparently, Dr. Fletcher didn't either. He had heard about her. Everyone had. She was the first woman doctor any of them had ever seen. "Doc" McFarlane didn't know quite what to make of her request to see him. She didn't say why, and he couldn't really think of any reason other than she just wanted to rent a horse. So why all the mystery?

The mystery was about to be solved. Here she was, standing in the doorway of his dusty stable, surrounded by a pungent mix of odors from steamy manure, urine and liniment. Main Street was often graced with steaming piles of horse manure in the winter. McFarlane's stable was far cleaner than the street, but the smell was still strong. She didn't seem to mind. He was surprised, pleasantly so, at her attire, particularly the wool pants and high lace-up boots that added another two inches to her commanding height. The western attire favored her. She was not at all what he had expected, but then he wasn't sure what he expected for a lady doctor.

"You are John McFarlane, Doctor McFarlane, as I have been told?" Sarah asked.

"John, yes, but not Doctor, ma'am. That's just something the townspeople call me for fun," he said somewhat sheepishly.

"I am Dr. Sarah Fletcher," and she offered her hand. "I know we have not had the pleasure of meeting, although most people would consider that a blessing with a new physician. I wonder if I might have a moment of your time to seek your guidance?"

"Certainly, ma'am, er, Doctor," Mr. McFarlane said, pulling himself up to his full five feet and six inches of height and brushing his shock of sandy hair into place, trying to look as respectable and professional as he could. She was intimidating beyond her height with her piercing eyes and high cheekbones. "But what might I have to offer you in the way of guidance? Are you in need of a horse?" he asked.

"Yes, but not in the way you imagine. The livery out in the meadows has been quite helpful in providing transportation when I must venture away from town to visit patients in their home. But I have asked around and understand you have some medical skills with animals that might prove helpful for some interesting research I wish to conduct."

"I am happy to assist," McFarlane said uncertainly, baffled as to what he might be asked to do. "But I am unclear what skills I might possibly have that you yourself would not have as a real physician." He was amused by being called "Doctor," but he was, in fact, proud of his skills with animals. McFarlane was intrigued by Dr. Fletcher, impressed with her demeanor, serious but with a gentle and professional style that was compelling. She seemed to be suggesting that they might collaborate in some way, something scientific perhaps. He was a curious man, and her reference to research interested him.

"I would like to learn how to draw blood from a horse," she said.

It was easily the strangest request John had ever heard. He now had no idea where this conversation was heading, but wherever it was going was now making him nervous.

Sarah continued, "I want to develop a new approach to fighting the disease of diphtheria that currently claims the lives of so many children, as well as not a few adults. This involves exciting new discoveries from scientists in Germany, as well as work by my professors in Michigan. The approach requires a horse, into which I make injections and then from which I later draw blood."

McFarlane's brain couldn't process this strange request. The more he thought about what she was saying, the more bizarre it sounded. This could be even greater quackery than he was used to hearing from the many supposed healers and dispensers of miracle cures that regularly passed through town. He thought maybe he'd been unduly intrigued by her as a woman physician, causing him to assume that her request would be somewhere in the realm of reasonableness, but injecting horses and drawing their blood was way beyond anything he considered reasonable. "I'm sorry, ma'am, er, Doctor," still catching his mistake, but now not even sure she deserved that honor anymore. "I couldn't imagine letting you do that to one of my horses."

"I expected you would say that. I hope you will let me explain. I want to develop here in Park City a technique that has been developed by scientists in Germany, as well as in Michigan where I studied. A professor in Germany developed an approach to treating diphtheria by growing a substance, mysterious to be sure, an antitoxin we might call it, that would fight the effects of the germ that causes the disease. He did this by injecting horses with the diphtheria bacteria, a type of germ grown from the phlegm of patients sick with diphtheria. The horses only become mildly ill, for whatever reason, and they develop a resistance to the disease that is carried in their blood. This antitoxin is carried in their serum, the clear part of the blood that can be separated, which is then injected into patients. In many cases, although not all, this reverses the downhill course of the disease, and the patient will recover from a disease that might otherwise kill them.

"I will also note," she continued, "that my professor in medical school with whom I studied, and in whose laboratory I worked, developed the same technique, possibly even before the German professor. He used pigeons to which he gave small doses of snake venom to protect them from being poisoned if they were bitten, to the same effect." She added this extra bit of information mostly to impress McFarlane with her training and background. She could tell by the look on his face that she was not making much progress in convincing him of the legitimacy of her plan. She couldn't blame him. She thought it sounded crazy at times, but she was a scientist and she trusted the data and the scientific methods that produced the results. She hoped she could convince him the same way. However, she had learned at even this early stage in her career that Elizabeth Blackwell's admonition was accurate. She needed to work harder and be better than any man, and impress people with her credentials, just to be given a chance to be taken seriously.

She sensed McFarlane was a man of logic and had a scientist's heart. She needed to impress him with her scientific background and bring him around to trusting her. "The German professor, a Dr. von Behring, and a partner in Japan, Dr. Kitasato, purified the small germ, grew it in the laboratory, and used the growth to make a solution that they injected into horses. They tried guinea pigs, sheep, and goats first, but the amount of blood produced was too small. So, they tried it in horses to prove that it was safe, because horses had a much larger blood volume for harvesting the antitoxin. Two weeks after the injection, they drew blood from the horse and injected the serum into children. The first such successful treatment of a child with diphtheria was conducted just three years ago. The treatment must be administered as early as possible in the course of the disease, otherwise the physician may be required to cut a hole in the windpipe and insert a tube to help the child breathe. I would like to develop this new technique in Park City and hopefully avoid such traumatic emergency care."

That last comment did it. McFarlane was being slowly won over by Sarah's clear command of the scientific details, but mentioning the possibility of having to cut a hole in a child's windpipe was far more persuasive. He was impressed with her dedication to caring for her patients, but her somewhat off-handed comment about cutting a hole in a child's neck just about caused him to faint. Just thinking about such a gruesome act sealed his decision. "Uh, well, yes, that would certainly be a good thing to avoid, wouldn't it? This new approach sounds much better than that! What about the horses, how sick do they get?" He was past the point of deciding whether to collaborate with the doctor and had moved on to the details.

"Not much at all, a mild fever for a day or two. I would feel obliged to buy a horse, so the risk is mine not yours, although I guess to be fair the risk is actually the horse's. What I was hoping is that you could care for the horse and teach me about horse anatomy, how to inject them, and how to draw blood from them," Sarah said. "I will have to modify the technique used by Dr. von Behring that I described, because I do not have a proper laboratory or equipment to grow the bacterium and harvest the antitoxin for injection, but the basic approach is the same for injecting the horse."

McFarlane thought for a bit about Sarah's sincerity and impressive demeanor, and the way she had explained this radical treatment with both scientific precision and personal warmth. Her manner was both commanding and compassionate. He had heard some whispering among the women about town that her medical care was excellent, although sometimes the women didn't seem to want to talk openly about consulting her. He guessed this had something to do with keeping it secret from their husbands. He was honored that she had come to him as a sort of colleague. It didn't bother him that she was a woman. In fact, that made this all the more interesting. She was winning him over.

"I am willing to do as you suggest," he said, "although, I trust you understand that the whole idea does sound a bit unusual, to say the least."

"I am so pleased," Sarah said. "I will look for opportunities to collect samples of phlegm and pus as children become ill, which will sadly happen soon I suspect. We will need to develop an experimental plan for varying the dose and volume of the injection so the horse becomes just sick enough, not too little, not too much. We will also have to vary the strength and volume of the injection for the child until we find the right combination. I have not been able to find much information about the side effects of such an injection in children, which I will have to explain to parents to gain their permission. We have a lot of work to do!"

McFarlane liked the sound of "we"!

There was no lack of children who were sick with diphtheria. Sarah saw such a child the very next day, the six-year-old daughter of a mother she had seen recently. Despite being mostly ignored by town leaders and businessmen, Sarah was developing a presence in town. She was not at all invisible to the wives of those town leaders, nor to other women in town. Her practice grew by first seeing the mother in a family, often for a problem ignored or minimized by other doctors, just as had been the case with Flora's complaints of weakness and fatigue.

This sick child's mother had recently consulted Sarah with questions about why she had not become pregnant again after the birth of this child. Sarah had listened carefully to the woman's story, more sympathetically than the woman had experienced from other physicians. She made some general suggestions about diet and activity, as well as timing her sexual relations with her husband at a more fruitful time of the month. The woman had become pregnant quickly and was so appreciative that she sent all of her friends to Sarah. Now the woman was seeking care for her daughter.

"Tell me what is happening with your daughter," Sarah asked.

"Doctor, I am very worried she has diphtheria. She started with a fever, hot to the touch, and then a scratchy throat and a little cough, now three days ago. I waited a bit to consult you because she did not seem to be getting sicker. She was still able to take water and soup, and I could not see any swelling or obstruction of her throat. I hope I did not wait too long," she said with some guilt.

"Let me examine her, but it does not feel like this is a rapidly-progressive case. A serious case usually progresses quite quickly." Sarah examined the child carefully. "Her skin is a bit warm, but she does not have a high fever. She is well-hydrated and her lungs sound fairly clear. There is a very small amount of gray pus in her throat. Would you allow me to extract a small bit of it for my laboratory?" It sounded so much more impressive to Sarah when she phrased it that way, as if she actually had a laboratory. She made the child gag with a tongue depressor and snatched a small bit of pus, placing it in a glass dish to be saved for processing later. "I think this appears to be a mild case for now," she said reassuringly. The mother breathed a huge sigh of relief. "Keep doing as you are, water, a sip of soup, and rest. I will come to the house tomorrow to check on her, unless I hear from you before that."

"Thank you so much," the mother said. "I am so glad you came to town!"

Sarah smiled with appreciation.

After they left, Sarah macerated the lump of pus in a small amount of salt solution made from boiled water and let the membrane dissolve. She added more salt solution to make a larger quantity, mixed it as thoroughly as she could to make a clear solution, and drew it up in a glass syringe. She walked out the front door of her house, across Park Avenue to Fourth Street and over to Main Street to McFarlane's stable. It was time for him to teach her how to inject her now newly bought horse.

"The best place to find a vein in a horse is along the angle of the neck, behind the large jaw muscle," McFarlane explained. "Just trace the vein down the neck about six or eight inches behind the muscle to feel the swelling of the vein, and then push into the skin at that point to block the vein so it fills with blood. Here, give me your hand." He took her hand, ran it down the angle of the jaw, and then pushed her hand in hard. He noticed the strength in her long, supple fingers. He had never felt a hand so soft and so powerful at the same time.

"Oh, look, just as you described," she said with delight. She was rewarded with a large swelling running up the lower margin of the neck. She shaved a patch of hair surrounding the spot, washed the area vigorously with soap and water, dried it, and then occluded the vein again. She easily inserted the needle and injected the solution quickly.

"Well, that's the first part of the procedure," she said, "but now we have to wait for two weeks before drawing the horse's blood. I really have no idea if we will get any response, but the only way we will know is to inject the horse's serum into a sick child. The response might be too vigorous or dangerous in some way. What we need at the moment is for this lovely horse to get just a little sick, not too much, not too little, just the right amount. Based on how sick the horse gets, we can decide whether to use the horse's serum or adjust the amount of the next injection and go from there."

There was that word "we" again, and McFarlane smiled.

Sarah stopped at the home of the little girl the next day and found what she expected. The girl was no worse, maybe a little better, and she appeared to be on her way to recovery. It had occurred to Sarah more than once to wonder why some children did not die from the dreaded disease. Perhaps some children developed resistance to the disease like horses did, maybe from a prior infection. Somehow, some children could fight it off. She would have to think about that.

Sarah thanked the child and her mother for contributing to science and to the treatment of the next child sick with diphtheria.

They had no idea what she meant.

Sarah could barely control her excitement during the two weeks she had to wait before assessing the potential value of the horse's serum, but she did have a medical practice to run. Most importantly, she needed to follow up with Flora, so she stopped by Flora's home the next day.

"Thank you so much for coming to my home to see me," Flora said. "I am not feeling better, worse if anything, weaker, and I have fainted twice. I did finally discuss your recommendation with James, my husband. I was worried about doing so. He himself seems to be getting worse, more erratic in his behavior, sometimes angry, sometimes sullen. Mostly he is just moody and irritable and doesn't seem to know where he is. I have no idea how he can even work. I worry every morning when he leaves for the mine. It is so dangerous down there. I was worried about even talking to him about my problems." She paused, eyes downcast, solemn. "It did not go well at first."

"What happened?" Sarah asked, alarmed. "Perhaps I should have been with you. Did he harm you?"

"Oh no, not that, but he was very angry. He wouldn't even discuss the surgery. Then, when I said it had come from a lady doctor, he became even angrier and more belligerent. He couldn't imagine that a woman could be a doctor, and he certainly was not going to let a woman operate on me. I dropped the issue and decided I just had to live with it. I did not know what else I could do."

"Perhaps I should talk with him directly," Sarah said. She was even more sure of her suspicions of lead poisoning as the husband's diagnosis because of her description of his erratic behavior.

"I thought of that," Flora said, "but then something happened at the mine. He wouldn't say what exactly, but it had to do with other miners getting sick, and some sort of confrontation between the mine manager and the mine doctor. There was a lot of talk among the miners about how dangerous the Ontario had become, and how many miners were getting sick. I think he started to wonder if he was getting sick because of something at the mine. So, then he started to pay more attention to me getting sicker and weaker. He shocked me by then saying he was open to discussing the surgery."

"That's very good news," Sarah said, but she was mostly paying attention to this report of what she knew to be a confrontation between Gibson and Thomas. "It sounds like we need to be worried more about his health as well. Will he come to the office with you so we could meet?"

"Yes, he said he would. Could we come tomorrow?" she asked.

"Absolutely, I will see both of you then."

Flora and James appeared at the door of Sarah's office the next day, in the early evening, after James's shift. Flora walked in with familiarity and comfort. James was tentative, halting, as if he was entering some strange and dangerous place. Flora wore a plain dress and sweater, a blue, flowered pattern, and her pale skin contrasted sharply with the deep blue color of her dress. James had come straight from his shift. He had changed out of his mining clothes, but his shaggy hair and mustache were still full of dust and his face was grimy.

"Dr. Fletcher, I am pleased to introduce my husband, James," Flora said, proud to take the lead in the conversation.

"Ma'am, er, Doctor, er," James said, and tipped his hat, shy and sheepish, clearly uncomfortable talking to her. "I'm not sure what to make of a hen medic, um, sorry ma'am, er, Doctor, just a phrase. But my wife likes you and trusts you. She has not been herself for some time and she says you have an idea for how to fix that. I am concerned about her health and appreciate what you are doing for her." He paused, clearly wanting to say something else. "But, um, I also have questions about myself. I have not been myself either. I have learned that some of my friends at work have had some sort of mysterious ailment, and I wonder if I have the same trouble. So, I have some questions about my own health if you would permit." He talked quickly, wanting to get out what he had been thinking before he lost his nerve.

"Of course, James," Sarah said. "I would be happy to consult on your care. But let's start with how Flora is doing." She turned toward her. "Please tell me how you are feeling."

"Even worse than when you saw me yesterday. I fainted again this morning, and I am just so tired."

"Are you still in agreement about the surgery?"

"I, uh, we would like to proceed with the surgery," Flora replied. "James and I talked after you came by yesterday, and he understands now how sick I am. James and I discussed the plans we have for our family, and we agree that not having more children would be acceptable. Personally, I think it would be a blessing, at least for me. I am exhausted, even beyond my low blood."

"Very well," Sarah replied. "We will proceed. Let me explain a bit about the procedure. The operation to remove the uterus has been done for hundreds of years, but often unsuccessfully and with tragic outcomes. More recently, new ideas about how to prevent infection in patients undergoing surgical procedures have led to new techniques of cleanliness. The operation has become much safer, although not without risk. We will, of course, be using an anesthetic, a medicine to make you fall asleep so you will not have discomfort during the operation. There will be several weeks of recovery following the procedure, and you will need help at home."

"That can be arranged," James said, his eyes darting around, looking everywhere and anywhere but at Sarah, like he couldn't really believe he was talking to a lady doctor. "There is a neighbor girl who can help. The operation sounds risky, but it is clearer to me now how sick my wife is."

"Thank you, sir," Sarah said. "That sounds good. Now, let's talk about you for a bit. Please tell me what you are experiencing."

"I started in the mines fifteen years ago, happy for the job, better wages than most jobs and never had a problem. Hard work, but I am strong, and I got stronger. I was good with a drill and sledge. In fact, I once won the double-jack contest that is held every year in the city park. Have you watched that? It can be very exciting. I sunk a hole fifty inches deep in fifteen minutes two years ago. Set a record!"

"I'm sorry, sir, I really have no way of knowing how impressive that is, but I trust your assessment! I look forward to watching the contest next year as I settle in," she said, sincerely. She had come to love her new home and practice. She had no idea what this contest and his performance were all about or whether it was impressive or not, but she could see that James was proud of his skill. "I hope you will be competing in good health! Please go on."

"About six months ago, I started using a mechanical drill. It was faster and more powerful than hand drilling, even for me. It drilled holes faster so we could blow more rock faces, crush more ore, and make more money, for someone anyway, not for me. What it did for me was create huge clouds of rock dust. The mine said they would get a water line in to wet the rock and keep the dust down. Never did. A couple months after we started using that drill, my wife says I changed. I was jumpy, irritable, like I couldn't focus. Sometimes, I get real mad for no reason." He hesitated and looked worried about what he had just said. "I didn't hit her, just so you know." He turned to Flora to get her confirmation, and she nodded and touched his arm again. "I would never hurt her, but I'm sure I scared her. What I noticed was mostly pain everywhere, headaches, joints, everything seemed to hurt. Then my memory started going. I couldn't remember a thing, as I think Flora told you." He paused. "I forgot the name of one of our children last week for a few minutes," he said, shuffling around, embarrassed. His voice trailed off, "My stomach hurts real bad sometimes."

"I am sorry to hear of so much difficulty, and I would be happy to help. But why are you consulting me? The mine has a physician, Dr. Wilson, as you know," Sarah replied. She was interested in taking on this medical challenge, but she knew the right thing to do was remind James of Thomas's role.

"I was going to ask him, seemed like maybe he would be able to help. But then there seemed to be a big blow-up with him and Mr. Gibson. A bunch of miners, including my partner, had seen the doctor for some type of lung problem. He was trying to sort it out, and he seemed to have some ideas that he took to Mr. Gibson. The doctor was told it wasn't the mine's problem and to drop it. Friend of mine overheard the conversation in the Administration Building. Gibson was real mad. My friend couldn't tell how the doctor handled it. He didn't say one way or another what he would do, but he's still the mine physician, and nothing has happened. Looks to me like the doc didn't have the guts to stand up to Gibson; although, I can't blame him. No one else will stand up to him either. Miners aren't so sure now if they should trust Dr. Wilson, but all the talk got me to thinking about how badly I have been feeling."

He paused for a moment, trying to decide how comfortable he was with everything he had said. That was more talking than he usually did, and to a woman at that! But he knew something was wrong, and he hoped someone would do something about it, even a lady doctor.

"I am sorry to hear about your uncertainty with Dr. Wilson," she said, not sure what to make of James's report. "I know Dr. Wilson well. In fact, he trained with me at the

University of Michigan and is quite experienced. But I do not know what is happening with his position at the mine." She hoped he was still pursuing the matter. Sounded like maybe not, she thought. And then she wondered why she even cared.

"In any case, I am happy to be of assistance. May I examine you?" Sarah continued. Her exam was detailed and thoroughly embarrassing for James. She touched him all over, asked about tingling, pricked him with a pin on his arms and legs, tested his reflexes, looked in his eyes. She was so close he could smell her perfume. The doctors he had seen in the past hadn't smelled that good.

"Could you please pull up your shirt and pull down your pants?" she asked.

"Well, maybe the first, not a chance for the second," he said with the faintest of smiles. He was warming to her and her gentle but persistent approach.

She examined his abdomen and said, "Nothing very specific here, which eliminates a lot of possibilities, just a general soreness. I have some ideas for the source of your troubles, but I would like to read a bit further in my textbooks from medical school. It is possible this could be related to the dust from your drilling. There may be appropriate treatment available, but there is also the issue of how your illness is the responsibility of the mine. What will you do with the information if I confirm my suspicions?"

"I don't know," he replied. "You let me know what you think, and I will think about what to do next."

"Very well, please return in a week, and we can discuss my thoughts." Then Sarah turned her attention back to Flora. "In the meantime, ma'am, I would like to schedule the surgery when you are ready. I will need an assistant for an operation of this complexity. Your mention," she turned toward James, "of Dr. Wilson is quite a coincidence, because I would like to ask him to assist, if that would be acceptable. There really aren't too many other choices, but fortunately, Dr. Wilson is very well-trained," she said. She hoped that James or Flora didn't ask about Dr. Stout. She had heard enough about his drinking and rough ways to know she wasn't going to ask him, as if his disgusting office wasn't already enough reason.

"Hmm," James said. "If you must. I suppose he is fine, but I don't trust anything having to do with the mine."

"I believe he would be very helpful in this situation, if you will permit me," Sarah said. "It will not involve his mine responsibilities, and I will be quite clear about his role as my assistant for the surgery. He is indeed an excellent physician with outstanding surgical training." She wondered why she had felt the need to keep extolling his skills and training, although it was certainly true enough.

Flora and James looked at each other and nodded. "We are comfortable with your recommendation," Flora said. "Let's do the surgery next week, and you can talk with James then as well."

"That sounds like a good plan. Let's make it Tuesday. I will see you then," Sarah said, and escorted them to the door. "Good day."

As they walked out the door, Sarah was already thinking about explanations for James's symptoms. She was fairly certain he was suffering from acute lead poisoning, possibly from the heavy lead content in the rock being drilled and the dust being produced by the mechanical drill. She recalled a lecture about this very disease from Professor Sewall who had an interest in toxic poisoning like this. James's symptoms seemed to fit exactly the picture the professor had described, but she would need to confirm her suspicions with some further reading. That was the fun part of what she needed to do next.

What was not going to be fun was having to talk with Thomas about James, as she rocked back in her chair and looked up at the ceiling thoughtfully. *I need to think carefully about how to approach this with Thomas. He is not going to be pleased about James consulting me, but even more importantly, I really need him to assist me in Flora's operation. I have performed enough hysterectomies to be comfortable operating on her in general, but doing so in an office in a remote mountain town is an entirely different matter. I really need to be very careful and thoughtful about this procedure, and I really need Thomas as an assistant. A mistake could be fatal for Flora.*

She would visit Thomas's office the next day.

CHAPTER 12

Park City, 1897

Sarah knocked gently on Thomas's office door, closed against a cold winter wind, opened it and walked through. He was sitting at the desk in his consultation room. "Dr. Wilson, might I have a word?" she asked, formal, proper. She did not feel like they were yet on a first-name basis. She was as uncertain about how her visit and discussion would be received as her knock was tentative. She assumed that he was not feeling particularly warm towards her about the mine physician issue, but she hoped he would agree to assist her in the hysterectomy. Even if she had more choices, which she did not, she would have asked him. Despite how damaged he seemed to be personally, she knew him to be well-trained and smart, better than he probably knew himself.

"Please, come in out of the wind. So good to see you," Thomas said, surprised to see her. *Hmm, I wonder why she is even here. What could she possibly want after our last conversation? I wasn't sure I would be seeing her anytime soon after that meeting on the boardwalk, but I am happy she's here, especially so I can tell her about my exploration of the lung disease issue. I hope she is pleased I am pursuing it. But then why do I care so much about what she thinks?*

Despite Sarah's anxiety about the visit, she couldn't help but look around his well-appointed office with envy. She noticed the substantial furniture, a new and modern operating table, and a cabinet full of what looked like new instruments, not to mention the now elaborately carved and permanent wooden sign she had walked under as she entered. *Gibson has set him up well in practice,* she thought. *Wish I had an office that was as comfortable and prosperous-looking. Being employed as a mine physician has its advantages.*

"How might I help you?" he asked, also formal and proper, more so than he really intended. *I will just forget the confrontation on the boardwalk,* he thought. *I am just happy she is here.*

"Two matters, sir," she said, also more business-like than she really intended. "The first has to do with a need I have for assistance at a surgical procedure. I have a patient with severe anemia from uterine blood loss. She bleeds almost daily and has done so since her last child. She has what I hope are simply large, benign muscle tumors in a very enlarged uterus, although cancer is, of course, always possible. Her red blood cell count is very low, perhaps less than a half of the normal level. My hemocytometer and microscope are likely not of the quality yours appear to be," she said, unable to completely control her resentment as she motioned toward the new equipment and microscope in the cabinet, "but it is clear she is profoundly anemic. I have discussed my recommendation with her that she undergo a hysterectomy, and she has agreed to proceed. I have performed this operation several times in the women's infirmary in New York, but not without assistance and not alone in a remote office. It is not clear that I can remove the uterus through the vagina, because of its size. An abdominal procedure would, of course, entail much greater risk. Hence, my request."

There, she had gotten it out, but this was the easy part of the conversation.

Thomas was immediately touched and honored by the invitation, even though her reluctance in asking something of him was obvious. Her sarcasm about the appearance of his office stung; now he felt even more guilty about how he had been intimidated by Gibson and ordered to cease his investigations into the lung disease. He had convinced himself he had a plan that justified continuing as the mine physician, but the plan was rudimentary at best. His conviction was shaken by every little event, perhaps most by Sarah's obvious disdain for his decision. "I would be pleased to assist," he said, one doctor to another, professional, business-like. "I have observed this procedure and performed it once with assistance. I am honored you asked and happy to accept." There, he had said the right thing. He was pleased to be asked and excited to be part of this complicated surgery.

"Very well," she said. "I have arranged to have her come to the office Tuesday next. Will that be suitable for you?"

"Yes, of course." He paused, waiting for more, but she hesitated as well.

"Em," she said, and stopped. They looked at each other in several awkward seconds of silence.

He broke the silence finally. "You said something about a second matter?"

Sarah caught a small breath and composed herself before she spoke. "Thank you for being willing to assist. The other matter has to do with this woman's husband. He has consulted me about symptoms he has been having, now for over six months, starting shortly after the Ontario mine installed a new mechanical drill."

She could see that the moment she said the word "mine," Thomas heard little that came after. She knew that he would be angry that one of *his* miners had consulted her. Nonetheless, she pushed ahead. "I know nothing about mining, but I know you do," a purposefully ingratiating ploy that she hoped would mollify him. Mostly it just annoyed him because her attempt was so transparent. His face darkened, but he said nothing.

"He reports," Sarah continued, "that the drill creates a large cloud of rock dust, and he blames the dust for his troubles. He is forgetful, has headaches and abdominal pain, and sleeps poorly. His wife says he is moody and irritable. My suspicion is that he is suffering from lead poisoning. I wonder if you know anything about these matters in the mine?"

She was trying so hard to act like this was a normal collegial conversation among fellow physicians. Maybe it would have been a routine chat in another time and place, but this was his mine and his responsibility as the mine's only physician. She had little hope that her strategy had much chance of success. She knew that he would resent her contact with this patient, perhaps rightfully so. She was particularly sorry to see what she took to be his initial hostile reaction. She interpreted his reaction to mean that he was not wavering in his commitment to serve as the Ontario physician. She feared that her report about the miner was just going to make him dig into defending his role that much more. She was right.

Thomas's pleasure at being asked to assist at surgery was short-lived. "Why was he consulting you at all?" His tone was sharp, the look on his face more so, eyes narrowed, mouth tight. His anger spread between them like a dark fog and swirled around the room. As much as he knew Sarah was right about the ethical dilemma in serving as Gibson's mine physician, he felt compelled to defend his authority. "He knows I am responsible for medical matters in my position as mine physician, and he should be consulting me. I know of no such consultation about this matter."

Thomas knew he should be less touchy, less territorial, more professional, just one physician to another discussing an interesting diagnostic challenge. *I should be more generous,* he thought. *But I just can't. And it's not about her. The miner is free to see any doctor he chooses. She is just doing what any good doctor would do. I wish the miner had consulted me, but I should just let it go.*

"I knew you would be concerned," she replied, trying her best to be sympathetic and conciliatory. "The first thing I asked him was why he had not consulted you. He said there were concerns by the miners about a conflict you may have had with Mr. Gibson. He wondered whether you were in the best position to help him."

"Of course, I am in such a position." He couldn't help himself. Her mention of the conflict with Gibson just stirred up his defensiveness all over again. He was also embarrassed that she knew about Gibson attempting to shut down his investigation. "It is my job to be concerned about the welfare of the miners. That is my responsibility. I have, in fact, had conflicts with Mr. Gibson about this, but that is not the business of the miners, nor is it of yours," he added, more harshly than he intended. He tried to soften his accusation. "I, of course, wish he had consulted me, but I am pleased he is seeking help."

His anger had peaked with his sharp words, and now he could feel it draining away. He felt like he had to say those things, but now he was sorry he succumbed to the temptation. He didn't even necessarily mean them. He was just sad to hear that the miners were not sure of his commitment to their welfare. They were not altogether wrong. He was committed, but he could do little about it in the face of Gibson's resistance, so now he felt guilty about both continuing in his role as mine physician and failing in that same role. He realized he was incapable of holding his initial resentment that the miner had consulted Sarah. He held her in high regard, and the scientific issue she was raising about the miner was, in fact, very interesting. The fact that she shared it with him, knowing that it could cause a conflict, was actually a compliment, of sorts. It would be a shame to let his little tantrum get in the way.

"But, putting that aside for the moment," he said, trying very hard to restore a professional calm to his comments and put the conversation on a more collegial footing, "I share your concern about the safety of the new drilling method, but for different reasons. I have observed the mechanical drill in action and there is indeed a large cloud of rock dust produced. The silver veins being pursued by the mine foremen seem to run with lead ore as well. It is apparently as valuable as the silver itself, sometimes even more so. I think we should assume that there is considerable lead in that dust, which could have an adverse health effect. However, I actually have a different concern about the dust that I had thought I might share with you."

I think I just found the ally I needed, he thought. *Perhaps there is more of a partnership possible here than I realized. Sharing clinical dilemmas with another physician, especially with someone as smart as Sarah, could be very rewarding. She was a fellow scientist after all—curious, brilliant, and dedicated. A very attractive combination.*

Sarah saw Thomas's anger cooling, and she was relieved. She very much wanted to discuss this matter with him as a colleague, not as a competitor. "Please, tell me more about those concerns."

"I have now seen more than a dozen men with a breathing and lung issue, something different than that of your patient."

Hmm, she thought. *He referred to "my" patient. The miner is, indeed, for the moment at least, my patient, and maybe that is fine where it is for now. I like where this conversation is going. I never thought much about him in medical school, or what he thought of me, but this could be interesting.*

"These miners all have a similar pattern of shortness of breath and cough," he said, "but also something unusual, cyanosis. Their lungs sound dry, not wet as in tuberculosis or pneumonia. They all drill at the rock face as opposed to working jobs on the surface, such as lift operator, and all use mechanical drills as opposed to hand drilling. I think the distinguishing feature in this group is their exposure to the rock dust generated by the drill, which is causing some sort of lung damage. I was told that two men with similar troubles died in the prior few months. The disease apparently can be rapidly progressive in some patients."

Sarah's fascination with this report overcame all of her previous tension and uncertainty. This was an important and serious health issue, something not previously reported in the Park City mines, as far as she knew. This was a problem worthy of their skills as scientists, a place they could apply their combined energy and expertise. As had been the case for her entire life, she felt empowered and energized by the challenge and the mystery of science and medicine, by the opportunity to be fully engaged as a curious scientist and physician. And now, she had a colleague who might be equally committed to solving this diagnostic puzzle and finding ways to help these patients. In an odd way, they were now responsible together for solving what appeared to be possibly two dreadful diseases affecting their respective patients.

"I understand you may feel a certain resentment about how the miner consulted me," she said. She wanted to let go of the tension between them, when he seemed to have done so, but she decided it was better to address it head-on so they could be done with it. "It appears we have separately uncovered two potentially serious harms befalling these miners, perhaps two entirely different, but equally threatening, diseases related to their jobs. If you agree, I think we have an obligation to pursue this health issue both scientifically and with Mr. Gibson. Perhaps we can join forces here."

Thomas was pleased that she wanted to bring the conflict to a more formal closure, although he himself would not have done it so directly when the tension seemed to have already faded. "I am fine if we let this issue drop and move on to more important medical and scientific issues. I agree we need to do something here, but I am not sure what. Gibson has already made clear that he does not acknowledge the existence of any lung disease, and pursuing it is not in his best interest. I had heard of some of these concerns from miners when I first arrived, so I raised the topic when I first met Gibson." He felt at least a small need to defend his integrity. "It is clear that he has absolutely no willingness to bear any responsibility for the welfare of miners in general, or especially those employed by him in particular. He was vigorous in his admonition, quite painfully and unpleasantly so, I will add, that I should drop the matter. He hinted, not too subtly, that my job was at stake. He also appears to have enlisted at least one ally in delivering this message. Marshal Bennett visited me very shortly after my meeting with Gibson and, shall I say, strongly reinforced Gibson's message. If the message was not clear previously, it certainly was after his visit."

Hmm," she thought, *Gibson is just another blowhard and bully, like many men I have met, not deserving of serious attention. So why is Thomas reacting like this? And why do I care?*

"This is a far more serious situation than I might have imagined," she admitted, "because of both the severity of the disease and the number of miners afflicted, not to mention the politics of the matter. But we must do something on behalf of our patients. That is our fundamental responsibility, whatever the consequences."

Thomas knew very well what the consequences would be. "But I trust you understand the difficult position I am in here," he said, trying hard to not sound weak and pleading. "I have to be very cautious about how I proceed. I will give it careful thought. Perhaps we can discuss the matter again next week."

"I have no idea why you have to proceed cautiously," Sarah said. She did not intend to be mean, just blunt. She truly could not imagine how there was anything more to say about their responsibility to their patients. There were certainly threats from Gibson and the town marshal, but Thomas's higher responsibilities to the miners seemed so obvious to her. Having Thomas uphold what she believed to be his obvious professional obligation should have required no thought on his part. She understood that challenging Gibson might result in the loss of his job and the fancy office and equipment that came with it. So what? Maybe he felt vulnerable, that his practice would fail without Gibson's support, but that was for another day. All she said was, "We can talk again next week. I look forward to operating together and will see you then."

She had learned something about Thomas. He was intriguing in some ways, certainly smart and well-trained, as she knew when they last left off in medical school. He was investigating a complex and unexplained medical phenomenon in an expert way. However, she found him annoying in other ways: his uncertainty about his ethical obligations and his equivocation in the face of Gibson's threats. She just did not understand why he was struggling with what seemed to her to be easy decisions about caring for the miners. Perhaps this was the first time he was being tested in his values and character as a physician. He did not seem to be prepared to accept the consequences of doing what was so clearly right. She knew she should probably feel some faint sympathy for the difficulty of his position, but she felt far more sympathy for the plight of the patients.

"How is our horse doing?" Sarah asked McFarlane as she walked into the livery stable.

"I am not seeing much change," McFarlane said. He was so pleased by how Sarah was including him as a full partner in this exciting venture. She visited the stable each day, and they conferred regularly about the horse's condition. "Unfortunately, at least for any sick children you may see, the horse seems fine, probably too fine."

"I agree," Sarah said. "It seems likely that the horse will have produced too little, if any, of whatever the mysterious antitoxin was. It will likely not be effective when used in a child, but that is the only true test. For better or worse, I hope we will have opportunities to conduct that test."

That very day, the mother of a sick five-year-old boy asked Sarah to visit them in their home.

She walked up Daly Canyon, nearly to the top before the dirt road gave way to a trail the miners walked each morning up to the Judge-Daly mine, nearly a mile and several hundred feet above. She saw the run-down miner's cabin on the east side of the dirt road, with a creek running behind the cabin. The house had a small porch along the front, the porch roof sagging a bit in the middle where a post had broken. The paint on the walls of the cabin had peeled so badly that it was mostly bare wood. She knocked on the door and was let in by the father who had apparently stayed home from work. She was met by a blast of hot air from the fat-bellied, wood-burning stove. The boy laid close to the stove, bundled in blankets, shivering despite the heat. It was dark and grimy in the cabin.

"Please help, Doctor. Our boy is so sick," the mother and father said simultaneously.

"I am so sorry your boy is ill. May I examine him?" she replied. She unfortunately found what she expected. He was flushed with wheezy breathing, unable to swallow, saliva drooling out of the side of his mouth. He was feverish and laid in a soggy puddle in his sweaty blanket, looking at her with vacant eyes. His throat was lined with gray pus.

"Your boy is indeed very sick. I am afraid he has diphtheria." Sarah said. "It appears to possibly be a serious case. We will start by trying to lower his fever, with cool wraps on his forehead from the stream behind your house. I will leave you with some liniments to relieve the rigors and discomforts, and potions to sooth his throat, the treatments you likely already know about. However, I have another approach I would like to discuss with you."

The parents looked up eagerly. "Please, anything. We are so scared." They left unsaid what all three of them knew: their boy would likely die if nothing could be done.

"I would like your permission to treat your son with a serum, a clear liquid extracted from the blood of a horse." Just saying those words for the first time to these parents made her realize how truly preposterous it all sounded, just as it had to McFarlane when she had told him. The parents just stared at her, stunned, mouths agape.

Sarah paused, allowing their astonishment to settle at this shocking statement, and then described the procedure and what she proposed to do.

The parents reacted as she feared they would. They looked at each other with shock and horror, and then at her with disbelief. "You couldn't possibly be serious," the father said. "What kind of crazy treatment is that? Are you really a doctor?" he said, incredulous, angry, scared. "You don't even look like a doctor!" His wife nodded in agreement, her face twisted in a grimace. Their deep appreciation that Sarah had come to the house had quickly faded.

Just then, the boy gasped, coughed, and stopped breathing for several seconds. The mother screamed and the father shook the boy before Sarah could intervene. As the boy finally took a breath, the father pleaded, "Please, Doctor, isn't there anything else you can do?"

"I'm sorry, nothing more than you already know. I would be happy to tell you more about my research," she said gently. "I understand this is all quite confusing but let me explain." And she did.

The questions came hard and fast. "How could this possibly work?" the mother asked. "Isn't it bad if the horse is sick? Is it safe to inject blood from a horse into a person? How do you know this will work?"

"All good questions," Sarah said, as she answered them, but their questions and resistance started to fade as the boy continued to gasp and wheeze. The more questions they asked, the more Sarah knew they were just postponing their inevitable permission.

Finally, they ran out of questions, looked at the boy, and looked at one another, both exhausted. They simply nodded. "We do not really understand what you are proposing. It is all so strange," the father said, "but our boy is so sick. We really have no choice. We understand what will happen if he gets sicker. Please proceed."

"Thank you," Sarah said. "I cannot guarantee that the serum will help. It may, in fact, cause some adverse event itself. If there is no response, I have one final method of intervention that may be required. It is used infrequently but may become necessary. Let's try this new approach first. I will prepare the materials and return soon."

She nearly ran down Daly Canyon, going first to the stable to draw blood from the horse. "John, can you assist me with drawing blood?" She was quite pleased with herself for how quickly she had learned to find and block the neck vein for either injecting the diphtheria solution or drawing blood.

She withdrew two large syringes full of blood, returned to her office, placed the blood in a manual centrifuge tube and spun the centrifuge over her head to separate the serum from the red blood cells. She drew up a full syringe of serum and walked briskly back up the canyon to the boy's house.

She was pleased at how much fitter she had become in walking uphill in these high mountains; she was breathing barely harder than usual. She couldn't say the same for the poor boy when she arrived. His breathing was so much worse. He was exhausted from the fever and the work of breathing, so he needed little comfort when she injected the serum into a vein in his arm. He barely whimpered.

"I will return in the morning," she told the parents. "The next day will tell whether the antitoxin was sufficient to help. I will bring other equipment in case it does not work." She did not describe exactly what would be required, but when she returned to her office, she organized her surgical kit to perform a tracheostomy.

The next morning did indeed reveal whether the antitoxin had worked. It had not. The boy's breathing was labored and harsh, with long pauses and gasps. He would not live through the morning if she did not act.

"I am sorry to say that the treatment does not seem to have worked," she told the parents. "The strength of the horse's serum was likely too weak, with too little of the special compound that fights the disease. I believe the only recourse is to perform a tracheostomy, to open a hole in his throat and insert a metal tube so he can breathe." She had seen this procedure done twice but had not performed it herself, a piece of information she did not share with the parents.

The parents were even more horrified to hear what Sarah said than John McFarlane had been. Cutting a hole in their son's throat was just unimaginable. "What? Is that the only choice?" the father said. "That is horrible!"

"I'm sorry, it really is the only choice at this point. His airway will soon close completely."

The mother's eyes were wild with fear and exhaustion. "Do what you must," she sobbed. "I can't stand to see him suffer more."

"Thank you. I need to move quickly. Please boil some water so I can sterilize my instruments." She positioned the boy with his head extended over a pillow so his neck was exposed. She washed her hands, his neck, and her instruments all in the same hot, soapy water. It was the anesthetic that most worried her. He needed some, but not much, or he would stop breathing altogether. He was still conscious, but barely, yet the procedure was painful, and she did not want to cause further suffering, to either the boy or his parents. His eyes were closed, and he was barely responding. All of his attention and energy was directed to his next breath. His eyelids barely fluttered as she laid out her instruments on the wobbly kitchen table.

The parents cowered in the corner of the meager shack, barely able to look.

The family was too poor and the shack too far up the canyon to have electricity as others in town did, and the kerosene lamp was too dim. The two small windows were smeared with dust. She could see bits of morning sun streaming through the gaps in the rough wood walls, fortunate given how deep Daly Canyon was. She positioned the boy's neck so it caught a bright shaft of light. She carefully arranged her surgical kit on a clean cloth, laying out a scalpel, spreading forceps to insert into the incision to open a hole into the airway, a probe to explore the airway, and a curved metal tube about four inches long and a little less than a half-inch in diameter, the smallest one she had. It would be a tight fit on a boy this size.

She placed a clean cloth over the boy's mouth and dripped ether very slowly. He responded almost immediately, with a long, snoring breath, and was asleep, breathing slowly and quietly, but not a good quiet, quiet because so little air was moving. His chest barely rose with each weak breath. She could hear the faintest whisper of his breathing. She had only a minute to open his airway before he would die. She used a few seconds of that precious minute to open the boy's mouth and extract a large chunk of the gray membrane lining his throat, as she had done with the sick girl, but this time a much larger, thicker, and more inflamed piece. She placed it in a glass dish and turned her attention to his neck.

She palpated the large cartilage over his airway, much softer than that of an adult and difficult to fully feel with the puffiness of his neck. She felt carefully for the space below the cartilage and just above the next cartilage ring of the trachea. She took the knife and made a careful cut across the trachea in the small space, directly into the airway, making a hole barely more than a half inch long, just the size of the tube.

She was committed now and had to get the tube in quickly. She swiped at the blood around the wound so she could see the hole. The boy was so dehydrated that his blood was thick and barely oozed across the wound. He was sucking air hard through the hole in the trachea, pulling strings of thick blood with it into the lower airways. She ran the probe into the wound and downward in the direction of the boy's lungs. The space was clear minus the blood smears. She placed the spreading forceps into the wound and opened up the space, creating just enough room for the shiny metal tube. The fit was close, but she ran the tube smoothly into the space, better than she expected. She pushed it down the trachea toward where it branched, the air now moving hard and fast into his deprived, fragile body.

She knocked the cloth off his face and ran bandages around his neck to stabilize the tube in place. The tube had a surrounding flange to stabilize it across the throat, and Sarah bandaged it tightly in place. She pulled him into her arms, hugging him tightly with feelings of both relief and victory. She had held patients like this many times in her New York practice, for reasons of both great happiness and great loss. She had been taught, as had her one hundred forty-nine fellow medical students, that it was not professional to share emotion with patients or touch them like this. Physicians were supposed to remain aloof and keep complete emotional distance from their patients. It had always sounded to her like something stupid that men would say. Every time she hugged a patient, she thought about all the hugs that her male colleagues were passing up, a loss for both physician and patient.

The boy tightened his small, pale arms around her as he awakened. He fought a bit and then settled, aware at some subconscious level of the air now flooding his lungs. His sallow color brightened, his cheeks pinked up, and he looked up at Sarah, understanding as only a child can that this unknown woman was his savior. She loved him as the beautiful child he was, and as evidence of the power she had as a physician to be part of the miracle that had just occurred. Sarah and the boy looked at each other adoringly.

The parents were dumbstruck at what they had just witnessed, appalled at the gruesome trauma and joyous at its outcome, their boy breathing easily through the tube, relaxed and pink. They stared at Sarah as if she were a god-like apparition. They could not speak.

"I am pleased he is now breathing so much better," she told the parents, sounding more relaxed than she felt. "I believe he will get through the rest of the illness without difficulty. I will return tomorrow to check on him, and then in a week to remove the tube. Please keep the area very clean and change the bandages around the tube every couple of days. Can you do that?"

They could only nod.

However miraculous the tracheostomy was, Sarah knew that not every child could be saved like this. Diphtheria often affected other organs, especially the heart, in ways that no surgery, however dramatic, could fix. She needed to continue her experiments with the horse. Producing antitoxin was the key to unlocking the secret of saving the lives of these children. She savored this moment with the boy, but her mind was already looking ahead to injecting her horse with the slurry made from this boy's pus, with the hope that the horse serum would work the next time she needed it.

But before that, she needed to read and prepare for the upcoming hysterectomy. This would be the most complicated surgery she had ever performed. She was pleased that Thomas was willing to assist, despite the somewhat awkward conversation that had followed her request. Working with him in a delicate surgery would be a professional pleasure, but there was something else. She wanted to know why he was in Park City, why he had left Michigan, and what he was looking for. She didn't know why she cared.

Chapter 13

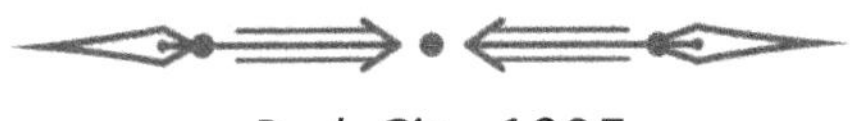

Park City, 1897

Thomas kept turning over in his mind the last conversation with Sarah. He knew she was right. They were absolutely obliged as physicians to carry the issue of lung disease in miners as far as, and in whatever direction, was required. He was just not sure he was as strong as he needed to be to do what he knew was right, or as strong as she wanted him to be. He was also not sure whose expectations were most important. His? Hers? Was he more concerned about what she thought of him, or what he thought of himself?

At first, the job offer from Gibson had seemed too good to be true. He should have known immediately that it was. He wanted to believe that the offer confirmed the rightness of his decision to leave Michigan. The guilt at leaving his family in a whole field of graves was buffered by Gibson's generous offer. The possibility of new opportunities for success in his practice was so seductive, but the excitement of the new position had lasted for what now seemed like mere minutes. He knew it was wrong almost before he had all the details, and it started coming apart almost immediately. If he stood up to Gibson for what was right, right for the miners and right for his responsibilities as a physician, he would certainly lose his employment. However, if he lost his job, he would lose any chance to do the right thing. He tried not to think about the loss of financial security as well.

Perhaps there was another choice. Perhaps he could keep his job and still do the right thing—or maybe keep his job *so* he could the right thing. The idea was rough and needed more work, but he thought there might be something there worth exploring.

He needed to start over with his notes about the miners' illness. He reviewed them carefully, paying close attention to where they worked, the duration and nature of their symptoms, and what he had found upon exam, particularly the notable blue shade of their lips. He visited each miner in the evening after their work shifts and repeated his exam. He did not go out of his way to hide his visits, but he didn't go out of his way to be visible either, slipping up and down the side streets and side canyons to avoid Gibson and Marshal Bennett, hopefully without being obvious about it.

The miners were suspicious, probably rightfully so, Thomas thought.

"How do I know you aren't going to run to Gibson with everything I tell you?" one miner said. "Gibson doesn't care a thing for me. How do I know you do?"

"Fair enough," Thomas said. "All I can say is that my obligation as a physician requires me to care for your illness in the best way I can, no matter the political issues. You are sick, I am a doctor, and you need the help I can give." Thomas might also have said that he needed this opportunity to show that he cared, that he was committed to helping, that he needed to prove his worth to himself. And maybe to Sarah.

"OK, maybe, if you say so," the miner said grudgingly.

"I want you to believe what I said," Thomas said. "I feel very strongly about this obligation, and I will fulfill it to the best of my ability. But I have a question for you. What would you think if I brought together several of the miners with the same problem so I can share my findings?"

"I guess. These guys aren't much for meetings, except in the pubs. You will need to be quick. But why not?"

Thomas arranged for a meeting, including the wives of those who were married. They agreed, albeit reluctantly. Several miners said they were not sure they trusted him, but the wives were worried about their husbands' health and pushed them to attend. The miners could not shake the fear that Gibson controlled their jobs, their families, their livelihood, their very lives. But they agreed to attend, reluctantly, when pushed by their wives.

As they each approached the front of Thomas's office one evening, they looked carefully up and down Main Street before entering. Thomas did not understand why.

They all crowded into the small front room of Thomas's office, the miners toward the front, the wives behind, everyone standing and shuffling as Thomas began.

"I asked to meet with you tonight so I can tell you what I have concluded about the lung disease that all of you are experiencing," Thomas opened. "I thought it would be most helpful to come together as a group to discuss my findings."

Before he could continue, a miner interrupted, "Make it quick, Doc, I don't want to be here too long. We might be seen, and it wouldn't go well with Mr. Gibson. He doesn't care about our lung disease, or about us for that matter. If he knew we were here, we would be fired in a minute."

The other miners nodded and murmured. They all looked scared, and the wives picked up on their fear. The worries about their husbands' health teetered in the balance with their fear about their husbands getting fired, the net result of both outcomes being their inability to feed their children. There would be no other jobs in town if they were fired. Gibson had the ear of the other mine owners, and most of them feared him as much as the miners did.

Thomas could feel his control of the meeting quickly spinning away and tried to recover. "Very well, I will be brief. I believe you are all suffering from some type of new lung disease that we have not seen before. I think it comes from the dust you breathe when you work the mechanical drill. It doesn't seem to occur in men working on the surface or away from the rock face, and it didn't seem to happen before when you used the single- or double-jack manual drilling. I don't know what is in the dust, but I think we need to investigate that. I also think you should stop using the mechanical drill until it has a water stream to suppress the dust." Thomas talked fast to get as much of his thinking out as he could before the miners reacted. He barely made it.

Several miners responded at once, and one won out, "That's all well and good, Doc, but there is no way the Ontario is going to do that. We have already asked for water suppression, and Mr. Gibson made clear that was not going to happen. It's expensive, more expensive than replacing us. But we appreciate what you're doing." He looked around and there were a few nods. "It's just not possible to do what you recommend."

Thomas was about to respond when he heard quiet, but distinct, footsteps on the boardwalk outside his office. The town was strangely still, and the late winter evening breeze had settled. The snow had melted off the boardwalk, and footsteps were easily heard. The dim glow from the streetlamp outside the office door seemed to darken for a moment as a shadow passed the open door. The light from inside the office reflected off a brooding face set on a large body. Thomas could not see the face clearly in the murky shadows, but he was certain it was Marshal Bennett. He could feel the evil and intimidation radiating from the hulking body more than he could see the face. The shadow paused briefly, then moved on with the same soft boot steps on the boardwalk. Thomas shivered. Several miners looked at each other and their wives with fear.

"We got to be going," several miners said simultaneously. They rushed to the door in a small mob, the wives dragged into the crush, each crowding to get out first. As each one passed through the door they looked up and down the street before passing into the night.

Thomas understood why this time.

After the miners left, Thomas sat in his office, in the dark, alone, knowing that something had changed. His investigation had taken a new and threatening direction. What should have been a straightforward, albeit scientifically challenging, medical investigation was now something else, dangerous beyond just the risk of losing his job. Calling the miners together had taken disagreement with Gibson to a level he would now view as insubordination. Thomas shivered again.

Sarah visited the boy recovering from the tracheostomy the next day, and again a few days later, making sure the metal breathing tube was still clear. She cleaned it, rebandaged the wound, and examined his throat. The gray membrane was slowly disintegrating, and with each day, the boy was more comfortable. His fever broke and the pink color that had blossomed across the boy's face as she had placed the tube became permanent. The parents watched Sarah work with continued adoration and wonder. What she had done seemed so dramatic and frightening; they had stood there and watched this woman cut a hole in their son's neck. But no matter, their boy had recovered.

At the end of the week, Sarah brought back her surgical kit and ether. "Could you please corral your young man?" she asked the parents. She was always amazed at how quickly children recovered and how adaptable they were, even with a tube in their throat. The boy paid no attention to the bandage around his neck or to the tube buried in it. He was running around the small shack like he used to do, to the parents' great delight. They placed him lovingly in her arms. "Give me a good cough, son," she asked the boy, which he did, strong and loud, a fine mist of debris spewing from the tube. He would be able to breathe with the tube out.

"Do you want to get rid of this tube?" she asked. He nodded vigorously. She had endeared herself to him with her visits, and he paid attention to everything she said. He couldn't talk with the tube in place, but his meaning was clear.

She unwrapped the bandage around the tube and took one last look at his throat. It was clear. Some air was moving around the tube as he breathed. "Take a big breath," she told him. As he came to the end of a full breath in, she removed the tube in one long quick pull, and clamped a cloth over the hole. The boy bucked, coughed out all the debris in his upper airway, cried once, and took another long deep breath, just as she wanted.

Once again, he settled comfortably in her arms, subdued, frightened, but mostly happy to be breathing without the tube. He had become comfortable settling into a puddle in Sarah's arms each time she visited, and he did so again. He looked up at his parents with his large, brown, and trusting eyes.

She let him breath and settle a bit. "I have to do one more thing," she told the boy. "You need to go asleep for just a short time." She put a cloth over his mouth and nose and dripped a little ether. As soon as he was asleep, she placed three small sutures to close the hole in his neck and bandaged him back up with a tightly folded cloth to make sure the opening was completely covered. He awoke, and she returned him to the loving arms of his parents.

"Here you go, back to you," she told the parents. "Just keep the area around the stitches dry and clean, change the bandage every day or two. He should be fine. I will stop by again in a week to take out the stitches."

Taking out the tracheostomy tube was one more reminder that she hoped never to have to place another one anytime soon. She had to get the proper reaction from her horse so the next dose of serum that she had made from the boy's pus would work, but that was not her most immediate concern. Flora would be coming back the next day for her hysterectomy. Sarah was confident in her skills, but the operation was difficult enough under the best of circumstances. Her office on a side street of a rough mining town did not qualify as even close to the best of circumstances. Operating with Thomas should be interesting, she thought. It would be a very efficient and revealing way to find out just what kind of physician he was.

Flora and James arrived the next morning at the appointed time, and Thomas arrived shortly after. "I believe you may know of Dr. Wilson," Sarah said to James, "But I would like to introduce him to you, Flora. Dr. Wilson is an outstanding physician with several years of experience in Michigan," she said, as she smiled at Thomas.

"Ma'am," Thomas said and nodded to her. She nodded back with a smile. Thomas offered his hand to James who took it briefly. Flora was clearly more comfortable in the office than James was, even though she was the one about to undergo major surgery.

"May I examine you, Flora?" Sarah asked.

"Certainly," Flora said. She went into the back room and undressed, coming back with a clean sheet wrapped around her.

Sarah thought the uterus was perhaps just a touch larger, now certainly too large to be brought through the vagina.

"Let me explain the procedure, just to make sure you are both comfortable with the plan," Sarah said. "You will be asleep, as I discussed, and we will make an incision in your abdomen to remove the uterus, the womb. Dr. Wilson will assist me because of the difficulty with removing such a large uterus. Most hysterectomies in the past were performed due to extreme prolapse, when the womb drops down into your vagina, your private area, and protrudes through the opening of the vagina. It was relatively easy to remove the uterus through the vagina. Unfortunately, your uterus is too large now. We will need to operate through your abdomen," as she motioned across her own abdomen.

They nodded as if they understood. She was certain they did not. It was all so overwhelming. The idea of taking out a whole part of her body was so preposterous to them that they did not even know how to respond. "Do you have any questions?" They looked at each other and shook their heads. Sarah figured they were so overwhelmed they just couldn't think anymore. "Will you be staying in the office?" Sarah asked James.

"Good Lord, no!" he said, then gave Flora an awkward hug and left.

"Please get on the table," Sarah requested of Flora. "You are going to sleep now. Are you ready?"

Flora nodded, confident and frightened all at the same time.

Sarah placed a clean cloth over Flora's mouth and nose and dripped ether until she fell asleep, breathing slowly and deeply, slightly snoring.

"Are we ready?" Sarah asked Thomas.

He nodded, nervous but not frightened. Sarah had already prepared her instruments, washed and laid out on a clean cloth. They washed their hands together at the sink. They both felt the gravity of the moment but did not talk. They were about to perform an operation that was done infrequently and probably never in a setting like this. It was dangerous, difficult, possibly life-threatening, and potentially lifesaving. And they were going to perform it together. They each felt the power of the bond that all physicians feel when they work together to contribute to miracles.

They washed Flora's abdomen thoroughly, and Sarah positioned herself along Flora's right side, easiest for a right-handed surgeon. Thomas was on the left side, where it was much harder for him to assist since he was also right-handed. He had reviewed the procedure and the anatomy in his medical school textbooks the night before. He trusted Sarah and her experience, but he knew experience was sometimes not enough. Luck and a higher power sometimes had their say.

"This is it," said Sarah with excitement and just the right amount of tension to keep her focused.

"I'm ready," Thomas said and nodded again. The anticipation for the surgery they had planned to perform was about to get very real.

Sarah picked up her scalpel and made an incision through the skin and scant fat, starting just below the breastbone, coming down the midline, around the umbilicus to the left side, and continuing to finish just above the pubic bone.

"Not much fat," Sarah observed. "Not enough calories in the family diet to be overweight, not to mention the work of caring for her house and children."

Thomas blotted the blood oozing from small vessels as Sarah carried the incision down to the peritoneum, the shiny translucent membrane lining the abdominal cavity. They could see the uterus underneath. She pulled the peritoneum away from the underlying uterus with a clamp, and carefully cut through it. The uterus pushed up through the incision and nearly filled the opening, as if it was trying to escape.

"Looks like about a four-month uterus," Sarah said, comparing it to the size of a pregnant uterus. "Lots of fibromas," she said, pointing to the whorls of uterine muscle tissue, some small, the size of a thimble, some larger like the bottom of a small cup. "Exactly what I was hoping we would see."

She pointed to the round ligament on each side of the uterus that suspended it in the abdomen and Thomas nodded. She double clamped each one and cut between the clamps. Thomas placed sutures in the tissue around both cut ends of each ligament and tied them off as Sarah removed the clamps. "OK, here we go." Sarah said, "The broad ligaments will be much trickier," nodding toward the wide ligaments on each side of the uterus through which the blood supply passed. "If we are going to have trouble, this will be the time."

The arteries to each side of the uterus were normally large to begin with, the diameter of a pencil. But in this case, the arteries were supplying blood to a massive amount of uterine muscle tissue and the benign tumors. The arteries were correspondingly larger, the thickness of a finger, even a thumb. "If we don't get these clamped and tied off properly, we will be in big trouble." They could pump blood several feet into the air like a small hose, and the massive hemorrhage would kill Flora in a minute or two.

Sarah reached across the abdomen to Thomas's side of the table, double-clamped the broad ligament on Flora's left side, and cut between the clamps. She placed a heavy suture in the tissue beneath each clamp around the large uterine artery and tied each suture as Thomas carefully removed each clamp, tying off the cut ends of the large artery on either side of the cut as the tension was released when the clamp came off. Sarah turned to the broad ligament on her side of the uterus and repeated the process. It was easier to work across the table on the patient's left side, and more awkward securing the artery on her side of the uterus. After double-clamping and cutting between the clamps, she placed a suture in the tissue near the artery as it came in from the larger arteries deeper in the abdomen and pelvis.

"OK, I'm ready to tie it off," she said. "Remove the clamp." As Thomas did so, the suture tore out of the loose tissue, leaving the uterine artery free, spurting a fountain of blood with each heartbeat. Whether Thomas released the clamp too soon, or Sarah tore the suture out of the tissue, could not be said.

"Oh my God," Sarah gasped. Blood pumped vigorously, filling the abdominal cavity, shiny, coating everything. The cut ends of the ligament disappeared into the pool of hot blood. The suddenness of the life-threatening bleeding paralyzed both of them but only for a moment. In that moment the patient lost a pint of blood. The sharp metallic smell of blood filled the room, triggering flashbacks for Thomas to the smell of Emily's blood seeping from her head in the barn. The memory could have paralyzed him. It did just the opposite.

"I've got it," Thomas said softly, decisively, a second faster than Sarah. He used the clamp he had in his hand to grab the tissue around the artery and pull it out of the rapidly filling pool of blood in Flora's abdominal cavity. He grabbed a second clamp off the tray of instruments with his left hand and clamped it securely across the artery. The bleeding stopped. The quick and sure movements of both hands working in synchrony were stunning in their precision and breathtaking for Sarah to behold.

"Oh my God," Sarah said again, but this time for entirely different reasons. "That was impressive! Thank you!" she said in a whisper, as if Flora was awake. Sarah realized at that very moment that Thomas was indeed as outstanding as she had expected, maybe better.

The doctors looked up at each other, relief in their eyes but for very different reasons. Sarah could have felt guilty that she had made a mistake, and then resentment that Thomas had to cover for it, but she felt only gratitude. Sarah was simply thankful that Flora's life had, in fact, been saved. She didn't care that she wasn't the one who did it. Thomas felt the thrill that all surgeons feel with a dramatic life-saving intervention. The rush of adrenalin permanently imprinted his incredible split-second response in his memory. But the adrenalin also called up the flashing images of his dead family, this time his mother, sweaty, gray, incoherent, dying of a uterine infection. He pushed it down quickly.

"Thank you," Sarah said, quietly, with a small sigh of relief. "I don't know why the suture tore out."

"It happens. Not your fault," Thomas simply said. He knew she was feeling badly about what happened, and he sought to minimize it. "The tissue was just a bit loose and stringy there. No problem, we recovered quickly. She lost some blood, but she should do fine now that she will not be bleeding from her uterus anymore."

Sarah appreciated Thomas's reference to how "we" recovered so quickly, but she did not feel she deserved to be included. Now that the crisis was over, she immediately wanted to understand why the suture tore out of the tissue, and how it could be prevented next time. She just wanted to get better and be better prepared if it ever happened again. She had learned something from Thomas about how to respond technically to this near disaster, stabilizing the tissue with one clamp so he could clamp the artery with the other, and to do it calmly and composed under duress. He had acted coolly and decisively, not too slow, not too fast, just the right sense of urgency to solve the crisis effectively. She would remember that for the rest of her career.

"Shall we finish?" Sarah said. She continued on with the procedure, clamping, cutting and suturing the remaining tissues that supported the uterus. At the end, Sarah dissected the peritoneum overlaying the uterus as far down toward the cervix as possible, cut across the uterus without damaging the bladder that lay just above, and closed the loose tissue around the passage that ran down through the cervix into the vagina. They removed the uterus to the table, to dissect and study it later, and prepared to close the abdomen. Before doing so, Sarah washed the abdomen with a solution that she had previously prepared by adding just a few drops of carbolic acid to water, the same technique Thomas and his father had used so many years ago with Evelyn as she lay dying from sepsis. It would work far better this time.

She removed the gauze with the ether from Flora's face and she slowly awakened, moaning with the pain. "Flora, we're done," Sarah said as she leaned over and whispered quietly in Flora's ear. Flora looked around with some confusion, not clear where she was or how she had gotten there. The grogginess and confusion slowly cleared. "Let's help you off the table and over to the couch to rest." Sarah gave her a small dose of laudanum, and she fell back asleep. She would stay overnight in the office so Sarah could check on her.

The doctors washed their hands and moved to the back room of the house.

They looked at each other and both started speaking, Thomas just a moment faster. "I am impressed with your surgical skills and your confidence in taking on such a major surgery like this. This operation is the largest and riskiest I have ever seen, but you managed it well. A vaginal hysterectomy is one thing, but removing a uterus this large through the abdomen is another thing altogether. She is fortunate to have received such good care from you." He seemed to completely ignore his critical part in averting a potential tragedy.

"You are very gracious, thank you. I appreciate so much how you responded to that little crisis we had. Things could have gone much differently," she replied.

"I am happy I could help. Thank you for the opportunity." They each silently reveled in the complicated operation they had just performed. To have done it together magnified the satisfaction.

Thomas savored the pride at his contributions to the operation, but the pleasure quickly faded as he thought back to the meeting with the miners. He expected a summons from Mr. Gibson at any moment. He was not exactly sure what he was dreading about the likely meeting with Gibson, because it was becoming clearer to him what the right thing to do was, and how he could go about accomplishing it. He was even more certain about his plan after working together with Sarah in this dramatic surgery, but the image of the shadowy presence passing by his door the previous night kept pushing into his thoughts. He was sure it was Marshal Bennett and equally sure that the marshal had gone to Gibson to report what he had seen.

Sarah's pleasurable satisfaction lasted longer and flowed in different directions. While she was pleased with the surgery and the outcome, she was more interested in Thomas. His skills were brilliant, and she sensed that Thomas did not fully realize until now just how skilled he was. She replayed the surgery in her mind, making a mental note to pay more attention to where and how she placed the critical ligatures around the uterine artery. She let the self-recrimination slide away as good surgeons do. She had learned what there was to learn about the surgery. Now she was more interested in learning about Thomas.

Thomas walked up Park Avenue and over to his office on Main Street in the late morning after he and Sarah had finished the hysterectomy. He passed a woman on the boardwalk, a woman he had treated in the office in the past.

"Good morning, Doctor," she said and nodded.

"Good morning to you," Thomas said. "It is indeed a good morning!"

She wondered why the doctor had such a big smile on his face. It wasn't that nice a morning!

Thomas was still reviewing the drama of the morning's surgery, proud and happy about how he and Sarah had performed. He had amazed himself as much as he had impressed Sarah with the speed and precision of his response to the potentially catastrophic bleeding episode.

But that's not what he was really thinking about, and not why he was smiling. He was thinking about standing at the sink washing his hands with Sarah after the operation. *What happened at that moment?* he wondered. *The triumph of operating together has taken our relationship in some new direction. But where? I'm more confident and comfortable with her, not like how she intimidated me in medical school. More like her colleague, more worthy of her. But worthy of what? It's very confusing. Was this just the euphoria of the moment, or something more? Personal? Professional? Both? Neither? The only time I don't feel lonely is when I am with her. I wish that happened more often.*

If Thomas had known that Sarah was having the exact same thoughts at that moment, he would have been even more confused.

He had decided to not share with Sarah his evening meeting with the miners, especially the intimidating specter of Marshal Bennett passing the door. He thought it better to spare her for the moment. Mostly, though, he just wanted to spare himself reliving the ominous specter of the marshal's intimidating shadow lurking at the office door. The more he thought about it, the creepier it seemed. His assumption that the marshal went straight to Gibson to report on the meeting was confirmed with the arrival of a messenger as Thomas walked into his office.

"Doc," the young man called out as he walked in the office right behind Thomas. "I'm here from Mr. Gibson's office. He requests a meeting with you at your soonest convenience."

"Did he really ask about my convenience?" Thomas asked, his smile fading.

"Not really, sir. I just made that up."

"As I expected, son. Thank you. Please tell Mr. Gibson I will come straightaway."The tone of the summons was clear, even coming second-hand from the messenger. Gibson was not asking to meet to tell him how pleased he was with his work, but Thomas didn't really care anymore. Something of Sarah's strength and passion seemed to be oozing into his consciousness. Or maybe he was finding his own. The power of operating with Sarah was transformative.

Just as Thomas dismissed the messenger and was about to leave for Gibson's office, a man ran breathlessly into the office. "Doc, come quick. Something terrible has happened down at the train depot. A child fell under the train!"

"Tell Mr. Gibson the meeting will have to wait," Thomas yelled at the messenger as they both ran out the door.

The Union Pacific railroad had pushed a spur from its transcontinental line down through Ogden and Coalville and up Echo Canyon into Park City, giving the mines a new option for shipping their crushed ore out for smelting in Salt Lake City or to San Francisco. The line came out of Echo Canyon, ran southeast through the meadow along the hills to the east and then turned southwest along a small creek that came down through town from high up in Empire Canyon. The route brought the train as close to the bottom of Main Street as possible. The mines still had to bring their stamped ore from the mills down the middle of Main Street on wagons to load on the train, but now the wagons did not have to continue on down Parley's Canyon to Salt Lake City, a long, slow, expensive process. The financial benefit to the mines was tremendous. The danger to Park City children was equally so.

On this day, two ten-year-old boys had been playing on the tracks and around the train that had come in the night before. They were jumping back and forth over the hitches between cars and crawling underneath the cars on the tracks. The engineer was working the gears in the cab, and the train unexpectedly lurched. The wheels of the second car caught one boy on the tracks. His piercing screams were easily heard by the engineer even over the noise of the engine. He frantically reversed gears, afraid of what might have happened.

It was worse than he could have possibly imagined. He jumped off the cab to run back to the boy and vomited when he saw what the train had done, really what he had done. Where once there were the spindly prepubertal left arm and leg of a ten-year old boy, now only jagged stumps of muscle and bone were left, the crushed muscle dripping blood on the dusty ground. The left arm had been severed just below the elbow, and the left leg just above the boy's knee. The boy's screams could be heard throughout the lower part of Main Street as he writhed in pain, drawing a huge crowd. Fortunately for the onlookers, the boy went into shock, lost consciousness, and stopped screaming.

Thomas arrived at the bottom of Main Street breathless from his run. "Men, your belts, now!" he yelled at two men. He tightened a belt around the upper arm and another to the thigh to stop the stumps from bleeding. "Find a wagon and get him to my office!" Two men found a wagon in the railroad shed, and the boy was hauled quickly up Main Street to Thomas's office. The men carried the boy into the office and placed him gently on the table in the front room. His pure face and tousled brown hair gave him a certain angelic sweetness, even with the coal soot and blood smeared across his pale skin. Thomas could not hold the vision of the boy's innocent face and the jagged bloody stumps of his arm and leg in his mind at the same time. Emily's face and crushed skull loomed over all of it.

Thomas worked quickly before the boy regained consciousness, sawing off the jagged spicules of bone, rinsing and cleaning the stumps, ligating the cut ends of the larger blood vessels with sutures, and bandaging each stump tightly. The bandages turned red quickly as blood seeped through the clean white bandages. Thomas could not find and clamp all the small arteries.

As the boy awoke, Thomas used a small amount of ether to put him back to sleep, to spare him the agony and pain of his injuries for another hour. He thought about trying to complete the amputations with proper excisions and closures, as if the amputation had been done purposely, but the boy's condition was too unstable, plus the amputations were not the entire problem. The limbs above the amputation were crushed and the bones broken. Thomas also suspected a crush injury to the boy's pelvis, likely with substantial internal bleeding, none of which he could do much about. The boy was just a limp sack of crushed tissue and broken bones, and he was going to die.

The warmth of Thomas's earlier morning was a distant memory as he looked at the boy's shattered body. He was back in Michigan, watching Emily's blood seeping into the straw on the barn floor, and his mother's cold face slowly turning gray. He could feel the cold stone of the dying fireplace as he sat next to his father. The swirling collage was frightening, but he was not that young, scared boy anymore. He was the physician responsible for this boy's life and for talking to the boy's parents when they arrived. His past life both frightened him and strengthened him.

A crowd had gathered outside the door of the office, watching as people do during tragedies, saddened for the boy and his family, and shamefully happy it was not their son. They watched admiringly as Thomas worked quickly and expertly to stabilize the boy, murmuring and nodding among themselves.

The boy's parents had been summoned, but only the mother could be found. The father was at his shift in the mine and would not get the news for some time. She ran into the office and screamed at the sight of the bloody bandages on the stumps of her son's amputated limbs, fainting and slumping to the floor. As she revived and was helped to a chair, she looked up at Thomas with agony in her eyes, unable to comprehend what was happening.

"Ma'am, please tell me your name," Thomas asked softly, pulling a chair close to her with an arm on her shoulder.

"Caroline," she said, "Caroline Roberts," she said softly. "What happened?"

"Caroline, I am so sorry." Thomas replied. "Your son has suffered a terrible tragedy at the train depot. He has extensive injuries to his arm and leg, as you can see, but I also fear internal injuries as well."

The full impact of what she was seeing broke through her disbelief, and she let out a wail of pain, a shriek, not human.

She collapsed in a massive wave of tears, caught by a woman in the crowd, a friend. As she consoled Caroline, Thomas saw that he could say nothing to help. He returned to monitor the boy. The friend told Caroline what Thomas had done to try to save the boy's life. The crowd offered their positive opinion of Thomas's impressive work as a way to reassure Caroline that everything possible was being done. They talked respectfully amongst themselves as the friend consoled her.

Thomas turned back to Caroline. "Caroline, pull your chair over close here so you can hold your son." Thomas pulled his chair close as well, so both were nestled up next to the boy. His arm wrapped around her shoulders again. "Caroline, I am so very sorry. I have done what I can for the moment, but I will not leave him."

"Will he live?" Caroline asked, sobbing, eyes darting back and forth from her son's bloody bandages to Thomas's face, looking for clues about her boy's fate.

"I cannot say, but I will do everything in my power to help him. What is your husband's name?" Thomas asked gently.

"Fred," she said. "He is at work. I, uh, don't want him to see this. This boy is his whole life."

"And the boy's name?" Thomas asked, holding Caroline even a bit closer.

"Michael," she said. "We call him Mikey. He's the oldest of our four children."

"Let me explain what happened," Thomas said. "He was playing around the trains with a friend, and the trains jumped, rolling over him on the track. The damage to his arm and leg are obvious, but I am also worried about damage to the bones of his pelvis, and possibly elsewhere in his abdomen. The bones of the pelvis can bleed heavily and there is little I can do about it. I have done everything possible for now to stop the bleeding and make him comfortable. All we can do is pray and hope, but I will be honest and say that the situation is very dire."

Thomas always tried to be hopeful, but there really was no hope. To offer too much hope would not be humane.

"I will sit with him until we see what direction this takes. Only time and God know what will happen now." The same God his father had hated every time the name was invoked. The same God that looked away as each of his family members had died. He remembered the physicians at each tragedy as crude and insensitive, blunt to the point of cruelty, using God as an excuse for their impotence, lacking any empathy or warmth. Their professional demeanor was cold and their words hard. He tried to do better, although he was never sure if he was successful. At least he tried. The words seemed to come out the same, but he hoped they were received differently.

"I think it would be best for you to go home for now and be there when your husband arrives. I will be staying with Mikey in the office tonight, and you can come back at any time. I will be keeping him sedated with anesthetic to lessen his misery. I cannot do that for long, but at least a few hours will help him be more comfortable."

Thomas did not need to tell Carline the obvious. Mikey would be comfortable until he died.

Caroline nodded numbly, not really hearing what Thomas had said, but mumbled her thanks for his kindness. "Please save him, Doctor, whatever you have to do. If we lose him, it will kill my husband. Thank you for everything you have done."

Thomas helped Caroline to the door, waved the crowd away, and closed the door quietly. The silence of death settled over the room. He pulled his chair next to the bed and watched Mikey. The boy moaned from time to time, and when he did, Thomas dripped a bit of ether. The bandages continued to soak with blood, and Thomas changed them.

Caroline and Fred returned later that evening, stood at the side of the bed, and stared silently at their son. He was pale and sweaty, now under the sedation and haze of a heavy dose of laudanum that Thomas had dripped into his mouth. He was delirious, not awake but crying out for his mother. Caroline cringed and cried each time he asked for her. She sat near him and hugged him, smearing the bloody bandages on her clothes. Mikey's eyes fluttered, unseeing. Caroline and Fred looked back at him with helpless love. Fred said nothing, pacing the room, trying to find some way that his misery and agitation could be put to good use. "Doc, whatever happens, I know you did your best. Thank you for trying." It was clear to Fred how this would end.

A few hours later, in the faintest glow of early morning light, as Thomas sat next to the bed, nodding off, Mikey died in Caroline's arms. But it wasn't Mikey. It was Stephen, his brother. And it wasn't Caroline. It was his mother. And he wasn't Dr. Wilson. He was Thomas and he was twelve. And he was scared. And then Stephen and his mother were gone, and Thomas was chilled with sweat.

CHAPTER 14

Park City, 1897

Thomas's energy ebbed as he cleaned up his office after the undertaker took Mikey's body away. He shuffled across the room and looked aimlessly around. He had done everything he knew how to do, to no good. He would remember the pain in Caroline's and Fred's eyes forever. Mikey would probably be buried later that week in the city cemetery on the side of the low hill in the meadow, along with so many other Park City children. Thomas would attend and stand quietly in the back, as he did frequently with patients who died. That would bring closure, but no relief, to his parents, and to Thomas. For now, he needed to sleep.

It wasn't just the night with Mikey that weighed on his mind. That was sleep-deprived physical exhaustion, doing what doctors do. More exhausting, for different reasons, was the summons from Gibson the day before. He had tried to ignore it as he nodded fitfully through the night with Mikey, but it laid over him like the layer of hazy smoke that covered the town. He would have to deal with it now.

After a nap, Thomas walked up Main Street, slopping through the snow and mud over to Marsac Avenue and up the hill. His step was slow as he trudged up the hill. He barely noticed the pounding of the Ontario stamp mill. It was just always there, a constant reminder of the power and success of the Ontario mine, as its influence followed the pounding sound, up and down the canyon and throughout every building and activity in town.

The power of the Ontario mine became more explicit and personal as Thomas walked into Gibson's office. Standing off in the corner, shaded a bit even as the rest of the room was filled with the hazy light of a winter sun, was Marshal Bennett. He said nothing. Thomas thought he saw the slightest nod. The light did not warm his cold and black eyes.

"Thank you for meeting," Gibson said, a weak attempt to be courteous and polite. The insincerity was obvious to both Thomas and Gibson. "I wanted to discuss your recent meetings with my miners, about which the marshal here has told me. It appears you did not heed our previous conversation and are continuing to dig into work issues that are better left alone. I thought I had made it clear that your concerns about some mysterious lung disease are simply a medical fantasy and none of your business."

"Good morning to you, Mr. Gibson," Thomas said, responding with the same facade of professional courtesy. "I apologize for my unkempt look," he said. "I was up most of the night with an emergency."

That's all it took for Gibson to drop his façade of courtesy. "Of which I am well aware," Gibson said, his voice rising, "as I am aware of everything that happens in this town. Why you responded to this emergency instead of my request for a meeting I do not understand. You are the mine's physician, *my physician*! There are others to take care of these minor medical matters. Get that woman to do it next time."

Thomas could not help but be in awe of Gibson's malicious arrogance, even as he detested him. "My responsibility is to respond to the medical needs of anyone who requests me. And it was no minor matter! The boy died this morning!"

"Of which I am also aware," Gibson said. "My condolences to the parents." His tone was stunning in its lack of compassion.

"I am sure they will appreciate hearing from you," he said, with a level of sarcasm equal to Gibson's insincerity. "My responsibility for the needs of my patients includes the miners. I have completed my initial assessment of the miners' illnesses and appreciate the opportunity to discuss my findings with you." Thomas smiled to himself at his little lie. "May I describe to you what I have found in our miners?" He asked, purposely framing the miners' welfare as a joint responsibility.

He continued before Gibson had an opportunity to answer. "I believe there is some substance in the dust created by the mechanical drills that is toxic to the miners' lungs. They develop shortness of breath, chest pain, cough, difficulty sleeping, and a peculiar blueness around the lips. It seems to affect only those men who drill at the rock face, not to those who work elsewhere." He speeded up, knowing he had only a few more seconds before Gibson would interrupt. "And as you likely know, at least two of our miners have apparently died of the condition. I would like to explore further what happens with the drilling and obtain samples of the dust for examination."

The longer and faster Thomas talked, the more agitated Gibson became. He slammed his fist on his desk, making Thomas jump. The marshal did not move. Sunlight reflected off the dust as it flew into the air. "No! No to your assessment, no to your conclusions, and no to your proposed next steps! I am aware that two miners have died, likely of tuberculosis or whoring around, or they drank themselves to death, but it has nothing to do with the mine. Your job is to protect the mine and keep it making money, not to stir up trouble where it is not wanted. And I assure you, it is not wanted by me, by Marshal Bennett, or by the mine owners." His plethoric face matched the flaming anger spewing from his mouth. The marshal shifted just enough in the corner to remind Thomas of his presence.

Thomas was shaken by Gibson's violence and by the marshal's hawklike stare, but he was not intimidated. "I believe there may actually be two problems with the dry mechanical drill," he said. "Dr. Fletcher and I have discussed a patient who has consulted her about a different issue. We believe this man may be suffering from lead poisoning, also from when he started his job on the mechanical drill."

"What?" Gibson roared, even more loudly, "why is that woman digging into my mine's business? It is even less her business than yours, and it is none of yours!"

Thomas immediately regretted bringing Sarah into this mess. He had thought, or hoped, that he could address this issue head-on with Gibson. He believed in the power of science and data and had the fantasy that Gibson did as well. He hoped that his rational argument would be persuasive, both in getting permission to continue his investigation and in keeping his job. He should have known better. It was now becoming obvious that this plan had no hope of success.

He felt his commitment draining away in the face of Gibson's anger, but he pushed ahead. "Well, whether it is her business or not, it is certainly mine. I am responsible for the miners' welfare." His words sounded good, even to him, but he was not sure they were matched by sufficient conviction. He wished Sarah was standing with him.

"No, no, and no! You are not responsible for their welfare," Gibson said. "Where you got that notion, I have no idea. Your job is to protect the mine, to protect me, and to protect the financial interests of the owners. You will cease all of this nosiness immediately!"

"And if I do not?" Thomas asked. His resolve was hardening even as family images flashed in front of him, this time of his father humiliating him with criticism of his medical skills. He had shrunk in the face of his father's harsh words, but no more. He had the responsibility and the obligation to do the right thing, however futile it might be, as it had been with Mikey. He understood even better now the source of Sarah's passion and righteousness.

An image of Sarah standing with him in front of Gibson's desk gave him strength, and the strength gave substance to the rudimentary plan that had been lurking in his mind. He was filled with the goodness of his responsibilities and the skills he possessed to address them. He knew what the right thing was to do, and he would do it. He would do what physicians are obligated to do, to conquer death when he could, to console the living when he could not, and to care always. He had the sudden realization that applying to medical school had been, in a strange way, preordained. It gave him the opportunity to add some virtue to a world that often seemed so cruel.

"Oh, there could be many consequences," Gibson said, with a cold grin. "We could start with taking away all that expensive equipment I bought for you. A few well-chosen words to the right people and you would find the flow of patients to your office dwindling quickly. The same might happen to that lady friend of yours, now that I know she is involved in this mess. You both would be driven out of town in a month."

Thomas momentarily smiled to himself when Gibson referred to Sarah as his "lady friend." It bolstered his resolve even further. "I can buy my own equipment, and I think my reputation is already established in this town, certainly with the miners I have evaluated. They are very interested in what I have to say." He knew immediately that he had made yet another strategic error, referring to the miners' support, about which Gibson cared not at all.

"Well," Gibson said, an unmistakable smirk on his thick face. "As far as those miners are concerned, you won't be seeing them again. They have come to understand from Marshal Bennett that engaging with you that night was a mistake. They have expressed their great appreciation for their jobs and are pleased to continue working at my mine under the current conditions."

Thomas did not back down. "I will rebuild my practice with new patients. The town is booming and there will be increasing need for my services, whatever lies you intend to spread about me." Thomas's defiance was rising now, even in the face of Gibson's hostility and threats.

"Assuming you have a place to build that practice," Gibson said. "I have noticed occasional small fires popping up in several businesses lately. Must be due to the owner's carelessness. It's amazing how fast a fire can burn down an entire building, even with the response of our excellent fire brigade in town." A pause, just to let the threat take full hold. "I encourage you to be careful." Again, the thin smile that wasn't a smile.

"Thank you for your concern," Thomas said, not even trying to conceal his sarcasm. He thought of his family one more time before he steeled himself to say the words that he knew would be painful, but right. What he was about to say would give him the opportunity to continue his investigation. He composed himself and said in a flat voice, "I believe it would be best for all concerned to continue in my role as the mine physician. I accept your directives and instructions."

Thomas's words caught Gibson off-guard, and he looked sharply and quizzically at Thomas.

Thomas himself was almost as shocked as Gibson to hear the words said out loud. He was not at all sure about all the details of this new approach, but it started with keeping his job and, therefore, his access to the mine and the miners. He hoped that he was not simply deceiving himself for convenience, that the plan was not just a delusional excuse for avoiding Gibson's anger. Even as he felt more certain about his new plan, his verbal acceptance of Gibson's prohibitions still brought shame. He knew Sarah would be disappointed. She would make quite clear that he had just committed a complete abdication of his ethical responsibilities as a physician.

Gibson recovered from his surprise. "A wise choice," he said, "and somewhat unexpected I might say. And tell that Fletcher woman to mind her own business as well."

"Will that be all?" Thomas asked, now with his own cold smile.

"I believe we have concluded our business satisfactorily," Gibson said. The marshal had not said a word.

Thomas shook with disgust, his heart racing with anger as he left the mine and walked back down the hill. He was already thinking ahead to his next conversation with Sarah. The weather seemed to reflect his vacillating mood, at one moment a bright sunny sky, warm for a mountain winter day even with the hazy smoke. And a moment later, heavy clouds scudding across the sun, the temperature dropping twenty degrees as a dark cold descended. He had so much to discuss with Sarah, much of which he knew would not be well received. He would need to be especially persuasive about his plan, even more so now that he had dragged her into this conflict with Gibson.

❧·❧·❧·❧·❧

While Thomas had been called to the train accident, Sarah was cleaning up her office and relaxing at her desk in the front room, lost in thought about the success of the surgery and Thomas's dramatic contribution to that success.

In her reverie, she was not sure how long the man had been standing in her doorway, silently surveying the office, but she startled when she looked up and saw him. Despite the surprise, she was not scared, more curious because she had not yet been consulted by a Chinese patient since settling in town. She knew where they lived, in the hollow between Main Street and Rossie Hill, but she knew nothing about them. Parkites were scathing in their prejudice, critical of the Chinese, their customs, their clothes, their food, the way they worshipped, critical of them being in Park City at all. The *Park Record* endorsed their prejudice with its scathing and racist editorials and news stories. Everything about them was strange and wrong according to the newspaper. She had cared for patients of all kinds in New York City, and thought of herself as lacking any prejudice, but she knew that it was sometimes hard to know. She would find out now.

"I am Sam Sing," the man said. "You are the lady doctor?" He seemed intrigued and perplexed at the same time, hoping she was a physician, but not sure what to do if she was.

Sarah was immediately fascinated by him. She first noticed the long, braided queue in his hair. She had been told those who wore such a queue were accorded respect as an elder for their mature wisdom. He wore a round silk cap, baggy, blue, cotton pants and shirt, and flat-bottomed wooden sandals. His face was kind, with the anticipatory look of someone who hoped she could help.

"Yes, I am Dr. Fletcher, and I am indeed both a woman and a doctor. Please come in. How can I help you?"

"Can you come and help a woman? She has been hurt. She has no family here."

Sarah waited, expecting more information to be forthcoming, but Sam Sing's face suggested there would be nothing more. "Yes, I can come now," she said. "Let me get my emergency bag."

She followed Sam Sing out the door, east on Fourth Street and across Main Street. Instead of taking the China Bridge as she had done previously to get to Marsac Avenue and Rossie Hill, she followed Mr. Sing down the hill, under the bridge, to the hollow below Main Street. Her office was not more than a hundred yards from Chinatown.

Mr. Sing led her along the hollow, past several wooden shacks with corrugated tin roofs to one painted a bright yellow. Chinatown itself was quite festive, neatly kept, with brightly painted one-room cottages, smoke from charcoal fires coming out of chimneys, and a few light poles with electric lights dangling. She had heard that the Chinese had developed their own electrical system and contracted with the power company separately from the town and mines. She was struck by how tidy and comfortable the entire area felt, in contrast to what she had been told by nearly everyone in town, that the Chinese were a dirty heathen people. The *Park Record* regularly reported on Chinese opium dens, exotic funeral processions, and Chinese men who left their family in poverty to pursue their gambling addiction. All she saw were industrious people taking care of their neighborhood and their families.

"We are here," Mr. Sing pointed to the home, motioning for her to enter.

Sarah entered what she expected to be a dark, smoky room. She instead found modest light from an electric light bulb dangling from the ceiling, a spotless and neat living area, a mat near the fire to sit on when cooking, and a bed in the corner. On the bed a small woman was curled up in a ball, rocking and moaning. She could have been fourteen years old or forty-four. Sarah could see blood on her face and arms, with bloodstains on her white blouse and cotton pants.

"Do you speak English?" Sarah asked. The woman nodded. "And what is your name?"

"Ma Choy."

"Madam Choy, please tell me what happened."

The woman looked at Mr. Sing with a questioning eye. No white person had ever called her "Madam" and shown her such respect. It was confusing. He nodded and motioned for her to answer. "I was beaten by a man," she replied. Nothing more.

"When?" Sarah asked.

"Last night."

"Where did he hit you?"

"My face, my arms, my legs. He kicked me in the stomach."

"Why did he do this?"

"I cannot say. He does this when he is angry. It was not the first time. Most times he is angry about work. He is a very important man."

"Why were you with this man?" Sarah asked, but she already knew the answer.

"It is my job. I work for Madam Urban."

Sarah knew the name and knew what kind of work Madam Choy did. She was a prostitute. Mother Urban was one of the most successful business owners in town, with a large brothel dominating the row of cribs and brothels along Heber Avenue leading to Frog Valley. Madam Choy had been beaten by her customer.

Mother Urban was widely respected in a perverse sort of way, in part because she gave generously to many social and school causes. She also paid her considerable taxes on time. Taxes and fees on her brothel and the others lining Heber Avenue supported much of the city's budget. Beyond respect, she was feared because she knew the secrets of nearly every prominent man in town. The secrets were the best protection she could have. Her business was not respected by most of the townspeople, but she herself was feared by all of her customers.

"May I examine you?" Sarah asked. Madam Choy nodded. Sarah found blood smeared everywhere, scratches along her face from which blood had dripped and dried, bruises on her upper arms where she had been tightly grasped and her arms twisted, and more on her chest and abdomen and along the fronts of her thighs. Sarah could picture the violent assault that Madam Choy had suffered. With careful palpation of the woman's abdomen and a listen with her stethoscope, she concluded that there was no internal damage. Madam Choy was breathing comfortably, if in pain, and her pulse was slow and regular.

"May I examine your private area?" she asked. Madam Choy nodded again. Sarah covered her discreetly with a sheet, and Mr. Sing turned away. A brief exam under the sheet showed shallow radiating stellate lacerations along the sides of the opening to her vagina, and a spot of blood at the opening. Sarah's clinical assessment fed a rising anger at what had been done to this woman. Her physical wounds would heal, but the emotional trauma might not. She had been forcibly penetrated, beaten, and abused. She had been raped. While she had suffered no serious internal organ damage, her mental recovery was far from clear.

"Can you bring a basin of warm water and some clean cloths," Sarah asked Mr. Sing. He nodded, disappeared out the door, and returned quickly with a large metal pitcher filled with warm water and a bright blue ceramic basin. Sarah carefully washed and dried Madam Choy's wounds. Sarah wanted to ask many more questions and get to the information she really wanted, but she knew it was not the right time.

"Madam Choy, you have been abused badly, but I see nothing broken or any serious damage. I think you will recover. Mr. Sing, can you care for her overnight and I will return in the morning? I would like to see how she sleeps and feels in the morning so I can ask more questions."

Mr. Sing nodded, gratitude in his face for Sarah's discretion. He knew she was mostly coming back for the questions. He knew what she really wanted to know, and he was impressed with her sensitivity to not ask it now. "Yes, I will watch over her. What instructions do you have?"

"Light food, easily digestible, lots of water, and rest," Sarah replied. She knew that the Chinese diet was already far healthier than that of most Parkites: rice, vegetables, a little meat, not much fat or sugar. "What you normally eat is fine, just small amounts."

"I understand. Thank you for coming."

"Crash!" A sharp explosion came from the corrugated tin roof over their heads, like a rifle shot only louder, more like a heavy gauge shotgun blast that echoed around the inside of the small home. Sarah jumped and screamed. Mr. Sing and the woman did not move.

"Just boys throwing rocks from the bridge onto the roof," Mr. Sing said. "They do it every day coming and going from school."

"That's terrible," Sarah said. "Can't you report it to the marshal?" She knew immediately how silly her question was.

"There is no point," Mr. Sing said. "He would do nothing. Most Parkites hate us, including him. They say they want us to leave, except of course for all the people whose houses we clean and those for whom we cook and do laundry. They do not speak up."

"That's terrible," Sarah said. "And so unfair. Why do they treat you so badly?"

"Because we work hard and so we are resented because of it. I make more money in my laundry than a miner makes, by several times. They are threatened because they think we want their mining jobs, but that is the last thing we want."

"Why do you stay?"

"Because life is still better here than in China. We simply want to take care of our families. But when we die, we will go home."

"But the bridge? Why is it even there?"

Mr. Sing responded with repressed emotion and a clenched jaw. "So the good people of Park City can walk from Main Street to Rossie Hill, their large homes, and the school, without having to walk through our neighborhood."

Despite his attempt to be diplomatic, his anger was easily felt. She was honored that she had been trusted to care for the woman, but she was even more embarrassed at how her fellow white Parkites treated these good people. "I apologize for the prejudice and hateful behavior of the townspeople. It is embarrassing."

"It is not your responsibility to apologize. I see your care and concern for Madam Choy's welfare. That is all that matters. You are a good doctor." Mr. Sing knew he had taken a chance in even asking her to see Madam Choy. Most doctors in the past had refused to provide care for the Chinese. He had thought that a woman doctor might be more receptive and helpful. He had been right.

"I will return tomorrow morning," Sarah said as she walked out.

⁂

That night, Sarah came down from her upstairs bedroom quarters every hour or two to check on Flora. She was still angry about Madam Choy's beating, but she was exhausted and slept well, if intermittently. Flora's sleep had been restless, but small doses of laudanum had helped. She became more comfortable in the dawn light before the morning sun peeked over Rossie Hill. The winter sun was cold, but it bathed the first floor in a morning glow. Sarah made coffee and slowly awakened from her own jumbled sleep.

"Good morning, Flora. How are you feeling?" Sarah asked.

"Oh, not great, but good enough to go home. I hope James was able to get the day off so he can come get me. I sort of remember you checking on me from time to time. The night is a bit of a fog. Thank you for everything."

"I am pleased at how well the surgery went, and now how well you got through the night. I think you will be fine at home, whenever James can make it."

"Please thank Dr. Wilson for me as well."

"Absolutely," Sarah said. "Happy to do so."

Flora's husband, James, had asked permission from his foreman to have the day off so he could come to take Flora home.

Surprisingly, his request was granted. He wondered if the mine was taking a new, more positive approach to its employees. As both Flora and Sarah brightened with the morning sun, James arrived as he had promised.

"Good morning, James," Sarah said, feeling the surge from her early morning coffee."Ma'am," James said, mumbling, his eyes on the floor. "I need to get back to work. Is Flora ready to go?"

"Certainly," Sarah replied. "I know you had to get special permission to take the day off. Can I ask how you are feeling?"

James did not respond and looked away. "James!" Flora said sharply. "The doctor is asking you how you feel."

"Fine," he mumbled. "We need to go."

Sarah looked at Flora, her eyebrows raised in question. Flora shook her head nearly imperceptibly.

"Flora, you need to rest," Sarah said. "Lots of fluids, water, soup, that sort of thing, until you come back next week. James, have you arranged for some help to come in, a neighbor or someone?"

James nodded but did not speak. Flora glared at him.

"Thank you so much, Doctor," Flora said. "I will be fine at home. I look forward to seeing you next week."

They walked out the door, and Flora grabbed James's arm as soon as they reached the road. "What is wrong with you?"

"Nothing," James said. "Just need to get back to work." He paused as if he wanted to say more.

"What?!" Flora said sharply.

"I'm sorry I told that woman so much about how I was feeling. I'm glad she took good care of you, but I can't talk to her anymore. Mr. Gibson made that clear. We are not to have anything to do with that woman. So I do what I am told. I need that job."

"Mr. Gibson has no right to keep you from talking to her. Dr. Fletcher is a good doctor, and she may have saved my life! She could save yours if you would just stop being so stubborn!"

❦·❦·❦·❦·❦

After Flora and James left, Sarah took a nap and then strolled down into the Chinatown hollow to visit Madam Choy. She had rested well and eaten a bit, but Sarah could still see the trauma and sadness in her eyes.

"Have you been harmed before, Madam Choy?" Sarah asked.

"Yes, but not this badly. I do not know if I can go back to Mother Urban's house," she said. "But I have nowhere else to go, and no other work I can do." Another rock hit the roof. Sarah didn't scream, but she still jumped, although a little less than the day before.

"If I may, Madam Choy, I would like to ask you the name of the man who did this to you?" Sarah asked.

"I cannot say," she replied. "He would kill me."

"You must tell me so we can tell the proper officials."

"It would not matter," Mr. Sing interjected. "The marshal and county sheriff ignore us when we have problems like this. No good will come from telling them. Just like the boys who throw rocks."

"I will see that they respond properly," Sarah said, turning back to Madam Choy. "It is important that you tell me, important for you and for other women. I promise I will not tell anyone else unless I ask your permission first."

The reference to helping other women was the key. Madam Choy's face brightened slightly, and her eyes opened a bit wider. "I understand. Then I will tell you." She paused, still considering the wisdom of saying the name. "Mr. Gibson," said Ma. "He is the head boss at the big mine above town."

Sarah could not speak for several moments. Her eyes darted around as she processed the shocking news. Finally, she composed herself. "Thank you for being willing to tell me this information. I know it scares you, but this man must be stopped. He cannot hurt other women."

"I told you so you can help my friends," Madam Choy said. "It does not matter to me. I will die."

The brutal simplicity of Madame Choy's statement was chilling to Sarah, and she feared the truth of it all the more so.

And then there was the name itself. Sarah's mind spun with this revelation. *Oh my God,* she thought. *Of all the names. What can I do with this information? What should I do? Gibson's lack of caring about the miners is the least of my concerns now.* She looked at Madame Choy's face again, defiant in its resignation and calm in its acceptance of whatever fate awaited her. *I said I would not reveal the name without her permission, particularly to the marshal. But I have to do something.*

CHAPTER 15

Park City, 1897

Sarah was still struggling with the shocking revelation about Gibson as she walked over to the livery stable the next morning. She needed to do something positive and satisfying after the trauma of caring for Madam Choy. "What do you think, John? It's been a week since we injected him with the diphtheria solution from the sick boy. Seems to me he's a bit off, not terribly sick, just a bit sluggish."

"I agree," McFarlane said. "Not eating quite as much, but he still has good energy and responds well to you." The horse nuzzled Sarah as she stroked his head.

"I'd like to see just a bit more evidence that the diphtheria was having an effect," Sarah said. "Not too much, just enough to know that he was developing the resistance in his blood that would be needed to treat the next sick child with diphtheria."

She had grown fond of the horse, and it seemed he was equally fond of her. She felt a bit guilty about purposely making him sick, but she knew at the worst it would be a mild illness, while the horse's mild discomfort could be responsible for saving the life of a child with diphtheria. She knew it would not be long before she would have the opportunity to test whether her experiment was a success. The infection continued to circulate in the community, made worse by the transient nature of the town.

She came back a few days later. "John, good to see you. How's he doing?" She always felt good walking into the stable, like it was her own little laboratory and John was her lab partner.

"And you," he replied. "I think he got a bit sicker since last week but he's recovering now. Not too sick, just a little, off his feed. His nose was wet, and his ears were laid back. I think he was a bit warm, and he was standing off in the corner of the stall by himself. But now he looks good, seems to be fully recovered. Time for another blood draw?"

"Indeed," she said, "but more this time." She had changed her protocol slightly based on the prior experience with the boy whose injection had not worked. She intended to withdraw a much larger quantity of blood so she could treat more than one sick child, each with a larger dose.

She attached a washed needle to a length of clean tubing and placed the other end of the tubing in a clean glass container on the floor, sweeping away the straw to make a clean spot.

"Shh, shh," McFarlane said as he soothed the horse.

Sarah easily punctured the horse's neck vein and drained off two pints of blood, which would give her more than a pint of serum once the red blood cells were separated. She really had no idea how much was needed, but she had enough now to conduct tests with at least two children.

As Sarah was finishing the blood draw, she reflected on the last couple weeks of remarkable events. She had saved a boy's life, albeit in a crude way, and engendered the everlasting admiration and appreciation of his parents, admiration that would surely spread through town and generate new requests for her care. She had made progress in developing what she hoped would be a more elegant and safe approach to saving the lives of children sick with diphtheria. Somewhat perversely, she was looking forward to identifying the next child with severe diphtheria so she could see if her suspicions were correct about the potency of the serum.

What was really interesting to her, though, was working with Thomas. They were engaged in a collegial and productive discussion about a potentially major occupational and public health problem in the Ontario mine. More immediately, she had observed him perform brilliantly in a stressful and potentially catastrophic surgical event. He was very impressive.

He's an interesting man, she thought. *If I had not been so fully admonished by Dr. Blackwell with the impossibility of having both a career as a physician and a family life as a wife and mother, I might be interested in a personal relationship with Thomas. But Dr. Blackwell was clear. Being successful in one's career was just too important to run the risk of being subjugated to family life. I wonder if that is true for everyone.*

"Nice job with the blood draw," McFarlane said. "You have a smile on your face."

"Hmm, I guess I do," she said, smiling even more broadly.

❧·❧·❧·❧·❧

Flora returned for a follow-up check later that day, and Sarah invited Thomas to see the patient with her. Thomas appreciated the courtesy, but dreaded the visit. He would have no choice but to reveal what had happened in the meeting with Gibson. He knew, but more importantly feared, that Sarah would not be pleased. Her reaction mattered to him, and he wanted to please her. Or perhaps not please her exactly, just gain her respect.

Flora arrived alone. James was at work for his usual shift. She looked happy and energetic.

"It is good to see you. Thank you for returning," Sarah said. "You remember Dr. Wilson?"

Flora nodded. "Thank you so much, Doctor, er, Doctors, for everything!"

"Tell us how you are feeling," Sarah said.

"So much better. I have so much more energy, even with the recovery from the surgery. My appetite has improved, and my sleep is better. I am so thankful to you." She nodded in the direction of both of them.

"All the credit goes to Dr. Fletcher, ma'am." Thomas said. "She made the correct diagnosis and performed a difficult operation with great skill." Thomas was sincere in his flattery, but he admitted to himself that he hoped his comments might smooth the next conversation he would have with her. He did not like to think of himself as manipulative in that way, but anything he could do that would help Sarah think better of him, as well as his developing plan, would be good.

"Thank you both," Sarah said, modestly, but beaming with pride. "Shall we examine you now?" She washed her hands and conducted a brief exam, including a vaginal exam to assess the cervix and how it was healing after removal of the uterus. She did not exactly exclude Thomas from the exam, but she conducted it discretely under a sheet, just a habit she had developed to respect the privacy of her female patients. The cervix was a bit tender but healing well, with no evidence of infection.

"Please let me know of any further difficulties," Sarah said. "You can resume your normal activities as you wish, although you may still be a bit tired after a day of housework. You may also resume intimate relations with your husband."

"Oh, I am so appreciative!" she said brightly, slightly embarrassed, slightly amused. Then her face darkened. "But I'm not sure that other issue matters. Can I ask about my husband?"

"Certainly, tell us how he is doing," Sarah said. "He didn't seem to want to talk much last week."

"Indeed, he did not. He was very rude, and I apologize for him. Unfortunately, he seems to be the same, maybe worse," said Flora, her smile and brightness long faded. "More moody, more forgetful."

"Dr. Wilson and I have discussed your husband's condition only briefly," Sarah said, "but we have both explored his condition in our textbooks, and we would like to discuss his case in more detail this morning. We will talk, and then I will come to your house to discuss our recommendations with you in the next day or two." She paused, not sure she wanted to pry further, but she pushed ahead. "Why was he so unwilling to talk last week? Has something changed?"

"I am very appreciative of anything you can do for him. Yes, something has clearly happened at work. I don't know what, but things changed after a meeting Mr. Gibson had with all the miners. My husband became even angrier and moodier after that. He snapped at me as we were leaving your office that he didn't want to talk about it anymore, that he was told by his foreman to stop complaining. I don't know what to do. I thought he trusted you and was willing to let you try to help, but not anymore. Please, could you come to the house and try talking to him again?" Flora asked.

"I will be happy to do so," Sarah replied.

"Thank you for everything. Thank you both. I feel so much better," Flora said.

"So," Sarah said after Flora left the office, "sounds like something happened with you and Gibson. Tell me."

This was a more abrupt transition than Thomas hoped for, but he decided to just get the bad news out quickly. "Mr. Gibson forbade me to have anything further to do with the miners and their health, under threat of losing my job, losing my office, losing my practice, and basically being run out of town. I agreed to stay on as mine physician and obey his requirements." He knew he could have presented this in a more positive way, but too late. He saw her startle, eyes wide, jaw dropping, and he wanted to say, "wait, wait, let me finish!" He didn't talk fast enough.

Sarah gasped and blurted out, "What?!" She could say so much with a single word. The anger flashed in her eyes. They narrowed, hard, accusatory.

Thomas could feel the sting and it hurt. He pushed on and said, "But I did so for a reason. I do not have the plan fully developed exactly, but I think staying connected to the mine is part of it."

"What kind of plan could that possibly be?" she said, less angry, but not warm. Flat, hard, but at least she seemed willing to listen.

"I don't know exactly," he replied, "but I think staying connected to the mine and the miners will help us in our investigation. Perhaps I can investigate a bit on the side since it would be acceptable for me to be in the mines. I know you are disappointed, perhaps even angry, and that makes me sad. Your opinion matters to me, but I am just trying to figure out how best to do what we both know needs to be done." It was so hard to say those things, but he was sincere, and he wanted her to know that her view of him mattered.

Sarah seemed to cool quickly, but not because of what he said. She was already thinking about how her information from Madam Choy could have an impact here. She was also puzzling over why she was disappointed. There was no real reason why she should have cared at all about Thomas or his decision, but she did. She heard the sincerity in his voice and felt the pain he was suffering with his decision. Why did it matter to her what he decided? Why did her disappointment seem to affect him? This relationship was taking new turns that she did not fully understand.

"Well, I guess I understand the dilemma here, maybe, and I look forward to hearing how you can make this plan work for the miners," she said, a touch more warmly, barely.

He could tell she was already on to something else, and he wasn't sure whether he was relieved or regretful that she was moving on so quickly to another matter, especially when he heard what she said next.

"I have an additional piece of information that may be helpful here. I was called to see a Chinese woman a few days ago. She works for Mother Urban, and she was severely beaten by a client. She told me the client's name." She paused. "It's Gibson, 'an important boss man at the mine,' as she said. I am going back to see her again later today." Retelling the story stirred her anger all over again. "I think we have no choice but to report this to Marshal Bennett. I know it is likely to be futile, but I see no other option."

"Oh my, that is terrible. I am so sorry for this woman," Thomas said. "I suppose it should not surprise me that she named Gibson, but it does. However much I have come to hate him, this is even shocking beyond that. Gibson is a truly bad person. What he has done is horrible. However," Thomas said, his voice dropping in volume almost to a whisper, "this news is also potentially very useful from a strategic perspective."

"Yes, exactly what I was thinking. Just telling the story makes me angry all over again," Sarah said. "She only told me because I said we need to stop Gibson from hurting any other women, and that's what we need to do, but I also said I would not tell anyone else without asking her permission. I have already violated that request by telling you, but I con-sider you a partner of sorts here."

Thomas warmed at the mention of their partnership, "of sorts." "But why report this to Bennett?" he replied. "You just said it would be futile, and I agree. He all but works for Gibson. Anything that might threaten the mine, including something as politically explosive as this, is his business to fix. Perhaps we should go to the county sheriff, or maybe the mine owners."

"I thought of that, all good ideas, but I think we have to start with the marshal. Anywhere else or anybody else will simply send us back to him. The proper authorities should at least be aware of what Gibson did to this woman."

"I don't know, it seems like we simply lose the best card in our hand, for no good purpose," Thomas said. "The marshal won't do anything here except tell Gibson."

Sarah paused to give it some thought. "I see your point. We don't want to lose the element of surprise here. Perhaps we should hold this information for a bit and give you some more time to investigate in the mine. Then we can decide what to do and when, especially if you start to uncover important information about how the mine's decisions are hurting the miners," she suggested.

Thomas was warmed by her increasing use of the word "we." "I like that approach. I think we will have to do all this on our own from here on. Gibson has clearly gotten to the miners, and they will not talk to me anymore. James made it pretty clear that he had been told to drop the issue. Gibson says the miners have expressed their appreciation to him for the way he manages the mine. It's obvious they will lose their jobs if they say otherwise."

"So what do we do?"

"Let me have a week to see what I can learn."

"OK, let's meet again then."

The conversation had taken them past midday and the sun was high as they left Sarah's office. Thomas turned right and headed back up to the mine. Sarah went straight on Fourth Street and across Main Street to make her way back to Chinatown. As they walked away from each other, they each thought to themselves that something important had happened in this encounter. Neither was sure what, maybe a new level of partnership, a new honesty in their communication, more trust and more respect. Thomas felt a bit of empathy from Sarah for his predicament. Sarah thought Thomas was growing, albeit slowly, into what she thought was the proper approach to his professional responsibilities. But something was missing, she thought. He's damaged in some way. She wished she knew why.

When Sarah entered the tidy yellow home, Mr. Sing was there waiting with Madam Choy. Sarah had not expected to see him. His presence told her something was wrong, but it did not appear to be with the woman. She looked more rested and comfortable, more composed, but there was something in her eyes, anger maybe, but more fear.

"I am scared," Madam Choy said, unasked. "I should not have told you who hurt me."

"You did the right thing," Sarah said. "This man must be stopped before he hurts other women."

"I understand, do what you have to do," Madam Choy said. "The gods will know what is best for me. Which is why I am scared." Sarah admired her bravery but cringed at Madam Choy's bluntness. *Just like the way everyone thinks whether a patient lives or dies is in God's hands. Maybe a different God but the same outcome. How can she be so accepting of her fate and so helpless all at the same time?*

"Tell me more about yourself. How did you come to Park City?" Sarah asked gently. She needed to understand this woman better before she decided what to do about the assault. She glanced at Mr. Sing, who nodded discretely to Madam Choy, encouraging her to respond.

"I came to this country from China with my husband, when he worked on the railroad, the big railroad that goes across the country."

"And now here? How?"

"When that job was finished, he looked for more railroad work and we moved here when the railroad came to Park City. We were happy here."

Her reference to the past did not go unnoticed by Sarah. "But your husband? Where is he?" She was afraid to hear the answer.

"Dead," she said matter-of-factly. "A heavy iron beam fell on him," Madam Choy said, again matter-of-factly. "Many Chinese died building the railroad. He was just one more to the owners. We sent his body back to his relatives in China. Now I am alone," she repeated.

"How did you end up with Madam Urban?"

"I was hired to clean the home of a nice family up on Woodside," she replied. "They were very kind to me, and I liked their children." She paused, and her gaze wandered upward in memories.

Beneath her seeming calm retelling of her story was a deep sadness. Sarah could hear it in her voice, halting, soft, as if she herself still could not understand how she found herself in this sad place. "And then?" Sarah was almost afraid to hear what came next.

"I could not support myself cleaning houses, so I had to start working for Mother Urban." She was not ashamed talking to a woman as she might have been to a man. She knew Sarah would understand.

"I am so very sorry about your husband. I understand why you are doing what you are doing, although I am sorry it is necessary. I promise I will protect you," Sarah said, her eyes moist, although she had no idea what that meant or how she could promise it.

Madam Choy thought about her husband, as she did every day. He would want her to do the right thing, but she was so scared. "My husband would tell me to do this, if he was here," she said. "Do what you have to do," Madam Choy said, resigned, but also resolved, "or he will hurt my friends."

"May I examine you again?" Her abrasions and bruises were clean and healing well. "Please continue to take care of yourself as we have discussed. I will return in a few days for another check. I understand you are scared. You have reason to be. I will consider this issue carefully before I do anything."

Madam Choy gave a small bow of her head but did not look back up.

Sarah packed up her bag to leave. Mr. Sing gently stepped into the conversation. He was trying to be patient but was anxious to get the doctor's attention. "Doctor, would you be willing to see another patient?" he said.

"Of course," she replied. "How can I help?"

"A child three houses down is very ill. The mother is worried that it is diphtheria."

"Please take me there." Sarah was immediately sorry to hear about another sick child, and then she felt guilty just as quickly as she thought about the opportunity to try out what she hoped was a stronger dose of antitoxin.

Sarah and Mr. Sing walked just a few steps down the tidy street and entered the house. She knew immediately that the mother was right. The girl, perhaps six or seven years old, was pale, sweaty, gasping for breath, and coughing hard. The mother looked terrified and desperate, both for good reason.

The child had a severe case, and the mother knew what the outcome would likely be.

"The mother speaks no English," Mr. Sing said. "May I help with translation?"

"Please. Can you ask her when this started?"

Mr. Sing had a lengthy and strangely lively conversation in Chinese with the mother, far more than would be necessary to answer Sarah's simple question. Somewhere in the middle of the conversation Mr. Sing introduced Sarah as a doctor and the mother looked at her with thankful eyes. Sarah bowed slightly.

"The girl became sick two days previously with a slight fever and cough," Mr. Sing said. "The cough became much harsher and more painful last night, the fever was higher, and the girl could not drink. The mother says sometimes her daughter's chest hurts. The mother is sick with fear that there is nothing to be done and her daughter will die. The mother pleads with you to do anything, any medicine, that could possibly help. She said she sought the opinion of a Chinese healer who offered traditional herbal remedies, but she wants your help as well, any possible help, from anyone. She has already heard how kind and helpful you have been with Madam Choy."

Sarah's mind moved quickly. She had nothing to offer the girl at this point except a tracheostomy as a desperate last possibility. But it was very high-risk and could have a catastrophic outcome. She was also worried about some cardiac involvement with the child saying her chest hurt. The tracheostomy would do nothing for that. The horse serum sitting in her icebox was the only hope, if it was strong enough, stronger than the first batch. The only way to know was to try it, and this was the opportunity she needed. This was the time.

"Please ask the mother if I may examine the child."

Mr. Sing talked to the mother quickly. "Anything, anything, she says."

She quickly examined the child and found what she expected: dehydration, the dreaded gray membrane, and poor air movement. She needed to act quickly.

"Is there anything you can do to help the child?" Mr. Sing asked. "The mother says again that she is desperate and willing to try anything."

"There is a new approach that could potentially save the girl's life," Sarah replied, hesitantly, carefully, already more encouraging than she should have been. "But it is very new, somewhat unusual, and will seem strange to the mother." She described her experiments with the horse. Mr. Sing could not quite grasp the details of such a strange approach to treatment, but then he was always a bit perplexed by the ways of the white citizens of Park City. He translated as best as he could. Judging by the look on the mother's face, Sarah was sure that much had been lost in the translation, but she was seeing the same sequence of reactions when she had described her research to the parents of the boy she treated—shock, disbelief, curiosity, acceptance, and finally hope.

With this mother, though, there was an additional level of confusion and curiosity as she considered the strange ways of these strange people in this strange country. The mother could not really understand as Mr. Sing explained what this woman doctor proposed to do. How could a horse possibly save her daughter's life? But what choice did she have? She knew her daughter would die, and soon. She nodded vigorously to Sarah and talked rapidly to Mr. Sing to express her confusion, but also to be clear that she agreed to what the doctor was proposing.

Mr. Sing simply said, "Please proceed."

"I will return in less than an hour," Sarah told Mr. Sing.

Sarah nearly ran out of the hollow, across Main Street and along Fourth Street to her office. She had recovered over a pint of serum when she had manually spun down the two pints of blood drawn from the horse. The serum was clear with a yellow tinge. She drew up a large glass syringe of what she hoped would be a life-saving miracle, wrapped it in a cloth, grabbed a rubber tourniquet and left the office to return to Chinatown.

As she crossed Main Street, Marshal Bennett was coming down the boardwalk and they met at the intersection. She tried to hurry past him, but he blocked her way. His sheer bulk was threatening and his glowering face more so. "I understand you are mixed up in this business with the miners and their supposed lung disease," he said.

"I'm sorry, marshal, I haven't the time. I have a patient to whom I must attend urgently." As she spoke, the flap of cloth fell away in the mountain breeze and the syringe was clearly visible. The marshal looked down at the syringe, and then back up at her. He did not fully understand what the syringe was, but it looked suspicious, and that was his job, to be suspicious, especially of this so-called woman doctor. His eyes narrowed as she edged along the boardwalk to get past him. It looked like she was going down the hill from Main Street, not over the China Bridge.

"Are you taking care of those Chinks?" he asked.

"It's none of your business who I care for and what I do," she replied angrily. He was large and threatening, but she was a doctor, and she was not going to be intimidated by his threats.

"Whatever, if you want to waste your time on those Celestial heathens, it's no matter of mine. Just keep your nose out of the mine's business. The so-called lung disease Wilson is fussing about is no business of his, and even less of yours."

She did not reply. She brushed past him and hurried down the hill.

As she entered the child's house, she quickly explained again to the mother, through Mr. Sing, what she intended to do. What Mr. Sing translated was just as preposterous to the mother as it was the first time, but she nodded her agreement again.

Sarah wrapped the tourniquet around the child's pale and thin upper arm, waited a bit for a dehydrated vein to fill with blood, washed the arm quickly, inserted the needle, released the tourniquet, and injected the serum slowly. And then she settled in to watch and wait. Whether a miracle or another tragedy, whatever happened, she would be there.

Thomas went straight from Sarah's office to the mine, thinking up as many reasons as he could for why he should be loitering around the mine and hanging around the miners as they came up in the cage from their shift. One of the miners he had already evaluated turned away and would not look at him or talk to him.

"Charlie," Thomas said, remembering the miner's name. "Can you tell me how you are feeling?"

"Sorry, Doc, can't talk," the miner said.

Thomas approached others who looked as if they were sick, hacking cough, sucking in air noisily, but he received no response. He looked up at the lift operator. "Can you let me down into the mine?"

"Sorry, Doc, no can do. Foreman's orders," waving to the man standing off to the side.

The foreman turned to Thomas, the same foreman who had thanked him before when Thomas cared for the miner with the injured hand. "Sorry, Doc, orders from Mr. Gibson. Only way I am allowed to let you down into the mine is if there is an injury, or if some type of medical care is needed."

And that is how he got into the mine the next day.

He was called to the mine to attend to a miner who had tripped on a sledge left on the floor in the murky lighting of the tunnel, smashing his face against the rock wall. Thomas was called to the mine, and when he arrived at the changing room, he was offered a set of a miner's wool undergarments, a heavy yellow waxed slicker, a felt helmet, and rubber boots. The clothes were not as clean and fresh-smelling as the set Gibson had given him on his previous trip down. The smell of sweat from the previous user was nauseating. He didn't want to think about what else was dried on the stiff undergarments.

With his medical bag, he entered the cage and descended into the blackness. At the underground station, he found the injured man who had been brought out from the rock face where he had been working, laid on the ground as comfortably as possible, and covered with a blanket.

"Sir, what is your name?" Thomas asked.

The miner was conscious but groggy, moaning and swiping at the blood on his cheeks and mouth. "Calvin," he said.

"Calvin, let me check you out," Thomas said. He examined his skull and face carefully, and suspected he had a broken nose, probably a crushed right cheekbone, and several deep lacerations on the forehead and cheeks. "Do you know where you are, Calvin?" Thomas asked.

"Well, that's a stupid question, Doc. In the Ontario mine of course," the miner replied.

"Good, glad to see your sense of humor hasn't left. Then tell me what happened?" Thomas asked.

"Well, I really don't know. Someone told me I fell on my face."

"And after that," Thomas asked, "before I arrived?"

"I don't know," the miner mumbled. He was irritable and grumpy but not necessarily more so than most miners were most of the time.

"You have several injuries on your face, and some broken bones around the nose and eye. We'll get you to my office where I can fix you up."

Thomas dressed the wounds temporarily with some bandages from his bag. "Take Calvin to my office and I will be along shortly to repair the wounds more carefully," Thomas directed the workers standing around. Quite a large crowd had gathered as the shift was ending, just about exactly the capacity of the cage, and Thomas told them all to take the lift up. "I will gather up my equipment and be along on the next cage." He knew they were all anxious to get out of the mine at the end of their shift, to the boardinghouse to wash up, and to the bar. It was the perfect opportunity to send them along and stay behind alone in the station.

A few men gathered up Calvin and loaded him into the cage, the cage filling up as the gate closed. Up they went as Thomas looked around carefully to make sure he was alone. He lit his carbide lamp, peered down each dark drift and could see no one. He chose a drift from which he had seen miners emerge when he had come down. There was an ore car full of rocks waiting at the opening to be taken up at the next shift. He started down the drift and soon came to the rock face at the end. A mechanical drill was mounted and ready to be used the next morning, under which had collected a thick layer of fine dust from the day's work. Thomas pulled a clean glass jar out of his medical bag. He scooped up as much dust as he could into the jar, screwed the lid on tight, and tucked it back into his bag. As he made the final turn of the lid, he thought he heard a scuffing noise along the tunnel behind him. He turned and looked but saw nothing in the receding darkness. Probably just the mine rats.

Thomas retraced his path back to the underground station. The lift cage was on its way back down. As he waited, he looked nervously around the station. The openings to each drift were dark and shadowed, and he could see little even as he turned his head with the lamp stuck to his helmet. The lift arrived with a jerk and stopped just inches above the floor. He climbed in, gave the bell instructions to the operator as he was taught to do, and up he went. Just before he cleared the high-ceilinged station to enter the narrow rock shaft, he thought he saw movement at the opening to one of the drifts. It was just the briefest flash of something or somebody, and then he was into the shaft. He gave a little shiver, perhaps because of the clammy penetrating cold of the mine, perhaps because of what he thought he saw.

Thomas left the lift cage quickly as it came to the surface and hurried to his office. He found the miner, Calvin, resting comfortably with a friend. He excused himself and went through the front room to his office in the backroom, pulled the jar filled with dust out of his pocket and tucked it in the corner behind his desk. He came back out to the front room, moved the patient to his medical table, removed the dressings, and washed the wounds clean. "You have some deep lacerations that will need stitches," he told Calvin. "Do you want to be put asleep?"

"Naw, don't bother," Calvin said. "I've had worse before after bar fights."

Thomas placed several sutures into each gaping laceration. Calvin winced with each one but made no sound and stayed still. Thomas redressed the abrasions on the patient's face and covered the entire face with bandages except for holes for his eyes, nose, and mouth. "You will heal up fine," Thomas said, "but your face will look a bit rugged. You have a fracture of the cheek bone, and I can't do much about that."

"No worries," Calvin said. "It will give my face more character!"

"I will see you in a week to take out the stitches. No work until then. Someone needs to stay with you tonight because you were out cold for a while. No trips to the pub tonight!" Thomas said, knowing that the miner would disobey every single instruction he had just given.

Thomas was only half paying attention to the suturing and care of Calvin's wounds, because he was mostly thinking about what he would do next with the rock dust. He would contact Sarah the first thing next morning and they could discuss the possibilities. He wondered if there was someone in town who could assess the dust. Perhaps the mining assayer in Park City could help. Assayers were some of the most powerful and best educated people in town. Fortunes were made and lost and mines were bought and sold based on the assayer's report of rock sample assays, the composition of silver and other valuable minerals, and his calculation of the potential financial yield of the mine. Thomas felt better having advanced his plan to continue his investigation, even under the guise of continuing his employment with the mine. But something was nagging at him from the corners of his consciousness. He couldn't identify exactly what.

Several minutes after Sarah's injection, the Chinese child had a wrenching shiver across her entire body, almost a seizure with violent shaking and sweating. Her face was flushed, and blotchy red swellings popped up on the skin of her abdomen and chest.

The mother looked at Sarah with terror in in her eyes. The girl said something to her mother.

"The girl says her muscles hurt," Mr. Sing translated. The shivering lasted for a couple minutes. All three adults barely breathed as they waited to see what would happen. Finally, the child settled down and the mother's terrified look settled with her. The child's pulse became a bit stronger and slower, and she fell into a deep sleep.

The mother looked at Sarah, eyes wide and eyebrows raised in a question. "Tell the mother I believe this is a reaction to the horse's blood," Sarah told Mr. Sing. "It could be a good sign that the treatment will work." She really had no idea what that reaction had been, but this was a reasonable guess. It might reflect a higher concentration of whatever the powerful antidote was in the horse's blood that attacked the diphtheria. Her lack of full understanding did not stop her from looking calm and reassuring as she said, "I believe the shivering reaction and skin splotches might mean the medicine is working."

Sarah found a comfortable spot in the corner of the room and dozed a bit. She awoke with a startle later in the evening, sensing that something was happening with the child. The child was awake, sipping some broth as she nestled in her mother's arms. Her eyes were brighter, less sunken, the skin around the eyes less dark. "May I examine your daughter?" Sarah asked. Mr. Sing had asked to stay the night as well so he could help with translation, but the mother understood and nodded. Even with the faint light from the dangling light bulb, Sarah could see the girl was better. Her throat was less swollen and inflamed. The gray membrane was still there, but the tissue around it was less puffy. The child could swallow better, and her breathing was less raspy.

The child was still sick, a sheen from the feverish sweat still on her forehead, but something good was happening.

"Tell the mother I think the child has improved, that the treatment appears to be working," Sarah told Mr. Sing.

The mother collapsed with relief from Mr. Sing's translation. She brought herself up to her knees in front of Sarah and lowered her head and hands repeatedly in a small bow. "The mother expresses her deepest appreciation to you," Mr. Sing said, "and praises your magical power as a physician."

"Not magic," Sarah said. "Science. Tell her I am most grateful for her appreciation. I do indeed believe that her child may have started on a path to recovery, but there is much to go before we know if she has recovered. I would like to spend the rest of the night here with her if I may."

The mother nodded vigorously at Mr. Sing's translation and bustled around to gather some blankets to make a bed. She ladled steaming broth and vegetables out of a pot hanging over the fire into a bowl for Sarah. The soup was delicious. She saw for herself what she had heard; the Chinese were far healthier than most Parkites she knew. They bathed more regularly, cleaned their houses more carefully, and ate healthier food. She wondered why there was so much prejudice against them. She drifted off to sleep, satisfied in all ways gastronomic and scientific.

CHAPTER 16

Sarah's morning brought more sun and a refreshing breeze that blew away the usual murky smoke. The warmth of the sun matched the joy and life in the room. Sarah knew that the child was better before even looking at her. The room was quiet but not death-quiet. It was the comforting murmur of a child softly breathing and not gasping for air. She was not fully recovered, but better, much better. Sarah rolled out of her duck feather-filled mattress and saw the child's skin, rosy now, not the slate gray of the day before. Her moist lips savored a small spoonful of porridge.

The mother looked up at Sarah with wide, adoring eyes. She said something Sarah could not understand, but it didn't matter. The mother was happy. "May I?" Sarah asked, motioning toward the child to exam her. The mother held the child out to her. "No, no, she can stay in your arms," motioning the child back into its protective cocoon. Her exam confirmed her informal assessment. The girl's throat was less swollen, air was moving, although still a bit raspy, and her skin was fresh and smooth because her fever had broken. She had lost the harsh scale of dehydration.

The mother's face as she looked at Sarah was a swirl of emotion—confusion, curiosity, gratefulness, relief. But not fear. She didn't know who this strange woman was, and a strange white woman at that. Somehow, she knew the doctor was good and her daughter was safe. A white woman had never been in the house, but this white woman had brought a miracle. She had no basis for understanding exactly what had happened or what the doctor had done, so it must indeed be a miracle. All she knew, and all she really cared about, was that her daughter was now resting comfortably in her arms. Her daughter would live.

Mr. Sing had left late the previous evening when the child and Sarah were both sleeping comfortably. He poked his head through the doorway and took in what he knew immediately to be a remarkable scene: the sun, the smiles, the soft happiness in the room.

"Mr. Sing, please tell the mother I think the crisis has passed," Sarah said. "I will return later today to check on the girl again, but I expect she will continue to improve."

Mr. Sing translated, and the mother replied with what appeared to be a long question and some confusion. "The mother says she is deeply grateful, but she does not know how to properly thank you. She thinks God has sent you as his messenger to bring this miracle to her daughter," Mr. Sing said.

"The color in the child's cheeks and the smile on the mother's face are thanks enough," Sarah replied. "I think a miracle from God is as good an explanation as any. Science heals, but I am sure God helped," she said with a smile.

Mr. Sing translated, and the mother smiled and nodded. Sarah smiled back even more broadly. She recognized that she had, indeed, contributed to a miracle with this child. Sarah was a woman of science, but she could not deny the power of faith. The relief and happiness of everyone in the room did not care why the girl had lived.

Mr. Sing said, "The mother thanks you deeply again."

Sarah nodded toward the mother and to Mr. Sing and excused herself. She nearly flew out of the door of the small and happy home, floating on the euphoric energy of having done something extraordinary and powerful. However, miracle or not, she knew that much more work was required to understand this new treatment, how it worked, and what risks there might be. Most importantly, she needed to standardize the process so she could do it again, because, for better or worse, she would certainly have more opportunities. A diphtheria epidemic was sweeping through the surrounding communities; it would not be long before she was called again. For now, she had one more dose of serum left from the batch that had just saved the girl's life.

The news spread quickly from the bright Chinatown home, through the owners of the many Chinese laundries as they delivered their clean clothes around town, through the Chinese women who cleaned the homes on Rossie Hill and above Main Street, through the workers in the one Chinese restaurant other Parkites thought fit to visit, and through the cooks in the boardinghouses. It was not long before the miraculous event was known throughout Park City.

Sarah was bursting to share the news with someone, someone who would understand the magnitude of this miracle. She went straight to Thomas's office.

❦·❦·❦·❦·❦

Thomas was about to leave his office to find Sarah when she ran through his front door and nearly knocked him over, talking as she entered.

"Thomas! Thomas! It worked! It worked!" Sarah nearly yelled. "I used the horse serum on a Chinese girl, and she is recovering!"

Thomas was certainly excited by the science and medicine, but he was far more interested in Sarah's excitement and passion. Her joyous voice was mesmerizing. "I am so happy for you, and, of course, even more so for the girl! Tell me the whole story," he said. It was a remarkable story, and he had many questions, but all he really wanted to do was gaze at Sarah's beautiful smile, illuminated by her glow of triumph.

Sarah reviewed her work from medical school with Professor Sewall, which Thomas recalled, and what had happened with the girl. "What we most need to pursue, now that we know that the antitoxin works, is the cause and nature of the shaking chill and puffy rash that happened after the injection. It must be some sort of reaction in the child's blood against some compound in the horse's serum. It appears to be transient and not serious, but there is a very distinct reaction of some sort."

Thomas loved her reference to how "we" needed to investigate this reaction. "Sarah, how do you think we should proceed?"

"I think I need to try this again as soon as an opportunity arises," she replied. "One event, however remarkable, really tells us nothing. Maybe it was a fluke. Maybe the child would have recovered anyway. Maybe the next child will have a more severe reaction. We should consider administering the serum to a small number of children, maybe ten or so, and write up our observations as a medical case report. We could send this to Professor Sewall. Perhaps it would be suitable for publication in a medical journal."

"I would very much enjoy being part of that in whatever way you think I can help," he said. "I doubt very much this was a fluke. I think you have done something remarkable, and we should pursue it as you have described. Congratulations!"

She swelled with the praise and the pride of what she had accomplished. His support meant more to her than she expected. "Thank you," she said, simply but sincerely.

"Can we discuss our other matter? I have some news to report," Thomas continued. "I had the opportunity, or more correctly created the opportunity, to make a clandestine trip into the mine." He couldn't resist the need to emphasize how his decision to stay in the mine helped them to advance their investigation. "I was able to collect samples of the drilling dust. I wonder if we might learn something from the assayer about the composition of the dust."

He did not tell her about the shadowy figure he might have seen as the lift went up. He wasn't sure what he saw or what he could really say.

Sarah did not ignore Thomas's bit of continued defensiveness about how he was handling his employment, but she did not want to come down from her cloud of euphoria, so she just let it go. "Excellent plan, Thomas. Let's see what he has to say."

The two doctors walked down Main Street to the assayer's office, just a few doors down from Thomas's office on the opposite side of the street, next to the Dewey Opera House, the pride of the town. Park City was well-known amongst traveling entertainers, and they often stopped on their way from Denver to San Francisco. The Opera House boasted performances of some of the best singers, lecturers, magicians, and other entertainers in the country, as good as any big city. Parkites considered the Opera House to be a measure of its sophistication and success.

Mr. Frank A. Bird, Assayer, was another measure of that sophistication. He was known across western mining towns as one of the best assayers in the business, well-trained, precise, honest to the point of bluntness, and incorruptible.

An impressive carved and painted sign hung from the office's overhanging porch, *"Mr. Frank A. Bird, Assayer."* The doctors felt immediately at home as they walked into the assay office. "What does this remind you of?" Thomas asked Sarah as they walked in.

"Medical school," Sarah replied immediately. "The building looks like our school, and this room smells like school. The solvents and salts, the formalin, the sweet smell of carbolic acid. Just like our laboratory. It smells good."

The building was one of the most substantial in town, layered quarried stone for the walls, heavy wood paneling inside. The front room was filled with evidence of Mr. Bird's work, seemingly in disarray to the eye of an uneducated observer but in perfect order to Mr. Bird. There were large bags of ore samples stacked on the floor and tables covered with smaller labelled bags containing the dreams of prospectors roaming the hills looking for the next big bonanza. The shelves lining the walls were filled with reference books, arranged neatly with the spines flush with the edge of the shelf. An air of solemnity hung over all of it, like a church, a church where the religion of money was celebrated. The sunlight glinted off flecks of silver and quartz dust. This was a place where important decisions were made and where fortunes could be made or lost based on the accuracy of Mr. Bird's work.

A bell hung from the wall near the door, and Sarah gave the cord a pull. The assayer was nowhere to be seen, but they heard steps through the door in the back wall, from which Mr. Bird appeared. Behind him, through the doorway, they could see what looked to be his assay lab. A tall, thin man with a heavy drooping mustache, he was as sparing in his dress and speech as he was in his work, focusing his energy on the careful, scientific work his clients expected. He wore a heavy, canvas apron that had several burned spots and holes. His bare arms had dozens of small, white scars from the burns caused by splattered molten rock from his assay furnace, the mark of a good assayer who does his own smelting and sampling.

"Yes?" he asked. "May I help you?"

"We hope so. We have not met but I am Dr. Wilson and this is Dr. Fletcher. As you may know, we have each come to town recently and established our medical practices."

"Oh, yes," Mr. Bird responded. "I know of both of you well, for different reasons. You, Dr. Fletcher, were quite a surprise to everyone," as he nodded to Sarah. "No one here had imagined that a woman could be a doctor. I was much amused when I heard the townspeople whisper about you. Personally, I measure professional men—and women—by their work, and only by their work. I have heard good things about yours.

And your reputation, Dr. Wilson, long precedes you from your interactions with Mr. Gibson and the Ontario miners. I have heard good things about your work as well. Several Parkites have commented favorably, especially about that terrible tragedy with the boy run over by the train. Your caring and concern were widely admired. Park City appears to be fortunate that both of you have added to the quality of medical care in town."

"Thank you," Sarah and Thomas said together.

"We are pleased to hear that," Sarah continued.

The doctors both blushed in their embarrassment. They were becoming aware that they were more a topic of discussion than they realized, a fact about which neither of them was particularly happy. They both wished the townspeople would just focus on their medical skills.

"You are quite welcome. But I assume you did not come just to hear such embarrassing pleasantries. I actually have no interest in any of these dramas. I consider myself a scientist and geologist, and I am only interested in the accuracy of my assay work."

"We are pleased to hear about your commitment to scientific accuracy, because we wish to consult you about a scientific matter," Thomas said. "You may be aware that we are studying a disease in miners, actually two diseases, one chronic and one acute, that may be related to the lead content of drilling dust. We have a sample of dust from the rock face where the drilling occurs." He pulled the jar out from beneath his coat. "We would like to know about its properties and chemical make-up, both its lead content and any features that might lead to lung disease."

"I could do some of that, but you understand that I am not a biologist or a physician. I do not have expertise in these medical matters of which you speak. But I have a more immediate and practical concern. I am aware that this is an issue not lacking in controversy, and one about which there are many opinions. I depend on the goodwill of all mines and mine managers, in particular that of Mr. Gibson and the Ontario mine, for my living. The Ontario mine is my largest client. I do not necessarily enjoy interacting with Mr. Gibson, but business is business. Performing this assay could compromise that relationship in an adverse way."

"Yes, we understand," Sarah said. "But you should also be aware that miners have died from this lung disease, at least two to our knowledge. Other miners have been unable to work because of their severe lung symptoms. We believe we have an obligation to help. We hoped you could see fit to do so as well."

Mr. Bird sat down behind his desk and fussed with the laboratory logs laying there, rearranging them and tidying up the piles of paper and reports. They didn't need tidying. He fussed some more and avoided looking at the doctors. After a long and awkward pause, he chose his words carefully. "Hmm, maybe, maybe not. I understand the gravity of the situation. And I am also curious about this matter as any scientist would be, but I can only imagine what Gibson would do to my business if he found out. As I said, the Ontario is my largest account. Without their business, mine would fail."

"We understand that," Thomas said, "perhaps better than you might think. Our practices are equally threatened."

Mr. Bird paused and stared at both of them without blinking for a few moments, internally weighing the pros and cons. It wasn't clear which side would win. "Were I to do this, and I am not yet sure I will do so, my work and report would have to be kept in the strictest confidence, never to be revealed as to its origin. Whatever you think necessary to do with the information, it cannot be attributed to me." He paused and his stern look softened, and he smiled faintly. Thomas and Sarah were silent as they watched him struggle with his dilemma.

"I guess my scientific curiosity is stronger than my fear of Mr. Gibson."

Ah, the power of science, Thomas thought. *Mr. Bird faces the same ethical and political conundrum as I myself face. Somehow, he seems to be working through those dilemmas more expeditiously than I seem able to do.*

"Thank you, Thomas said. "We do understand, me particularly so because of my role as the mine physician." He couldn't stop defending his decision in Sarah's presence. "We are prepared to pay your fee for this work, to make it clear this is a business relationship. Will that be satisfactory?"

Mr. Bird nodded. "Very well, leave the sample and return tomorrow. I will have a report prepared by then."

After the doctors left, Mr. Bird took the sample and divided it into three portions so he had back-up samples should the analysis go awry. He assumed the sample had a high lead content, partly because of prior analyses he had done for the Ontario mine, and partly because of the doctors' concerns, so he chose a wet method of analysis using a sequence of sulfuric, nitric, and hydrochloric acids. He precipitated the lead with acid washes and the addition of a zinc rod.

When he finished, he found what he expected: a lead concentration in the dust of nearly fifty percent. That itself was not surprising. The dust was very fine, more so than seemed to be the case with manual drilling in samples he had analyzed previously from the mine. Mr. Bird could easily imagine how it could be inhaled and absorbed into the body. He had no idea how the inhaled dust would harm lungs, but he suspected the doctors were correct in their hypothesis.

Next, he spread a small sample of the finest portion of the dust on a slide for examination under his microscope. He had less experience with this type of exam, but he was struck by what he saw. The slide was covered with sharp-edged crystals of what looked like silicates, shiny flakes of mineral that were microscopic versions of the quartz veins seen in the rock outcroppings prized by prospectors looking for silver. Outcroppings of quartz were what prospectors first found in Bonanza Flats by the Fort Douglas soldiers, which led to the rush of prospectors, the filing of claims, the sinking of shafts, the bustling town of Park City, and Frank Bird's successful business. The microscopic version of that same quartz was now apparently being produced in abundance by mechanical drilling.

He was still anxious about the potential repercussions of performing this analysis, but he would report his findings as accurately as he could. He prided himself on his professional integrity, and he would not waver here. He hoped the doctors would return as quickly as he had asked so he could deliver the report and have nothing further to do with this sample. He was already at risk if the doctors had been seen visiting his office.

Mr. Bird fidgeted around the office all the next morning until the doctors returned.

"I have prepared a summary of my findings," he said, handing them a single sheet of paper with handwritten comments and numbers. "As you can see, the lead content of the dust is very high, which itself is not surprising, because we know that veins of galena are common throughout the Park City district. Galena is lead sulfide, and it is often contaminated with enough silver to make mining it worthwhile. Lead itself is increasingly valuable, so following and drilling into veins of galena is common. I know enough about mining and drilling to know that this type of fine dust was not formed from drilling by hand, or least not in the same quantities. Even a rapid double-jack pace could not throw clouds of dust into the air like mechanical drills do. As you can see, I also looked at the dust microscopically and saw shiny, sharp crystals that look like silicate, but I am not a chemist. I think you will need to pursue additional expertise there, perhaps at the University in Salt Lake."

He paused to let all that sink in. "Having said all this, it is the last you will hear from me about this matter. There are only two copies of this report, one of which I always keep as a record of my work, and the one here I am giving to you. I am returning the dust samples that were left from my analysis. There is no other evidence of my involvement here." He did not want to sound rude, but he wanted to be clear about his concerns. "I fear retaliation and the potential consequences if my involvement is exposed." He held the jar with the remaining dust out at arm's length, as if the jar itself could harm him.

"We understand," Thomas replied, "and we appreciate very much what a sensitive matter this is for you. You will hear no more from us about our request. We appreciate the recommendation about consulting a chemist at the university. We thank you."

Mr. Bird locked up at the end of the day and strolled down Main Street to the China Bridge and across to Rossie Hill to his home. Assaying work paid well, and he was proud of his fine home on the Hill, along with those of other prominent townspeople, including, ironically, his neighbor, Mr. Gibson. As he was about to turn off Main Street to the Bridge, Marshal Bennett came up Main Street toward him. He tipped his hat to Mr. Bird as they passed one another, and Mr. Bird turned right to the Bridge. He shivered as he always did when near the marshal, something about his dark and brooding face that always seemed set in anger. The marshal continued on up Main Street.

The next morning, Mr. Bird unlocked the storefront door to open his office. He immediately knew that someone had been inside. Others would probably not notice the slight difference in position of the books on the shelf and the papers on his desk in the front room, but he did. He could also tell that the jars and tins of chemicals on the shelves in his assay lab had been moved. Small arcs of clean bare wood, untouched by the fine layer of dust that covered everything, had been exposed when the jars were moved. He also saw that his file of reports from past work had been opened. The reports had been replaced in the file, but the last one, the copy of which he had given to the doctors, was sticking partway out of the folder. No reports were missing, but he was quite sure an intruder had examined just this report, no others, and taken nothing else.

The doctors huddled in Thomas's office over the assayer's report. They felt like they should whisper, although no one else was in the office. They felt both the fear and the excitement of their conspiratorial investigation.

"This report from Mr. Bird is interesting," Sarah said, "but I am much more concerned about how we should handle the assault on Madam Choy. She is taking a great risk in telling us Mr. Gibson's name, and she rightfully fears retaliation. Under normal circumstances, we should be reporting this to the marshal, but that just won't work."

"I agree," Thomas said. "Gibson was not subtle about the potential harm that could befall me and my practice if I continued to push the lung disease issue. Charging him with assault is way bigger than that! He made vague references to the risk of mysterious fires. If he will do that with the medical investigation, I can't imagine what he would do if we brought evidence to the marshal that required Gibson to be charged with assault.

I have a thought," Thomas continued. "What about bringing Dr. Stout into the discussion? He is highly respected, whether justified or not, and is known by all the mine managers and owners. Maybe he can offer some guidance here."

"Hmm," Sarah said, yet one more of those vague utterances that Thomas was coming to understand could mean so many things. "Maybe," she continued, cautious, not convinced. "This issue eventually has to find its way to some sort of law enforcement, but some guidance from another source might be helpful. I was pretty disgusted by his office, and what I have learned about his medical practice, but I guess we don't have a lot of choices. When I introduced myself to him after operating on Mr. Miller, he did seem quite collegial. I doubt we have much in common medically, but let's start there.

"But tell me something, Thomas," Sarah continued, "something strange happened on the sidewalk yesterday. The marshal threatened me because of my involvement in the lung disease issue as I was on my way to Chinatown. How does he know I am involved?"

"I am so very sorry, Sarah," Thomas replied sheepishly, eyes downcast. "I made the mistake of mentioning to Gibson your concern about lead poisoning in one of your patients. I knew immediately I should not have done so. It did not help to convince Gibson of our concerns, of course, and it has now exposed you to the same threats. I apologize."

Sarah shook her head and waved her hand dismissively. "I am not sorry you did that. Gibson and now the marshal need to know that we are together on this issue, that it is not just your individual campaign. But we should let that issue sit for now until we know more about the assay from the university chemist. Let's go see Dr. Stout first."

Thomas was certainly relieved that Sarah was not angry, but more inspired by how beautiful she was in her toughness.

They walked down Main Street on the west side to the bottom of Main Street and Dr. Stout's office. As they entered the office, Sarah had just the briefest flash of panic from her traumatic memory of operating in Dr. Stout's stained and dirty office. It was just so unkempt and cluttered. They rang the bell hanging near the door and could hear a heavy body thumping down the stairs. Dr. Stout's bulk filled the doorway as he came into the front office.

"Doctors," he boomed heartily. "Please have a seat," he said as he settled himself heavily into his wood and leather desk chair. "So good of you to visit. To what do I owe the pleasure?"

"We have a delicate matter to discuss with you as professional colleagues. We are hoping you can provide some guidance," Sarah said.

"Well," Dr. Stout said, "happy to help in any way I can. We doctors should always be supporting one another, eh?"

Sarah tried not to be annoyed by his pompous heartiness. "I have attended to a Chinese woman who works for Madam

Urban. She was severely beaten by a client recently. Her injuries will heal but she was terribly traumatized. She has accused a prominent man in town, which presents some difficult issues."

"Hmm," Dr. Stout said, "that is a very serious charge indeed. Why do you believe this woman? Do you have any proof?"

"We knew you would ask that, and, no, we do not have proof. But I do believe she is trustworthy. She has no reason to lie. She is exposing herself to a substantial risk of retaliation."

"Yes, yes, of course," Stout said. "Are you willing to share the name with me?"

"I said I would ask her before sharing the name, but I am comfortable doing so with you as a matter of professional collegiality." Dr. Stout smiled and nodded. "She claims the perpetrator is Mr. Gibson."

"Oh my," Stout said, an immediate look of concern on his face. "That is a serious charge indeed. I, of course, know Mr. Gibson well, as I do all of the prominent leaders in town. I always thought of him as a principled and decent man. But of course, we never know, do we? We doctors have the burden of seeing the best, but also the worst, in people. We see them in ways unknown to more casual acquaintances." He paused, looking thoughtful. "But, no proof, you said?"

"Not yet" Sarah replied. "She is recovering from her injuries, but I am very concerned about her safety, as well as the safety of the other women who work there."

"Yes, yes, of course," Stout said. "I can't really imagine Mr. Gibson being involved in a matter like this, so some sort of proof would be quite compelling. But no matter, we certainly should be concerned about all the girls who work with Madam Urban, shouldn't we?" He looked deep in thought as he pondered this news.

Sarah and Thomas were hopeful that Dr. Stout seemed to be taking the news seriously. Perhaps he really could be a source of wisdom and guidance. They gave him a moment to digest it.

"Do you have any guidance about how to proceed here?" Thomas asked. "It seems to us that telling the marshal will serve no purpose. The marshal all but works for Gibson and will simply pass the news along."

"Yes, I can see how that would be a problem," Stout replied, pausing once more in thought. "We certainly want to pursue justice, but the prominence of Mr. Gibson's position does present some problems. We may need to consider some other law enforcement options. I, of course, know a wide range of officers in the region, as well as the US Marshal in Salt Lake City. But we will need to proceed very carefully."

Stout maintained his look of thoughtful concern, but his mind was racing as he worked through this shocking information, like a duck paddling frantically beneath calm water. Gibson would be far from the first prominent leader in town to frequent Madam Urban's establishment and enjoy the hospitality of her girls. Dr. Stout himself had done so on occasion, but he always required a medical exam beforehand. This would not be the first time that a client took out his frustrations on one of the Urban girls. It happened with some frequency, but charges had never been filed. No one outside of Chinatown cared what happened to them. Dr. Stout was pleased that these doctors were seeking his support and guidance, and he needed to think carefully about what do with this provocative information, even without clearcut proof at the moment. All Sarah and Thomas had for now was the prostitute's accusation, and that wouldn't go any further than such accusations had in the past. The emergence of more objective proof would make this an entirely different matter indeed, and it was prudent that he be involved.

"I am thinking it might be best for me to make some discrete inquiries," Stout finally said, "perhaps with Judge Lawson, the local district court magistrate. He is a fine and wise man and could be quite helpful as we sort through this sticky situation. Do you know Judge Lawson?"

Sarah and Thomas looked at each other and shook their heads. "No, it appears neither of us do," Thomas said.

"He might assist me in approaching the US Marshal as well," Stout continued. "I think it best if I do this, since I am well-known to both men. It might be awkward for the two new doctors in town to be raising these concerns. But I promise you, I am taking this very seriously and will keep you informed of what I learn. Please let me know if any hard evidence becomes known."

"Thank you, sir," Sarah said. She noticed his now third reference to a lack of proof, but she did not acknowledge it. "We are so appreciative of your willingness to assist with this 'sticky' situation, as you call it. We were not sure of how you might respond."

"Not at all," Stout said. "We need to do the right thing here, wherever the matter leads. I appreciate very much that you reached out to me. Good for us doctors to stick together, eh?"

Sarah and Thomas bid their goodbyes and left his office.

"I'm quite pleased with how he took our news," Thomas said.

"Maybe, maybe not," Sarah said. "He did seem quite thoughtful and acted like he was taking us seriously. I was worried that he was too enmeshed with Gibson and his crowd. But something about his manner is nagging at me. Did you notice how he asked three times about whether we had any proof?

And he didn't ask for details when I said, "not yet," like he already suspected Gibson might be guilty."

"I did notice that, but perhaps he is just being appropriately cautious. It is, in fact, at the moment, just Madam Choy's word against what Gibson would likely say in denial. I believe Madam Choy as you do, and she has no reason to lie, in fact, just the opposite. But it does seem that Dr. Stout is taking this seriously, and his suggestion that he approach the local magistrate seems sound."

"I guess you're right. I suppose we should take him at his word for now. I don't know, something still bothers me." Sarah paused as she pondered Thomas's assessment and what her intuition told her, her brow furrowed in thought. "Alright, let's push ahead. I guess we don't have too many other options. What's our next step?"

"I understand your concerns," Thomas said, "but let's give him a few days and see what he says. In the meantime, let's send off our samples to the chemist at the university, as Mr. Bird suggested. Otherwise, I guess we just have to bide our time for now."

CHAPTER 17

Park City, 1897

$\mathcal{A}$ few days after the meeting with Dr. Stout, Gibson's messenger reappeared in Thomas's office. Sarah happened to be in the office at the time, visits by each to the other's office occurring with increasing frequency. They regularly shared discussions about their most perplexing patients, as doctors do, but there was a personal warming that was also perplexing.

"Another request by Mr. Gibson for your presence at a meeting, Dr. Wilson," the messenger said.

"No mention of coming at my convenience this time?" Thomas asked with a smile.

"No, sir," the messenger said, "I'm afraid not, sir," also with a smile.

"Did he ask for my attendance as well?" Sarah asked the messenger, without a smile.

"No, ma'am, er, Doctor, he made no mention of you."

"Please tell him I will be attending as well," Sarah said, still no smile.

"Yes, doctor, as you wish."

The messenger had barely walked out the door when Thomas gave Sarah a questioning look.

"I couldn't possibly let you go to that meeting alone," Sarah said. "We are in this together now. I am as deep into it as you are, maybe more so."

"But all we know at the moment is that he wants to discuss the lung disease issue. He has no way of knowing about your patient, nor any way to know about my snooping around the mine to get the dust samples. I don't want to pull you into any of that more than necessary. And we need to wait for the results of Dr. Stout's queries." He paused. "But," he said with a smile, "I am always happy when we can work together."

Thomas was indeed happy to work together on this matter or on anything else. He would not have blamed Sarah if she had not wanted to go with him to Gibson's office. By asking to go, the fullness of her commitment was that much more powerful. He liked the way they were becoming full partners in whatever happened. It energized Thomas's step as they walked up the hill together.

The late-winter day was cold, tempered by the late-morning sun. The warming sun and the spring in their step died with the grim and icy look on Gibson's face as they walked into his office. They were used to Gibson's plethoric bluster. His hard face was more frightening.

They were barely in the door when Gibson yelled across the office. "You," he said, pointing at Sarah, blustery, spittle flying. He stared at her, but turned away, unable to hold her piercing gaze. "The messenger said you would be coming. Why? What are you doing here? I did not summon you!"

"I do not need your permission to demonstrate my collaboration with Dr. Wilson!"

Gibson glared at her with contempt. *How dare this woman defy me! She is no better than a common whore! I don't tolerate this kind of backtalk from such a woman, or any woman for that matter.* Gibson replied through clenched teeth. "Fine! Just makes it easier to get rid of both of you at the same time." He turned back toward Thomas. "You're the one I summoned. We discussed what would happen if you did not drop your investigation of the miners' complaints. I understand you were observed prowling around the mine recently, without my permission and without any reason to be there. Surely you must understand that my foremen are everywhere, protecting the interests of this mine and its shareholders. I believe you obtained samples from the mine that you had analyzed by our local assayer. Mr. Bird apparently forgot who he worked for, so now he does not work for me, or likely anyone else once I talk to the other mine owners. We will be hiring our own assayer soon. As a result, his business is finished."

Gibson enjoyed the meanness of his words, and his twisted face matched the evil spewing from his mouth. Thomas and Sarah took a step back in the presence of his vicious hostility. They realized immediately that they were responsible for Mr. Bird losing what was likely his entire livelihood for simply doing his job.

"That is so unfair!" Sarah nearly shrieked in anger and surprise. "You have no right to punish him like that."

"I have every right to do whatever I want to protect this mine and its shareholders!" he yelled back. "He forgot who he worked for when he did your analysis and gave you that report!"

"It is our professional and ethical obligation to try to uncover the cause of the miners' illnesses, wherever it takes us," Thomas said. "I felt compelled to obtain samples of the dust so we could have it analyzed. You have no business retaliating against Mr. Bird for simply doing his job. It's your rock dust he was analyzing! You should want to know his results! Do what you have to do, but we are going to take this wherever it leads."

Thomas's pushback was not what Gibson expected based on their last meeting. He was shocked, maybe even perversely a bit impressed, by Thomas's aggressive response, but the surprise lasted only seconds. "I have absolutely no interest in what you believe to be your ethical obligation," declared

Gibson. "But I hope your dedication to those obligations will help you as an unemployed mine physician, because you are hereby terminated." He paused so his cruel words could sink in. "That is, however, not the least or last of your problems. We will be reclaiming your office equipment later today. It will matter little to you anyway because you are soon to have no need for any of it.

In addition, a number of prominent colleagues will be making clear to the fine people of this town that your skills and medical abilities are inadequate, that you are a charlatan like many so-called "doctors" that seem to pass through town, and that Parkites would be wise to seek their medical care elsewhere. Dr. Stout was fine enough for this town before you came, and he will be just as fine after you leave."

"And why do you think the fine people, as you call them, of this town will change their opinion so suddenly like this, given that they have seemed more than satisfied with my services to this point?" Thomas asked, the anger rising in his voice.

"Well, it will start with the parents of that boy who fell under the train and died a few days ago. They will be telling their friends that his life could have been saved, that you showed little care for the boy's life, and that they believe your skills are not what are needed for this town."

"What!?" Thomas yelled. "You know that is not true! The parents, as well as the townspeople who had gathered around the office, expressed their strong approval of my care!"

"Of course, they did", Gibson sneered. "I know that, but who am I to argue with the changing opinions of grieving parents, especially with a father who works in my mine."

Thomas felt the temperature drop from the cold deceit in Gibson's face. "So, you told him to change the opinion that he expressed to me that horrible night, the night when I did everything possible to save the boy's life, the night when I held him in my arms as he was dying, the night when he and his wife expressed their deepest appreciation to me for everything I did?"

"Not at all," said Gibson. "I expressed my deepest sorrow for their loss, and simply mentioned that a small increase in the husband's wages, perhaps a half dollar a day, might be forthcoming as an expression of the mine's support, especially if he had any concerns about your care he wished to express."

The corruption flowing out of Gibson's mouth flowed across the room like a sour fog. Sarah watched admiringly as Thomas stepped up his resolve. "We will not stop our investigation," he simply said. "We still have the same obligation to the welfare of the patients who consult us, irrespective of what harm you may cause to me."

"Do as you wish," Gibson said, turning to Sarah. "And you! No one will listen to you, especially once everyone finds out that you are taking care of a Chink whore, especially a whore who lies."

Sarah and Thomas were stunned by the revelation and threw shocked looks at one another. How could Gibson know about the assault? The only person who knew besides Madam Choy and Mr. Sing was Dr. Stout. It could only be Stout. As the reality of Stout's treachery became clear, their faces were transparent in their realization of what had happened.

Gibson's triumphant smile spread across his face as he saw Sarah and Thomas come to grips with the understanding that Stout had gone straight to Gibson with Madam Choy's accusation. "I see you are beginning to understand how this town works. You are not part of it, and now you will never be part of it. The Chinks are never believed, especially in this type of matter for which there is no proof, just one word against another. Just the word of a prominent business leader in town against that of a miserable Chinese whore. Your insubordination is now compounded by your naïve belief in justice. I am the justice in this town, as is the marshal."

"You are disgusting," Thomas said, with quiet sinister, "disgusting and evil."

"Well, the good news is that you won't have to worry about me, or meeting again, or any of this anymore because you will soon be gone. You have no further obligation to the miners since they will be consulting Dr. Stout for their care, and you will soon have an unequipped office in which to see any other random patients who may stumble in. And you," he said as he turned to Sarah, "You won't be here much longer either. I will see to that! Now, enough of this, pick up your final wages from the cashier and be gone."

"We are not done with this!" Thomas said, as they slammed the door on the way out.

The doctors walked slowly back down the hill, stunned, silent, pondering the corruption and brazen evil that had just assaulted them, aimless in their walking as well as in their discussion about what to do next. They could now only feel the cold wind, not the warm sun.

"Well, what do we do now?" Sarah asked. "I'm so discouraged I can't even think."

"I don't know," Thomas replied. "It's all quite overwhelming. All of our well-intentioned efforts, on both matters, have come to a dead end. Stout clearly betrayed our confidence and told Gibson about Madam Choy. We really have nowhere to go now with the assault charges without definitive proof. We may have exposed Madam Choy to possible retaliation, without any good coming from it. We could send the dust samples to the university, but to what end? Where would we go with the results? And what if microscopic silicate crystals were confirmed? How does that relate to the miners' lung disease? It is indeed so discouraging."

"And now we have more immediate issues," Sarah said. "Do we even have a future in this town? How do we even make a living?"

"I don't know," Thomas said. "But I take some heart that we are in this together." He turned and smiled softly at her. Sarah smiled back. Neither knew what the smiles meant exactly, but they were comforting in the face of so much treachery and intimidation. They were partners now as the threats around them seemed to multiply. The partnership had started with their admiration for each other's skills as physicians and scientists. Now there was something more.

Sarah warmed to Thomas's comments. She herself wondered about whether some sort of personal relationship was budding here, but Dr. Blackwell's visage loomed in her mind, admonishing Sarah that any personal relationship that detracted from a woman physician's responsibilities was forbidden. Sarah was beginning to wonder if that was the right advice for her.

As they turned down Main Street, they looked ahead to Thomas's office. The marshal had gotten there ahead of them, with two men and a wagon. Thomas noted, with not a small amount of irony, that the two men were part of the group with lung disease that he had examined in that very office. Or perhaps it was calculated irony on Gibson's part. He would do that.

It was obvious from the timing that this plan had been prearranged. The marshal had simply been waiting for the word from Gibson to proceed. They were moving every bit of Thomas's medical equipment out of this office—metal table, surgical instruments, medications, even the desk and furniture—and into the wagon.

Thomas thought about objecting but knew there was no point. *What am I going to do? Call the town marshal?* But then the marshal went a step too far, pushing by Thomas with his black bag that contained everything he needed for house calls and emergencies.

"Stop!" Thomas yelled. "That is personal equipment, not bought by the mine. It has nothing to do with your corrupt collaboration with Gibson!"

Marshal Bennett dropped it on the ground with a snort. "Ha! Won't matter whether we take it now or not. You won't have any need for it soon enough anyway. I'm not done with you! Nor you, lady!" he said, turning his attention to Sarah.

Thomas and Sarah stood on the sidewalk and watched with dismay as Thomas's medical equipment was hauled out of the office and loaded up. The workmen wouldn't look Thomas in the eye. They seemed to be as embarrassed as he was. A small cluster of townspeople had gathered at the commotion. When they came to town to shop this afternoon, they had not expected to witness such a scandalous event. The news would be all over town by the next morning.

The next several days proved how powerful Gibson's influence was in town. Thomas borrowed a few instruments from Sarah, cobbled together some furniture, and sent an order down to Salt Lake City to finish out his office. But visits to both of their practices fell sharply. Patients they had seen previously did not return. People turned their heads as they passed the doctors on the street, appearing to be in deep thought or conversation. Some even stepped off the boardwalk and crossed the street to avoid having to greet them as they walked by.

Gibson's influence reached to the farthest corners of Park City society. His lies about both doctors had been spread wide and deep throughout the community. Most Parkites either worked in the Ontario or had a business that supplied the mine, or had an interest in another mine with the same mining practices as the Ontario. They had reason to pay attention to Gibson's advice that they seek their medical care elsewhere than the offices of Doctors Wilson or Fletcher.

But there were a few who ignored the advice. They liked the doctors, liked their care, and liked doing exactly the opposite of what Gibson told them to do. Both doctors saw enough patients to pay their rent and put food on the table, barely. Women would sneak into Sarah's office so they could not be seen by their friends. The doctors knew, though, that neither of their practices were sustainable in the long run.

The lack of medical business had the unexpected benefit of giving them more time to be together. They were often seen walking together, deep in conversation, sometimes not even noticing how they were being shunned. Their conversation was usually about medicine, about the few patients they were still seeing, and about the miners' health problems. Talking about medicine was always engaging, but over time, they started to talk about their families, about how they grew up, and how they found their way to medicine.

"I have a feeling," Sarah said, "that you must have experienced great pain and loss as a child. It may not be apparent to you, but it seems to me that you have carried this trauma into your adult life as a physician. You seem tentative about your role at times."

"I think that is a fair assessment," Thomas replied. "But what causes you to think that? I haven't told you that much about my family."

"It seems to me that your confidence in your skills has been shaken by something, that you are reliving something from the past, something that takes away from the confidence that we all need so badly to stand up to the rigors and demands of a physician's life. That lack stands in sharp contrast to your actual skills and knowledge. You are an outstanding physician and surgeon."

"Well, you are correct, very impressive diagnostic skills," he said, hoping to lighten the mood. "I do mourn for the loss of guidance and love from my parents. The death of my mother when I was so young, and the deep melancholy into which my father sunk were great losses. He was so depressed and brooding that we talked little in his later years. I still see images of my family in my dreams, although they are more properly called nightmares. I thought they might decline over time and after moving here. They haven't."

"I am so sorry," Sarah said, placing a light hand on his shoulder. "Tell me what happened."

Thomas turned to her and told her his family's story. He managed a smile, a weak smile, but a smile, nonetheless. "My schoolteacher, Ms. Easton, filled in as best she could, but I know now I really needed more. I am so envious of the nurturing nature of your family and upbringing. They seem so supportive."

"Well, yes, they were, but I have my own issues. My family provided everything I could possibly need, but it turned out to still barely buffer what happened after I left for school. My family was wonderfully supportive of my ambitions. I just thought everyone was like that. Apparently not," she said kindly. "And then, of course, there was Dr. Blackwell. I have thought of her many times since we met in college. She was a powerful influence, but now I wonder whether she was maybe too much of an influence. I wonder if I learned the right lessons from her."

"Given the extraordinary barriers you had to overcome to follow in her footsteps, it seems that her wisdom and inspiration were very important to you."

"Maybe. Dr. Blackwell made clear that I had to be as good or better than any man as a physician. The pressure to succeed is enormous, and failure is unthinkable. She was clear that women needed to pursue the most difficult training and take on the most difficult patients just to be seen as being as good as men. That's why I came here, to be challenged with the most demanding cases possible. I think it is fair to say that I have not been disappointed! But I wonder at what cost."

What did she mean? Thomas wondered. *Is she talking about us in some way, something about our relationship? She is just an incredibly attractive woman, attractive both physically and personally. I am sorry she keeps mentioning Dr. Blackwell.*

"The medical challenges have been very satisfying," Sarah continued, "but now I have more immediate worries about how to pay my rent. Mr. Miller had been particularly gracious of late, making clear to me that I have a secure lease for my home and office for as long as I wish, but that is not fair in the long run, albeit very kind of him for now."

Thomas was relieved that Sarah shifted the conversation to more immediate worries about paying her rent. Their casual chat had been heading in a direction that was more personal than he could manage at the moment.

Sarah had turned to the Chinese community for support, and it was freely given, which deepened her shame at Stout's treachery. She could not bring herself at first to tell either Madam Choy or Mr. Sing about what Dr. Stout had done. Mr. Sing continued to ask Sarah for her help, and an increasing number of Chinese patients started to fill the many gaps in her now nearly empty schedule. She was often paid with vegetables, chickens, and beautiful pieces of embroidered cloth. It didn't pay the rent, but she didn't mind as long as she was doing good work. It helped buffer her distress at how she had failed Madam Choy. She often visited patients at home because she liked the quiet, clean, peaceful Chinatown neighborhood. She even learned to not jump every time a rock crashed on the tin roofs.

Finally, one day, the weight of her shame was too much, and she felt compelled to reveal her failure and her disgrace. "Mr. Sing, I need to tell you something that happened. Dr. Wilson and I tried to pursue guidance from Dr. Stout about Madam Choy's assault, believing that he was a trusted fellow physician. I am sorry to say that I was horribly wrong. I have learned that he informed Mr. Gibson and shared what I told him in confidence. I am terribly sorry. I fear I have put Madam Choy at some risk."

Mr. Sing said nothing. He did not look angry, but also not forgiving. Finally, he spoke. "I am very sorry to learn of this. Have you told Madam Choy?"

"No, I have not. I am so sorry again, Mr. Sing. I am pleased Madam Choy has recovered physically, but I have failed to achieve any sort of justice for her. In the absence of any proof of her allegations, I have nowhere else to go. What do you recommend?"

"It is only fair that Madam Choy is made aware of this. I fear now for her safety as well. If you agree, I would like to be the one to tell her."

Sarah could only nod silently, her throat tight and eyes red.

❈·❈·❈·❈·❈

Gibson summoned Marshal Bennett to his office. "Tell me what is happening with Wilson and that woman," Gibson asked. "I assumed they'd be gone by now."

"Not sure," said the marshal. "They are around town, seen together a lot. They took a trip to Salt Lake a few days ago. Not sure why. The rumor around town is that they are still seeing a few patients, mostly the woman going to Chinatown to take care of those Chinks. She seems to have quite a following there. Not sure why any self-respecting doctor would even go to Chinatown, let alone take care of those slant-eyes. I heard that she cured a kid with diphtheria. My wife heard it from the woman who does her laundry, but it must be a lie. Everyone knows there is no cure. Supposedly, the treatment had something to do with a horse. Just some fantastical lie like a lot of what goes on in Chinatown."

"I think it's time that they both leave town for good," Gibson said. "I tried to force Miller to evict that woman, but he told me off in a rather disgusting fashion. Not sure why he is so protective of her. I wasn't worried that much about the woman until I heard that she was seeing so many patients in Chinatown."

The marshal threw a sharp look at Gibson. The marshal knew why Gibson was worried. "She could stir up trouble there," Gibson said vaguely. "We don't need a bunch of uppity Celestials thinking they deserve medical care, or anything else for that matter."

The marshal's thoughts raced in several directions, protective of his employer's generosity, anxious about covering up a serious crime, and, increasingly, embarrassed at how completely he was in Gibson's control. It was shocking, although not surprising, when Gibson had confirmed Stout's news that the Chinese whore named Gibson as her assailant. Something about how casually he talked about it nagged at his conscience, more so than all the horrible things Gibson had done in the past. The marshal wasn't sleeping well, he couldn't discuss it with his wife, and he didn't know if there was the line that had now been crossed. Was there a line? What was next? Where would it end?

"I heard that Wilson bought some of his own equipment after we took back what we bought for him," Gibson continued. "He is clearly not getting the message. Maybe it's time for one of those mysterious fires to pop up in his office. Or maybe the woman's office needs to be disrupted a bit so she can't take care of her Chink friends."

"Surely you are not suggesting that an officer of the law would be involved in that type of harassment or coercion?" the marshal replied, trying to sound clever and facetious. Being Gibson's flunky was wearing thin.

Later that afternoon, all of the marshal's ethical ponderings were brought to a crashing halt by an urgent message from his wife, Effie, to come home immediately. The marshal was dismissive and abusive to nearly everyone he came across in his duties, but there was one person to whom he would always respond with such a request—his wife. Not even Gibson commanded the marshal's attention like Effie did.

He walked briskly up Main Street, over to Park Avenue, and up to his house. As he walked in the door, he was immediately overwhelmed by the wail of Effie sobbing and crying, holding tight to their eight-year-old son. The boy was coughing hard and sweat ran off his forehead. Effie was rocking the boy, trying to soothe him, to no noticeable effect. He had a greasy poultice on his chest. There were dishes of various brown and pasty liquids near the bed that she fed to him in small doses.

He mostly just sank into her arms and sobbed with each raspy breath. The cough was harsh and ugly.

The marshal's conflicts about Gibson were swept away by the fear in Effie's eyes. "When did he get sick?" he asked.

"Last night, but I didn't go in to see him until after you left this morning," Effie whispered, her voice hoarse from crying. "He started with a fever, then a little cough, then more fever, harder to breathe, now what you see. I am sure it is diphtheria." She could say no more but returned to holding and rocking with the boy.

Their other three children, two girls, five and seven years old, and a boy, four, cowered in the corner, hungry, scared. The marshal fed them as best he knew how, while Effie held the older boy, her tears dripping on his sweaty cheek. As the weak, late-winter light faded into evening, there was little to do except put the other children to bed and watch over the boy. They took turns overnight holding him, now in and out of consciousness. Everyone slept fitfully as they listened to him cough. The cough became harsher, deeper, more grinding. It hurt his sisters and brother just to listen to the coarse cough and breathing. And then they all heard the dreaded bark in the pre-dawn darkness. Doctor Stout was summoned, but he sent word he would not attend. He told the marshal they were doing everything known and he could do nothing more. It was in God's hands.

God decided it was time for the boy to die, which he did later that next afternoon, pale, wet, and then cold. Effie held him tight, rocking and sobbing, hysterical with tears. The marshal never cried, never shed a single tear, never a break in his grim face, but now he cried. He wailed to God, tore at his clothes, and cursed Dr. Stout. His face twisted in pain, and then he abruptly stopped. The pain was too much, and he felt shame for showing it. He composed himself as he thought a father should. He pried the boy from Effie's arms and wrapped him in a clean blanket. The marshal tried to hug Effie, but she did not respond. She was nearly as cold and lifeless as their dead son. She wept but had no more tears, and she had no more time to grieve.

Before the undertaker had even arrived to take the boy, wrapped in a clean blanket, the seven-year-old girl started coughing. The parents' desperation found no respite as they turned their attention to the girl. The mother held her in her arms as she had her son. The marshal was frantic and disorganized in his attempts to help, pacing aimlessly in despair. Effie mixed the same potions, used the same cool cloth on the girl's forehead, and rocked her in the same chair. The day passed in silent agony, except for a constant gagging cough.

The other two children cried in the corner of the living room as they watched their helpless parents. The girl's cough got worse, louder, gasping. The disease was moving fast. The marshal put the other boy and girl to bed, but no one slept. They all heard the barking harshness of the girl's breathing in the morning. Effie was out of her mind. She looked to her husband with wide and frantic eyes, and he looked back but had nothing to offer. The child held on to her life as hard as she could throughout the next day into an even more painful night, and finally gave up the next morning. They wrapped her in another clean blanket, waiting again for the undertaker.

The marshal and Effie held each other without words. They knew of a family that had been wiped out by diphtheria, six of seven children dying in a week, one a day until only one was left. They had seen the row of headstones for that family in the city cemetery and wondered what their row of stones would look like, each one headed by "Bennett Family."

And then the four-year-old boy started coughing.

Their Chinese cleaning lady came later that morning and walked into a silent house, Effie holding and rocking the four-year-old. The marshal sat with their remaining child, the five-year-old daughter, in the corner of the living room as they listened to the younger boy coughing.

"You," the marshal yelled at the Chinese woman, "out! Out of the house!"

The woman was taken aback by the anger in the marshal's voice but stood her ground.

"You," she said, unfazed by the marshal's belligerence, "you talk to lady doctor."

"Why would I do that, you stupid woman?" he asked. His exhaustion, but more his fear, just made him that much meaner, but he was desperate. He listened.

"She treat Chinese girl with cough, girl live," the woman replied.

"Is that the same horse story my wife heard at the laundry?" he asked. His shame at his helplessness was overpowering. When he had heard about the miracle of the girl who lived after receiving the strange horse treatment, he had reacted with his usual sneer and scorn, but that was then. Now he had two dead children, cold, lying in blankets waiting for the undertaker. The nightmarish vision of his remaining children being loaded into the undertaker's wagon flashed before his eyes and he gasped, wiping his eyes to make the image go away. The fear that he could not protect his remaining children fought with his hatred for everything about the Chinese. Hatred won out, for the moment.

"Get out!" he yelled at the woman, who bowed slightly and crept out.

And then Effie spoke. "What did the cleaning woman say?"

"Nothing," the marshal said dismissively. "She is just talking nonsense. I am going to try to get Dr. Stout again."

"What. Did. She. Say?" Effie demanded, more loudly, crying with both fear and anger.

"She said to get the woman doctor, the one who supposedly cured the Chink girl. I would never consider doing such a thing."

"What?!" Effie screamed. "You would ignore even a small chance to save our child just because you hate the Chinese? What kind of a father are you?"

The marshal cowered before Effie's anger, and he felt ashamed. *What kind of a father am I indeed? And what kind of a husband? I would do anything for Effie, for her expectations of me, for my family. But a Chink girl recovered from some treatment that involved a horse? Really?*

At that moment, there was a soft knock on the door, and the marshal yanked it open.

"What?" the marshal yelled, tortured with his feelings of shame and helplessness. Gibson's messenger stood there, small, cowering.

"I'm sorry, sir, I know you have sickness in the house, but Mr. Gibson requests your presence at his office. A matter has come up that requires your attention."

"No, what? I can't, tell him I must attend to my child," the marshal replied, barely controlling his anger.

"Mr. Gibson is aware of your sick child but demands your attendance to an important issue."

"Is he aware that two of our precious children have died? Is he aware that we are out of our minds with grief? What kind of man is he to think that his work is more important than that? This is my answer to Mr. Gibson's request," he bellowed as he grabbed the messenger and threw him toward the door. The marshal fell against the wall, exhausted, his heart aching, his emotions raging as the messenger staggered out the front door.

"And you will go out right behind him and get Dr. Fletcher!" Effie yelled as she pushed him toward the door. His mind was wild with fear, but he would do what Effie told him to do.

Sarah sat at her desk in the front room of her office, mulling over the report she and Thomas had received from the chemist at the University of Utah. The report, short and precise, described the examination the chemist had conducted on the dust. He had confirmed the level of lead found by the assayer, with exact agreement as to the percentage, and went on to report on the crystals seen under the microscope. He compared them to other known samples of dust and rock in his library and concluded with fair certainty that they were indeed silicates, as the assayer suspected. What that meant, he could not say, but he speculated that inhaling dust with those crystals could have harmful effects on the lung. Like Mr. Bird, he was also not a biologist nor a physician, but he suggested that a microscopic examination of the lungs of a miner who died of the lung disease might be useful as a way to understand how the crystals interacted with the lung tissue.

She pondered this recommendation and wondered how they could possibly conduct such an examination. Postmortem examinations conducted for the sake of understanding why a patient died had been performed in Europe for centuries and in the United States as early as the 1500s, but they were still viewed with some suspicion. While the postmortem examination of patients who died was thought by physicians to be a way to understand how disease caused death, it was seen by society and family members as a way to cover up for the physician's failures. Securing a lung specimen from a miner who died with the same symptoms they had identified, especially the blue lips, seemed impossible. It was time to discuss next steps with Thomas.

As she swiveled her chair to walk out of her office to see Thomas, a large shape appeared in the doorway, backlit by the glare of the morning sun hitting the front of her office. She didn't need to see the hulking body's face to know who it was.

"If you've come to take my medical equipment, I will remind you that it was not purchased by Gibson. It is all mine!" she snapped at him. There was no response.

The man walked into the shadowed room slowly, dragging his feet. Sarah could see that it was indeed Marshal Bennett, but it was not the marshal to whom she had become accustomed. She had never seen him like this, fear on his face, weakness in his limbs. He looked exhausted and small despite his size. Her personal anger faded quickly, replaced by her innate clinical curiosity. She was not sure what had happened to him or how to inquire, so she simply nodded slightly to the marshal and asked in a softer voice, "Is there some other matter with which I can help?"

"Ma'am, er, uh, Doctor, I need help. My wife needs help. Effie's her name. Our son is dying. We need you." His voice cracked and she barely heard the last three words. They were so hard for him to say, and he could barely get them out. This was not the marshal she knew, not the marshal she feared sometimes and hated always. This was something else and someone else.

"How can I help?" she said. While the marshal struggled to be the father he needed to be to help his family, Sarah had no difficulty easing naturally into her role of physician. But she was cautious. She had never seen the marshal like this, and it was confusing. She saw his tortured face, creased with hope that she held magical powers, fighting with his deep hatred for her. She could see him wanting her to be a physician like any physician, duty-bound to care for him, his family, and their needs. Most of all, she could see his deep anger that he had to ask for her help at all. He needed her, and he hated needing her.

"My son is sick, maybe dying, probably dying," the marshal said, in a weak whisper. He continued in short, wheezy gasps, able to get out only short phrases with each gasp. "Diphtheria, two children have already died. Now our youngest son is sick with the fever. My wife is out of her mind.... I am out of my mind," he cried, sobbing, rocking back and forth. She was afraid he would collapse. He was far too large for her to catch if he did.

"Please sit, marshal. Have you consulted Dr. Stout?" she asked. The marshal collapsed in the chair.

"For the boy, the first one to get sick. Stout was no help, said it was in God's hands. God or no, the boy died. Then the seven-year-old. My wife and I cannot bear to lose another." He paused, not sure how to push on. "I, uh, heard you fixed a Chink, er, sorry, I mean Chinese girl with diphtheria. Our cleaning lady told us."

Ah, Sarah thought, *now I understand. And now I see exactly the dilemma that I need to face.* "Yes, I did indeed successfully care for a Chinese girl a few weeks ago. I have some training from medical school in a new treatment for diphtheria. It is highly experimental, but it has shown some promise in one child, the Chinese girl you mention. There is much yet that we do not understand and need to explore."

The marshal looked sharply at her when she referred to "we do not understand." He hated having to consult her in the first place, and now he was even more sorry he had to ask for her help.

"But the situation is more complicated than that," Sarah continued. "I would not want to penalize your child for the conflicts you and I have had, but I would not be comfortable using an experimental treatment like this on your child. There is an inevitable risk that you would distrust my motivations and decisions, including blaming me for any complications. To be blunt, I do not trust you. I am appalled by the way you do Gibson's bidding at the expense of the health of the miners. Our relationship is just far too complicated given the nature of this experimental approach."

Sarah's comments about Gibson revived all of the marshal's uncertainties about his own behavior, but he needed Sarah's help. He couldn't allow his past allegiance to Gibson, however much he now despised it, get in the way of receiving the help he so desperately sought. "What about your professional obligations?" the marshal cried in desperation. "Obligations that you yourself have emphasized more than once with Mr. Gibson. Don't those apply to my son, no matter what has gone on between us? Was everything you told Gibson about your responsibility to the miners just a sham?"

Sarah was stunned by how right the marshal was. She felt shame that her first reaction was to treat the marshal and his family differently because of who he was, but she couldn't help it. The hatred was just so deep. It was difficult to suddenly feel compassion for someone she detested so much, but he was right. The situation was actually quite simple. The marshal's son was sick, very sick, and she had a potential treatment that could save his life. Her decision should be obvious.

The marshal saw conflicting emotions fly across her face, as she had seen the same in his. "I am begging you, Doc. My wife is begging you. We cannot bear the loss of another child," he sobbed. "I understand we have had our problems, but I am pleading as a father with you as a doctor to do whatever you can. I understand this is an experimental treatment, but we have no other hope. Please give Effie and me hope!"

How could such a corrupt and disgusting man still love his wife and family so much? she asked herself. *He is clearly suffering so much, as his wife must be as well. She should not be punished because she is married to the marshal. And the boy not at all in his innocence.* "Very well," Sarah conceded. "I am willing to exam your child and explain to you and your wife what I might do. I make no promises, but you are correct. My ethical obligations require me to do this."

"That is all I ask," he said, quietly, carefully. "I make no promises, either. I am simply a grieving father and husband who seeks your help and expertise. Thank you for agreeing to come."

CHAPTER 18

Park City, June 1898

Sarah followed the marshal up Park Avenue, just a few cross streets south from her office to his home at 137 Park Avenue, near the St. Mary's church. She had no idea that he lived so close, yet the neighborhood was so different. As they proceeded up Park Avenue, the houses became larger and more established, not the modest, faded buildings like her office. She admired his house, large, well-kept, generous for a marshal's salary it seemed to her.

She walked up the steps behind the marshal and entered the front room of the house. Death suffocated her with its weight. The room was dark, the shades closed, and dust drifted in the small shafts of light that cut across the room. The house smelled of sweet sickness, and the only sound came from Effie, sobbing in the far corner, holding and rocking her son. Clothes were scattered around, dirty dishes piled on the kitchen table, the house unattended. The normal rhythms of family life in this fine house had been destroyed by the diphtheria germ. The house itself was dying, just as the third child was dying. One more death could be the end of the family itself.

Effie looked at Sarah with unsaid questions for which there were no answers. Sarah approached and knelt down next to her. She laid a hand on Effie's shoulder and the other on the child's head. She could both console and assess with one tender movement. The child's skin was hot and dry, past sweating, a sign of impending crisis. His breath was rasping and harsh, the wheezing rattle of death. Sarah heard the high-pitched musical notes of air moving through his small and diseased airways, not in the lungs but higher up, in the throat and trachea. Air was whistling through the narrow airways, now almost closed. Sarah had always thought the musical notes from the breathing of a child with diphtheria were really quite beautiful, if only they were not the song of death. The child's eyes were sunken from dehydration, the spaces between his ribs sucking in with each breath.

Sarah turned away and walked back to the marshal. He had stayed back, afraid to approach. He could not look at his dying son. His eyes pleaded with her to do something, anything.

"You understand that the treatment I have developed is very experimental?" Sarah asked, but not really asking, more a warning. "I don't know if the serum will be strong enough. Or perhaps it will be too strong. I cannot be certain. Your son is very sick, and he is far along in the illness." Then she paused to choose her words carefully. "It might just be too late. Or he could have a severe reaction to the serum. There are many uncertainties and risks." She described the treatment in more detail.

The marshal had the same look as did the other parents to whom Sarah had told this story—shock, disbelief, resignation, and finally acceptance of something that he could not comprehend. He nodded, almost imperceptibly, torn by competing feelings of fear and hope. He was embarrassed that he was asking for help from a woman doctor, particularly this woman doctor. But he could not help himself from doing so, and he found himself oddly reassured by her calm and authoritative manner. She had a steely resolve he found calming, not overly rigid but clearly in command, different from the male doctors he had known. While she explained the treatment with expertise, her dark eyes held his with a confident kindness.

The earth had tilted, and he had no other choice than to trust his child's health with this doctor, woman or no. He nodded to Sarah to continue, his mind made up.

"You wish for me to proceed?" she asked to confirm his agreement.

"Yes."

"I will return within the hour."

"I will come with you," he said. "There may be problems at your office."

"What kind of problems?" she asked, afraid of the answer and especially afraid of what it might mean for the serum she had stored in her icebox. The marshal did not answer.

They walked back down Park Avenue, both hurrying in fear, one being the potential cause of the fear, the other the potential victim. They came up to her office just as two men kicked open the locked front door.

"Stop!" the marshal yelled sharply at them.

"But we're just doing what you told us to do," one man said. The marshal was both embarrassed and angry, angry at them for what they had revealed, angry at himself for the truth, embarrassed for how his family's life was now so dependent on the object of Gibson's hatred.

"Just go!" the marshal yelled. They did, looking at the marshal as if he had lost his mind. Perhaps he had.

Sarah ran into her office, through the door in the rear of the front room and to her icebox in the back. She gasped with relief. The serum was there, safe, clear, yellow-tinged, ready for use. She grabbed the entire bottle, two large syringes, and a rubber tourniquet, and threw it all into her medical bag.

They ran back up the street to the marshal's home. Sarah gently pried the child away from Effie and placed him on the bed. She thought she should be explaining the same issues to Effie as she had to the marshal, but the mother collapsed when

Sarah took the child and could not be aroused. The marshal just nodded and told Sarah to go ahead.

She tightened the tourniquet and waited for the dehydrated veins to fill with the boy's thick blood. As she waited, she filled a syringe with serum. When a vein finally revealed itself, she inserted the needle, released the tourniquet, and pushed the plunger on the glass syringe to the hilt. And as before, she settled down to wait.

"I will be staying to monitor the child, if that is acceptable," she said.

The marshal nodded, too tired to speak, but he was thinking about something else. He could not ignore the embarrassing incident with the men at her office. He felt obliged to address the tension that hung over both of them like a dark curtain. "You know I was just doing what I was told," he said, meekly, defensively.

"I understand you believe that to be true," she replied. "What I don't understand is why the town marshal should feel obliged to do the bidding of a mine manager." *I know he wants to smooth over our relationship,* she thought, *but I'm not having it. I'm not letting the past fade away just because he is suddenly so appreciative of my care.* "I am committed to caring for your child in any way I can, because that's what responsible physicians do, as you so clearly reminded me. But, however appreciative you may be of that care, it doesn't change anything about my opinion of your conspiring behavior with Gibson."

She was so fierce in living her value system, the marshal thought. *I wish I could do that with Gibson. Maybe it's not just an issue of my disgust with being controlled by Gibson. Maybe I have some ethical obligations as well. Her obligations mean my son may not die. What do mine mean?* "Perhaps I can talk with Mr. Gibson, and you and he could find some sort of compromise," he said.

"Do as you wish, but there is no compromise for my obligation to do my job, which is what Gibson wishes for me to stop doing. I will not accept any so-called compromise that prohibits me from fulfilling my responsibilities to my patients. Nothing either he or you could say or do will change that responsibility."

She turned away from him. She had no interest in continuing this conversation, and certainly no interest in giving the marshal sudden absolution. The marshal had no response, whether from agreement and understanding, or just sheer exhaustion, but Sarah thought she saw a fleeting, thoughtful look before the usual scowl returned. She settled in for what she knew would be a long day and night.

Like the Chinese girl, the boy had a shaking chill several minutes after the injection and cried out in what seemed like pain, but he was barely conscious. Sarah examined him and found his heartbeat to be strong and regular, perhaps a bit faster with the outcry and shaking, then a bit slower than with her first exam. There were some raised splotches on his skin, also similar to what happened with the Chinese girl. Sarah hoped this was a good sign, that the serum was still active and doing its good work as before.

The marshal gasped as the boy shook, certain this was the end of the boy's life. He looked at Sarah with eyebrows raised, mouth open, expecting her to tell him the worst.

"I think the reaction has passed," Sarah said, anticipating his unspoken question. "I have seen this in one of the two children I have previously treated, and it did not cause any permanent harm."

"Two children?" the marshal asked. "I know of only one, the Chinese girl who was cured. What happened to the other child?"

"Let's just focus on your son for now," she replied.

The day eased on. The sun arced across the sky and dropped behind the western ridge. Evening came early in the deep canyon, and the temperature outside dropped despite the coming of spring. Sarah dozed. Then the quiet room started to stir. Effie awakened and took some soup and bread.

"The doctor has administered her treatment," the marshal explained to Effie. "The boy had some sort of reaction, shivered, a rash, but she seems to think that is a sign the treatment is working. It happened with the other girl."

Effie just nodded numbly. She was groggy and had heard none of Sarah's explanation to the marshal. All she knew was that this woman doctor offered at least the potential for hope, hope that her precious son would not follow his brother and sister to the grave. Effie would allow Sarah to do anything for that small shred of hope. She didn't need to know more.

But she had another agenda that had nothing to do with her son, but everything to do with her husband. She pulled him off into the corner.

"I have heard around town that Mr. Gibson is trying to run these new doctors out of town. Are you involved in that?"

"Don't ask me about my work," he snapped at her. "I have told you, it's my business, not yours." His anxiety about his son, concern for Effie, and waning devotion to Gibson were no match for his innate meanness.

"It's my business if this doctor is taking care of my son!" she snapped back, in a shrieking whisper. "She is a good doctor. She is kind, she is smart, and she has shown love for my child!"

Her reference to "my" child was not lost on the marshal. He could feel Effie drifting away. Sarah stirred in the far corner. "Shh," the marshal shushed her with a finger to her mouth.

"Don't shush me! What are you doing to her?"

"Mr. Gibson doesn't want her, or that new guy, Wilson, messing around in the mine's business. They have some wild ideas about how the drilling is making the miners sick. Gibson just fired Wilson, and she is kind of a partner, so he wants her out of town as well." The marshal anticipated an explosive reaction. He was not disappointed.

"What?! What do you mean leave town? She is a good doctor, and we need good doctors. We certainly didn't get any help from old Doc Stout! You have no business being involved in something so disgusting, especially now!"

She looked at him in a way he had seen many times before, a look that required no further words for her to send a message, a look as legible as if she had written it down. With just that one look, he knew what she expected him to do. She stared at him, waiting for him to respond, to acknowledge she was right, anything.

The marshal looked down, sheepish, embarrassed. He knew exactly what she wanted to hear, but it wasn't that easy. With Effie, it was an issue of emotion. With Gibson, the issue was financial, something Effie knew nothing about. The only way they lived in this fine house, the only way Effie shopped at the finest stores, was because of Gibson's payoff for the marshal's loyalty. But how could he possibly equate that to what he hoped was Sarah saving his boy's life? He struggled to find some sort of equivalence there, but he couldn't hold two competing thoughts in his head at the same time. He was too exhausted. He nodded slightly to Effie. She nodded back and laid down next to the boy, asleep almost before her body settled on the blanket.

Sarah slept fitfully, turned and tossed on the blanket on the floor, and woke from time to time to listen. Each time she awoke, the boy's breathing sounded better, quieter, less harsh, a little slower, a little deeper. She fell back asleep, reassured.

The morning light woke Sarah, and she immediately knew that the boy's progress had continued. His breathing had slowed and was almost quiet. Effie and the boy were sleeping comfortably nestled with one another. The marshal was not to be seen.

Sarah examined the boy briefly. He was warm, but not feverish, perhaps just from lying next to Effie. His color was better, some pinkness in his cheeks. The boy looked at the doctor with no recognition, really just seeing her for the first time. He gave the doctor a small, wan smile. Sarah smiled back and stroked his thin hair. Effie awoke with Sarah's light touch.

"Effie, please continue to give him fluids, but no food yet, just water and broth, a little milk if you wish. I think the disease may have turned and your son will continue to improve, but I do not want to be prematurely optimistic. I will return at the end of the day to check him."

"Thank you, thank you," Effie said, grabbing Sarah's hand. "I don't know what you did, but my boy is better, and that is all that matters." She paused, and a different look came over her face, strong, confident, commanding, a look Sarah had not seen before. "I know you have had a difficult time since you arrived. I think my husband is responsible for some of that, for which I am sorry. I did not know women could be doctors, but you clearly know what you are doing, whatever it has to do with the blood of horses." She gave Sarah a small smile. "I have made it clear to my husband that he needs to make things right with you. I am quite certain he will do so." The smile got bigger, more confident, a knowing nod of her head that Sarah understood completely. Effie stroked Sarah's hand and gave her a hug.

"Thank you," Sarah replied. "I am committed to this town and everyone who lives here, no matter what others may think of me. Any help that would allow me to continue to do that would be most appreciated."

Marshal Bennett walked into Gibson's office. He had left the house early in the morning, knowing even without medical training that his son would live. His heart was full of gratitude for what Sarah had done, and equally full of shame for all that he had done to her and for Gibson. Gratitude, or shame, or both or neither, Gibson's financial control over the marshal and his life returned to the front of his thoughts. He was back in Gibson's office, subject to his whims and anger, and most immediately afraid of Gibson's reaction to his refusal to meet with him the day before.

"Mr. Gibson, might I have a word?" the marshal asked.

"Certainly, if you think you have time for me now! Where were you yesterday when I sent for you?"

"I apologize, sir. I was with my wife and ill son, as I think you were told. We are still grieving the loss of two of our children in the previous days, and I had to stay to help care for my family. What is it I can do for you now?"

"Yes, I am aware of your family's loss. You have my deepest condolences." The marshal thought Gibson had never sounded so insincere.

"It is laudable that you feel your fatherly responsibilities so strongly," Gibson said. "You should remember your responsibilities to me equally so! Are those troublesome doctors still here?"

"Yes, they appear to be. That is what I wanted to discuss as well. Doctor Fletcher has been caring for my son, and she was very impressive. I implored her to try the treatment that apparently saved the life of another child, an injection of serum from a horse infected with diphtheria. She did so and my boy is better this morning, his breathing eased up. He had some sort of shivering reaction right after the injection, but no harm ensued. He is clearly better now. My wife is so relieved!"

"What?! What did you let this snake-oil huckster of a woman do to your son?" Gibson said with dripping shame. "You let her treat your child with blood from a horse?! You are as stupid as those Chinks, and as gullible as she is deceitful. This is even more reason for you to help her see the benefits of leaving town."

That's it, the marshal thought. *It's one thing to use me, or to abuse the woman doctor, but it's quite another when Gibson thinks I would carelessly risk my child's life. This man has humiliated me for the last time. I know I have done some things of which I should be ashamed, but I do have limits, money or no, not to mention what Effie thinks of this.* "All I know is that my boy was going to die twenty-four hours ago but is now alive and recovering. This 'huckster,' as you call her, saved our son and saved our family," the marshal replied defensively. His resolve hardened, and he now felt only the indignation of Gibson's abuse.

"I can't believe you fell for her crazy ideas!" Gibson spit back. "The child was clearly going to survive anyway, with or without horse blood, whatever drivel that is. We all know there is no treatment for diphtheria. You said so yourself when you told me about that Chink girl. All of this is even more proof that this woman is a dangerous, babbling charlatan," Gibson bellowed. "If I want the doctors gone, it's your job to make it happen. You will do what I tell you to do. Or perhaps it would help if I pulled out the balance sheet for the so-called loan I made to you, the loan that will never be repaid. You do recall that, I assume?"

Gibson sounded as blustery and harsh as ever to the marshal, but he knew him well. He heard something else. It was fear. Gibson hid the fear in his plethoric face and abusive words, but the marshal could see a fine sheen on his rough forehead.

Gibson reached for the ever-present fine silk handkerchief in his coat pocket to wipe his face, but it was not there. He looked confused as his eyes scanned the room. Then his gaze locked back on the marshal again. The marshal might need some further encouragement to do his bidding. "I trust you understand that our financial arrangement is not permanent and can be withdrawn at any time?" Gibson hissed, snake-like.

The marshal seethed inside. "You would hold my entire family, or at least what's left of it, hostage to my continued collaboration at this time of grief and loss? I won't have it! You do not own me!"

"Oh, I disagree. I absolutely own you. I can have the same workers who gutted Wilson's office do the same to your home. Your family could be out on the street in an hour! And never forget it!"

The marshal's internal rage started to seep out of his pores, bitter and acidic. His son's life, Effie's anger, Sarah's compassionate care, his pride as a man. All of it washed over him in a cleansing heat. He clenched his fists, aching to strike Gibson. The brutish way Gibson exerted his control over the marshal was now fully visible in all of its ugliness. At the very same moment, he realized now was not the time for violence. He paused for several moments, letting his anger and shame settle, letting the boil come down to a simmer, before he spoke.

"No need," he said, seemingly suddenly contrite, eyes on the ground in front of him. "I will take care of it." What he meant by that he did not fully understand, but it did not mean the same thing to him as it did to Gibson. In some subconscious, ill-formed way, much like the decision Thomas had made under similar circumstances, the marshal knew that he needed to maintain the relationship with Gibson, at least for now. It all came down to his own pride, to his resentment at being Gibson's stooge, no better in Gibson's mind than any of his other lackeys. It was all so clear to him now, for the first time. He had slowly become nothing but a shell of his former self. He would not put up with Gibson's abuse any longer, but to do so meant he had to swallow his shame for just a little longer.

"That's what I wanted to hear," Gibson bellowed. "I know you are not that bright, but I am pleased to see that you are smart enough to understand where your loyalties lie." He waved off the marshal, as if he was throwing out trash. "You are dismissed."

The marshal returned to his office, wrestling with his confusion and his shame, pondering where to go from here. He wished he could ignore the charges of assault made by Sarah. He had done so many times in the past with the most upstanding Parkites, and there was still no proof in this case. He knew at some subconscious level that the Chinese woman was telling the truth, but that was not the point. He didn't really care about the prostitute, nor about Sarah for that matter. This was about him now, about his pride as a man. This was between him and Gibson. Charging Gibson might lead to a solution to his resentment, but without proof, nothing would come of it.

The marshal left the office to return home later that afternoon. His wife had sent word that their son continued to improve, sitting up, eating, smiling. The marshal looked forward to hugging Effie and holding his son. He would thank Sarah. That was only the right thing to do, but he would not apologize. He had already moved on. This was not about the doctors anymore. It was between him and Gibson. He had to figure out how to get rid of Gibson. If that solved the doctor's problems, so much the better.

As he approached the front door of his home, Sarah came up the street from her office. The two of them met at the front door just as the marshal's deputy ran up, breathless from the hill up Main Street.

"Marshal, I just heard from Mr. Sing, the Chink, er, I mean, Chinese elder," as he looked sheepishly at Sarah. "Sorry, ma'am," he stammered.

"Yes, yes, what?" the marshal asked sharply. He wanted to see his wife and son.

"Mr. Sing asked that we come to attend to someone who died," the deputy replied.

"Why can't you take care of it?" the marshal demanded.

"Mr. Sing was quite specific that it was you who needed to come," the deputy said. "I'm sorry, sir. He wouldn't say why."

"Perhaps I should be coming along as well," Sarah said. Something told her there was a reason she should be there.

"Yes, please. In fact, Mr. Sing asked for you as well," the deputy said.

"Alright, if we must," the marshal said. The marshal was puzzled about why Mr. Sing asked for Sarah. Something lurked in the shadows of the marshal's mind, but he was too tired and couldn't quite make sense of it all. The combination of his son's near-death illness and Gibson's abuse was exhausting. He turned to Sarah. "Please, come along if you wish."

"Of course," Sarah said, worry in her voice. She had slept fitfully but she was used to long nights. She was way ahead of the marshal in understanding the implication of Mr. Sing's request.

The two turned back down the street, followed the deputy down Park Avenue, turned right over to Main Street, and down the hill into the Chinatown hollow. Mr. Sing was waiting at the bottom and motioned for them to follow him. He led them to a bright yellow shack.

Sarah pushed ahead of the marshal and was hit with the sickly-sweet odor of carbolic acid as she entered the home. In the corner, in the same bed where Sarah had seen her many days ago, lay Madam Choy, dead. She lay curled-up in the corner of the bed, her skin gray and cold, a frothy yellow liquid and streaks of blood dripping from her mouth and nose. Sarah knew immediately how she died.

A few drops of carbolic acid, diluted in water, was an effective disinfectant for skin wounds. In stronger concentration, with the addition of benzalkonium chloride, it made a widely-sold and effective disinfectant for floors and toilets. At full strength, it was the preferred method for committing suicide by women and especially by prostitutes. The acid destroyed the esophagus and stomach, causing massive bleeding and eventually perforation and leakage of the acid throughout the chest. There were few more miserable and agonizing ways to die.

Madam Choy's face was twisted in the final agonies of her death. She had black discolorations around her mouth where the acid had burned her skin. A bottle of the sickening chemical solution lay over on its side on the floor near the bed, the acid dripping out. Madam Choy clutched some sort of white cloth that she had used when she gagged on the carbolic acid, the cloth now black and slimy.

Her pupils were markedly dilated, and the inside of her mouth swollen and raw. The smell of carbolic acid coming from the woman's throat was overpowering, and Sarah had to turn away before she gagged. As she turned, she saw a scrap of paper on the floor. She saw Chinese characters on the paper and handed it to Mr. Sing.

He read it, his face hanging in sadness. "It says," he read aloud to no one in particular, "I cannot live in the same world as this man. Please make sure he does not hurt anyone else."

Sarah carefully pried apart Madam Choy's lifeless fingers and pulled away the cloth. It was a handkerchief, delicate and of a fine weave, but it did not belong to a woman, more to a wealthy man. The corner was not stained black like the rest of it, and Sarah could see embroidered initials, "JGS", the "G" in the middle larger in the fashion of indicating the owner's last name.

All three looked at the handkerchief, each with their own racing thoughts. The marshal knew he now had the proof he needed to escape Gibson's control and restore his dignity. Sarah knew that she was responsible, at least indirectly, for this tragic death because of her naive trust of Dr. Stout. Mr. Sing felt only deep sadness for the miserable death of yet another desperate member of his community.

Sarah's guilt took her eyes first to the marshal. He could only nod, acknowledging the hate in her eyes. The handkerchief confirmed the accuracy of her charges of assault against Gibson. Had he believed Dr. Fletcher and done his job, Madam Choy would not have suffered this horrible death. The marshal's excitement that he now had proof to take down Gibson was overwhelmed by her piercing stare.

Sarah turned to Mr. Sing, her hate for the marshal and guilt for her actions turning to tears. "I am so sorry, Mr. Sing. This is my fault, at least in part. It is the marshal's fault as well for not believing us, but that does not absolve me. My trust in Dr. Stout was not justified, and Madam Choy has suffered as a result of my failure. I don't know how I can expect a patient to trust me ever again."

Mr. Sing looked at her silently, not angry but not forgiving, just the deepest sadness and then compassion, a soft and wise look on his face. "Our community has benefited from your care and from your kindness, and I hope we can continue to do so. We have a saying, "Better a diamond with a flaw than a pebble without." Please do not let this tragedy detract from your caring."

Mr. Sing's kind words released a flood of emotion and more tears from Sarah. She felt his blessing flow over her, and she reached out for his hand. He held her hands with both of his, and they held each other's gaze with warmth.

The marshal looked expectantly at Mr. Sing for some kind words.

"I am sorry," Mr. Sing said sternly to the marshal. "I have no wisdom for you."

CHAPTER 19

Park City, June 18–19, 1898

The Dewey Opera House buzzed with self-congratulatory conversation, hearty back-slapping, and the clinking of glasses filled with some of the best whiskey the Towey Bar could provide. The occasion was the monthly meeting of the Park City business elite—mine owners, managers, and the businessmen who supplied them. For one night each month, the town leaders set aside their conflicts, competition, claim-jumping lawsuits, and petty resentments so they could celebrate their power and success. Above all else, they were all committed to doing whatever was necessary to make sure their power and success continued. Ego-driven quarrels and personal animosity were one thing. Making money was something entirely different. The mood of forced goodwill and fellowship swelled along with the whiskey consumption.

The speaker this month was the mayor, and he was pleased with the opportunity to speak to this group of powerful business leaders. He was running for re-election, proud of how Park City had grown and thrived, and happy to talk about the role he played in that success.

"The city is growing and growing fast," he opened in his best campaign voice. "Close to four thousand residents, including several hundred of our Chinese brethren, call Park City home." The mayor's entirely gratuitous nod to the Chinese residents was his attempt to demonstrate his inclusivity as a liberal and welcoming mayor. No one in the audience cared.

"We have weathered the downturn in silver prices, disproved predictions of our own demise, and thrived when other towns have failed, and now like never before!"

There was wild shouting and applause at the last line, by all except one attendee. The marshal wasn't listening. All it took was the mayor referring to the Chinese residents for the marshal to flash back to the gruesome image of the dead Chinese woman, the blood and froth oozing from her mouth over her black coagulated lips. The images had grown more lurid with each flashback, as if the woman was reaching out to him in her death throes, mocking him for his corruption, begging him for help. Her anguished grimace was burned into the marshal's brain for all time. Since that horrific scene, he had thought a hundred times about the agonizing pain the woman must have experienced, her chest exploding with acidic fire before she died.

Her miserable death was traumatic enough, but finding the fine silk handkerchief clutched in her hand was shocking in a different way. It clearly belonged to Gibson, and it was the final piece to this tortured puzzle. The mayor's voice faded into the background. *I have the proof that both Gibson and Stout thought, or hoped, did not exist. Now what?*

The marshal paid no attention as the mayor continued to boast about the signs of Park City's success and strength as a community. "We can claim amenities and community organizations that no other mining town can claim, not even towns of far greater size," he said. "Our athletic association sponsors several sporting events each summer, including our great baseball team! The Irish, the foundation of this successful mining community and on whose backs this town was built, celebrate St. Patrick's Day with a thrilling parade and the most festive dance. We are proud of our hard-working Chinese residents and enjoy the pageantry, music, and drama of their New Year celebration." More gratuitous lies.

How best to bring Gibson down? the marshal asked himself. *I am so sick of his demands and tired of his assumption that he owns me. But he does own me, at least financially. There is no way we could have such a fine home for my family without Gibson's help.*

"Our schools are outstanding," the mayor continued, "both public and private, and I think we can agree that we all enjoy hearing the laughter of an increasing number of lovely school children at play." Sufficient whiskey had flowed at that point that the attendees cheered the mayor's treacly comments about the schoolchildren, even though many of them cared little about children, and certainly not about being asked to pay a school tax. The only reason they supported the schools was their necessity for attracting a fresh supply of new miners to town.

The mayor's self-important bragging continued, boasting about the town's fine hotels, a couple dozen markets and dry good stores carrying the finest food and clothing, jewelry stores with all manner of beautiful baubles for the businessmen's wives, butchers selling the finest meats and cheeses, several excellent restaurants, two banks, a telephone exchange, a gambling hall, and more than twenty saloons. The mayor carefully skipped over mentioning the same number of brothels in town. "Why, we even have a fire brigade, something of which much larger towns are envious."

The mayor knew his audience well and played to their greed. "The mines and town have thrived, even despite the national depression of several years ago, because of your outstanding business management skills. The miners are happy with their work and how they are treated." There was not even the slightest hint of ironic laughter at that comment.

That's it, the marshal thought. *It's all so clear now. I don't need to worry about the legal system to take Gibson down. The mine owners will do it for me. There were other sources of power in town besides the law, less accountable sources, more powerful sources. And I know how to use them.*

The marshal silently thanked the mayor for showing him the way.

The attendees applauded politely, pleased with themselves, amused by the mayor's blatant pandering and hypocrisy, and reassured that his re-election would guarantee the continuation of their generous lives. They retired to the back of the auditorium for cigars and samples of an even finer brand of whiskey that the Towey Livery Stable and Bar had held back just for this occasion.

The mayor's meeting finally wound down at about one o'clock in the morning, mostly because the attendees had finished off the last of Towey's fine whiskey. Patrick Fitzpatrick's night shift at the Towey Bar normally ended at ten o'clock, earlier than the bar's closing because he had worked up over the year since his amputation to be promoted to the position of bar manager. For that same reason, he had been assigned by the bar owner to staff the meeting and reception at the Opera House. He was depressed as always with the ostentatious arrogance of the assemblage of town leaders—wealthy, powerful, full of confidence in their abilities, and completely oblivious to the plight of the miners on whom their success depended, and for whose misery they were responsible. His repressed anger at how he been treated following his amputation welled up as it did nearly every day, every time he ran into something he used to do and now could not. He resented everything about the meeting and the participants, including the quality of the special Roxbury Rye Whiskey shipped all the way from New York City that the Towey Bar owner brought out for the event.

The quality of whiskey far exceeded the quality of the mayor's presentation, in Patrick's opinion. All he heard was a lot of blather about how happy the miners were and the high quality of life that was had by all in Park City. Maybe for others, but not for him, at least not since the accident. Working at the bar was fine, but nothing like the money he had made in the mine. He wished he could go back, perhaps as a lift operator or a foreman. He was more than qualified, but he knew Gibson would never allow him to be re-hired. It was too embarrassing to have a miner around who lost his leg in a mine accident, in Gibson's own mine.

Patrick was very observant and always paid attention at these events to the clusters of mine owners and leaders who huddled together during the reception to conduct the real business of the town. He wanted to know who was making deals and about what. The most powerful deals were not sealed with pen and ink but with a handshake.

Tonight's eavesdropping had revealed the most shocking news he had ever heard.

He had noticed a particularly interesting group of men gathered off in a corner, chatting in a hushed and conspiratorial way. The group included the marshal and the owners of the Ontario mine, as well as the owners of other large mines, including Thomas Kearns, the owner of the Silver King mine, and his superintendent, David Keith. What was notable was the absence of J. S. Gibson himself. Patrick busied himself around the group, cleaning up the dirty glasses and spilled whiskey. A measure of the arrogance of the mine owners and business leaders is that they never noticed people like him, unimportant people, poor people, people who worked for a living. He bustled around the group, busy but unobtrusive, listening carefully.

The town was riven with lawsuits, every mine owner suing every other owner for infringing on their claims, for following veins of ore into someone else's mine, for causing floods that shut down adjacent mines. Owners sold mines, bought other mines, merged, and demerged. It was chaotic, but purposeful chaos, always with the goal of making money. Gibson was the loudest and most obnoxious litigant of all, always complaining to everyone about everything. There must be a reason he had not been included in this group. The marshal was doing most of the talking, and the mine owners were paying close attention. The group would sometimes look furtively across the room to Gibson who was in another group.

After a spirited discussion with nods and handshakes all around, the marshal walked across the room to approach Gibson. He laid his arm across Gibson's shoulders, like a friend might, but Patrick could see that the disgust on the marshal's face. He whispered in Gibson's ear and pointed to the group of mine owners. Something important was happening.

The marshal gently guided Gibson over to the group.

One of the owners of the Ontario touched Gibson's arm, in yet another insincere gesture. "Mr. Gibson, a word please before you go. You have served this town admirably for many years, and you have managed our mine in a productive and effective way," the gratuitous words delivered with not the slightest embarrassment. "The marshal has informed us of some regrettable behaviors that cause us to think that the mine and the town would be best served if we transferred you to another one of our properties. They would certainly benefit from your expertise."

"What behaviors, what are you talking about?" Gibson yelled. Everyone in the room turned toward the group.

"Please, Gibson, lower your voice."

"I know of no reason why I should not continue in my current position," Gibson continued in a lower voice, but Patrick could still hear perfectly as he hovered around the nearby tables.

The owner did not reply, but simply tugged at his own silk handkerchief and pulled it partway out of his coat pocket. "You may be missing one of your fine handkerchiefs," the owner said. "The marshal told us where he found it."

Patrick had heard gossip about a prostitute who had been assaulted, and then died in a horrible suicide. There were whispers about a handkerchief. Could it have been Gibson's?

Gibson turned to confront the marshal, but the marshal's cold stare stopped him. He turned to the mayor and others, all of whom had the same icy glare. There was nowhere to turn for support or sympathy. But this had nothing to do with the Chinese whore. Gibson knew the owners hated him. He had amassed enormous influence over the town, but, more importantly, over even them as owners. He could see that the owners had finally had enough. They wanted to take back control, and the marshal had given them something with the leverage to do so.

Patrick quietly slid away, out of sight and out the side door. *Well,* he thought, *something interesting is going down here. Maybe there is justice in the world after all for people like me.*

Patrick had barely fallen asleep when it was time to wake up, four o'clock as always, his usual time no matter when he got to bed. As he did every morning when he awoke, he massaged the stump of his amputated leg. Doc Stout had said the pain would eventually fade, but it hadn't, at least not yet and that was more than a year ago. He still felt the electrical buzzing that shot around the stump and sometimes up his leg after working each night. Every once in a while, it felt like his foot hurt and he looked down in amazement to see if his foot had somehow reappeared, but it was never there. He had a decent wooden leg, but standing at the tavern bar for several hours every night made his leg tired, which made him tired, and caused the fiery pain to flare even more. With a little massage each morning, he could get back to sleep for a few hours before he had to be up and around. More massage later in the day would get him back to the bar in the evening when he would do it all over again.

As he lay in his boardinghouse bed trying to get back to sleep, thinking about the shocking news about Gibson that he had overheard, with the smells and snores of a hundred miners all around him, he suddenly smelled something else, a whiff of wood smoke. He came fully awake with a startle. Coal smoke was one thing, and a few wood stove fires were normally burning this early in the morning as the boardinghouse kitchens fired up. But this was different, fresher, closer, bigger. He was frightened.

Fire was the greatest threat to the very survival of a mining town, more than the landslides, avalanches, thunderstorms, deep snow, and economic downturns. The town was built entirely of wood and not that well. The wooden storefronts on Main Street looked prosperous, as the mayor had described so exuberantly, but behind the fronts was a maze of shacks and rundown buildings. The entire town was really just one big bonfire waiting to explode, driven by the canyon winds that flowed up the canyon during the day and down at night. There was a fire brigade in town, as the mayor had noted with pride, but the brigade's capabilities were modest at best, and a fire could easily expand far beyond its capacity if not caught in time. Once it took off, the entire town could become one huge pile of ash. It had happened to other mining towns, and they had died, never to recover. Their success had turned out to be fleeting and meteoric, and their resilience lacking.

A few minutes before Patrick awoke, a Chinese cook had been walking up Main Street, going south, to the American Hotel to start his prep work before the hotel served breakfast. He liked the sights and sounds of Park City coming to life in the pre-dawn darkness as he trudged uphill. People stirred in their homes, getting ready for the day. Two dogs barked, and a horse at the McFarlane stable whinnied.

But then he saw and heard something else, something garish and exotic, something he had never seen. A golden light flickered and reflected off the buildings behind the hotel. He could hear a crackling sound. Only a few steps farther on he saw the flames directly, flaring up from the kitchen and shooting out the back of the hotel. The flames lit the alley behind the hotel and the buildings backing up to the alley from Park Avenue, shooting higher and higher. He stopped, stunned, unable to comprehend what he was seeing. The shooting flames were beautiful in the darkness, beautiful in a horrifying way, paralyzing him. But he had to tell someone.

He screamed, turned and ran back down the street to the marshal's office, racing through the door panting and yelling in Chinese, waving his arms wildly. The deputy on duty at the city jail was asleep on his cot at the back of the office. He came awake groggily as the cook ran through the door. The deputy knew no Chinese words, and he was amused by the frantic arm-waving and jabbering. He always found the excitable nature of the Chinese entertaining. It didn't really matter that he couldn't understand the cook, because he generally didn't believe anything he heard from them anyway. But the cook was persistent, grabbing at him and trying to pull him out the door.

The cook's yelling and waving became even more frantic. The deputy begrudgingly stood up from his cot, pulled on his pants and boots, slowly buttoned his shirt, pulled up his suspenders, and walked casually out the door and moseyed up Main Street to investigate. The cook kept grabbing his sleeve to urge him on. And then the deputy understood why. In the short time since the cook first saw the fire, it had already consumed the back of the hotel, flames now licking at the edges of adjacent buildings.

"Did you do this?" The deputy yelled to the hysterical Chinese man. But the Chinese cook didn't understand, and the deputy didn't wait for an answer. He was focused on his one really important responsibility, maybe his only real responsibility, and that was to awaken and warn the town. He pulled his revolver and fired it three times quickly in the air to alert the town. He paused for several seconds and then fired the remaining three rounds. He had fulfilled his one responsibility and done his job. Now it was time for Parkites to do theirs.

Patrick heard the shots as he laid in bed. He knew now that the smell of wood smoke was not from Gertrude starting her own breakfast preparations downstairs. Less than a minute later, he heard the three high-pitched, screaming whistles from the Marsac mill. The mill security guard had the responsibility of reinforcing the deputy's revolver shots by pulling the steam whistle cord. The three shrill whistles could be heard for several miles around, up every canyon and down through the meadows, even more penetrating than the mill's constant pounding. The whistles awakened the entire town, including the volunteers in the fire brigade who started to gather.

Patrick jumped out of bed, pulled on his pants and shirt, and ran down the stairs from the dormitory and out the back door to see what was happening. He could see the glow of the flames reflecting off nearby buildings from the back of the hotel. The American Hotel was just a few buildings down from his boardinghouse, just below Dr. Wilson's office. The fire had already jumped to the building behind the hotel. The early morning down-canyon wind whipped the flames down the hill toward the north end of Main Street, but also up the side hill to the west, attacking the houses along Park Avenue.

Patrick saw the fire brigade coming up Main Street from the meadows below. They had a small wagon with a water tank and hand pump, and a small hose to match. Their dedication was admirable, but their efforts would inevitably be futile. They had no chance of stopping the fire, even responding as quickly as they had. What little water the fire brigade could spray on the fire seemed to spread it more quickly because of the kitchen grease.

The fire jumped to the next building to the north, a particularly unfortunate event. The building housed a hardware store, full of highly flammable and volatile paints, oils and thinners. When the fire burned through the store's wall, the building exploded as if a bomb had gone off. Strangely, the fire paused, as if it was thinking about where to go next. It seemed like it might die down after the violence of the hardware store explosion almost blew it out. Patrick watched the fire's brief pause, and it caused him to pause as well. The building explosion meant something, but he couldn't quite say what. The pause was brief, and the fire roared on to the north and west.

Every Parkite had poured into the streets and gathered at the sound of the Marsac whistle. They watched the fire with horror and looked back and forth at each other, speechless with fear and paralyzed with their impotence in stopping it. They tried to be productive by hauling their belongings out into the street, emptying their stores, businesses, and homes.

The publisher of the *Park Record* rounded up several townspeople to help remove the new printing presses that he had just bought and installed only months before. They failed because of the speed of the approaching fire, the weight of the presses, and the substantial way they had been installed. The purchase and installation of the presses had seemed like a good idea at the time, a reflection of the stability and permanence of the town. The loss of the *Park Record* presses and building might mark the end of the very stability it had tried to promote.

The assayer, Frank Bird, enlisted the help of several bystanders to remove the most important scales, equipment, and chemicals from his laboratory. Some of the chemicals and acids were highly flammable. He also managed to haul most of the bags of samples left in his front room out onto the street. Not at all randomly, and in fact quite purposely, he removed all the samples except those that had been left by workers at the Ontario mine. Mr. Gibson had made clear that the Ontario mine would have no further need for his services. The only redeeming part of his firing was that he would have no further obligation to deal with Gibson, always an unpleasant event. Gibson complained that Frank's assays were too conservative. Frank had barely removed what he could when the fire came roaring down the hill, jumped from the west side to the east side of Main Street pushed by the canyon winds. His shop was turned to ash, with small explosions from the chemicals in his laboratory.

As the fire worked its way downhill, it burned through the Episcopal Church on the west side of Park Avenue and then jumped on to the next house and the next. It eventually found its way to Sarah's office. When she heard the Marsac whistle, she had run downstairs to her office to try to salvage her medical and surgical equipment. Her surgical instruments were most important, especially a new set of instruments to perform trephination. Boring holes in the skull to treat brain injuries and bleeding was an ancient practice that had been restored anew by a few prominent surgeons on the East Coast. It seemed so radical to her, especially in a frontier mining town, to perform such a procedure, but her confidence was boundless, and she wanted to explore the surgery. There was no lack of head injuries in a mining town. She had read extensively about it and felt prepared should the need arise. She swept everything up in a large leather satchel and fled.

The fire roared down Main Street and created its own wind, flaring so high that it lit the entire town in its red-gold horror. It destroyed every building and business in its path, including Dr. Stout's office toward the bottom. He was not as quick as Sarah and had almost no time to evacuate his office. It was turned to ash like its neighbors, equipment and all. The fire flowed downhill from Frank Bird's office and down into the Chinatown hollow. It worked its way both up and down the hollow and burned all of Chinatown to the ground, leaving only the cast iron stoves, kettles, and stone fireplaces standing lonely in the deep piles of ash.

The Park City townspeople cared little about the loss of Chinatown, but they cared a lot about Rossie Hill, the neighborhood that lay beyond. In addition to the threat to the fine mansions on Rossie Hill, the neighborhood was the shortest route down the hill to the Marsac mill. The townspeople hoped that Chinatown would be a firebreak of sorts and the fire would stop, but it didn't, climbing quickly up to Rossie Hill.

The Marsac mill stood proudly at the bottom of Rossie Hill. If the fire reached the mill, it would shut down the stamping operations for months, perhaps more than a year. The productivity of nearly every mine in Park City, except the Ontario, would be severely reduced. The town's lifeblood would drain away. Revenue would fall and dividends would be suspended. The mines would fail, and therefore the town would fail, as had happened to so many mining towns in recent years. Rossie Hill was important to the comfortable lives of the wealthy families who lived there. The Marsac mill was essential to the town's very existence.

The fire spread up the Rossie Hill ridge to the south, consuming one large mansion after another, and at the same time, the down-canyon winds kept pushing the fire north. As each mansion turned to ash, the fire strengthened as it headed for the last few mansions at the bottom. After that, there would be little to stop the fire from consuming the mill.

The townspeople and city leaders looked on helplessly, searching for any answer to stop the fire. The call had gone out by telegraph to fire departments in Salt Lake City and Ogden. Their firefighters and equipment were loaded on trains and on their way to Park City. The response was admirable and well-intentioned but would be far too little and too late. By the time they arrived, perhaps by late morning, the town would be gone, likely never to reappear. The firefighters from Salt Lake City would arrive just in time to see the Marsac mill burn and collapse.

The city leaders, mine managers, and owners gathered in the apocalyptic piles of ash and debris in the Chinatown hollow. They had barely gotten to bed from their celebratory reception the night before, and now they looked with horror at the possible end of everything they had been celebrating. They huddled in the ash as the weak light from the early-morning sun tried to penetrate the lingering smoke of the Chinatown ruins. They looked up to Rossie Hill, murmuring among themselves, searching for ideas, finding none. They were masters of their lives and destinies but powerless in the face of the fire. They were confronted with a catastrophe for which they had no useful solutions. It would not be long before the fire took all the mansions, including the one owned by J. S. Gibson, the grandest on Rossie Hill.

As the leaders stood paralyzed, Patrick Fitzpatrick edged closer to the cluster and said just one word, "Dynamite."

The mayor and others turned to him. "What? What did you say?" the marshal asked.

"Dynamite," Patrick said again. "The only way to stop this fire is to blow a firebreak in its path and deprive it of fuel."

"And I suppose you will tell us you know how to do that," the marshal said, not only dismissing the suggestion but also its source. How could an amputee bartender possibly have anything useful to contribute to solving this disaster? But then he had a little tickle in the back of his mind, and a different thought took hold and started to grow.

"I do," Patrick said quietly. "Worked with dynamite all my life, until this," pointing to his leg. "I know how to do this." He couldn't believe he had spoken up, but the idea had just come to him in a flash as he recalled the hardware store explosion. It just seemed so right. Besides, no one else had any better ideas. Speaking up felt good, like he had something to offer, like he was useful. He hadn't felt like that in a long time.

"And where would you propose to create this firebreak?" the mayor asked, trying to look like he was taking charge, like he knew what he was doing, even if he didn't. He didn't really expect an answer, but he got one.

"There," Patrick said, pointing immediately up the side of the hollow and a little to the north at J. S. Gibson's home. "That house is at the crest of the hill. Once the fire takes that house, nothing will stop it until it runs straight to the stamping mill." Patrick amused himself that he had actually selected, mostly unintentionally but not quite, what turned out to be Gibson's house. It would serve him right for refusing to pay

Patrick's medical bills or considering him for other jobs at the Ontario. Plus, Gibson was getting fired anyway, so why would he care.

"What? No! You can't do that!" Gibson yelled. He was still processing the confrontation just a few hours ago, still trying to understand how his power and influence had suddenly disintegrated with the simple tug on the owner's silk handkerchief. He looked frantically from one person to the next, looking for support, looking for friends, wondering why they were all paying attention to this cripple. He looked pointedly at the marshal, who ignored him.

"You can't!" Gibson yelled again, but his anger was starting to sound like pleading.

The marshal backed away from Gibson, not responding to his screaming and abuse. Gibson grabbed the marshal's coat lapels and shook him, screaming spittle into his face. "That's my house, I won't allow it!" he said, the combination of arrogance and whining becoming even more awkward.

The marshal looked furtively at the mine and town leaders as they silently shuffled their feet in the dust. He saw subtle nods that Gibson missed in his desperation and anger. "Take your hands off me!" the marshal yelled back. "This man is right. We will do as he recommends. Besides," the marshal said with a vicious chuckle, "you have no family, and you're leaving town soon anyway!"

"No," Gibson screamed again. "You can't do this! I won't allow it! You work for me!" He took a swing at the marshal. The marshal easily ducked away, and Gibson missed in his blind rage.

What Gibson said was true, the marshal thought. It was also embarrassing. The secret amongst the town leaders was now out in the open for all to see. "I don't work for you," the marshal said softly, barely heard by the others over the roar of the fire. He was now fully dedicated to solving this festering part of his life once and for all. The deal he had sealed with a handshake at the town meeting the night before was a good start, but the fire was a bonus, a whole new way to hurt Gibson. He was not going to waste this opportunity. "It's not your decision. This is the only way to save the town. It is also the only way to save the mill. Your fellow mine leaders and owners will thank you," he said with the greasiest sarcasm he could muster.

The marshal turned to Patrick and said, "You have our support. Get to it!"

Patrick skipped along on his wooden leg as fast as he could to the mining supply store at the bottom of Main Street, safely out of the fire danger for now. He gathered friends he had known before from the mines as he went along. They pulled a wagon down Main Street to the supply store where they found the stock of dynamite safely stored in a locked shed behind the store. They knocked the lock off with an axe and loaded the dynamite into the wagon. They pulled the loaded wagon back up Main Street, down into the Chinatown gully, and up the edge of the hollow to Rossie Hill below the northern margin of the fire. The fire moved fast and was closing in on Gibson's mansion. The down-canyon winds would turn soon with the warming morning sun and the heat of the fire itself, but not soon enough to save Gibson's house.

Gibson was blind with confusion, looking at his magnificent house on the hill and back to the gathered town leaders. First the embarrassment last night, and now this! He never thought of them as colleagues, but they had been useful as his power and influence had grown over the years. Now they had turned on him. No one cared about his home, or about him anymore for that matter. He turned to run up the hollow toward his house.

His only hope now was to save whatever he could of his possessions. He ran along the Chinatown hollow through the ash, blind with rage, following the same route Patrick and his miner friends had taken with the wagon full of dynamite. He turned up the hollow toward the ridge, heedless of the debris and charred wood that littered the way.

CHAPTER 20

Park City, June 18, 1898

Gibson was blind with a steaming rage. He knew he should be focused on removing as much of his valuable furniture and as many possessions as possible from his house before the crazy bartender blew it up, but he just couldn't think. Where that stupid bartender got the idea to blow up houses to save the town Gibson had no idea, but picking his house as the target was not just a random event. He was sure of that, and he would not forget it. The cripple would get what was coming to him.

As he ran toward his house through the deep layers of debris in the Chinatown hollow, he passed a tall Chinese man digging through the ashes of his home. Even in Gibson's disoriented mind, he could see that the man was dressed as a distinguished elder. The man stared at him as he ran by, a hard, flat look on his face, as if the man recognized him, and not in a pleasant way. Gibson ran on, ignoring the man, angry, frantic, not noticing the rocks and debris buried under the ash. He tripped on a hidden cooking pot and fell forward, landing hard on the mudpack underneath the dust. He slammed the right side of his head on a rock that was buried in the hardened mud and was knocked unconscious. He laid in a crumpled heap for a minute and then came to, groggy and confused.

Why am I lying here on the ground? he wondered. *Where was I going? The marshal was telling that cripple bartender something. What was it? Ah, I know. He is supposed to blow up my house.*

Why? Why are they doing this? Why did the mayor agree? Why are they blowing up my house? Ah, my house, I have to save my house.

Gibson slowly got to his knees, brushing off the ash. The elderly Chinese man stood over him.

"May I offer some help?" he said in a deep and elegant voice.

Gibson slapped his hand away. "I'm fine!" he shouted. "Leave me alone!" He slowly stood and staggered up the hollow. His fuzzy thinking kept coming back to his house. *Must get to my house, save it from that cripple,* he thought. Shouting at all of the miners he could see along the way, he ordered them to help him evacuate the house. Most of the men were not Ontario miners, but they all looked the same to Gibson. They all looked away and pretended to not hear him. They had their own worries about their own homes and families.

But there was something else, something about Gibson's futile arm-waving and desperate cries that told them they could ignore him without consequences. He didn't come screaming at them like he usually did—no more bluster, no angry, inflamed face. His yelling subsided to a confused mumbling. This was the first time anyone could remember that someone spoke up to Gibson and got away with it. He seemed small and faded, unable to understand or cope with his fall from power. The miners turned to the many others who were in true need of their help, as they piled their possessions in the middle of the road.

Gibson ran inside his house and worked to drag his furniture out into the road, struggling, sweating from the heat of the fire consuming the house next door. He wondered why he had bought such heavy, massive furniture. It was almost impossible to move, and no one was helping. He dragged what he could out into the street. His fog had not entirely cleared, and he had difficulty deciding which of his many possessions were most important to save. He saw Patrick working around the foundation, which inflamed his mind even more.

Patrick studied the house carefully, thought about how the house was constructed, and what he knew from his former life blasting rock faces. Just like he used to drill a pattern of holes so the rock face would blow inwards and collapse, now he placed the dynamite at different spacings to cause the house to implode and collapse inward. He knew that the timing of the fuses would be most important, sequencing the explosions so the house fell into its foundation and out of reach of the fire. He directed the men confidently, and they followed him willingly, seeming to recognize his expertise and the authority conferred upon him by the marshal and mayor. He told the miners where to place the dynamite and how long to cut the fuses. The fire was now next door, and he could feel the heat. They didn't have much time.

They placed two dozen sticks of dynamite at key points on the corners of the foundation and under the house, about the same number as what they would use on a rock face. Confident that he was ready, he approached Gibson and gave him the courtesy of a warning that he was about to light the fuses. "Sir," Patrick said, "just to let you know, the dynamite is placed and will be lit in the next minute or two."

"Yeah," Gibson snapped. "You think you're so smart, getting that worthless mayor and marshal to give you permission to blow up my house! I know you didn't pick my house at random!"

"No, sir, I did not," Patrick said with a smile, quietly. No one else could hear them talk over the crackling and roaring of the fire.

Patrick's smug response was the final blow. He could have raged at Patrick. That would be his normal response. Instead, he simply stood on the road, slumped, small, knowing at some subconscious level that he now no longer occupied his rightful place in town, his rightful place in the world. The miners refused to obey him, his former employee was about to blow up his house, and the mayor and marshal were nowhere to do his bidding.

Gibson's muddled mind tried to focus on this sudden change in his fortunes. *What has happened to me?* he thought. *What do I do? Where do I go? Why am I am scrounging around my house. Why is that damned bartender setting dynamite around my house?*

Patrick watched this turmoil and confusion play out on Gibson's face, but then he saw something else. A dark shadow like a window shade dropped over it. Gibson's eyes rolled upwards as he let out a garbled scream and collapsed on the road. Several men, including Mr. Sing, ran up as Patrick leaned over to find him barely breathing. Patrick felt for a pulse at Gibson's neck and found it, weak but there. He shook Gibson but got no response.

"I saw this man fall and hit his head a few minutes ago," Mr. Sing said, to no one in particular. "I think he lost unconsciousness briefly."

A miner ran for the cart they had used to haul the dynamite, and they lifted Gibson carefully onto it. They rolled him down the hillside back into Chinatown, and then up the side of the hollow onto Main Street, where Thomas and Sarah were huddled together watching the flames. The physicians had responded so they could help anyone needing medical attention, but, amazingly, there had been no injuries or need for their services—until now.

"He just passed out," Patrick explained. "Some Chinese man said he fell a few minutes ago and hit his head on the ground." Thomas examined Gibson quickly and found bruising and dirt on the right side of his head where he had first fallen. He was unresponsive, his heart rate slow, and his breathing shallow. The pupil in the right eye was wide and dark.

Thomas turned to Sarah and motioned toward Gibson. "Please," he said.

She examined him quickly. "I think he has an intracranial bleed," Sarah said, "probably a tear of the middle meningeal artery where it runs in the groove along the skull's undersurface. What do you think?"

"I agree," said Thomas. "If the blood is not removed, he'll die."

"I know about trephination, but I can't imagine doing that here. Have you studied the procedure?" Sarah asked Thomas.

"I have read a bit about it," Thomas replied, "but certainly not performed it. You?"

"Strangely, I have been reading quite a bit about it, just seemed intriguing to me given all the head injuries we see here. I actually purchased all the necessary equipment recently, never thinking that we would be called upon to use it so soon. It's right here in my bag. But I think we should be worried about a much bigger issue, whether we should consider such a procedure at all."

Thomas turned toward the miners who had pulled Gibson up in the cart. "Take him to my office quickly!" He turned back to Sarah. "We have no choice." Thomas and Sarah looked at each other as they considered the complexities of performing such a surgery. It was exciting and appalling all at the same time. Their thoughts swung wildly back and forth for what seemed a moment frozen in time as they considered the options. This was an operation with the highest imaginable risk, on a man they both detested, in circumstances far from ideal.

"I agree," Sarah said. "I think we can do this, together. But he is not just any patient."

Thomas nodded, "I understand there is no easy answer here, but if we do nothing, we could be faulted for our inaction, especially by those who know of our conflicts with him."

Sarah knew he was right. She nodded her agreement. It was her call because they both knew that she would be the primary surgeon.

"Let's go," she said decisively.

"I would be honored to assist you," Thomas said with an encouraging smile.

The marshal had walked up from the hollow after consulting with Patrick about his progress. As the marshal approached the doctors, he saw the miners carrying Gibson up Main Street toward Wilson's office, and Thomas and Sarah deep in what appeared to be a complicated discussion. He approached them cautiously, unsure of where he stood with them. "I understand Gibson collapsed and is unconscious. Is there anything you can do to save him?" the marshal asked, trying not to be obvious about the answer he hoped to hear.

Thomas and Sarah looked at the marshal, trying hard to be civil. "Possibly," Thomas said in a flat voice. "The risks are very high, but without it he will surely die. It is not an easy call."

WHOOM!

The explosion echoed up and down the canyon. The three of them, and everyone around them, jumped and looked toward Rossie Hill, everyone except for the miners. They had heard hundreds of dynamite explosions in their careers. Gibson's mansion came apart like a doll house, wooden siding and timbers blowing upwards and inwards as Patrick had designed. It all came down in a pile of rubble. Patrick's dynamite placement worked perfectly, collapsing the house into its foundation, away from the licks of flame leaping off the next-door house. Gibson's grand mansion was no more.

No one saw the small, discrete smile on the marshal's face as he turned to walk back down to the hollow. "I'm sure you will do the right thing," the marshal said to Thomas and Sarah as he turned away.

The fire was no more, at least on Rossie Hill. It had nowhere to go, no fuel left to feed it. Patrick and his team moved quickly to Main Street to work their counterintuitive magic again as the fire spread across town.

Thomas and Sarah found Gibson lying on the table in Thomas's office where the men had brought him, breathing slowly, too slowly, still unresponsive. The miners had fled, having no desire to expend more time or energy on a man they hated. Sarah and Thomas looked at each other as they silently confirmed their decision.

Gibson's pulse was weak. His sallow skin was a sharp contrast to his usual plethoric face. There would be no need for ether.

They positioned him on his left side, exposing the right side of his head. Thomas shaved bare a patch of skin over the ear, about four inches square. The oily wet hair fell away in piles. The scalp was white with smears of dirt.

Thomas washed the entire scalp with soap and water, and then he and Sarah washed their hands, vigorously and thoroughly, as well as the drills in Sarah's trephination kit. Thomas placed large clips through the skin of the scalp in the shape of a square centered on the shaved area, pins that clamped over the skin and would reduce the bleeding when they cut into the scalp. They placed clean cloths over Gibson's skull to cover it completely except for the shaved area.

Sarah held her scalpel for a moment, poised over the white skin. She looked at Thomas and he nodded. The scalpel descended. She cut a square flap, two inches on each of three sides of a square, leaving the fourth side near the ear intact. The scalp easily peeled away from the skull, and the flap of scalp flopped over the cloth covering Gibson's ear. The skull underneath was white and shiny. There was a small, jagged mark on the skull, the hairline fracture they suspected.

Sarah's kit had a selection of hollow drills, and she selected one a little less than an inch in diameter, a hollow cylinder with finely-ground sharp teeth at one end welded to a T-shaped handle on the other end for turning. She placed the drill on the skull and started rotating it, carefully but persistently, boring into the skull an eighth-turn at a time. She worked quickly and precisely. Her hands were quiet and confident as she turned the drill, cutting deeper and deeper into the skull. She estimated the thickness of the temporal bone of the skull and worked even more precisely with smaller and lighter turns as she approached what she expected to be the bone's full thickness.

Thomas dabbed at small bubbles of blood oozing from the cut edges of the scalp. Sarah bent over Gibson's head as she turned the drill in even smaller arcs. She looked up at Thomas and he looked back, each with a mixture of awe and amazement. They did not need to speak to know that they were doing the right thing and doing it as well as they possibly could. Their faces showed the respect they each had for the skills of the other at this remarkable moment and the love they shared for the opportunity to do it together. They shivered with the power of their emotions.

Sarah continued to turn the drill with a light touch, not slowly but carefully, purposefully. Gibson's breathing slowed even more, and the small spurts of bleeding at the edge of the cut bone slowed. He would be dead in minutes. She made a final turn of the drill, just a few degrees, and then three things happened, all at once.

The core of bone in the hollow cylindrical drill moved just slightly as it disconnected from the surrounding skull. A gush of dark, partly-clotted blood pushed the cylinder of bone out farther and flowed out around the bone.

And WHOOM! Another explosion. Their ears exploded in a sharp crack that rocked the building. Sarah's hand did not twitch even slightly, strong and steady.

Patrick had just blown up the store two doors down from Thomas's office and stopped the fire as it worked up the hill. One more firebreak on Park Avenue, just below the marshal's home, and the fire would die.

Sarah removed the core of bone, and a clot of blood the size of a small egg protruded through the hole. She removed the clot with forceps and was met with a spurt of red blood that arced out of the hole and across the table.

"I've got it," Thomas said, calmly, quietly. He blotted the blood in the wound and saw the artery and its partial tear. "Here it is, a small tear in the middle meningeal artery." He applied pressure with a clean cloth in his left hand and held out his upturned right hand. Sarah knew exactly what he wanted and slapped on his hand a clamp with a curved needle onto which she had threaded a fine suture. Thomas rotated the curved needle under the artery above the tear and tied it quickly over the top of the artery. The bleeding stopped.

They looked at each other with mutual thanks and admiration. Their movements in stopping the bleeding and tying off the artery were stunning in their beauty and precision. "That should hold," Thomas said, "but it is vulnerable to any new injury. He will need to be very careful. Any fall, any bump to the head, could disrupt the suture or damage the brain and kill him."

With a clean cloth, Thomas explored the cavity that had been formed by the bleeding. The tough fibrous covering of the brain was depressed into the brain from the pressure of the clot that had laid over it, but Thomas could see that it was already recovering its normal contour. He inspected the ligated artery and found the suture holding well. Small collateral branches off the main artery were already filling and compensating for the blocked flow of the ligated trunk. Gibson's breathing picked up a bit, a little faster, a little deeper. Sarah could see the pulsation of the meningeal artery, the rate picking up and the pulse a little stronger. They had saved Gibson's life.

They left the hole open. They had no way to suture the cylinder of bone back in place, or any good materials to cover the hole. They laid the scalp back over the skull, sutured it in place, dressed the wound, and bound Gibson's skull tightly to prevent bleeding. He would always have a soft spot under the skin where the bone of the skull would not entirely fill in. The torn artery and brain were vulnerable to any new injury, but he would live.

Sarah's pulse slowed as Gibson's pulse picked up. She sighed quietly, feeling the thrill that all physicians feel when they have saved a patient's life, the deepest satisfaction from an accurate diagnosis and a near-miraculous surgical intervention. There was always regret for the patient, even for this patient, for the suffering he had endured and the potential consequences of his injury. But the regret was small, especially for this patient, and faded fast compared to the thrill of doing something so special and dramatic.

But even this deep thrill of success paled in comparison to operating with Thomas. That was a whole other level of emotion, bordering on love.

Thomas's pulse slowed as well as he recovered from the drama of the surgery, surgery that seemed to mark the culmination of a remarkable journey. In the face of unimaginable loss and sadness, he felt strong and confident, able to give of himself at the highest levels and to receive love and admiration in return. His skills and expertise had been on full display, and it felt good. And the woman he had seen striding into the lecture hall on that first day of medical school had shown him the way. *The dead visages of my family are fading,* he thought. *Maybe they will eventually stop. Maybe...because of...Sarah.*

They sat silently next to each other as they recovered from the tension of the operation. Something had happened between the two of them, and each considered separately what it was. They had contributed to a miracle and saved the life of someone they hated because it was the right thing to do. They were able to save Gibson's life because of their surgical skills and judgment, but also because of how smoothly and precisely they worked together. The respect each held for the other's skills opened up the possibility of something more, but what that was, and how it would be revealed, was not yet clear. They had more to discuss, but not until they recovered from the exhaustion of a day of miracles—the miracle of saving Gibson's life, the miracle of Park City saving itself, and the miracle of finding themselves as physicians and finding each other as partners.

CHAPTER 21

Park City, June 25, 1898

The offices of the *Park Record* were burned to the ground, but it published its regular weekly issue six days after the fire, thanks to the generous assistance of the *Salt Lake Herald*, which provided printing services. The June 25, 1898, issue included the following news and happenings from the front page and from a gossip column called *The Park Float*:

> *The Record is unprepared to go into detail regarding the losses sustained at this time, but when everything is taken into account, it will be found that the total money damage is not far short of $1,000,000, if it does not exceed that amount. We count hundreds of businesses and homes lost in the fire on both the sides of Main Street, Rossie Hill, and extending down Park Avenue.*
>
> *It is not often that men are called upon to face such wholesale disaster as was visited on the community Sunday morning last, and it is not often that a community so visited proves its moral worth and stout heartedness so completely as have the people of this town since the awful fire that made hundreds homeless and penniless. No description can adequately convey an intelligent idea of the scene of desolation and ruin that confronts one when a walk is taken through the once busy Main Street of this, the best-governed and best-taken-*

care-of mining town in the state. We understand the fine Chinese residents of this town have been similarly afflicted and we congratulate them for the strong spirit of citizenship they have shown in the many ways they have offered assistance to Parkites during their time of need.

When normal conditions again prevail in the camp—when our people have recovered from the sudden shock of the battle through which they have just passed—the same energetic, progressive, loyal, go-ahead spirit will be manifested on every hand, and from the ruins of the day, another splendid Park City will be reared and its people will be the same generous, honest, and honored host as of yore.

Thomas Kearns, the esteemed owner of the Silver King mine, a former miner and foreman at the Ontario, a former Park City councilman, and a close colleague of the well-known engineer David Keith, has always demonstrated his great concern for the welfare of his employees as well as of the fine citizens of Park City. He has once again done so by giving orders that no one in the city be allowed to suffer as a result of the fire. He will personally contribute the necessary funds to achieve that goal. Mr. Kearns has also been offered a stake in the Ontario mine, which will now benefit from his commitment to maintain the success of that important source of the town's economic success. His close working relationship with David Keith, who himself started his career at the Ontario, should also bode well for improving the life of the Ontario miners, leading to continued success of the mining industry in Park City."

The Record has learned that Parkites owe a

great debt of gratitude to Patrick Fitzpatrick, the well-liked bartender at the Towey Livery Stable and Bar. Mr. Fitzpatrick was the source of the radical but highly effective method of stopping the raging fire of last week by using dynamite. His suggestion was initially rejected by town leaders for its seemingly outrageous and perverse nature, but they eventually succumbed to the logic of his reasoning. Mr. Fitzpatrick has been rewarded for his creativity and bravery with appointment as a shift foreman by his former employer, the Ontario mine. The mine's new superintendent, Mr. David Keith, has indicated his desire to follow the lead of Thomas Kearns and the Silver King mine in providing the safest possible working conditions for the welfare of their miners, including taking advantage of the considerable expertise and intelligence of foremen like Mr. Fitzpatrick."

Fire or no fire, the mines continued to operate, including the Ontario. The day after the fire, Patrick Fitzpatrick walked up Ontario canyon with a quicker step than usual, even with his wooden leg. He was excited to begin his new job as a mine foreman. Maybe he should have been nervous, but he wasn't. He had no concerns about his ability to do the job. He was smart and observant, and he had paid attention to how mines worked in both the Ontario and in his former position in the Virginia City mines. He tingled with anticipatory excitement for his scheduled meeting with Mr. Keith to receive his instructions in his new job. He was particularly energized after more than a year of boredom as a bartender. He felt like he was about to achieve the level of responsibility he had been seeking for so long. He was returning to the mines, but with a fresh approach to a new job and working for a new superintendent who seemed to actually care about the miners. Patches of smoke still drifted around town, but the bright summer sun above matched his mood.

He walked into the superintendent's office where Mr. Keith met him warmly. "Mr. Fitzpatrick, welcome. Thank you for your service yesterday. Your solution to the crisis was, I must say, quite unexpected, but also quite effective."

Patrick swelled with pride. He couldn't remember the last time someone had addressed him as "Mister." "Thank you sir. I am pleased I was able to help. The fire was such a tragedy, but it could have been so much worse."

"Yes, indeed. Are you prepared to assume your new responsibilities at the Ontario?'

"Yes, sir, very much so, sir!"

Just then the heavy front door groaned as it was pushed open by none other than J. S. Gibson, who burst into the room, eyes darting around the office, fierce and frantic, looking around the office like he had not seen it before. Before anyone could stop him, he walked straight over to Keith who was sitting at what used to be Gibson's desk and started to throw around the papers and mementos strewn across the desk.

Keith sprang to his feet and backed away, unsure of what to do about Gibson's deranged behavior. "Gibson, what are you doing here? We expected you would be packing and preparing to move to your new position." Keith and Fitzpatrick looked at each other, eyes wide, a touch of fear, hands upturned in confusion.

Gibson ignored Keith and seemed not to even notice Fitzpatrick, as he looked wildly around the room, focusing on each piece of furniture as if to remember that it used to be his. He looked at Keith like he was about to speak, like he wanted something, then shook his head and focused again on the desk.

Keith moved toward Gibson and touched his arm carefully, afraid he would lash out from his disoriented reverie. "Mr. Gibson, sir. Are you well? What can I do for you? You need to stop, please." Keith pleaded.

"Don't touch me!" Gibson yelled as he jumped away, like he had just noticed Keith, his quiet agitation suddenly released in full fury. He pushed his way past Keith, grabbing at every random thing he could touch. His face was now steaming, sweaty, and turgid, made worse by the florid contrast with the clean white bandages wrapped around the top and right side of his head. "You may be sitting at my desk, but the rest of this is mine!" Gibson raged at Keith.

Patrick had tried to slide to the side out of Gibson's sight, but the movement caused Gibson to suddenly notice him. "You, YOU!" Gibson said. "You are the cause of all this. You blew up my house! You picked it out on purpose! You even said so yourself!"

Patrick let the slightest smile flash across his face, and then it was gone. Gibson saw it. Keith did not.

He exploded, charging at Patrick, swinging wildly with his rough, clenched fists, as Keith yelled for him to stop. Patrick easily side-stepped his deranged charge.

"Mr. Keith, please, do something!" Patrick said. "I mean him no harm."

Keith tried to grab Gibson as he turned and charged back at Patrick. Gibson swung at both Keith and Fitzpatrick with both fists and missed again.

"Please!" Patrick said again. "Mr. Gibson, I had no choice. I'm sorry. We had to blow up your house to save the mill!"

"Mr. Gibson, please, stop. Stop!" Keith yelled.

Gibson charged one more time, swinging and missing Fitzpatrick, losing his balance. He stumbled and fell hard. The right side of his head slammed into the corner of the heavy wooden desk with a sickening thump, hollow, like dropping a pumpkin on the floor. He fell to his knees and then slumped over on his back. Patrick saw the same cloud pass over his face that he had seen the day before during the fire. The bandages on the right side of his head suddenly oozed with a rapidly widening stain of bright red blood. Gibson made no sound as he lay on the floor, arms flung out, legs crooked. Keith knelt down and shook him. There was no response. Patrick could see that Gibson was not breathing, and he checked for a heartbeat. Nothing. The pulsating blood slowed and stopped. Gibson was dead.

Fitzpatrick immediately turned to Keith and cried, "You saw, Mr. Keith, it wasn't my fault."

"I know, son, don't worry. You didn't do this. I saw the whole thing. He died like he lived, angry and mean. I will summon the marshal and Dr. Stout as the medical examiner, but you go ahead to your new job."

Patrick walked out toward the headframe, breathing hard. The small smile returned as Patrick savored the justice of Gibson's death, but he wasted little time thinking about Gibson's hateful demise. All that mattered now was that he had a new job as foreman, and he was going to make the most of it.

The marshal and Dr. Stout arrived later, conducted their duties in an entirely officious and unnecessarily formal manner. The marshal in particular went to some lengths to extol the business and personal virtues of Gibson, as unnecessary as it was untrue. Stout was not much better in his gratuitous compliments. Keith was annoyed at the sleazy disingenuousness that had oozed from both men. He had heard the rumors about the marshal's loyalty to Gibson, for which the marshal appeared to have benefited handsomely. He had also heard rumors that it would be prudent for his partner, the new part-owner, Mr. Kearns, to examine the mine's books. He suspected they would find reasons for the marshal's gratuitous behavior. For now, he needed to get Gibson's body to the undertaker. He supposed he should feel responsible for some sort of memorial service for Gibson since he had no family, but he was having no part of it.

Amazingly and fortunately, only one person suffered injury during the fire. Mr. J. S. Gibson, the well-known and highly regarded manager of the Ontario mine, suffered a serious injury during the fire from a fall in which he struck his head. The circumstances are unclear as to the sequence of events, but sometime after the fall he experienced a sinking to the ground and a loss of consciousness, necessitating emergent intervention by Dr. Fletcher and Dr. Wilson. Park City is fortunate to benefit from the medical expertise and learned acumen of such fine physicians. The Record has been told that the doctors performed an operation on the brain of Mr. Gibson that has heretofore never been performed in this state. The operation was said to be completely successful and to have saved the life of Mr. Gibson.

Sadly, we now have to report the subsequent news that Mr. Gibson suffered some sort of additional injury, not attributable to the surgery or other mischief, and has died. We mourn for the loss of this great business leader.

The next day, two days after the fire, the marshal relaxed in his temporary office just down the street from where his old office had burned to ashes. He was feeling very pleased with himself. *Telling the Mayor and Ontario owners about Gibson's assault of the Chinese prostitute—what was her name, Chen?*

Chow?—was brilliant, if I do say so myself. Things could not have worked out better. The loan Gibson had made would now disappear. From the lowest of lows, children dead, Effie devastated, to a complete resolution of the Gibson problem. How fortunes can turn!

Just then, the new owner and new superintendent of the Ontario knocked softly at the door of the marshal's office. "Marshal," Thomas Kearns said as he tipped his hat, always courteous and gentlemanly. "Might I have a word?" David Keith was at his side. He nodded politely to the marshal.

"Certainly, gentlemen, please come in," the marshal replied. "Have a seat." *What is this? What could Kearns want?*

"Thank you, again, marshal, for coming to investigate the Gibson death yesterday," Keith said. "Tragic, as I am sure you agree."

"Yes, indeed, terrible tragedy," the marshal said with forced goodwill.

"As you know, Marshal," Kearns said, "I now have an investment stake in the Ontario mine. As part of that transaction, I reviewed the financial position of the mine and examined its books yesterday."

"Certainly," the marshal replied, trying to seem as agreeable as possible. "Due diligence, like any good businessman." *Gibson told me that my little deal was buried so deep it could never be found.* The marshal's eyes dropped to the floor as his fingers clenched. He dreaded Kearns's next words.

"We see an entry for a substantial payment of funds to you some time back, labeled as a loan, followed by regular monthly payments by you to the same account since that time. Can you explain the reason for this loan and the payments?"

"Um, er, yes sir. Mr. Gibson was kind enough to make a small loan to me during a time of need. I am making repayment on that loan."

"I see," Kearns mused, "but the payments barely cover the interest on the loan. At this rate, it will never be paid back. Why would Mr. Gibson make such a loan in the first place? I doubt the Ontario shareholders think it proper for him to be making personal loans like this out of company funds."

"Yes, well, Mr. Gibson asked certain services of the marshal's office, not related to the loan, of course, just part of his responsibilities managing the Ontario."

"And what would those services be exactly?" Kearns asked.

"Well, it is a bit hard to describe. He liked to know that the marshal's office had the best interests of the Ontario mine and its shareholders in mind as we carried out our usual duties."

"I see. It has come to our attention that one of those services might be that your deputies acted on behalf of Mr. Gibson in his dealings with Dr. Wilson, and possibly Dr. Fletcher as well. There appears to have been some considerable pressure on them to leave town, including repossessing Wilson's medical equipment. Would that be correct?"

The marshal squirmed in his chair, trying to buy time before he spoke. "I, um, believed I was acting as an officer of the law, enforcing a legal contract and order by a local business against a contractor, meaning Dr. Wilson. He had been fired, and Gibson was simply recalling equipment that had been purchased for his use as the mine physician."

"I see," Kearns said, stroking his chin thoughtfully. "That would seem more properly handled by Gibson's employees. Do you consider yourself an employee, Marshal?"

Unfortunately for the marshal, he had run out of ideas for how to respond. Nothing was left but the truth. "I do not sir, but I behaved in a way about which I am not proud. The doctors were investigating the cause of the lung disease we have seen in the miners, something to do with the dust that comes from the mechanical drills. They had discussed the composition of the dust with Mr. Bird, as well as with professors at the University in Salt Lake. Mr. Gibson was adamant that there was no basis for their concern and wanted them out of the mine's business."

"Ah, yes, the matter of Mr. Bird. I have learned that you came into possession of a confidential report from Mr. Bird to the doctors. All of his reports are highly confidential to his clients, as I am sure you know. Can I assume you had something to do with that report and how it found its way to Mr. Gibson? I don't understand why any of this would be your business as the town marshal."

"I agree. It should not have been my business." The marshal tried to look as contrite and remorseful as he could, his eyes downcast, feet shuffling. He was not very persuasive. Kearns had conducted a thorough investigation in a very short time. There was nowhere else to go.

"Please tell us more about the incident with the Chinese prostitute."

"Ah, now that is an area where I think my behavior was more salutary," the marshal said proudly. "You recall from our discussion at the town hall Saturday last," the marshal replied, "that Mr. Gibson made clear that he wished for that incident to not be pursued, which is why I brought it to your attention." He pulled himself up to look as righteous and upstanding as he knew how. "I thought someone should know. I am ashamed about much of what I have done on behalf of Mr. Gibson, but the assault was just too much. I am committed to doing the right thing from this point forward." The marshal was embarrassed by his groveling, but he had to do whatever he could to extract himself from this mess.

The marshal's squirming voice was equally embarrassing for Kearns. The marshal had been quivering with emotion as he delivered his seemingly heartfelt speech. Emotion and length did not make the marshal's little speech any more persuasive.

"I am pleased to hear that, sir," Kearns said, hoping he did not sound as insincere as the marshal did, "but I believe it to be inappropriate for a public servant to be receiving supplemental benefits like this from a private enterprise. I am sure you would agree that the potential ethical conflicts would be difficult to manage."

"Yes, yes, most surely." The marshal spoke so softly Kearns could not hear the last words, but the marshal's whimpering look was all Kearns needed to see.

"The monthly payments will need to be raised considerably to a fair rate," Kearns said, "so I can close out the loan as quickly as possible. You will, unfortunately, have to make that restitution without your current marshal's salary. Your behavior was unacceptable and cannot be endorsed. I will be discussing with the mayor the installation of a new town marshal. Is that clear?"

"Yes, well, uh, yes sir, quite clear. But how can I possibly repay these funds without a job? And where will my family and I live now? I cannot maintain the home if my payments increase. We will need to leave, and there are nearly no homes left standing." His voice became shrill as he recognized the magnitude of what Kearns was saying. "Our lives will be ruined. How can I face my wife with this news, on top of the tragic deaths of our children?" He grieved for his children, but he was also not above using their deaths for his own purposes.

"Yes, of course, I am very sorry about the loss of your children, so sad, devastating to your family, I am sure. But I am committed to restoring justice and propriety to your office, and I must act in that regard. The mine has some small cottages that might be suitable, for which we would, of course, have to charge a fair rental fee. The loss of so many homes in town suggests you might wish to avail yourself of that offer quickly. I am also willing to take you on as a security guard at the mine. You know the property, and your policing skills should serve you well. We will, of course, be deducting your loan obligations from your paycheck. That would be most convenient," said Kearns, as he watched the marshal's face collapse.

"Yes, of course," the marshal whispered. He could barely speak as he drew into himself, small, diminished. *How am I going tell Effie? What will happen to us?*

"Good day, sir," said Kearns, as he turned for the door. Keith nodded silently at the marshal again, his face grim.

The marshal trudged up Main Street later in the day and over to his home on Park Avenue. He had spent the day agonizing over what he was going to tell Effie and how, all of it made worse by the depressing walk home. There wasn't a building left standing on Main Street until he got to the top, just below Dr. Wilson's office, where Fitzpatrick's dynamite had stopped the fire. Over on Park Avenue, he found the same thing just below his home. The charred timbers and ashes matched his mood. The heavy, smoky smell gagged him. His fine home stood proud and untouched amidst the street's rubble. But now not his home for much longer. It seemed to be mocking him with its upright arrogance.

"Effie, I'm home!" he announced with unnatural cheeriness. He had never walked into the house like that, as Effie knew well. She was immediately suspicious.

"You never say that when you come home. What's wrong?" the words expressing sympathy, her face not. "You don't look right."

The marshal knew that Effie would suspect something. "Mr. Kearns came to see me this afternoon. He expressed some, er, concerns about my relationship with Mr. Gibson that have come to his attention."

"What kind of concerns? What have you done? What kind of trouble are you in?"

"Mr. Kearns is unhappy about the loan Gibson made to me."

Effie's shock was matched by her anger. "I told you I didn't think that was right. You know I never liked Gibson. He was a mean and vicious man. I should be a more forgiving Christian, but I am glad he is gone. You should have stayed far away from him!"

"But, as you know dear, that was the only way we could afford our home."

"I don't care. However nice the house is, it's not worth the stain and embarrassment of being associated with him."

"Well, then," he said, "I guess you'll be happy to know that association is about to end. Kearns told me we have to move!" Even now his natural meanness could not be suppressed for long,

"What, why? What have you done?"

"Mr. Kearns has demanded full payment and disposition of the loan, and we cannot afford the payments."

"Well, then, that is what we will do. We will survive. At least you still have a good job."

"I used to," he said, his abusive tone turning back on itself to shame. "There's more."

"What?! Now what?"

"Kearns is going to make clear to the mayor that he wants a new marshal. He is not happy with what I have done at Gibson's bidding." The marshal's embarrassment was now complete. He shuffled over to Effie and tried to hug her. She drew back and pushed him away.

"What will we do? What will our family do? No house, no job. This is what you get for working with that disgusting man, but what about us? What have you done to us?"

"Kearns has offered a small house that the mine owns and a job as a security guard at the mine. We can probably figure out the money, but it will be tight." He paused, his face dripping with dishonor. "I am so sorry," he said, "so sorry. I have failed you and failed our children. I have brought shame on us."

"Not on us! Just on you!" she spit at him. "The good people of this town know whose fault this is."

"I am so sorry. I hope one day you can forgive me."

"No time soon," she snapped. "I have to go. My children need me." She turned with a flat look on her face, not angry anymore, just tired. Tired of everything, the fire, the deaths of their two children, her husband's failures.

Kearns added several items of business interest that demonstrate his personal commitment to the welfare of this town, including his concern about the loss of the business enterprise and laboratory of Frank A. Bird, Assayer. Prior to the fire, we were aware of a rumor of some disruption in the contract between the Ontario mine and Mr. Bird. Perhaps related to that rumor, and given the critical nature of Mr. Bird's services to the entire mining industry, Mr. Kearns announced that he will be establishing Mr. Bird in new offices and a laboratory on the premises of the Silver King mine while directing his full book of assay business to Mr. Bird. We have also learned that the Silver King will provide a suitable home for Mr. Bird to replace his terrible loss in the fire on Rossie Hill. Mr. Kearns has encouraged other mine owners to continue looking to Mr. Bird for their assay requirements.

Related to the above news, the Record has learned from Dr. Fletcher and Dr. Wilson that they have received a report from the University of Utah where they had sent samples of dust collected as part of an investigation into the nature of the mysterious lung disease killing our miners. The university chemists found crystals consistent with silicate dust, which could be the cause of the lung disease. The doctors have told The Record that they intend to lobby all mine owners in the district to mitigate the risk by adding water cooling and irrigation. This addition should improve the safety and the quality of life of our hard-working miners, while also contributing to markedly increased mine productivity and the success of this fine community.

Three days after the fire, Main Street was bustling, filled with Parkites clearing the debris from the houses and shops that burned, trying to restore some level of function to the businesses that had not burned. Piles of charred wood had been gathered, and soot stained the ever-present mud on Main Street. Neither the mud nor the soot stopped the children who ran back and forth in the street as their parents worked. Men yelled as they worked and wagons clopped by as the sun tried to burn through the smoke.

A wagon filled to bursting with ore from the Judge-Daly mine turned the corner from Daly Avenue onto the top of Main Street, where the pitch was particularly steep. The team of six heavy work horses were in a lather as they worked their way slowly down the middle of the street, the teamster yanking on the reins to slow them down on the steep grade. Thomas sat on the front porch of his office as the wagon passed by. A mother called to her five-year-old daughter to meet her on the other side of the street. As the girl ran with her dog, her blond curls blowing in the wind, she stumbled and fell directly in front of the charging wagon team.

The teamster yanked the reins, and the horses veered to the right. Thomas jumped off the porch and got to the girl just before the left front wheel of the wagon was about to roll over the girl's right leg. He snatched her off the soot-stained dust and away from the wagon into his arms.

The girl's mother screamed and came running as she saw her daughter stumble. Thomas gently passed the girl over, and the mother looked at him with thankful tears. The girl's sobbing settled quickly, and she nestled in her mother's arms.

"Please, come over to my office so I can be assured she was not injured," Thomas offered. The mother gratefully accepted. They were only steps from his office door. The mother carried her daughter in and laid her on the surgical table. Thomas could see her face more clearly now, and he froze, startled into paralysis. She looked just like his sister, Emily, the angelic face, the blond curls. All of the images of Emily that Thomas thought had left came roaring back. He could see her blood seeping into the straw on the barn floor, bits of brain tissue oozing from the gaping skull. He held his head tight between his hands and rocked, uttering a faint moan. The image slowly blurred and faded.

The mother looked at Thomas strangely. She could see his confusion and disorientation as he lifted his head from his hands. "Is there something wrong, Doctor?"

"No, no, I'm fine, thank you," he said awkwardly. "Just tired from the last few days. What is her name?" he whispered.

"Emmy," she replied. "Emmy Kelly. Thank you again, doctor, for saving her. Thank you, thank you!"

And then a collage of horror from times past came rushing back, Emily's sweet face, his brother's death rattle, the oozing stumps of the boy's amputations, the box of bloody body parts from the miner who fell to his death. Everything jumbled together in a tortured anguish. He squeezed his head again. Emmy and Emily became one. Emmy had died just like Emily had. Trampled by horses. Run over by the wagon. It was all the same. But look! Emmy had not died. She was alive, looking up at him with bright smiling eyes. Thomas shook his head and focused on examining her. She was fine, still clinging to her mother, uninjured. Her smiling face washed away the blood of his memories.

"You are fine to take her home," Thomas said. "A little extra hugging and loving this afternoon would be indicated," he said with a smile.

"With pleasure," the mother said with an equally big smile. "Her uncle will be so happy. He and Emmy are so very close."

"Ah, and who might her uncle be?" Thomas asked.

"David Keith," she replied.

> *As many Parkites learned over the last several weeks, Dr. Fletcher has been successful in bringing to Park City a new treatment for diphtheria, the respiratory illness that has killed so many beloved children in this town. This treatment was developed in Germany and Michigan and is being used in only a few places in the country. We understand Dr. Fletcher has now successfully administered this treatment to two precious Park City children. For reasons we do not fully understand, but which we find fascinating, this new treatment involves a horse in some fashion. Such a horse currently resides in the stables of "Doc" McFarlane and was saved in the fire, although, sadly, his stables were not. We have been told that Mr. McFarlane will*

rebuild his stables, in partnership with Dr. Fletcher, where she will board one or more horses that will become the source of this miracle substance.

Five days after the fire, Sarah walked up Main Street from the Park Hotel where she had been fortunate to secure a room. All she had to her name was the medical equipment she had managed to save and a few clothes she had grabbed on the way out the door as the fired raged. Mr. Miller was working hard to find a new space for her, but the choices were few.

Despite all that, her spirit was stronger than ever. She felt sorry, in a vague sort of way, for what had happened to Gibson, but not sorry that now he could not hurt anyone else ever again. She was proud of how she and Thomas had saved his life. What Gibson did with that opportunity was his responsibility, and he had squandered it. There were also rumors about a scandal with the marshal that somehow led to him losing his job and his home. If true, she felt most sorry for Effie.

So many challenges and conflicts that she and Thomas had confronted over the past year had come to a close. Gibson's blatant evil and the marshal's corruption had resolved with justice of a sort. The Ontario mine's new ownership and management seemed willing to discuss ways to prevent the lung disease that was killing the miners. Dr. Stout's deceit would need to be addressed, but not now. She certainly would never trust him again.

And then there was Thomas. She had been thinking about him almost continuously since they operated on Gibson, thinking about him as a physician, about him as a colleague, and maybe about something else. Their opportunities in Park City now seemed limitless.

She had not seen him since the fire, and they had much to discuss.

She walked into Thomas's office, and her pleasant reverie was stopped short by the shock of seeing Thomas slowly folding and placing his clothes into trunks. His equipment was laying loose in various crates and boxes. The shelves that had been full of books were now empty. He was clearly packing up to move.

"Thomas, what are you doing?" she asked, almost shrieking with the unpleasant surprise.

"I was just about to come and find you," he said, slowly, softly. "I wanted you to know that I have been offered a new position in Salt Lake City. Mr. Keith came to see me yesterday with a most generous offer, to become the new physician in charge of the St. Mark's hospital in Salt Lake. The hospital has moved recently, expanding to eight beds, and it is exploring the addition of x-ray services. I was quite taken by his vision of an actual hospital where patients could receive the latest advances in medical science. The mine owners have an interest in expanding the services there for miners, and they want me to lead that effort. I was most appreciative of Mr. Keith's generosity. It is a huge opportunity. I felt like I just could not pass it up." The seemingly joyous news did not match his affect, flat and halting. She heard no joy.

"What, what do you mean? Why would you leave? You're established here, successful! So much of our conflict and misery over the past year has settled. Why would you go now?"

"It has indeed been a remarkable time here. I have learned so much, much of it from you," he said with smiling eyes. "But Mr. Keith was most persuasive. The mine owners want to consolidate the best medical care in Salt Lake."

"But we could build a hospital here. The state considered funding for just such a project last year!" Her protests tumbled out into the space between them, every reason she could use for him to stay, except the most important one.

"Well, there is also the salary. It is much larger than anything I could make here. I would have more responsibility and the opportunity to do some real good for the miners. And I thought perhaps you could make use of my office. The town needs you here." His reasons for leaving tumbled out into the same space, without mention of the one reason he would stay.

"And the town needs you here!" She could not believe what she was hearing, just as she had been pondering the nature of their relationship. "Look at what you have done! Look at what we have done!" She sat down next to him, their knees close, but not touching. "You are part of this town now. Look at the amazing things you have done for your patients. Look at how grateful they have been. Think of them. Think of the patients yet to come who will be grateful." Her words came pouring out, anguished, pleading.

Thomas shook his head slowly, as if he hadn't heard her, or didn't want to hear. He changed the subject. "Did you hear about the girl two days ago, almost run over by an ore wagon on Main Street?"

"I did," Sarah said. "I heard you saved her life."

"Well, maybe. Not with my medical skills, just a reflexive reaction pulling her away from the wagon. It turns out that she is Mr. Keith's niece. He was very appreciative. I was happy I could help." He paused, looked around the office as if it would be the last time. "She is such a beautiful child, the girl, Emmy, Keith's niece." He paused, his vision clouded as he looked at Sarah. "She looks just like my sister when she died. I froze for a moment and couldn't think. The terrible memories and images I told you about that I thought were fading came roaring back, as bad or worse than before."

Sarah moved even closer and could feel him trembling as she laid her arm across his shoulders. "What did you see?"

"Everything. Emily, Stephen, my mother, everyone dying, pain, fear in their eyes, fear in my heart. And finally, my father, who was so kind before he died to tell me I was not good enough to be successful as a physician. Sometimes I wonder if he was right." Bitter and ashamed at the same time.

"You know that's not true. You have proven that beyond any doubt. Ask anyone in town, anyone you have treated." She paused and gently turned his face toward her. "Ask me."

"Thank you," he whispered. "I am slowly starting to believe that, thanks to you. But the memories, the nightmares won't leave. I thought that I had accomplished what I needed to do to live a new life. I guess I was fooling myself. I think the only way now is to move on and start again somewhere else. I need something or someone to replace my family's memories. Maybe I will find it in Salt Lake City."

"Of course it's time to live your life, but here! Your life is here! Here is where you will find the someone else!" She trembled inside, both hopeful and fearful that he could feel it.

Thomas looked up at her, wanting so much to hear her say who that could be and fearing she would not say it.

Sarah seemed about to speak, shook her head and looked away.

He was crushed with her silence. "I just think a fresh start would be good," his voice soft, trailing away.

Sarah would not, could not speak.

He did not break the excruciating silence, still hoping she would say what he wanted to hear, but he could not bear to think it.

Finally, softly, she said, "But what about us?"

"Is there an 'us'?" Thomas said. His wide eyes searched Sarah's face for an answer.

"I hope so," she responded sincerely.

Now Thomas paused, his silence just as discomforting for Sarah, who had the same hopes and fears.

He spoke but he could not be sure what he was about to say. "I, uh, I might hope for that as well. But I know what Dr. Blackwell told you. She was clear there was no room in the life of a woman physician for a family, no time for a personal life if you seek to be an outstanding physician. And you are indeed an outstanding physician."

"Yes, Dr. Blackwell was certainly emphatic in her advice. That doesn't mean it is correct, at least for me. You and I have shared so many struggles together. Do you have any idea how much it has meant to me to have done so with you?" She reached out and laid her hand on top of his. He turned it over, palm to palm, but she felt no response.

"No, no idea at all. You are so confident, so sure of where you are going and why. You seem to need little from others."

"You silly fool. I am as needy of others as anyone, as needy as you." She paused, then said softly, "and needy *of* you. Let me replace your family's memories. I beg you not to leave." She squeezed Thomas's hand gently. After the briefest pause that lasted forever to Sarah, she was sure she felt the smallest squeeze in return.

> *The business of recovery has already begun, with dozens of destroyed businesses committed to rebuilding in new facilities. As part of that recovery, Mr. David Keith announced that Dr. Wilson's appointment as the Ontario mine physician would be reinstated. More importantly to the fine citizens of Park City, the Record has learned that the aforementioned Dr. Wilson and Dr. Fletcher have joined their practices in the office of Dr. Wilson, the only medical facility in town not destroyed by the fire. Their intent is to combine their considerable*

talents in providing the best possible medical care for the fine citizens of Park City. We personally witnessed the installation of a temporary sign on Dr. Wilson's office just yesterday, proudly announcing the creation of their new medical practice, "Doctors Fletcher and Wilson, Physicians and Surgeons." The commitment of these good doctors to providing medical care for the fine people of Park City is a testimony to our resilience as Park City rebuilds into the powerhouse of the west that it once was. And will be again.

Acknowledgments

As is true for many novels of historical fiction, the events and characters in this story are all generally plausible, but none are exactly accurate. Most of the events come from somewhere in Park City's history, but not necessarily at the time or place noted, or in quite the same way. Several physicians came through Park City and stayed for various lengths of time in the late 1890s, but there were no women physicians to my knowledge in that era. There were, however, women physicians who came to mining camps in Montana, Wyoming, and other western states. Some characters are entirely fictitious, yet some bear a passing resemblance to actual Parkites of the times. The first names of several characters come from my extended family because of the fortuitous circumstance that many of my family members and ancestors have names common to the era. I am especially happy to be able to use the names Robert and Evelyn, the names of my grandparents. Other names are those of actual Parkites of the era, but the characters bear no resemblance to their namesakes.

The medical and surgical techniques and equipment described are generally accurate for the times, although simplified. I do not know if the use of pus from children sick with diphtheria to make a solution for injecting into horses would work as described here. The actual technique required a pure culture to be grown from infected children. Sarah had no capacity to grow pure cultures of the bacteria. At least one Park City physician of the era was known to effectively treat diphtheria with antitoxin, but how that antitoxin was produced is unknown, at least to me.

The Great Fire of 1898 generally behaved as described, but considerable license has been taken in the locations and names of buildings, though they do bear some resemblance to actual businesses. The story about how the Park City marshal lost his arm has been described often but could also be apocryphal.

Park City is rich in history, and it is equally rich in the documentation of that history. Several authors and historians provided critical details and stories that informed this novel, including *Treasure Mountain Home: Park City Revisited* by George A. Thompson and Fraser Buck, *Diggings and Doings in Park City* by Raye Carleson Ringholz, *Stories in Stone* by Colleen Adair Fliedner, and *The Trail of the Leprechaun* by William M. McPhee. The book *From the Ground Up* by Colleen K. Whitley included a chapter on Park City written by Hal Compton and David Hampshire that was also helpful. Gary Kimball is perhaps the dean of Park City historians, not to mention a descendent of the Kimball family who was responsible in part for settling the area. His books include *Life Under China Bridge, Of Moths and Miners, Saloons of Old Park City,* and *Death and Dying in Old Park City.* The last-named is a particularly fascinating account of the stories behind the tombstones in the Park City cemeteries.

The Park City Museum is a treasure, particularly its historical archives that are managed by Dalton Gackle. Dalton himself is an incredible repository of Park City history. He is also committed to making it more visible and accessible through presentations and newspaper columns. One of the truly great historical resources for Park City history is the *Park*

Record itself, which has been fully digitized since its launch in 1880 and is entirely searchable (https://digitalnewspapers.org/newspaper/?paper=Park+Record). Most of the medical events in this story come from those files, in one form or another. Some of the quotations in Chapter 21 attributed to the June 25, 1898, issue of the *Park Record* are direct quotations, used with the verbal permission of Don Rogers, the current editor of the newspaper, for which I am grateful. The quotations are then extended to account for the characters and incidents in the story.

A wide range of readily available websites documenting medical equipment and surgical operations of the era was used to inform the medical scenes. One of the most useful in addressing the treatment of diphtheria came from the National Museum of American History (https://americanhistory.si.edu/blog/2013/08/how-horses-helped-cure-diphtheria.html). Wikipedia, of course, was helpful for a wide range of fact-checking, particularly with regard to carbolic acid poisoning, antisepsis techniques of the time, and anesthetics. Bits and pieces about life in western mining camps and mining techniques came from many different readily available websites, but a particularly expert book is *Western Mining* by Otis E. Young, Jr.

The Horse and Buggy Doctor by Arthur E. Hertzler, MD, is a classic in the genre of biographies of rural Western physicians. *The Healers of 19th Century Nevada* by Anton P. Sohn is another rich resource for medical practices of the times.

The education and struggles of women physicians in the era were informed primarily by two wonderful books. The first, *The Doctors Blackwell,* by Janice P. Nimura, is a detailed and comprehensive biography of the lives of Doctors Emily and Elizabeth Blackwell, groundbreaking women physicians who influenced the entire field of women in medicine throughout the later 1800s and early 1900s. The second, *Women in White Coats*, by Olivia Campbell, expands upon the experiences of Dr. Elizabeth Blackwell with the addition of biographies of Dr. Elizabeth Garrett Anderson and Dr. Sophia Jex-Blake. The research in both of these books is as impressive as the stories are compelling. Olivia Campbell was also personally encouraging in my early days of researching and writing this book. A comprehensive history of the University of Michigan Medical School by Horace W. Davenport, *Not Just Any Medical School,* informed the description of the medical school experiences of Sarah and Thomas. I was a fortunate student of Dr. Davenport in the 1970s, and he bears a remarkable resemblance to Professor Sewall.

I am deeply appreciative to all of these authors and resources for many of the events and situations depicted in this book, including the description of the Great Fire, albeit often altered as to details, time, and location for the purposes of the storyline. The book itself is entirely my writing, and I cannot blame Chat GPT for any errors or deficiencies.

This book would not exist without the incredible patience and expertise of my publisher Katie Mullaly, the cover artist Michelle Rayner, Callie Miller, who provided proofreading and copyediting, and Stacy Dymalski, my editor and writing coach. These "four musketeers" were incredible teachers and coaches for this amateur author and helped so much in carrying this book through to completion. Katie is an expert in the broad range of requirements to get an author's interesting but ill-formed ideas to the finish line as an actual published and registered book. Michelle grasped the soul of the book immediately and brought it to vivid life with her cover art. Callie's meticulous proofing and editing detected a host of errors that would have detracted from the reading experience. I have published extensively as an academic physician, but, as I told Stacy, academic writing doesn't usually require much in the way of dialogue and character development! Any writing that the reader finds pleasing in this book is due to Stacy's tremendous skills as a teacher, coach, and mentor. Any times that I fell short of her guidance are entirely my responsibility.

I owe great thanks to our good friends Dee and Kevin McCarthy, who provided me with the most wonderful writer's studio imaginable. Looking at the mountains surrounding Park City through two years of changing colors and snow is an incredible source of writing inspiration.

None of this book happens without the experience of having practiced as a physician in Park City for six years, not long after the mines finally shut down. Some of the incidents in this book come directly from that experience. The early history of Park City was still immediately accessible in the 1970s and 1980s, including stories from a few of my patients who worked in the mines as early as the turn of the century and still lived in their original cottages above town, similar to the family who lived in the rundown shack up Daly Canyon. I thank them for helping me understand how Parkites have always been so passionate about their town and its history.

Finally, none of this happens without the love and support of my wife, Jane, and her constant encouragement to pursue this project. The book is better because of her comments and suggestions about what the story is really about and how to make it better, including her help in what became the most difficult part of the entire experience: choosing a title!

ABOUT THE AUTHOR

Dr. Schwenk recently retired as Dean of the School of Medicine and Vice-President of Health Sciences at the University of Nevada, Reno, having served in those positions since July 2011. He was previously on the faculty of the University of Michigan Health System for 27 years and served as Chair of the Department of Family Medicine from 1986-2011. He now holds a faculty appointment as Professor Emeritus, as well as an appointment as Dean Emeritus at the University of Nevada, Reno.

Dr. Schwenk earned his BS degree in chemical engineering and MD from the University of Michigan. Following residency training in family medicine at the University of Utah, he practiced in Park City, Utah and served on the faculty of the University of Utah for several years, where he also completed a research fellowship. He is board-certified in Family Medicine.

He has served on the Board of Directors of the American Board of Family Medicine (2000-2005, vice -president 2004-2005), and was elected to the National Academy of Medicine in 2002. He also served for four years on the Administrative Board of the Council of Deans of the Association of American Medical Colleges. Dr. Schwenk's research has focused on the care of patients with depression and mental illness in primary care, with a recent emphasis on mental health and wellness in medical students, residents and physicians. He has co-authored over 160 publications, and has consulted to over 50 medical schools and teaching hospitals in various capacities.

9 781947 459953